Praise for Molly O'Keefe

The F

D1020953

"If there is one con̶̶̶̶̶̶̶̶̶̶̶̶̶̶̶̶̶̶̶̶̶̶̶̶̶̶̶̶̶ ̶st read in 2013, this is it . . . this book, *this book* . . . I could go on and on . . . but I will just end with this: not only was the plot beautiful but the writing was as well."
—*Love's a State of Mind*

"One of my favorite things about [O'Keefe's] books is the way they refuse to shy away from messy, complicated characters and relationships. *Wild Child* is no different in that regard . . . It is a testament to O'Keefe's skill as a writer and a storyteller that she imbues Jackson and Monica's stories (as a fledgling couple and as individuals) with a tremendous amount of emotional depth and sensitivity . . . O'Keefe can bring characters . . . into vivid and compelling life as they stumble, sometimes joyously, often painfully, always passionately, toward love and mutual happiness."
—*Dear Author*

"I fell in love with this book from the very beginning . . . It has the right amount of romance . . . And the sex scenes were hot, too."
—*Night Owl Reviews*, 4 stars

"As I have come to expect from Molly O'Keefe, *Wild Child* is a deliciously steamy romance that has plenty of substance . . . Another fabulous book by a very gifted author that I highly recommend to anyone who enjoys contemporary romances."
—*Book Reviews and More by Kathy*

Crooked Creek Novels

Crazy Thing Called Love

"There is no stopping the roller coaster of emotion, sexual tension and belly laughs. O'Keefe excels in creating flawed characters who readers will root for on every page. Despite very serious subjects and tear-worthy emotion, the tone of the novel is a perfect balance of fun and heart."
—*RT Book Reviews*, 4½ stars

"O'Keefe's newest romance hits the high notes with a storyline that tugs on the heartstrings, maintains a sizzling degree of sexual tension, and plays on realistic, authentic conflicts that keep the audience emotionally invested from start to finish. Gripping storytelling and convincing character-building allow the story to unfold in the present and in the past, offering windows into the psyches of a damaged hero and his restyled first love. An intense, heartwarming winner."
—*Kirkus Reviews*

"*Crazy Thing Called Love* has become my all-time favorite contemporary romance! . . . Don't miss out on O'Keefe's Crooked Creek series! These are the books you will still be talking about in twenty years!"
—*Joyfully Reviewed*

"There is nothing lacking in Molly O'Keefe's *Crazy Thing Called Love*. I am glad to say that it has every possible thing a woman could want in a good romance story. The Crooked Creek series is something that you will definitely want to get your hands on."
—*Guilty Pleasures Book Reviews*

"Wonderful story . . . unlike anything I have read before . . . Highly addicting."
—*Single Titles*

"This was an absolute joy to read . . . Definitely a book worth picking up."
—*Cocktails and Books*

"O'Keefe keeps the momentum of the present story going at a breathtaking pace with well placed visits back to the past, providing insight into these characters."
—*Fresh Fiction*

Can't Buy Me Love

"Readers should clear their schedules before they pick up O'Keefe's latest—a fast-paced, funny and touching book that is 'unputdownable.' Her story is a rollercoaster ride of tragedy and comedy that is matched in power by believable and sympathetic characters who leap off the pages. Best of all, this is just the beginning of a new series."
—*RT Book Reviews*

"From the beginning we see Tara's stainless steel loyalty and her capacity for caring, as well as Luc's overweening sense of responsibility and punishing self-discipline . . . Watching them fall for each other is excruciatingly enjoyable . . . *Can't Buy Me Love* is the rare kind of book that both challenges the genre's limits and reaffirms its most fundamental appeal."
—*Dear Author*

"*Can't Buy Me Love* is an unexpectedly rich family-centered love story, with mature and sexy characters and interweaving subplots that keep you turning the pages as fast as you can read. I really enjoyed it. It's also got some of the most smooth and compelling sequel bait I've ever swallowed."
—*Read React Review*

"If you love strong characters, bad guys trying to make good things go sour, and a steamy romance that keeps you guessing about just how two people are going to overcome their own angsts to come together where they belong, then I highly recommend *Can't Buy Me Love* by Molly O'Keefe. You won't be disappointed."
—*Unwrapping Romance*

"A stunning contemporary romance . . . One of the most memorable books I've read in a long time."
—DEIRDRE MARTIN,
New York Times bestselling author

"Molly O'Keefe is a unique, not-to-be-missed voice in romantic fiction . . . An automatic must-read!"
—SUSAN ANDERSEN,
New York Times bestselling author

Can't Hurry Love

"Using humor and heartrending emotion, O'Keefe writes characters who leap off the page. Their flaws and foibles make for an emotional story filled with tension, redemption and laughter. While this novel is not a direct continuation of the first in the series, it makes the reading richer and more interesting to devour the books in order. Readers should keep their eyes peeled for the third book and make room on their keeper shelves for this sparkling fresh series."

—*RT Book Reviews*

"Have you ever read a book that seeped into your soul while you read it, leaving you feeling both destroyed and elated when you finished? *Can't Hurry Love* was that book for me."

—*Reader, I Created Him*

"*Can't Hurry Love* is special. It's that book that ten years from now you will still be recommending to everyone because it is undeniably great!"

—*Joyfully Reviewed*

"An emotion-packed read, *Can't Hurry Love* . . . is a witty, passionate contemporary romance that will capture your interest from the very beginning."

—*Romance Junkies*

Indecent Proposal

Bantam Books by Molly O'Keefe

Crooked Creek Novels
Can't Buy Me Love
Can't Hurry Love
Crazy Thing Called Love

The Boys of Bishop Novels
Wild Child
Never Been Kissed
Between the Sheets
Indecent Proposal

Indecent Proposal

MOLLY O'KEEFE

BANTAM BOOKS • NEW YORK

A Bantam Books Mass Market Original

Copyright © 2014 by Molly Fader

Published in the United States by Bantam Books, an imprint of Random House, a division of Random House LLC, a Penguin Random House Company, New York.

BANTAM BOOKS and the HOUSE colophon are registered trademarks of Random House LLC.

ISBN 978-0-345-54905-1
eBook ISBN 978-0-345-54906-8

Cover Design: Lynn Andreozzi
Cover photograph: Josep Mª Surin / ImageBrief

Printed in the United States of America

www.bantamdell.com

9 8 7 6 5 4 3 2 1

Bantam Books mass market edition: October 2014

With incredible respect and gratitude for their patience and hard work, I would like to thank everyone at Random House whose careful hands are placed on my books. Especially Gina Wachtel, Sarah Murphy, Jin Yu, Shona McCarthy, Lynn Andreozzi, and, with great affection—Shauna Summers.

Indecent Proposal

Chapter 1

"Ken Doll is back."

Ryan Kaminski didn't have to look to see who Lindsey was talking about.

Ken Doll had been Lindsey's obsession for the last three nights.

"Yeah? What's he doing?" *Talking on his phone? Texting? Ignoring the rest of the world?* She did not understand why people came to a bar to stare at their phones and ignore people. If they didn't want to talk to people, they should just hide out in their apartments like she did. Ryan scooped ice into the martini shaker and then poured in vermouth, followed by high-end vodka that cost about a week's worth of tips, and slid on the top before giving it all a good shake.

"Ken Doll looks sad," Lindsey added.

That made Ryan look over her shoulder at the handsome blond man at the far corner of the bar. For three nights he'd been coming in, working on two different phones. Making calls. Sending texts—never looking up. Never acknowledging that he was actually in a room full of people.

He ordered beer—Corona in a bottle. Tipped double the bill and usually left every night without saying anything more than "Corona" and "thank you."

Ken Doll would be totally unremarkable—there were plenty of men at The Cobalt Bar spending more time on their phones than actually talking to people, and wearing beautiful tailor-made suits that clung just right to their bodies while they did it.

But they were not nearly as interesting as Ken Doll.

Because Ken Doll was just so damn pretty.

His blond hair had a slight curl to it, just enough that you knew it probably made him crazy. Piercing blue eyes. Like they'd been computer enhanced, that's how blue they were. In the soft, smooth plane of one cheek there was a dimple—she'd only seen it by accident when he smiled at a woman who asked to take the bar stool to his left the other day. But the real kicker—the show-stopper—was how he moved, efficient and graceful, like there was simply no time to waste, because he was A Man Who Got Things Done.

Watching him unbutton his jacket before sitting down was like watching a mission statement. A planted flag.

Gravitas.

That's what Ken Doll had that every other man in this bar was lacking.

But tonight he didn't have his phones out. He sat there, hands pressed flat against the mahogany bar, as the raindrops caught in his blond hair gleamed red and blue under the moody lights. He was wearing a University of Georgia Bulldogs tee shirt under which his shoulders . . . oh, that slump, it told a very sad story indeed.

Ryan poured the martini into the chilled glass, took a twist off the fresh lemon behind the bar, and put the glass on a napkin before sliding the drink over to the woman who'd ordered it and collecting the twenty the woman had left on the bar.

These meaningless transactions made up her life. Over and over again.

"I want to ease Ken Doll's pain." Lindsey didn't even pretend not to watch Ken Doll while pulling a draft for one of the guys working the couches. "Like. Really."

Lindsey was well suited to that task. The bar's uniform—the short leather shorts, the fishnets and tall boots—took on a whole new level of sexy with her. She was a twenty-one-year-old party girl from the Bronx who could take care of herself and anyone else who wanted to have a good time.

Next to her Ryan felt old, way older than thirty-two. She felt old and crotchety and like she was only days away from yelling at kids to get off her lawn. Not that she had a lawn.

Ryan should just get out of the way and let Lindsey take care of Ken Doll.

But she didn't.

Once upon another lifetime she modeled, and she still did when she could get the work. When she couldn't, she worked at an overpriced bar inside the very swanky Cobalt Hotel in midtown Manhattan.

She knew all kinds of pretty.

But there was something about pretty and sad that got her antenna up.

"Switch sides with me," Lindsey said, referring to the neat-down-the-middle split between her side of the bar and Lindsey's.

"Nope."

"Come on," Lindsey pouted. "You hate the guys that come in here. He's wasted on you."

"This is true." Ryan had a fervent dislike for the posing and the posturing, the manicured and manscaped version of masculinity that walked into this bar. She hated the ego and the way the men watched her body—admittedly on display—but when she caught their eyes, no one was home. Or they were constantly looking past her for someone else.

For something better.

"But he's not like the other guys that come in here," Ryan said.

This was so true; other people in the bar watched him out of the corner of their eyes, as if they knew he was different from the rest of them. Or he was familiar and they just couldn't remember why.

She didn't want to ease Ken Doll's pain, at least not in the way that Lindsey did. But she'd been serving him for three nights and she was dying to know his story. "And he's on my side. Sorry, Linds."

She tossed a black bar towel toward a scowling Lindsey and sauntered over to Ken Doll's corner. There was a weird energy rolling off him tonight, and the air in this small part of the bar was electric and still. Humid, from the water burning up from the heat of his body.

"The usual?" she asked, waiting for him to look up at her so she could smile.

He ran a hand through his blond hair, sending water droplets into the air.

"I'll have scotch. Neat."

"Single malt?"

Finally, he looked up at her, and the distracted but polite distance she was used to seeing in his sky-blue eyes was replaced by a sizzling, terrible grief. Or anger. She couldn't be sure. Not that it mattered, really.

Because tonight, Ken Doll burned.

"Whatever," he said, his voice low and broken. "Just bring me whatever."

She poured him Lagavulin, and she barely had the tumbler on the bar in front of him before he grabbed it and shot it back. "Another," he said.

Two more shots later, she brought him a glass of water and a menu.

"Thank you," he said, glancing at her through impossibly long eyelashes. But he pushed the menu away.

"My name is Ryan," she said. "Apparently I'll be the woman getting you drunk tonight."

His laughter was dry, like wind through November trees, but he didn't say anything.

"And your name?" she asked. "That's usually how it works, in case you're unfamiliar. I tell you my name, you tell me yours."

"Harri- . . . Harry. You can call me Harry." His voice was laced with traces of the South, pecans and sweet tea.

She held out her hand, and after a moment he shook it. "Nice to meet you, Harry," she said.

There were no calluses on that hand, which wasn't all that surprising in the land of his-and-hers manicures. But every time she shook a man's hand she thought of her dad's big palms, the blisters and cuts, the thick calluses—a working man's hands.

Harry's palms were smooth and supple, but his grip was sure and strong and he didn't do anything skeevy—so points for him.

"You too, Ryan."

"Everything okay?" she asked.

He blew out a long breath, laughing a little at the end, as if he just couldn't believe how everything around him had turned to shit. "Have you ever done everything in your power and not have it be good enough? And not just a little bit, but have everything you are capable of be not even close to enough?"

"No idea," she joked, deadpan. "Ever since I was a girl I dreamt of making overpriced martinis for men who only stare at my chest."

It took him a second, the weighty stare of his checking to see if she was being serious or not, but finally he laughed. A weary *humph* that made her feel just a little victorious.

"Well, it's a first for me."

"It's no fun, is it?"

He shook his head, the muscles of his shoulders flexing under his shirt like he was about to twitch out of his skin. Empathy, something she very rarely felt at work, swarmed her.

"I'm . . ." he trailed off, his hands on the bar curled into fists.

"Angry?" she supplied, watching his knuckles grow white.

He nodded slowly. "And sad. Mostly . . . sad."

Inside, deep inside, a penny dropped and the complicated mechanism of her desire—of her elusive and rarely seen *want*—was engaged.

Well, shit, she thought. *Maybe I will be easing his pain after all.*

Later, she brought him the chicken and waffles, because while he'd slowed down on the Lagavulin, he hadn't stopped.

"I didn't order this," he said, looking down at their signature dish, guaranteed to soak up the alcohol in his stomach while making him thirsty enough for more.

"Comes with the scotch."

"Speaking of which." He held up his tumbler. At least he'd switched to scotch and water.

"Can I trust that your fancy New York City chef knows what he's doing with chicken and waffles?" Harry asked, not quite smiling, but not quite looking like the world was going to crush him.

"Well, our chef is from Mobile, so she might know her way around." She set the refilled tumbler back down in front of him. "It's raining out?"

"Yeah . . . I stepped out to get some air and it's cats and dogs out there."

Cats and dogs? she thought, swallowing her smile. *That's just adorable.*

Rain could go either way for business, and Lord knew she needed the money of a good night, but she was content at this quiet end of her bar.

"This is kind of you," he said, contemplating the food.

"Well, you seem like a nice guy."

"I've barely said two words to you."

"Well, I have a sixth sense about these things, and those two words were serious and well-meaning."

"Serious and well-meaning is exactly me." He cocked his head, watching her from beneath long lashes. "Or a pet dog; I can't be sure."

She laughed, happy to see that he was getting into the spirit of the banter. "I have never had a well-meaning dog in my life. Thieves and layabouts, all of them."

"I had one. As a kid. Daisey. She meant well."

Oh God, he was walking down old-dead-dog memory lane.

"You are just all kinds of sad tonight, aren't you?"

He spun his glass in a slow circle. "I guess so."

"You know," she said, "where I grew up there was this bar called The Sunset right down the street. A real dive bar. Guys went in after their shifts on Friday and didn't come out until Sunday afternoon. Well, they got this new daytime bartender. A real soft touch. She fell for every hard-luck story that sat down in the corner. And then word got out that Ben Polecka came in there crying after his wife left and the bartender gave him free beers all afternoon. Soon, everyone was going in there pretending to cry to get free beer. And my sister, always a bit of an entrepreneur, decides she and I should go stand outside the bar and charge guys five dollars to kick them in the balls. You know, as a kind of guarantee of real tears."

He laughed, which of course had been the idea, but it still came as a bit of a surprise.

"How much money did you make?"

"Five bucks," she shrugged. "We were out there for like three hours, and finally Bruce Dinkle took pity on us."

"That was his real name?"

"Yep."

"And Bruce Dinkle paid you to kick him in the balls?"

"He did. We bought some ice cream, and it felt like we were on top of the world."

His laughter faded and then the smile vanished, and then the weight of the world was rolled back up on his shoulders.

She leaned against the bar and crossed her arms over her chest, well aware that her breasts nearly spilled from the vest she wore, but Harry's eye didn't wander. They stayed glued to hers as if he didn't even see the body beneath her chin. "Okay, you sad sack. Tell me. Who is your best not good enough for? A wife?"

"No wife."

"Girlfriend?"

He shook his head, and she would be lying if she didn't say she was relieved.

"A boss?"

"I've never had a boss."

No boss? What planet is this guy from?

"Then who, my friend, is making you feel this way?"

"Why?" He smiled at her, looser than he'd been, but not yet totally unwound. The guy could hold his booze; she'd give him that. "You going to give them a talking-to?"

"I just might."

"What would you say?"

"I would probably say, listen . . ." She paused, waiting for him to fill in the blank.

He shook his head, that blond hair gleaming red and then blue under the lights. "I'm afraid it's . . . complicated."

Gary, her manager, glanced over from across the room, and Ryan reached for some unprepped garnishes under the bar and made a good show of stripping mint leaves off the stem for mojitos. "Give me the gist. You don't have to spill state secrets, but you might feel better getting some of this off your chest."

"You an expert on that too?"

"I'm a bartender, Harry. I am an expert on lots of things." She chucked the mint stem into the trash under the bar. "Lay your burdens down, my friend."

"It's my sister. She's in trouble."

"Ah, oddly enough, this is a subject in which I have plenty of experience."

"You have a sister who gets in trouble?"

"I *am* the sister who gets in trouble." Something buzzed up the back of her neck. A warning to shut her mouth and walk on, perhaps send Lindsey over. But she ignored it, despite having gotten so much better at heeding those internal warnings. She grabbed more mint just so she'd have something to do with her hands.

"So, is she in big trouble or little trouble? Like if one is dating a jerk and ten is living on the streets, where does she fall?"

"She isn't even on that spectrum." Something in his voice made her realize the jokes were soon to become offensive. That there was no part of this he was going to find funny. And funny was a huge part of her armor. And without her armor she was just vulnerable and sympathetic—two things that had gotten her in more than her fair share of trouble.

Leave, she thought. *Switch sides with Lindsey. Forget about Sad Ken Doll.*

But that was impossible. His anger and grief were magnetic.

She put down the mint.

"I'm so sorry, Harry," she told him sincerely.

"It's fine." His smile revealed the dimple, and for a moment she was distracted enough not to realize he was lying. But she had been a bartender for over a decade and she could smell a lie a mile away. And whatever the situation was with his sister, it was far from fine.

"That's what you've been working on for the last few days. With the phones? Trying to help your sister?"

"I couldn't stare at the walls of my room anymore. All day, every day, trying . . ."

He sighed, pushing away the plate with the half-eaten chicken on it. For a moment Ryan thought he was going to walk out; he was coiled, poised to just vanish.

And that would be for the best, she thought. For her. Maybe for him. Because the last thing he probably needed was a sister in trouble and a hangover in the morning. And the last thing she needed was this compassion—this empathy and curiosity, the rusted guts of her desire—making her decisions for her.

But then he relaxed back into his chair. Back into the moment with her.

She exhaled the breath she hadn't realized she'd been holding.

"Not that it's done much good. I don't know if I'm going to be able to help her."

There was an invisible barrier down the middle of the bar. This one and every other upscale bar in the five boroughs. The barrier was well documented not only in The Cobalt Bar employee handbook, but also in her own rule book: no fraternizing with the drinkers. A lesson she'd learned twice the hard way.

But she shoved her fist right through that barrier and put her hand over his. To her surprise, he grabbed her fingers and held them tight in his, like a lifeline he was terribly in need of.

"She's . . . she's my baby sister. And she hasn't needed anything from me in so long and now . . . now that she does, now that she really needs me, I might not be able to help her. It's killing me."

Everything, the empathy and the desire and the shock

of his touch, twisted and turned inside her, making her ache. Making her wish there wasn't a bar between them, that she could wrap her arms around him properly.

She squeezed his hand instead. "Do you have any other family?" she asked. "Someone else who can help you?"

"I am heading home tomorrow morning to talk to them." His tone indicated that this was a bad, bad thing.

"They won't be able to help?"

"Help or hurt—it could go either way. Smart money is on hurt."

She stood there, silently bearing witness to his grief. Letting him grip her hand so hard their knuckles rubbed up against each other's.

"It's so crazy, and my mother . . . Mother is not going to handle this well. She's never approved of my sister, and this is going to put her right over the edge." He shot her a wry look and then sighed. "The one bright spot is, I think I know a guy who can help."

"That's good," she said.

"Well, there is a decent chance that he will laugh in my face and tell me to go fuck myself. And then . . ." He hung his head, wiping his hand across his face. "Oh God, then I have no idea what I'm going to do."

Screw the barrier. Screw the rule book. Screw the rest of the bar. She lifted her hand from his grip and touched his cheek, the perfect bone structure of his jaw. The fine scruff of his beard felt good against her palm.

The man needed some sympathy. Some human connection. He'd been wrestling with what seemed like a nightmare for the last three days. And she . . . maybe she, who lived behind a solid glass wall of rules created by shitty past experience, could use a little human connection, too.

"He won't," she said. "You'll convince him."

He turned his face and whispered, "How do you know that?" into her hand.

The sensation of his breath between her fingers sizzled up her arm and across her chest, settling in her belly, where it smoldered and burned.

"Because I'm a little sister, too. And my big brother would tear down the world to help me. That's what big brothers do."

She smiled into his bloodshot blue eyes when he opened them.

The thick air crackled with the power of all the desperate grief and anger he was throwing off.

She felt the touch of his gaze across her face. Her lips and eyes, the cheekbones that had earned her quite a bit of money. Her hair pulled back in a high ponytail and falling over her shoulders like a luxurious cape.

What he saw wasn't really her. It was a quirk of genetics, a lucky break in the womb. To have her mother's nose and her father's eyes. Her grandmother's bone structure and her grandfather's outrageous thick, shiny hair.

It was just what she looked like. The tools she used to make a living.

And it had taken her years of destroying nearly every relationship that ever meant anything to realize that.

"You're the most beautiful woman I've ever seen."

She pulled her hands free of his. The moment of intense connection between them was fading to something slightly more manageable. Attraction and appeal. A rare camaraderie, but at least she wasn't ready to crawl over the bar into his lap.

"That's the scotch talking."

"Give me some credit. It's not just your looks, Ryan. You're lovely." For no good reason, that made her flustered, made her feel stupid for reaching across the barrier.

The rules were in place for a reason, after all.

"Ryan!" Lindsey said. "A little help?"

Ryan turned to see Lindsey inundated with gray-suited Wall Street types, so she gave Harry a quick smile and headed over to help her.

"Getting a little cozy, aren't you?" Lindsey asked, her eyes twinkling. She was a good sport, Lindsey. As long as someone had the chance to get lucky, she was happy.

"He's a nice guy."

"They always are. But listen." She jerked his chin across the bar where their manager, Gary, was talking to a few of the regulars in the corner. "Gary's watching you, so just be careful. He fired Will last month for going home with that crazy bitch from Saks."

As if he heard, Gary looked over. Gary was a nice enough guy, but the rules were pretty ironclad and he could lose his job for ignoring them.

The rush at the bar lasted a good hour and finally around ten p.m. slowed down to a trickle. Lindsey sent out another martini, a watermelon margarita, and three more Coronas and checked her watch. "It's cutting time," she said.

"You've been here since three," Ryan said, because the first one in was usually the first one to go home unless they were working a double. She set dirty glassware under the bar in the gray bins and then handed them to Sam, who was heading back to the kitchen.

"Grab me some lemons, would you? And more mint and more thyme. Thanks."

Sam, a notorious flirt, winked at her, taking the bins with him.

"Yeah, but I don't have a hot guy at the end of the bar waiting for me," Lindsey said.

Ryan looked over her shoulder to where Harry sat,

looking at his phone, nursing a Corona, the chicken and waffles forgotten at his elbow.

"I don't."

"Ugh, denial is so boring," Lindsey said, grabbing two more pint glasses and starting the intricate pour-and-wait system for Guinness. "Get into my back pocket."

Ryan reached into the tight pocket of Lindsey's shorts and pulled out two sticks of gum, a twenty-dollar bill, and a condom.

"Go," Lindsey said. "Stock my garnishes and then take Sad Ken Doll someplace and cheer him up."

It had been a long time since Ryan had gone home with a guy. Picking up at a bar was for other women, younger women. Women who hadn't been burned quite as effectively as she had.

There was also the small matter of losing her job if management found out.

But as with every job, there were ways of getting around management, if a woman wanted to bad enough.

She glanced back at Harry and caught him staring at her.

His eyes flared and the bar fell away again, the whole world disappeared. He had some kind of magical power when he really looked at her, a way of making her feel like the only woman on the planet. And hundreds of lesser men had tried and never, ever come close to doing that. Of engaging the old and rusted machine of her desire.

This man did it with one look.

A sudden breathlessness seized her, and the fifteen minutes she had left on her shift was too much. The time it would take her to get up to his room was too much. The fact that he—serious and well-meaning—might not take her up on what she was going to offer was a reality she had no interest in.

She wanted him—his scruffy face, the burning anger

in his eyes, the beautiful symmetry of his body, the delicious humanity of his grief.

Without a second thought, she slipped the condom in her own pocket.

"Thanks, Linds," she said.

"No problem." She wiggled her butt while Ryan tucked the twenty back in her pocket.

An asshole at the bar whistled.

"Oh, you wish, buddy," Lindsey said.

"Hey," the guy said, leaning across the bar toward Ryan. "You look really familiar to me."

"Because you were in here last week."

"No . . . My friend," he jerked his thumb over his shoulder, vaguely referencing one of the other guys in suits with manicured hands behind him. "He says you were the Lips Girl like fifteen years ago. Is that true? Can you do the thing? The slogan—"

"Your friend is wrong," she lied, and dismissed the guy by turning her back on him. There were bigger things on her horizon than trying to put a shine on ancient history.

Ryan walked over to Harry and picked up his plate of half-eaten dinner.

"No wife?" she asked. "No girlfriend? No woman waiting at home for you? Don't bother lying—I'll be able to tell."

He shook his head.

"Are you gay?"

That made him smile, and again she felt that little spike of pleasure. Of a job well done. "I'm not gay, and no one is waiting for me, Ryan."

"Are you staying at the hotel?" she asked.

His burning blue eyes met hers, and there was no confusion; he knew what she was asking.

"I am."

"I'm getting off in about fifteen minutes."

Harry stood, a new urgency in his movement. He tossed several bills on the bar, but she pushed them back at him.

"It's on me," she said. "The Sister in Trouble special."

By the shocked and blank look on his face it was obvious no one ever joked with him, and she wondered if he had any friends. Why would a man like him in what seemed to be the worst three days of his life show up alone at her bar?

But when he did laugh, it was a good one. Full-throated and deep, the kind of laugh that made other people smile. But not Manager Gary, who walked by giving Ryan a serious warning glare.

She took Harry's plate and stepped away.

"Room 534," he said.

She nodded once, the number tucked away.

"Ryan?" he said.

"Yes?"

"Hurry."

Chapter 2

It wasn't a hard thing to get up to the guest rooms from the bar. You had to go through the lobby and upstairs to get to the bathrooms anyway. She had changed out of her work clothes in the bathroom, the tight leather vest and dark shorts, and put on a camisole tank top and a gray jersey skirt. The boots stayed—overkill maybe, but they were too big to fit in her bag.

On her back, the top of her tattoo was visible just over the edge of her tank top. Ophelia's hands and the blue-green vines that bound them.

Her stomach fluttered with nerves, and her palms were damp. It had been . . . a very long time since she'd done this. There had been that two-year round-robin of questionable choices after her divorce six years ago. After which all the rules about guys from bars were formed and up to this point, easily unbroken.

But she found as she got into the quiet solace of the elevator, where she expected to be swarmed with second thoughts and serious misgivings, that she was only more excited. So much so that beneath the camisole her nipples were hard and her breath was short. Between her legs anticipation made her ache.

The door pinged open and she stepped into the opulent hallway that made up The Cobalt Hotel. Room 534 was just left of the elevators and down the hallway a few steps. Outside the door she took a deep breath and then knocked lightly.

The door swung open almost hilariously fast and

Harry stood there, backlit by the soft glow of the lamp in the room.

He'd showered. Shaved. He smelled woodsy and clean and rich. Masculine.

Her nipples really liked that and she was sure if he looked past her eyes, he'd see. But he was polite, very polite for a man who was going to fuck a bartender he'd just met, and he didn't break eye contact.

He wore jeans and a white tee shirt. His feet were bare.

His second toe was longer than the first. A little imperfection on all that perfection only made him more interesting.

"Come on in," he said quietly, shifting aside.

She stepped into the guest room, and the sound of the door clicking shut behind her was the sound of no return.

Here we go, she thought.

"Can I get you a drink?" he asked. "I nearly decimated the minibar before coming downstairs. But I think there's a bottle of white wine left in there."

"Am I taking advantage of a drunk man?" she asked, setting her bag down on the low dresser as she walked into the room.

"No." His voice was low. Serious.

Oh, her nipples were just approving everything this guy did.

She stepped farther into the room. A king-size bed.

Fun.

"No thanks on the drink."

"What would you like?" he asked. She could feel him behind her. Close, but not too close, giving her room should she need it. Room to get comfortable. Room to change her mind.

"Hmmmm?" She laughed and turned to face him.

There were high spots of color on his face. But those eyes, they were locked on hers, unmoving. Hot.

A test of sorts, she lifted her hands to her collarbones, pushing the heavy fall of her ponytail off her shoulder. With one finger she traced the demure lace edge of her black tank top. His eyes drifted from hers and followed the movement, but only for a second before his eyes met hers again.

The air in the room—filled with lust and danger—was hard to breathe.

I don't know you, she thought. She was alone in a hotel room with a man she'd just met, which was risky, but everything she did know convinced her that she was safe.

Secure and menaced, both at the same time. It was heady.

"You don't have to be so polite," she breathed, her finger finding the upward curve of her breast and tracing that, too.

"I'm a Southern gentleman, Ryan. I'm afraid that's how we're raised."

"I was born in northeast Philly." The implication that she was raised without manners wasn't true, but it certainly served her purpose right now. Hungry for him, her finger glided closer to the hard, aching edge of her nipple. She dropped her gaze from the magnetic appeal of his, and she looked shamelessly at his body. The way his chest filled out that tee shirt. The bulge of his erection beneath the button fly of his jeans.

"And the men from northeast Philly, what are they like?"

"Rough." She thought of Paul. "They have a certain 'take what they want' quality."

"Is that . . ." He tilted his head, as if sniffing her on the wind. And she felt suddenly . . . deliciously . . . at risk. "Is that what you like?"

"As a rule, no." She liked *him*. The way he'd been downstairs—split open and vulnerable. Human. Real.

His smile was sharp and fast, a flash of something predatory. "But tonight? From me?"

"I want you however you are," she said.

He flushed, and she got dizzy in the quiet before he charged across the room, pulling her up on her toes, against his chest. His mouth, those perfect lips, hovered just over hers.

"Who the hell are you?" His minty breath, with the tang of the alcohol he'd been drinking under it, swept over her lips.

She shrugged.

"Ryan Kaminski."

His fingers swept along her hairline, reaching back through her thick hair to cup her skull in his hands. "Thank you, Ryan Kaminski," he murmured. "For being here."

Oh God, she nearly melted right there. Right into him. With one hand cupped around her head, he took the other and placed it at her neck and then slowly, so slowly, dragged it down her chest, his fingertips brushing hard over a nipple.

Her knees buckled as her body, long asleep, awoke with a gasp. A raging fire. A sudden painful need.

His knee slipped between hers, the hard muscle of his thigh right between her legs. Right. Between.

She gasped at the pleasurable pain of it. His eyes were still on hers, but his gaze was no longer polite. It was demanding and hard, and she quaked beneath it. His hand slid downward over her stomach, setting all of the muscles there trembling over the rolled top of her skirt. He shifted his hand, his fingers pointing down, and stopped just before reaching the ache between her legs.

She rocked into his leg, biting her lip.

"That's still pretty polite," she whispered.

He smiled down at her and then pushed his leg up higher and harder against her.

"How about that?"

"Getting better."

Without warning he spun her slightly, so her back was against his chest and she felt the length of him against her ass. She pushed back against him and he groaned, surging up against her.

"You were very . . . kind to me tonight," he breathed into her ear. She closed her eyes against the electric pulses his voice and breath sent down her neck and over her body.

"You planning on returning the favor?" She looped her arm around his neck, pulling him down slightly while she rubbed herself against him. A cat in heat. Whatever. It had been a long time.

"I am," he said. His hands cupped her breasts. Not so polite anymore, there was demand in his touch, and she bit her lip. She felt the edge of her tank top get pulled down by one of those long, elegant fingers until her breast was revealed.

And then the other one.

She reached for the hem of her shirt, to just be done with it, be done with every bit of cloth between them, but he stopped her.

"Like that," he breathed, again against her neck. "Look."

He grabbed her chin, not hard . . . but not lightly either, and turned her head until she saw them in the mirror.

"Oh my God," she breathed. The two of them together, they were gorgeous. Like incredibly hot. Her arm around his neck lifted her breasts like she was offering them and his wide, lovely body was curved and curled against her. His hair gleamed gold in the lamplight, hers the color of mink.

"You are really the most beautiful woman I've ever seen." He slipped the hand that wasn't holding her chin down the front of her body, over those breasts, her stomach, and down between her legs, cupping her pussy in his palm, pushing her skirt between her legs.

"You watching?" He kissed her neck, his fingers moving out of the way. His thumb brushed her lips and she sucked it into her mouth.

His eyes, burning blue fire, met hers in the mirror and he groaned, pushing his erection against her, his legs flexing under the denim, and she reached with her other hand behind her ass to touch him through his jeans.

Those manners he'd been talking about, that Southern boyhood that required him to make polite eye contact even while a woman was fondling herself in front of him, were swept aside by the dark hand of lust.

He shifted them until they faced the mirror.

"Lift your skirt," he breathed.

"You do it." She squeezed his erection. "I'm busy."

His laughter was part growl, and instead of lifting the skirt he pulled it down, over her waist and hips, until she stood in front of him in a thin black cotton g-string and a tank top.

And the boots.

She tried to watch as long as she could, the way he soaked in the sight of her, how his hand looked between her legs, pushing aside that cotton and finding the heat and wet of her. The small muscles in his forearms flexing and shifting as his fingers found the hard stone of her clitoris and made friends. Slowly at first, with soft touches, light but growing heavier. Faster.

Her eyelids fluttered shut and she groaned.

Some switch got flipped in him and he pushed her backwards to the bed until she felt the mattress hit the back of her legs.

"What—?" Without the fire of him behind her, she was cold.

"I'm sorry." He tossed her on the bed and she was suddenly very aware of how big he was, how if he chose to exert his strength she wouldn't have a chance.

"Sorry?" Panic rippled through her.

But then he fell to his knees on the floor between her splayed legs. "I've got to taste you, Ryan."

He used his thumb to pull aside the cotton and she stared blindly at him, waiting for the damp heat of his mouth. And when it came, when it happened, there was nothing delicate, nothing careful—it was fierce and messy, his whole mouth devouring her, his hand spread wide over her tummy, holding her still as she nearly jackknifed off the bed—electrocuted by his tongue and lips. His fingers spearing inside of her.

She came and she came. Rolling waves picking her up and tossing her around like a rag doll.

His mouth gentled. He gave her a soft kiss, a slow lap, another. And she twitched under his attention. Shook as his breath ran hot over her fevered flesh. Finally, he sat back, his hands cupping her knees. His thumbs stroking the skin there, making her toes curl in her boots.

After a moment she sat up, light-headed. Feeling a little silly but very grateful. There were many beautiful things about a man's mouth that she could not recreate by herself.

And this man's mouth was particularly beautiful.

In the low lamplight, his chin was shiny, his eyes bright.

He looked pleased and dirty and totally delicious.

Quickly she contemplated what kind of luck pushed Harry into her bar.

She laced her fingers through his and tugged. "Come up here."

With that economic grace of his he surged up onto the bed, covering her piece by piece. Knees, thighs, belly. He stopped for a second, braced against her, and pulled off his shirt, kindly giving her skin to touch. And such fine, lovely skin it was, stretched over lean muscles, covered with hair as blond as what was on his head. She ran her fingers down his chest, across his nipples. He flinched slightly.

"You don't—"

"I do."

His thumb traced the curve of her lower lip. "I haven't kissed you."

"That's not entirely true," she laughed. Her clitoris still buzzed from his kisses. "I haven't kissed *you*," she said.

"Should we fix that?"

Leaning forward, she kissed his chest. The bit of bone at his sternum. He kissed her shoulder, a surprising quick, hard peck, and she laughed before kissing the tender skin near his armpit, which made him jump.

"Ticklish?"

"Yes."

He kissed the soft hollow at her throat, where the skin dipped between her collarbones.

Humming slightly, she lifted his hand and kissed the wide center of his palm.

Laughter, deep and dark, rumbled out of his chest, and he slipped his hand over her face and then up over her hair. Carefully he pulled out the dark ponytail holder and her hair spilled down over her back, across the white blankets of the bed.

The sight of her hair seemed to end some game for him and he shifted them so she was lying flat on her back in the bed and he came down over her, with his skin and his serious eyes and his gravitas, and she felt herself slip a little bit in love.

Just a little. It was something she did—fall in love. Quickly, easily, like a rib popped out of place by one wrong twist. Of course it wasn't real love. It was infatuation, lust. Camaraderie. A certain affection. Respect. All in all a potent mix.

Part of why she needed those rules, that hard glass wall of bad past experiences. Because she was always so ready to be in love. Always, despite pretending otherwise, wanting this feeling. This heady mix of the best of herself being called out by a man.

Which would be concerning if she knew his last name. Or who he was.

But they were just tonight. That was all.

And so a little infatuation was safe.

When he kissed her it was deep and thorough. Not so much a kiss as it was a possession. A slow and consuming takeover. He took his time, worked his way in slowly until it felt as if he'd always been there. Kissing her, the weight of him pressing her down into the superior mattress of The Cobalt Hotel.

His hand slid from her waist to her breast and she purred in her throat, slipping her own hand between them over the erection she felt behind his zipper.

The slow possession gained urgency. Gained need, and she fumbled with his zipper, growing frantic to touch him. To have him.

He reached down to help but only made things worse, and he laughed into her mouth before lying back, unzipping his pants, and pushing them down over his hips and legs. The hard length of his erection popped free and lay against his belly and it was as irresistible as the rest of him, and she slipped over him, lying on her stomach between his legs. He scooched up so she wouldn't have to twist awkwardly to stay on the bed.

Very considerate.

She cupped him in her palm, measured him with her

fingers, looked at every inch of him before curling her hand around the solid girth of his dick and leaning forward to lick, very slowly, the head. The salt and sweet of him flooded her mouth and she moaned at the taste.

He gasped and twitched and she smiled her wickedest smile, feeling her wickedest feelings.

She could sense him watching her so she settled into her work, easing up on the bed until her breasts rested against his leg, the rough hair teasing her nipples.

Slowly, she jacked him in her fist, testing her grip until she heard him hiss.

"Too hard?"

"Harder."

Oh, he was too much, just too much, and she lifted herself up slightly so she could take him into her mouth. Swallowing him deeper until she felt him against the back of her throat and his hands clutched into the thick fall of her hair.

Yes, she thought, *yes. Just like that.*

She hummed, hoping he would understand that she liked that.

He pulled her hair away from her face, holding it back with one rough hand.

"So good," he breathed. "You look so good."

Between her mouth and her hand she worked him harder. Faster. Lips, tongue. Both hands. Squeezing. Licking. Until he was pushing up into her mouth when she pushed down and she wasn't sure if maybe she was hurting him, or he was hurting her, but she couldn't stand it anymore.

He came out of her mouth with an audible pop and she got up on her knees beside him, staring down at the lovely flushed and sweaty delight of him.

"I want to fuck you."

He shook his head, his eyes wild, as if words were just totally beyond his ability to understand.

"Why not?" she asked. There simply wasn't any way this hookup was going to end like this. She was dying for him. Dying for the sensation of him sliding deep inside of her.

"I don't have any condoms," he said with a slight wince.

"Oh, you southern boys haven't gotten the memo—we northern women can take care of things." She got up off the bed, pulling off her damp and messy G-string, the tank top.

But leaving the boots.

From her purse she pulled out Lindsey's night-making condom before turning toward him, the condom between her fingers.

"Ta-da."

He smiled, then propped up on his elbows, his legs still spread, his ruddy cock lying against his abdomen.

"I like you northern girls."

Feeling like some kind of swashbuckling female pirate, she leapt on the bed and straddled him while ripping open the wrapper with her teeth.

"Your tattoo—?"

"Really?" she asked, holding the tip of the condom with one hand while sliding the rest of it over him. "You want to talk about my ink, now?"

Mesmerized, he stared like he'd never seen someone roll a condom on with such panache. Willing to give him more of a show, she hiked herself up his body, holding his cock still while she slowly, with breath-stealing, excruciating deliberateness, eased herself down him.

Despite her eagerness, despite the wetness he had inspired between her legs, there was still the small pinch and sting of taking this man inside of her. The strange reality that no matter what, sex was a matter of submission for her. Of accepting what on some level seemed unacceptable.

She was not and had never been very good at compliance.

"Oh . . . God, Ryan."

"Good?"

"Sublime. Fucking . . . perfect. You are perfect."

Let's not go overboard, she thought. But once he was inside all the way and she was seated hard in the cradle of his hips, she shook her hair out of the way and raised herself up over him, holding onto the headboard, nearly wild with a surge of power and sex and something old and womanly, and began to ride him.

Most men didn't know how to be on the bottom. They either held themselves still, letting her do it all, or they grabbed her hips, keeping her still while jackhammering into her from underneath

But not Harry. No, Harry understood. Making this work for both of them meant meeting her downward slide with his upward push. When she jerked forward against him, he pushed back until she felt the pressure of his body against her clit. He held her breasts, hard, his fingers careful but insistent vises against her flesh.

"Look at you," he breathed. "Fuck, look at you."

She was too busy looking at him, watching his face turn from pleasure-stoned to demanding. To animal. The pressure built from her clit and from deep inside where she was clenched so hard around him.

He reached up to hold her shoulder, pushing her against him, adding force to the incendiary grind they'd worked up. And it worked; pleasure spiked and she fell back slightly, holding herself up against his leg.

But then, predictably, she hit a wall—her pleasure built but went no higher. No matter what she did, it leveled off into a plateau.

She jerked and circled her hips, trying to wring every bit of pleasure from their bodies. But it didn't work. Between her legs she was growing numb.

The frustration moaned out of her.

"You need more?"

Stunned that he seemed to know, her eyes flew open, but he did know. Of course he did.

Words were about five minutes behind her and all she could really do was nod and twitch and want to come so bad she could taste it.

She dropped herself onto him, prepared for him to heave up and over her and end this, but he kept her there, one hand on her hip and the other slipping between her legs. His fingers found her clit and he pressed his thumb hard against her and she felt sparks drift outward from her skin, as if she were a torch held up against the night sky.

"Make yourself come," he breathed. "I want to see it."

With his thumb against her she smashed through the plateau; pleasure was a force living inside of her, ready to break through her bones and muscles and skin, ready to take her over and she couldn't stop it, didn't want to. She sobbed, sweat running down her back as she shook over him, no coordination left in her body. Nothing left in her body but this one stubborn strand keeping her on earth.

He surged up, wrapping one arm around her waist, and she felt his palm against her back, imagined it against Ophelia's body. Ducking his head, he caught her nipple in his mouth and sucked hard and the points of contact—the nipple, clit, tattoo—severed the strand and she was shattered. Simply shattered.

He held her while she shook, stroking her back, murmuring nonsensical things, her hair sticking to both of them, trapping them in a web. A cocoon.

I like it here, she thought, her face pressed to his chest. His deodorant smelled good.

He was still hard inside of her and there was no urgency on his part to finish, at least it didn't feel that way, and she nearly laughed.

Honest-to-God, who is this guy?

What were the chances that the best lover she'd ever had would stumble into her bar on a Tuesday night?

And be named Harry.

She leaned back, untangling her hair from around them so she could see him.

"Thank you," she breathed.

His smile was drawn tight; the poor guy was barely holding on.

Such a gentleman, she thought, lifting herself off of him so she could lie down on her back across the king-size bed. His eyes burned their way across her body, leaving trails of cinder and ash from her breasts to her waist, down the long length of her legs.

The boots.

Whatever remained of the polite southern gentleman in this man left town at the sight of those boots, because he growled and pounced. His body, hard and heavy, over hers, his cock, hard and hot, sliding right back inside of her. Deep. And then deeper. So deep she had to shift her head back to breathe.

His body slammed into hers, and she embraced the violence of it, the deeply erotic sound of flesh hitting flesh. The growling, grumbling roar in the back of his throat.

Yes. Yes, it should always be like this, she thought just before mindlessness slipped over her. Just before she was reduced to animal in his animal arms.

"Ryan," he growled. "God. Come on. Fuck. Come—"

He roared through four more hard, heavy strokes, so bruising, so punishing, she fell apart again under their lovely brutality.

And he collapsed against her, boneless and sweet.

It took a few moments for her heartbeat not to thunder in her ears. For the world not to sparkle in the corner of her eyes.

"Wow," he breathed.

She laughed, lifting boneless arms to wrap them around his neck.

"Yeah, wow."

After a long, delicious moment he shifted to the side to take care of the messy reality of the condom, and she began the slightly excruciating process of getting up and getting dressed and getting gone. But he stopped her with an arm around her waist, pulling her back into the muscular curve of his body.

"Stay," he breathed, and she could sense him starting to drift away on sleep. So she turned around, facing him, running fingers through his pretty blond hair with the slight curl. She touched his cheek, tickling him until the dimple made an appearance and his eyelids fluttered open.

"Hi," she breathed.

"Tell me another story," he breathed, shifting against the sheets, burrowing into the bed. "About your entrepreneurial sister. And your brother who would tear down the world for you."

"Why?" She laughed.

"It sounds nice." He yawned so hard his jaw popped. "Sounds like a nice way to grow up."

"It was," she whispered. "How did you grow up?"

"In a bowl. Without air," he whispered, but before she could ask him what he meant, he gave way to dreams.

Just a few more minutes, she thought, and closed her eyes to better enjoy the astronomical thread count and his strong arms and the rare illusion of care.

Chapter 3

She woke to a room thick with shadow. Alone. The white duvet pulled up to her chin. Her boots were gone—he must have taken them off her sometime in the night, because she didn't remember doing that. She stretched her toes in the soft, sleep-warm sheets.

Dawn, she thought, and listened for the sound of the shower, or of Harry quietly getting ready for the trip to find the man who would get his sister out of trouble. But then she realized the sunlight coming in under the blackout shades on the window was knife bright and she rolled over to see the clock on the bedside table.

Nine thirty.

Beyond the table, the closet was open and empty. The bathroom was dark. The sink counter empty of toiletries. Next to the TV were her bag and her clothes, folded and stacked.

Harry was gone.

The slice of pain was embarrassing and awful. And totally unexpected.

She sat up, clutching the sheet to her chest, trying to staunch the slow bleed of startling emotion.

It was a hookup at a bar. You can't go falling in infatuation just because he was sad and provided expert cunnilingus.

Though the truth was she'd fallen in love for far worse reasons before.

But there was a flash of white paper on top of her clothing, and she flushed with a sort of seventh-grade thrill.

A note!

She managed not to leap out of bed like the woman in a rom-com movie, but she couldn't stop the hard chug of her heart as she picked up the note, the dark scrawl of his handwriting not quite legible in the shadowy room.

She flicked on the light and sat down on the foot of the bed.

Ryan Kaminski. His handwriting was like the way he moved—no flourishes, but graceful in its economy. *I watched you for a few moments before leaving, debating whether to wake you up. But in the end I decided to let you sleep, because you are simply lovely and while sleeping you are only more so. Also I was in no great hurry to start a conversation about why I cannot see you again, or call you. Why anything more than this amazing night between us would be an impossibility. I arranged a late checkout, and breakfast will be arriving around ten. I hope you can stay to enjoy it.*

Thank you.

Harry

That had to be one of the most lovely kiss-off letters she'd ever seen. Really quite masterful.

Her stomach full of a weird kind of regret and morning-after melancholy, she made a quick call down to the front desk to cancel the breakfast. She would shower at home; the #7 train to Sunnyside would remove some of Harry's fairy-tale dust that still lingered on her skin.

She dressed, and after a moment of painful consideration, folded the note and tucked it into her purse.

The door clicked shut behind her and she checked her phone as she walked down the hallway toward the elevators. Luckily, she still had some juice left.

A text Lindsey had sent last night bloomed on her screen.

So? Did you make Ken Doll happy?

I gave it my best shot, she texted back hours after Lindsey's original note.

Atta girl, came the response fairly quickly. She imagined Lindsey in bed with her phone.

How was the rest of the night?

Gary asked some questions about you and Ken Doll. I threw him off the scent.

For some strange reason, that made her feel almost weepy. Talking to Harry last night about his sister when it had been years since she'd talked to her own. *Years.* She talked to her brother more often because he was pushy that way, but that she was closer to Lindsey, whom she'd known for only two months, than to her sisters, well, it hurt on this weird morning when she felt all raw and turned inside out.

Thanks, Linds.

The elevator doors opened and she turned left out of them, tucking her phone back into her bag, which was why she didn't see the men's bathroom door open and Gary come stepping out.

"Ryan?" His familiar voice made her stop in her tracks, her stomach slipping down into her boots.

"Gary." He really was a nice guy and if the bar were unaffiliated, what had happened between her and Harry probably wouldn't even get her hand slapped. But The Cobalt Hotel was a part of a conglomerate and there were rules about this stuff.

"What are you doing here this morning?" he asked, pretending to be casual, clearly trying to give her a chance to lie.

There was no point in pretending. That wasn't quite her style.

She smiled and shrugged. "What do you think?"

"Christ, Ryan," he said, stepping alongside of her and pulling her into motion, down the stairs toward the bar. "Couldn't you have taken him to your place? Why the hell did you have to stay here?"

"Because I'm a sucker for the free shampoo in the rooms." She had swiped it. She might be too proud for a free breakfast, but she wasn't too proud for travel-size luxury toiletries.

He paused in front of The Cobalt Bar's locked doors. "Do you even know who he is?" Gary asked.

"You're not my father, Gary."

"No. I'm not asking do you know his name and sexual history. I'm asking do you know *who he is*?"

"He's . . . someone?" She'd known that, of course. The gravitas. The way other people in the bar watched him from the corner of their eyes. She just chose to ignore it.

"Oh, Christ, doesn't anyone read the newspaper anymore? I thought you were smarter than the rest of the idiots who work here. He's Har—"

Some remnant of self-preservation made her hold up her hand. "Don't tell me. Don't. It's over. It won't happen again."

"But you did it here. And now you told me about it." He lifted his hands as if to show her how they were tied. *Poor Gary. Stupid Ryan.* "I have to fire you."

"Don't bother, Gary," she said. "I quit."

She patted his shoulder, because he was better than most, and headed out into the full summer reality of July in New York City. It was hot and close, though the smell of the garbage hadn't taken over yet.

The sun had heft to it and it fell over her bare shoulders like a lover's arm.

Instead of heading toward the subway, she turned east toward Central Park. A hike in heels that pinched her toes, but such was life.

In Ryan's reality, everything had a price. No pleasure came without its sorrow. No joy without its despair. And perhaps losing her job on top of the vague despondence she felt over the letter in her bag was overkill, but karma was a bitch, and sometimes she took more than her due.

Still, she thought, dodging a couple holding hands on their way to work, the fact that she'd gladly pay the cost for another night with Harry might indicate she wasn't quite done paying.

Chapter 4

Harrison Montgomery's hands couldn't stop shaking.

In his tumbler of water the ice cubes bounced against the crystal.

It wasn't the fault of the jet engines, or transatlantic turbulence. The ride, as ever, in the Montgomery family jet was smooth as silk.

The shaking was from him. From inside him. From his muscles. His brain. The damaged edges of his exhausted heart.

It's done. It's over. She is safe and we're taking her home.

That mantra had no effect on the shaking. He put down the glass and balled his hands into fists, hoping that might help. Exhaustion made him nauseous, but every time he slipped into a doze, all he saw was his sister, beaten and bloody, filthy and unconscious, and his eyes popped open, his heartbeat pounding in his throat.

Ashley had been kidnapped by Somali pirates.

The thought—even though he'd been living with it for the last three weeks—was still surreal.

Who gets kidnapped by pirates?

The statistics of that particular question got skewed by the fact that Ashley had spent the last year as an aid worker in Kenya and a friend had convinced her to take a vacation to the Seychelles. They'd rented a boat for a day and the pirates had picked them up.

In the last three weeks he'd negotiated her release, gathered the ransom, and found Brody Baxter, a former bodyguard for the Montgomery family, who was the man who actually went into the tiny desert village that had been armed to the teeth to get Ashley. They then spent twenty-four excruciating hours in a Nairobi hospital making sure she was okay to fly, that there weren't internal injuries or brain trauma.

Thank God there weren't.

He'd scheduled a more thorough exam to be done by their family doctor once they got back to New York City and called ahead to their grandmother's building, letting them know Ashley would be arriving and that she didn't have any keys. Or ID. Or clothes.

In front of him was all the paperwork that would allow her to enter the country without a passport with as little hassle as possible.

Luckily, being a Montgomery had a few perks, and he could count on some political friends on that score.

He'd done all of this—negotiating, ransoming, traveling, waiting—without the press finding out. Which was a miracle, really, considering he was a Montgomery and the press, as a rule, cared about what he and his family were doing.

He'd also done it without major international incident or a SEAL team.

Or sleep, really.

All while running for the United States House of Representatives.

And now, for some reason, with Ashley finally safe and sleeping in the back of the plane, he found himself unable to use his hands. The pen he'd picked up to finish the paperwork shook right out of his fingers.

"It's the adrenaline," Brody Baxter said from the seat

across the aisle. His eyes were closed and his head shimmied against the headrest with every small bounce and shift of the plane.

"What is?"

Harrison yanked further at his tie, trying to get some air.

Brody opened one dark eye. "You are jumpier than the Somali boys we got her from, and they were pretty damn jumpy."

Harrison stared down at the same passport paperwork he'd been looking at for the last twenty-four hours and the words blurred.

Tears stung hard behind his eyes and he had to gasp to catch his breath.

"She's safe, man," Brody said. "You did it."

Until the day he died, he would not forget his first glimpse of her in Brody's arms as he ran down the tarmac toward the ambulance. Unconscious, bloody, her dress in tatters, her hair a wild mess, filthy.

I'm too late, he'd thought, putting a hand against the ambulance so he wouldn't fall to his knees as nurses and paramedics swarmed Brody and Ashley. *If I'd worked faster, done more, she wouldn't have been hurt. Those men wouldn't have kicked her. Beaten her.*

"Harrison." Brody's hard voice worked on some instinctual level and he brought his head around to stare at the man. "You did it. You did it just right."

"It was you, actually," he said, his voice catching on emotion and exhaustion.

Brody had always been an impossibly cagey guy, and the years since he'd started working for the family only made him more so. His dark eyes both lauded him and damned him, which Harrison guessed was fair considering their history. The Montgomerys had not been kind to Brody Baxter.

"What you did," Brody said. "There aren't ten guys

in the world who could have done that as well. She's safe, because of you. I was just the muscle."

He thought of the days in New York, talking to senators and lobbyists. Retired generals. The assistant to the President's chief of staff. Had all of that been time wasted?

Trying to get all of that done on his own, holed up in a hotel room, avoiding press and family. Had that been a mistake?

They heard Ashley in the back, stirring. She'd been in and out of sleep, disoriented and confused, and Harrison didn't want her to wake up alone and scared. He began to shift to his feet, but his arms would not help him. His knees were jelly.

"I got it, man," Brody said, clapping his large hand on Harrison's shoulder. "Try to get some rest."

Harrison sagged back into his seat and let the big man go sit beside his sister. Briefly, he wondered if this was going to be a problem. Ashley had, at one time, caused quite a scene over Brody.

But Harrison found he did not have the energy to be worried. He couldn't even follow the thought to any conclusion.

He propped his elbows up on the small foldaway table and scrubbed his hands through his hair and down over his face. When was the last time he showered? Changed his clothes? Slept?

The answer to the last question came in a vision of a tattoo, a woman wrapped in seaweed and vines being pulled underwater, her blond hair a cloud around her composed, nearly blissful face.

Ryan.

Perhaps it was his general defenselessness, or exhaustion, but the thought of Ryan Kaminski slipped into his skull like an assassin.

He couldn't count that night as a mistake. It was the

first time in his life a woman had slept with him without knowing his family. Without one eye on his connections and his money.

Ryan had picked him, for him. And not at his best. At the very lowest point in his life, she'd held out a hand.

What kind of person did that?

What kind of person found such weakness and confusion interesting? And not just a little . . . What had happened in that room destroyed him. It wasn't just the incredible sex, but the honesty. The honesty had been addictive and erotic and rare. So rare he hadn't realized what a kingdom of lies and half-truths he ruled, until meeting her.

And ironically, he'd lied to her. A lie by omission was still a lie. Maybe worse because of its intrinsic cowardice.

Harry. No one ever in his life had called him Harry.

Oh God, he had to stop thinking about her.

It was one thing to cling to the mysterious woman and that charged night like a lifeboat while waiting to find out if his sister was alive or dead, but they were returning to the real world. Real life.

And in real life he was Harrison Montgomery, the favorite son of a fifth-generation political family out of Atlanta. And in three months about to be a congressman. The representative in the House for Georgia's fifth congressional district.

His father was finishing up his last term as governor of Georgia, and appropriately going down with the sinking boat of corruption and scandal that had been his life's work.

And in order to wipe the mud off his family name, to return some pride to his sister and himself and future Montgomery generations, Harrison's role, his mission, was to be without weakness. To give no rumors the chance to find foothold, no reporter trying to make his name even the slightest whiff of scandal.

And his night with Ryan to the outside eye was nothing but scandalous.

That night was an anomaly. Best forgotten.

He took a deep breath. Another. Stretched his hands out and then made fists. Pushed his messy, dirty hair back into some kind of order, straightened his dirty tie. Bit by bit he found himself back in control of himself. His body. His thoughts.

Ashley was safe. She was here.

Ryan was forgotten.

And he was Harrison Montgomery, with a family dynasty settled comfortably, familiarly, on his back.

Brody returned and sat down in his seat.

"She's sleeping again," he said.

"That's good." Harrison flipped the page on the passport paperwork and began filling it out, his mind clear. His hand steady.

"You okay?" Brody asked.

"Fine," he answered without looking up. "Just fine."

Chapter 5

"The good news! It just keeps coming!" Wallace Jones, Harrison's campaign manager, a whirlwind of spectacularly bad ties and genius brain cells, burst into Harrison's office without knocking.

"I could use some good news," Harrison said, sitting back from the dual, equally unappealing tasks of dealing with his mother and fundraising calls.

Financially, he was tapped out. Between getting his sister free and the campaign, he was running on fumes. And credit.

And his mother was here to harass him about Ashley. So, yeah, he could use some good news.

"Poll numbers!" Wallace said, lifting a handful of papers into the air. "The Education Initiative is working; so is VetAid. We're still up across all demographics. We're spanking Glendale in women under fifty, minorities, and college students."

Harrison left the jubilation to Wallace—he was far better suited for it. Punching the air felt stupid to Harrison. But the 100-proof relief poured through him all the same.

He allowed himself an unchecked smile and loosened his tie. Practically a party.

"College students don't vote," Patty Montgomery said. Across his small office, on the large couch where he'd been spending far too many of his nights since getting his sister back on American soil, sat his mother, Patty Montgomery. Her black suit matched the black of the couch and the gray light from the window illuminated her in a strange way, and he had the brief impression of her sitting on a stage.

And despite having grown up in Manhattan, her Georgia accent with its Buckhead polish was flawless. She sounded local. Several generations of local.

Wallace whirled to see Patty—his enemy in so many ways—on the couch and tossed his hands up in the air. "Jesus, Harrison. How many times do I have to tell you having your mother here does not help our campaign? We are trying to distance ourselves from the mistakes your father has made."

"Family issues, Wallace. Not political," Harrison said, though Wallace was right. The education scandal, the housing market, unemployment skyrocketing, increasingly disturbing race relations in Atlanta—all of it Harrison was trying to fix. All of it happened on his father, Ted's, watch.

"With your family it's always political!" Wallace sat in the chair across from Harrison's desk instead of flopping down on the couch, as was his usual practice, and glared at Patty. "I assume this is about your sister?"

"Ashley is safe. That's all that matters." Harrison was trying to finish the argument his mother seemed hell-bent on rehashing.

"All that matters?" She laughed, as if the safety and well-being of her only daughter was far down on her personal list of things that mattered. She ran a hand over her perfect, unmoving blond bob, the gold and diamond rings on her fingers gleaming, using all the meager light to her advantage. "You are running for Congress. Your father's approval rating is at an all-time low, and she is somewhere pouting because I asked her to answer a few questions. Runs off with that man without a word to us? Tell me, how am I wrong?"

"That man's name is Brody," Harrison said.

After Harrison and Brody got Ashley back into New York City, Brody had then whisked her away somewhere to recuperate after Mother bullied Ashley with press conferences. Ashley, concussed with bruised ribs and recovering from severe dehydration, exhaustion, and probably PTSD, had not been up for press conferences.

"I knew going to him was a mistake."

"He was the only choice we had. She'll call us when she wants to."

"Does this mean we can actually talk about business?" Wallace asked.

"Ah yes," Mom said, putting on the Steel Magnolia routine, something she did only when she was truly angry or there was a journalist in the room. "The spectacular approval ratings among people who just don't vote?"

"In the political stone age, that might have been true. But the world is changing, Patty." Wallace was young and black, a political street fighter with very little respect for the old guard. Mother would never say it, but Wallace was her worst nightmare.

"Well, one thing doesn't change," Patty said. "Money. And Arthur Glendale is getting some big money from contributors. His media budget is three times ours."

"And so far it hasn't mattered," Wallace said.

"You're foolish if you think it won't." Patty got to her feet. "A million will barely keep us on the air."

"I'm working on the money," Harrison said, lifting the call sheets.

"There's not a million on that list," Patty said. "Not even close. So we need a miracle."

"By miracle," Harrison said, "you mean I need to get

Ashley to show up to some campaign events. And I've already said I'm not doing it. She's been through hell."

"Your sister is a Montgomery," Patty said. "She knows her responsibility, and I'm not sure why expecting her to be grateful for your part in getting her out of Somalia makes me the bad guy in this."

Of course she didn't.

"The press release about her kidnapping and rescue gave us a bump," Harrison said. "Let's just give her some time to heal."

"You know," Wallace said, sheepishly running a hand over his dark hair. "While I appreciate you wanting to protect your sister and I dislike agreeing with the Queen Mum, Arthur Glendale has pockets deeper than anyone has imagined, and without something to break up the media message that you are too young, too inexperienced, too rich, too goddamned Montgomery, and somehow too handsome to be a trusted public servant, you might lose what started as a shoo-in run for the House."

"I thought you came in here with good news," Harrison said.

"Your mom killed it."

"Am I required to say it again?" Mother asked, holding out her arms. "All those problems would be solved if you were married."

"Mother—"

"It's true," she insisted. "If you were married, you would immediately be considered more substantial."

Marriage was Mother's Band-Aid. Respectability the solid wall she hid all the family sins behind.

"I can't just pluck a woman out of thin air."

"You're not even looking," she cried. "You've spent all your time in school or with VetAid and not enough starting a family. Waiting to fall in love is not helping your career." Her tone conveyed quite clearly her derision toward love.

Harrison had no feelings about love, derisive or otherwise. He had no time and no energy to waste on chasing something he felt quite convincingly was not meant for him. Not meant for anyone in politics. Or his family.

Marriage and family were tools.

Love was a yeti.

He was thirty-one years old and this was his entire experience. His entire life. Since he'd turned twenty-two, every minute of every day was spent becoming who he was right now. Every turn in the road led him here. Not to a family, not to a wife, but to correcting his father's mistakes. Making the Montgomery name something he could be proud of.

What else was he supposed to do but exactly this?

In the end, it didn't matter how he got into office. All that mattered was that he got in.

"We're in this and we're leading in the polls. If the matter is more money, we'll get more money. As for the Ashley miracle, I'll ask," Harrison said, bowing under the pressure because they were right. He looked like a kid standing next to Glendale. "When I get her on the phone. I will ask."

"Well, will you look at that," Wallace said, grinning at Mother. "Look what happens when we work together. We should channel our powers for good more often."

Mother did not smile. She picked up her purse from the couch and slipped the strap over her shoulder. If there was a prototype for politician's wife, Mother was it. Elegant, genteel, and calm. Stylish. Never flashy. Confident and contained. She gave the impression of still, deep waters. And even in his shabby, cluttered, crowded office that was basically just a cement box, she exuded a sense of Old World money.

There was a flash in his memory, the image of a woman in high leather boots and a thin tank top with a tattoo peeking over the edge.

Despite his efforts, he'd been unable to forget that night in New York City.

Raw. Rough. Unpolished.

Ryan had been the opposite of Patty Montgomery on a cellular level.

Perhaps that was why he'd been unable to stop thinking of her.

With effort, he refrained from smiling. Stopped that one flash from turning into a lightning storm of memory.

He stood and opened the door for his mother. Outside his office the campaign headquarters was crowded with staffers and interns, doing the hundreds of large and small tasks that made this campaign a real and tangible thing every day.

Outside the wide plate-glass windows was Peachtree and the downtown city center, cloaked in a gray rain. Mom's car and driver were outside waiting for her.

Noelle, her assistant, waited outside the door like a loyal pet.

"I've told your secretary to put a Friday luncheon on your schedule for the twenty-third," Patty said to Harrison.

"Fundraising?"

"Family."

"Our family?" Family meals were not something that happened at the Governor's Mansion. Not on Fridays. Not anytime.

"It's an article for *Southern Living*," Noelle supplied, glancing up from her iPad, where she seemed to have all her plans for world domination. "The Holiday edition."

Right. The only reason his family would sit down at a table together was if there was a chance someone would take a picture. Mother was very good at making them look like a typical family, with family dinners and vacations to the shore and trips to amusement parks, when in reality they didn't do any of those things without a camera crew making it happen.

"Distance, Harrison," Wallace said. "We don't need pictures of you and your dad standing arm-in-arm over a turkey, for God's sake."

"The magazine won't come out until after the election," Mother said. "And considering the way you've been tearing your father apart in speeches, a family photo shoot and article will go a long way toward showing there are no hard feelings."

She meant publically. Because personally, it was far more than hard feelings between him and Ted—there was a cavern of disappointment and anger. Of disgust.

Some men were created in the image of their father. Harrison grew up in his father's negative space. In the holes Ted had left behind. Harrison was who he was in spite of and to spite his father.

But Ted had clout and loyal followers—an Old World liberal guard that didn't like Harrison, and it would do his career good to get them on his side.

Harrison glanced at Wallace, who after a moment shrugged.

"What time do you need me?" Harrison asked.

"All day. I've had your schedule cleared." Mom glanced over her shoulder. "Goodbye, Wallace," she said.

"I can't come for lunch?" he asked.

"No."

And with that Mother was gone, down the center aisle of the room, a warship sending smaller vessels— interns and staffers—scrambling out of her way.

"Your mother terrifies me," Wallace said.

"You have a funny way of showing it."

"It's a very complicated fight-or-flight response. I can't explain it. I feel that way around most women."

Harrison smiled. Thought again of that tattoo and the long, silky brown hair falling over it, revealing and obscuring at the same time.

"Let's get back to work," Harrison said, walking back to his desk and the call sheets there. The destiny he'd been groomed for his entire life was waiting for him.

And there was no place in his destiny for that tattoo and the woman it belonged to.

Chapter 6

The nausea woke her up. The nausea always woke her up. A greasy, sick pull from sound sleep, from pleasant dreams about money and being able to go a day without barfing.

It was all-consuming, the nausea. Like an untrained puppy who kept jumping up when it shouldn't. Or a shitty friend with too much drama. It was, in fact, so paramount that it wasn't until she opened her eyes that she realized she wasn't in her own bed.

The ceiling was yellow and lacked the water stains from the time her upstairs neighbor left the sink running. Television news was on in the room and she didn't have a TV in her apartment.

The bed was funny. The mattress uncomfortable and beneath the sheets, covered in plastic.

She lifted her hand to find an IV tube stuck in her vein.

Uh-oh.

"Hey. You're awake." It was her brother's voice and she turned her head slowly, keeping the world steady, to find him sitting beside her bed.

"Hey," she whispered. Joy bounced through her, momentarily pushing aside the dizziness and exhaustion. Wes. Her big brother, who'd braided her hair after Mom died and forged Dad's signature on notes so she could skip school and go with him to Phillies games and showed up with pizza and milk at the end of the month when Dad's check had been stretched so thin it could barely keep the lights on.

It had been a few months since she'd seen him and as usual, it was a shock. Wes was a shock.

He'd always been an intense guy, an explosive kid and teenager. A lesson in extremes, that was her brother. Slow to love, quick to fight. Short temper, long memory. Smart brain, stupid heart.

But this man version of him seemed . . . dangerous. As if the years had worn away the middle ground between his extremes. He was all or nothing. In or out. All of his filters were gone, and he sat beside her bed in a sea of palpable anger.

Wes turned and pointed a remote at the TV in the corner behind him, putting the news on mute.

She reached out and touched his beard. Tugged it. An old welcome.

His lips curled in a familiar half-smile.

"Where are we?" she asked.

"Flushing Hospital," he said.

The world rolled off its anchors and her stomach pitched.

"You need to throw up?" he asked.

She breathed through her mouth until the wave passed. "No. I'm okay. It's just strange being the one in the hospital bed," she teased.

He smiled so sweetly at her. "It's a little strange for me too, but it's been a while since I was the one with the IV tubes."

"Allen Hayes?" she asked, remembering the last fight that got him in the hospital.

"I had no idea his sister could pack such a punch."

She ran a finger down the bumpy ridge of his nose. It

had been broken more than once. He grabbed her hand and pressed his mouth to the back of it.

"Do you remember what happened?" Wes asked.

"You were coming to take me to dinner." Excited, nervous, not exactly sure how she was going to break this insane news to her brother, she'd buzzed him up to her apartment, unlocked her door, and then run to the bathroom to vomit.

"I found you passed out on your bathroom floor. It looked like you'd vomited blood, so I called an ambulance," he said.

Blood she remembered, but that was all.

Oh God. She put a hand to her stomach.

"Did I—?"

"You're fine. Both of you." She could hear it in his voice, the lecture he was dying to give her.

She blew out a long breath, trying to get the sudden spike of her heartbeat under control.

"I'm sorry," she said. "That must have been scary."

"Well, it's not a moment I want to relive anytime soon, seeing my sister passed out in a pool of blood. You hit your head on the corner of the sink. Split the skin over your ear and knocked yourself out."

"I knocked myself out? On the sink?"

"At least it wasn't the toilet." Wes smiled. "You're still your own worst enemy."

Laughing felt good. Felt so good, like throwing open the window on a perfect day.

Wes picked up her hand and held it between his two. His hands were callused across the palm, worse on his right than on his left. And he was thin, thinner than she'd seen him in a long time. Whatever the mysterious computer work he wouldn't talk about required of him, it was taking too much.

"It's good to see you," she said, squeezing his hand.

"Talk to me, Ryan," he breathed.

She hadn't said the words out loud to anyone yet. A week ago what she'd thought was the flu turned into a missed period and a drugstore pregnancy test and finally a doctor's confirmation. So far the baby was a secret she kept to herself, and it still didn't feel real. She was in serious survival mode between the nausea and the joblessness and the fist-shaking minuscule failure rate of condoms that had not panned out in her favor.

Also surprising was how much she wanted this baby. It had been years since she'd thought of starting a family, and now certainly was not an optimal time, but none of that seemed to matter.

She was sick, scared, financially strapped, and emotionally vulnerable, but she was so damn *happy* about this baby.

Her new family.

"I'm pregnant," she said.

He opened his mouth to let out the lecture but she stopped him. "Don't," she said. "Anything you say about staying out of trouble will only be hypocritical."

"I've never been pregnant and alone and sick."

"I'm breaking new Kaminski ground." Even he had to smile at that.

"You've been sick like this the whole time?"

Her mouth was gummy, her lips dry and cracked. "I haven't been feeling great for a week. But it's only been like this for three days."

"The doctor said you were severely dehydrated."

"I haven't been able to keep anything down."

His hands squeezed hers and she pulled her fingers free, bracing herself for the outburst. "Jesus Christ, Ryan, why didn't you call me sooner? Why do things have to get this bad before you ask for help?"

"I don't know, Wes," she sighed. "But yelling at me isn't going to change anything."

He stood up and turned to look out the window. All she saw out that window was blue sky. Not a single cloud. Not a skyscraper or apartment building. It was as if they were floating above the city. Just a blue so dense and so deep it didn't seem real.

"The father—"

"Not around."

"You plan on telling him?"

"He is not around, Wes."

She wasn't about to tell her big brother that she didn't even know Harry's last name. *Oh God, he'd go ballistic.*

"Okay, so, no father. What is your plan?" The sunlight fell over his face, bringing out the red in his hair and tightly clipped beard, turning his eyes to amber. It was funny that she'd always been called the pretty one, had been able to make some kind of living for a while off of her looks—that stupid Lip Girl thing when she was seventeen—when Wes was the real beauty.

Half intellectual whiz kid, half well-groomed Viking berserker.

His look was popular and on Wes, extremely authentic. He'd make a killing if he wanted to.

"Ryan?"

Right. Her plans.

"I'm keeping the baby."

"Okay."

She pushed herself up to sitting because she quite literally wasn't going to take Wes's coming lecture lying down. "I haven't really had a chance to plan past that while vomiting my guts out."

"Are you working?"

She plucked at the edge of the thin hospital blanket; it was beige. The color of her life these days.

"Ryan?"

"No. I picked up a few shifts at a bar down the street, but once I started getting sick I was late too many times and the manager let me go."

"So, no job? Tell me you filed for insurance—"

"I did. I'm covered."

"Savings?"

"A few months' rent."

"That's it?"

"Wes—"

"You need to go home, Ryan."

She bristled. "No, I don't. I don't need to go back to Nora, pregnant, with my tail between my legs, so she can say I told you so."

"You realize you are a thirty-two-year-old woman? This sister fight with Nora is getting ridiculous."

"Tell her that," she muttered. "She's the one keeping me in exile."

But he already had. Wes had been trying to get them to make up for years, but the hurt Ryan had caused Nora was too bad. Too big. It wasn't a forgive-and-forget kind of thing. It was a carry-the-hatchet-to-the-grave kind of thing.

"There's a lot of money in pregnant modeling," she said, grasping at straws. She'd looked in the mirror, and what she saw there didn't say Happy Pregnant Woman About Town. She looked like she had barely survived the zombie apocalypse. "My agent says I'll probably be able to get some catalog work. Maybe some national spots."

"Right, as soon as you get off the bathroom floor."

"Morning sickness doesn't last forever."

"Then you don't remember when Mom was pregnant with Olivia."

The memory of her mother, shuffling around the house,

gray-faced and miserable during the entire pregnancy, gave Ryan's stomach a slimy twist, and she looked away from her brother's damning eyes.

"Women have babies by themselves in New York City all the time. I'm hardly alone."

But she felt it. She really did. So alone her entire life was just an echo chamber, her mistakes bouncing back at her.

Outside in the hallway, someone yelled and a metal tray was dropped. The noise was so loud she flinched.

"I can help," he said. "But even I can't support you and a baby in New York City. I don't have that kind of cash."

"I don't want your help."

"You've got to be kidding me."

"Don't yell at me, Wes," she cried. "You can't demand access and answers from me when your whole damn life is a secret."

"This isn't about me! It's about you and your baby." He threw his hands up in the air. "Day care. Schools. That one-room closet you call an apartment. You need help. Point-blank. End of story. And I know you've been living your life on your own terms for a long time, but if you plan on having this baby you're gonna have to get over yourself."

Get over myself, she thought, and nearly laughed. He said it like pride was a luxury when it was all she had left. The only thing that her family, her ex-husband, her life hadn't taken away from her.

The vague upset in her stomach that she'd gotten used to was suddenly eclipsed by head-to-toe chills, her skin breaking out in goose bumps.

The price of the baby, she thought, putting her hands over her stomach, *will be my pride.*

She'd known after the night with Harry that there would be more to pay.

Her brother's glowing intensity was suddenly too much and she looked away, staring blindly toward the silent news on the television.

Behind the dark-haired anchor with apple cheeks, the words *Kidnapped by Somali Pirates* flashed red and yellow.

Wes grabbed the remote from the bedside table and turned up the volume.

"What is this?" she asked, happily jumping on the distraction.

"You haven't been following the news?"

"Been busy, Wes. Puking my guts up."

The screen changed to a picture of a pretty woman with curly brown hair and a wide smile.

"That's Ashley Montgomery," Wes said. "She was kidnapped by pirates, rescued, and then vanished again."

"And I thought I had it bad," she muttered, pleased when Wes smiled at her.

"The worldwide media search for Ashley Montgomery has finally ended," the news anchor said. "Montgomery has turned up in a small town in Arkansas, where she's been recuperating after surviving three weeks in a Somali pirate camp. Apparently she's been busy organizing a series of senior citizen initiatives in the small town but has said that she will be stepping out occasionally to help her brother's congressional campaign."

A man, blond-haired and smiling, radiating a kind of poise and confidence that one would expect from a guy running for office, was shaking hands with people in a huge crowd as he walked toward a podium.

The crowd was holding signs that said *Harrison Montgomery for Congress* and *A New Hope*.

"Two months ago, Harrison Montgomery's run for Georgia's Fifth District seat in the House of Representatives seemed like a sure thing. But Republican candidate Arthur Glendale is giving the Montgomery Golden Boy a run for his money."

"Ryan?" Wes asked. "What's wrong?"

Harrison Montgomery.

Harry.

"I'm going to be sick."

Chapter 7

Ryan was proud of her apartment. It was an engineering/small-space lifestyle marvel and it had taken years to get it just right, to come up with all the clever space-saving tricks. The key was sparseness. Absolutely no clutter or mess. Having no attachments to things helped, too. No pictures in frames, no mementos to keep in boxes that took up space. Living this way required a certain ruthlessness, but she was suited for that.

The books were her only luxury.

Which wasn't to say her apartment was dour. No. She'd painted the kitchen part of the studio yellow to go with her red teacups, which went with her blue rug. The walls in the living area were lined with shelves filled with books and jewelry, along with some of her prettier shoes that she'd collected over the years. Her clothes were nestled in there, socks and underwear in a shelf basket. Her laptop was tucked under the couch.

After the divorce and selling the house in Jersey, she'd moved to this Queens apartment, thinking it was only temporary, hopeful she'd get some more bookings, maybe a national spot, and make some money that would let her move someplace else.

Someplace without water stains, and with a real closet and—dare to dream—an oven. Maybe a one-bedroom in Brooklyn.

But the big contract didn't come, and she'd stayed in Sunnyside and made her little apartment work for her.

"This place is worse than a college dorm room," Wes said as he walked in behind her.

"Like either of us has ever seen the inside of college dorm room," she muttered. She hung her keys on the hook beside the door and collapsed onto the couch underneath the loft bed she'd made with her own two hands last year.

Upstairs, her neighbor was screaming in Spanish at something on the TV.

And the smell of someone cooking cabbage seeped through the walls.

Home, sweet home.

"We need to talk about this," Wes said, pacing the four steps from her kitchen area to the bathroom door.

"There's not much left to say."

"Harrison Montgomery knocked you up and there's not much to say?"

Ryan sighed and rested her head in her hands. "You make it sound like I'm a victim, Wes. And I'm not. It was more than consensual, we used protection, something happened, and I'm pregnant."

"You're pregnant, broke, out of work, and sick as a dog."

She glared at him. "You don't have to stay. You can leave if this is so damn troubling to you."

"You know, maybe I *will* leave, and I'll head on down to Atlanta and let Harrison Montgomery in on what's going on with you."

"Don't, Wes." She stood, because these were not idle threats with her brother. Not at all. He would do just that and feel as if his actions were totally justified.

"Tell me why I shouldn't?"

"Because I need some time to think!" she cried. "Because this is my life, and I just realized that the father of my unborn baby is running for Congress. Maybe I don't want him involved in it!"

"You've got to be realistic. He is in a financial position to help you."

"I don't give a shit, Wes. He's in the middle of a campaign—this could seriously mess that up for him."

"You're kidding me, right? You're pregnant, alone, and broke and you're worried about his fucking campaign?"

Ryan sat back down on the couch, suddenly exhausted. By everything. The baby growing in her stomach, her tiny apartment, her brother.

Harrison Montgomery.

That explained the gravitas.

And the complicated family.

In fact, details of that whole night rearranged themselves into a different order. A different reality. She had a very hard-won sense of her own worth and it took some great weight to crush her, but Harrison Montgomery lowering himself from his lofty heights did it.

Harry had been slumming.

But even as she thought it, even as the proof seemed irrefutable, she didn't want to believe it. He had not been in that bar looking to score. Drinking away the pain of his sister's unsure future at the hands of Somali pirates had been his objective.

Christ, she thought. Amazed anew at how he'd kept his shit together that night.

There was not a chance in the world she would have had that kind of poise in the face of something that terrifying. She'd have been running down the streets of New York like a lunatic, not sitting so still in the corner of a bar like he was the axis upon which the world spun.

"Can we just take a break for a while?" she said. "You can go back to telling me how impossible my life is in a little bit. Okay?"

Wes braced his hands on his lean hips, his burgundy tee shirt worn and thin over black jeans and work boots. The Wes Kaminski uniform. She wondered if his secret job paid him at all.

"Fine," he sighed. "Take a nap. I'm going to go to the store." He opened the fridge and took quick stock. "You've been living on milk?"

"And oranges. Get lots of them. And sometimes I want peanut butter. Crunchy."

"What about meat?"

She gagged at the thought.

"Got it," Wes said with a smile, and she felt all her defenses get wobbly. Everything was wobbly, and she pulled the chenille blanket—red to match her teacups—from the back of the love seat over her tired and sore body.

"I'll be okay, Wes. I always am. I just need some time to figure this out."

"You don't have a lot of time, Ryan."

"I've got nine months."

Her eyes drifted shut and she didn't hear her brother whisper, "You've got until Friday."

Friday, August 23
The Governor's Mansion

Harrison's BlackBerry was getting hot in his hand, nearly burning his ear.

"We have got to do something, Harrison," Wallace was saying. "Glendale is killing us in the press. You look like a Boy Scout. Like literally, an earnest little boy in shorts with a stupid sash and knee socks."

"I get the idea, Wallace," he said, pacing the front porch of the Governor's Mansion in the bright noon sunlight. Inside, the bullshit was thick on the floor as his mother was telling the *Southern Living* staff writer all about her heritage recipe for Georgia Caviar, a black-eyed pea salad his mother had never made in her life.

And his father was pretending that these family meals had been a tradition for as long as he'd been in the mansion. There was even a baseball game playing on the television.

When Ted had been running for the Senate the first time and Harrison had been six or so, Mom arranged a press conference at a park so newspapers could get pictures of him and Ted playing catch. They'd had to send staffers out to buy baseball gloves because they didn't have any.

One of Ted's bodyguards taught him how to throw the ball, because Dad tried but got frustrated too fast and started drinking from the flask he always had in his pocket.

Mom had been furious. At Harrison. At Ted. At the world that was always so willing to disappoint her.

But no matter how awkward and truly false the event Mother was orchestrating, she used these little vignettes as a way to get work done. Today she was in there talking about Harrison's VetAid initiative to provide veterans returning home from war and their families much-needed legal aid.

You just had to wade through a lot of lies to get to the truth of his family.

"Ashley is coming to the fundraiser next week. That will help, won't it?" he asked. He'd finally gotten his sister on the phone and she'd agreed to do three events to help his campaign, on the one condition that he come to Bishop, Arkansas, to get her.

Have you ever in your life been just Harrison? she'd asked. *And not Harrison Montgomery?*

Once, he'd answered, thinking of Ryan Kaminski and that night that seemed more dream than real.

"Maybe we need another photo of you with your shirt off," Wallace said, pulling Harrison's thoughts away from tattoos and one-night stands. "Or a trip down to Manuel's Tavern to get your picture taken behind the bar."

"Don't be ridiculous."

"You are the new generation's JFK Jr.—let's not shy away from the sex appeal."

"That's a bit of a stretch."

"I'm getting worried, Harrison."

"Yeah, I get that. But I'm not going to take off my shirt. If we stick to the message: education, family—"

"Community, yes. The message is good. But Glendale has the same message and way more money. And his dad is dead."

And my dad is alive and still making mistakes.

Behind him he heard the scuff of footsteps on the brick porch and turned to see Noelle standing just outside the doorway.

"They're ready for you," she said, and he nodded at her.

"I've got to go," Harrison said to Wallace.

"Is Noelle there?" Wallace asked.

"Of course."

"What's she wearing?"

"You've got to be kidding me."

"What? I like her."

"You have a serious thing for inaccessible women."

"Wait . . . why do you think she's inaccessible? I could totally—"

"Goodbye, Wallace."

"Wait, wait—Jill down at Headquarters said a guy from Homeland Security came looking for you."

"For me?"

"Yeah. Is there a terrorist part of the résumé you forget to tell me about?"

"No. Of course not."

"Harrison," Noelle whispered. "We really need to get inside."

Harrison said goodbye to Wallace, tucked his phone in his pocket, and turned back toward Noelle, who stood there with her clipboards and her two phones and the pencil tucked in the bun of blond hair at the back of her head. She was an impenetrable wall of efficiency.

"Lead the way." Harrison's attempt at charm was met with blinking pale gray eyes.

"Your mother would like me to remind you not to bring up the education scandal," Noelle said as they walked back into the mansion. The first floor was a showcase used primarily for entertaining and tours. All the furnishings were a part of a historical federal collection and were hugely uncomfortable. Upstairs were his parents' quarters, and they were only slightly less formal. But they did have a couch that wasn't made out of horsehair, and the chairs when he sat on them didn't creak.

"Education reform is a major part of my platform because of the Atlanta corruption."

"Exactly."

"You're joking, right?"

"It looks bad on your father."

"It *is* bad on my father."

Noelle pushed her glasses up farther on her nose, her gray eyes steely, and he wondered, briefly, if there wasn't more to his mother's loyal pet. "There are other things to talk about."

They turned into the living room, where Mom and Dad, dressed in carefully calculated casual clothes, were sitting with the *Southern Living* staff. There was the writer, the photographer, and a videographer, because apparently there was going to be some special bonus material on the website. As well as a lighting guy and a sound guy.

And all of them turned to look at him when he walked in.

"Son!" Dad said, coming to his feet, his wide smile revealing the dimples Harrison had inherited. A former high school football star, Ted was still a big, strong man, with a barrel chest, who carried himself well. Harrison was the exact same height but without the football player build.

Ted's years of alcoholism were physically obvious only in the broken blood vessels around his nose and eyes. All of which were now carefully powdered over.

His blond hair was growing silver, his shoulders just slightly rounded. His blue eyes were still sharp.

There were times it was eerie looking at his father, times when the physical resemblance between them was so strong. So unbelievably real that Harrison lost himself for a moment.

That is exactly how I will look in thirty years, he thought for perhaps the thousandth time.

It was nearly surreal.

As a boy, watching crowds cheer for his father, men line up just to shake his hand, women press newborn babies into his arms so he could kiss them—it had only solidified his perception of his father as a hero. A god.

A man to emulate in all things.

And that's what he'd done. He'd emulated his father's overblown wealthy-white-man sense of privilege. His sense of destiny and entitlement. Of course he should get what he wanted. Of course he deserved the best. He was Ted Montgomery's son, after all.

And then he turned twenty-two and his father ran for Vice-President, and there had been Heidi and the car crash.

And Harrison found out who his father really was. Who all of them really were.

The memory of it, of finding out about it and feeling part of himself, his identity, his plans and goals to be just like his fucking father, shattering—it stopped his blood. Even years later, he looked at his father, remembered Heidi, and stepped away from Ted's outstretched hand.

"Harrison," Mom said, also coming to her feet, smiling so wide to cover the cold silence between the two men in her life. "We're so glad you could take a break from your busy campaign schedule to join us. I was just telling everyone about your work at VetAid."

Right. He would play the Montgomery game. Like he always did. Because it was a means to an end, a way into Congress and beyond that, the White House.

"I'm glad to be here, Mom. Are we ready to eat?" he asked, rubbing his hands together. "I'm starving."

By three o'clock in the afternoon they still hadn't eaten and Harrison was getting ready to end a ridiculous discussion on Montgomery holiday traditions, when Dad's head of security walked into the sunny room.

"Is there a problem, Jeff?" Dad asked.

"There's a man downstairs," Jeff said. "Says—"

In the hallway, someone yelled and another voice answered back, just as the door behind Jeff opened up and a stranger burst in.

"I didn't feel like waiting," the man said to Jeff, flashing a malicious grin behind a trimmed beard.

They all jumped to their feet, but Mom was the first one to speak.

"Can I help you?" she asked.

"No. Actually," the man said, and pointed to Harrison, "I'm here to talk to your son."

"I'm afraid you'll have to wait until we're done," Mom said.

"I'm guessing you didn't see my badge. Let me give you a good look." From the back pocket of his black jeans, the man pulled out a badge and held it out toward the family.

DHS. Homeland Security.

The guy wore jeans and a tee shirt. Beat-up boots. He didn't look like any agent Harrison had ever seen. *What the hell is going on here?*

"I don't care what your badge says; you can't come in here and harass my son," Patty said.

The bearded man shot Harrison a pointed look that somehow managed to call him out. *You let your mom fight your battles for you, you miserable boy*—that's what that look said.

"Please excuse me," Harrison said to the *Southern Living* staff before stepping to the door. "Let's talk outside, Mr.—"

"My name is Wes Kaminksi," the man said, glancing at the cameras and the witnesses before staring at Harrison, something unholy and bright in his eyes. "My sister is Ryan Kaminski."

Chapter 8

The name detonated in his chest.

And he stopped for just a moment, halfway across the room.

Wes saw his hesitation and grinned.

"Ah, so you do remember."

"Is she all right?" He imagined something awful. Something catastrophic. Something that would bring her brother, a DHS agent, to his door.

Wes blinked and then grinned, like the asshole had him by the short hairs. "If you do the right thing she will be."

Do the right thing?

Harrison inferred the only thing he could.

And a reality he wanted desperately to deny sucker-punched him, driving all the air from his lungs.

His savior that night had figured out who he was and was looking for her payout.

It was Heidi all over again.

"Outside." Harrison smiled with all his teeth and led Wes out the door, past security and the assistants.

Fuck. Camera crews. Journalists. There was a good chance someone in that room was getting on Google to figure out who Ryan Kaminski was. And within three hours there would be people camped out in front of her house, demanding to know how she knew Harrison Montgomery.

Normally, no one would care, but his sister was all over the news these days.

His heart pounding in his hands and behind his eyes, he opened the door to an old bedroom filled with boxes of holiday decorations.

"After you," he said to Wes, who eyed him warily as he walked in. Harrison slammed the door shut behind them so hard, a plastic elf carrying wrapped gifts toppled to the floor.

"How much?" Harrison asked through his teeth.

"What?" Wes asked. The man was full of a hot, manic energy, and in its presence Harrison only got colder.

"How much money do you want? I assume she took pictures somehow? Maybe while I was sleeping?"

"You think I'm here for money?"

"A sex scandal is hardly original. But I'll give your sister credit; she really had me fooled—"

Wes charged at Harrison, but Harrison grabbed him by the neck of his shirt and turned, pushing him into the wall. Feeling out of control. Violent.

Good.

It felt so good that he put more of his weight against the thinner man, pushing his knuckles into his chest until he felt bone.

"Yeah, you know what you need?" Wes sneered. "To beat up a DHS agent. That will make the shit storm of bad press about to rain down on your head better."

"What do you want?" Harrison bit out.

"Ryan is pregnant."

Harrison laughed, though the solid ground tilted beneath his feet. That night, that perfect, beautiful night, was being torn to pieces, ripped to shreds, and he wanted to walk away from the mess that was being made of those memories. He didn't want to say these things. He didn't even want to think them.

"You're pretty fucking silent for a guy who talks for a living."

"What makes you think it's mine?" he asked. If Heidi

had taught him one thing, it was that you couldn't hold
on to perception because you wanted to. Because it was
easier.

"Because she says it is."

"My guess is the other men she's slept with recently
don't have as much money as I do."

"Fuck you, asshole." Wes slammed his fist up under
Harrison's jaw and Harrison reeled back, but he didn't
let go of Wes's shirt.

"She didn't know my last name," Harrison said. "She
didn't even ask. You'll excuse me if I doubt her purity."

Wes growled and pushed Harrison back against the
other wall. They kicked aside a box, and red and gold
snakes of garland spilled across the carpet.

"I should make you eat those words," Wes sneered
into his face, doing a pretty good job of cutting off his
air supply. "She didn't want to tell you because she was
scared it would fuck with your campaign. She doesn't
want anything from you. Not one thing. She's sick, she's
broke, and she's alone, but she didn't want shit from you.
But I came down here anyway, because," he laughed.
"Because I thought you might do right by her. Because
there's no way my sister would spend the night with a
man unless she'd seen something worthwhile in him.
But my mistake. My fucking mistake."

Harrison shoved Wes back, breathing hard.

"Never mind," Wes said, jabbing a finger in Harrison's face. "Stay away from my sister."

Wes took a deep breath, wiped the sweat from his
face with the edge of his shirt, and left the room, slam-
ming the door so hard another box toppled. A Christmas star fell out at Harrison's feet.

He braced his hand against the wall. And then both
hands. His forehead.

A baby?

All his work, everything he'd done since he was twenty-two years old, was in ruins.

Because I am just like my father.

Unable to give that poisonous seed the space it needed to grow, he took a deep breath, pushed away from the wall, and straightened his tie.

Think, Harrison. Think.

Damage control. That's what he needed right now, because fucking Wes Kaminski with his badge had barged into a room filled with cameras and journalists and said the one name that could potentially bring down everything.

He grabbed his phone out of his pocket, nearly ripping the fabric in his haste and fury.

"Are you calling to ask me if I want leftovers?" Wallace asked. "Because I do. I really—"

"Listen to me," Harrison said. "I need you to find me everything you can on Wes Kaminski—he's a Homeland Security agent—and his sister Ryan. She's a bartender at the bar in the The Cobalt Hotel in Manhattan."

"What . . . why?"

"Just do it, Wallace. I'll explain later." He hung up. Finally, when he was calm, when he could wear the mask of dutiful son again, he went back out and joined the Montgomery Family Charade, feeling every moment like the worst of himself had been exposed.

Eight hours later

Ryan kept her eyes on the sidewalk in front of her as she walked from the corner store back to her apartment. The carton of milk—chocolate this time, because a girl needed a thrill now and then—was heavy in her hand. Far heavier than a gallon of milk should be, but that was the joy of pregnancy for her. A constant head butt against her new limitations.

But she was feeling better, thanks to the Compazine prescription the doctor had given her.

She could use a latte or ten, but the Internet seemed fairly divided on caffeine, so she was trying to err on the side of caution. For the first time in her life.

The summer night was thick and humid, and the streets were crowded with groups of Dominican girls in their summer clothes pretending to ignore the Dominican boys who were practicing their leers. Ryan smiled, remembering what it was like to be so young on a young summer night.

Best feeling in the world.

Even at ten o'clock at night, apartment windows were thrown open, letting out all kinds of music and the sounds of babies crying and moms yelling at kids and dads yelling that they couldn't hear the game over all the yelling.

She loved her neighborhood. It reminded her of her family, of where she grew up before everything went bad. When they were loud and rowdy and loving. Always loving.

It had cooled off with the sunset and the Korean barbecue place on the corner pumped out the sweet and meaty smell of bulgogi, which used to make her mouth water but now made her queasy.

She missed being hungry.

Missed loving food.

Missed coffee.

On the plus side, she wasn't throwing up anymore. And she was outside on a gorgeous summer night. So all in all, things were looking good for Ryan Kaminski.

Fantasizing about all the lattes she couldn't have, she didn't see the guy on the sidewalk in front of her building until she nearly tripped over him.

"Excuse me," she said, noticing the guy's big camera. Maybe her neighbor in 3B finally made good on the threats she'd been making at high volume for over a year to kill her no-good cheating asshole husband.

"You Ryan Kaminski?" he asked. His breath smelled like coffee and potato chips and he had crumbs in his mustache.

"Who wants to know?" she shot back, which made the guy grin knowingly.

"How do you know Harrison Montgomery?" He lifted the big camera around his neck to take her picture, blinding her with the flash.

Oh. Shit.

"I . . . I . . . don't," she said, stumbling up the path, glitter in the corner of her eyes.

She opened the lobby door and once inside, turned back around to see the photographer take out his phone and make a call.

"What the hell?" she breathed.

"Paparazzi," a guy said, and she turned to see a beautiful tall black man in a bad tie. He seemed vaguely familiar to her, but that was the life of a bartender. At some point it seemed she'd served everyone in the five boroughs a beer.

But so scathing was his gaze, she felt the need to pull the carton of milk to her chest, an extra layer between her and the hate he clearly felt for her.

"It will probably get worse," he said.

"Who the hell are you?" she demanded.

"Wallace Jones. I'd like to say I'm the man here to make your life hell, but I think that guy is waiting for you in your apartment."

In a great rush she realized why he seemed so familiar: in the footage of Harrison she'd been relentlessly watching for the last few days, this guy was almost always in the background. Looking nervous.

As she watched, he pulled a roll of antacids out of his pocket and thumbed one into his mouth. "Go," he said. "It's kind of making me sick looking at you."

"Listen, asshole," she snapped. "I haven't done anything!"

"You might not have done anything," Wallace interrupted, his dark eyes pulling her apart piece by piece. "But your brother sure has."

Her stomach fell to her feet. "Wes?"

"Bearded guy? Definition of a loose cannon? Paid a little visit."

She didn't stick around to hear the rest of the "How Wes Thought He Was Doing the Right Thing but Actually Managed to Screw Up My Life Even More" story. She bypassed the extremely slow elevator and went up two flights of stairs, pausing at the landing to get her breath back.

Once upon a time she used to run a six-minute mile, her body strong and fueled.

Now her ass was kicked by a flight of stairs.

The hallway in front of her apartment was eerily quiet, like a scene in some horror film in which she was the dummy too stupid to realize she should just leave. Vanish into the night instead of reaching out with a slightly shaking hand for that doorknob.

The door opened at her touch.

These days she was pretty much a stripped wire, exposed to every element, every emotional whim, and despite her efforts to prepare herself for seeing Harry . . . *Harrison* again, she was wasted at the sight of him.

He stood in front of her dark windows, the city a bruised landscape behind him. He seemed bigger in his suit than he had in that Bulldogs tee shirt. Or maybe it was because he was Harrison Montgomery now and not Harry, and that came with its own weight. An extra few inches.

At the sound of the door opening he turned to face her and she thought she remembered how handsome he was, how appealing his gravitas, but she hadn't remembered the half of it.

The lamplight gilded him in his tailored gray suit and his rich brown shoes, all of which cost at least four months' rent. Gone was Harry's grief and anger. This man was all cold and stony displeasure, his face carved in hard, unforgiving lines.

"Ryan," he said, and even his voice was different. Still laced with sweet tea and peaches, but there was an iron bar down the middle of it.

Oh, Wes, what did you do?

There were a thousand things she wanted to say and do, like ask him about his sister and brush that hair off his forehead, or cup that dimple in the palm of her hand the way she had that night.

And all of those things would tie this moment, this place, the two of them, back to that hotel room and maybe erase some of the anger on his face. This distrust that radiated from him.

She imagined a smile from her might set them down in this conversation with a kinder, gentler hand.

But there was nothing kind and gentle about Harrison at the moment. He looked like retribution dressed in a thousand-dollar suit.

And Ryan had been pushed into plenty of corners, so she knew when to come out swinging.

"Harry," she said, and his lip lifted, not quite a smile. No. It was far too mean to be a smile. "How did you get in?"

"Your landlord is very bribable."

"Well, that's troubling."

"You're lucky it's just me in here."

Considering the photographer standing outside her door, that was shockingly true.

"Did you give him your real name or your alias?"

"I gave him a hundred dollars and he didn't ask any questions."

"And I should have asked you a few more." That came out heavier than she'd intended. Hurt. Angry. Her swing had lost its power and she stepped over to the kitchen to set the milk on the counter.

He was watching her; she could feel the icy-hot touch of his blue eyes against her bare shoulder, the long revealed length of her legs, and she wished she had on more clothes. A snowsuit, maybe. Or one of those burka things.

Because she felt utterly naked in her cut-off jeans and thin red halter top, her hair piled on her head in a messy knot.

A bra would have been nice.

"That night," he asked, "did you know who I was?"

"No, *Harry*. I didn't." The plastic cap came off the milk jug with a loud snap.

"I don't know if I believe you."

"I don't know that I care." She took one of her red teacups and filled it with chocolate milk, not offering him any. Because that would be ridiculous, offering chocolate milk in a chipped teacup to future congressman Harrison Montgomery.

And because he's had enough, she thought. *More than enough of me.*

"This is quite an apartment." His tone was one shade away from a sneer.

Oh, could you be any more predictable? she thought.

"You like it? My uncle lived in his car in front of our house for a year. He had a microwave under his front seat. A foldout bed in the back. I learned everything about space-saving from him."

Her words were met with crackling hostile silence, so

she turned and saw Harrison looking over her book-shelves.

The problem with living a stripped-down existence was that the things she did keep around, that did survive the form-and-function test—they were precious. Tiny windows into her soul, and she wanted to grab all the psychology textbooks she'd gotten at the used book-store and her mother's Lucite jewelry and stuff them out of sight.

"You have some interesting reading material for a bartender. *Dictionary of Philosophy and Psychology, Social Psychology and Human Nature?*"

"Came with the apartment," she lied.

The look he sent her was scrutinizing and uncomfortable.

"Your sister," she said, and he stiffened, and she recognized the protective-older-brother stance. She'd seen it a million times before. "You did help her. In the end."

"I did."

"I'm glad." She lifted the cup to take a sip, but the smell made the tension in her stomach worse. The last thing she needed was to throw up in front of him. She lowered the cup but held onto it, so she had something to do with her hands. "When you said she was in trouble you weren't kidding. But I suppose the Montgomery family does things on a larger scale than average humans."

Silent, he just stared at her, his eyebrow arched, his electric-blue eyes soulless and dead.

Ugh. Enough.

"Why are you here, Harrison Montgomery?"

"Your brother came to see me." He stepped closer. The apartment—already small—was claustrophobic now. "He says you're pregnant."

She lifted her chin against his icy gaze. Her heart hammering at her rib cage. "So I am."

"Your brother seems to think it's mine."

"It is."

The muscles in his jaw flexed as if he were making gravel out of his teeth. That night they'd shared, the way he'd grabbed her hand like a lifeline, the way his cheek had felt against her palm, the way he'd kissed her like she was property he needed to know every inch of—it was gone. The sweetness. The kindness. The mutual respect.

That small slip into infatuation.

It was all gone.

All that was left was hostility and a baby.

Worst one-night stand. Ever.

"I don't care if you don't believe me," she said, setting down the cup with great care because she felt as if she were shaking apart. "I don't want a single thing from you. Not money. Not anything."

"That's certainly independent of you, Ryan. But it's too late for that. The press won't care. They will form their own opinions. And all they need for confirmation is to talk to the other girl behind the bar that night. Or perhaps the manager. A patron. Anyone who saw us."

"All they saw was us talking."

"It doesn't matter. Your brother stormed into my parents' home while my family was conducting an interview, flashed his badge around—"

"Badge? What badge?"

He blinked. "Homeland Security."

She laughed. Her brother ran in secret circles, but not that secret. "My brother is a computer hacker, Harrison. The badge was undoubtedly fake."

"It wasn't."

"Don't be embarrassed. He's fooled smarter men than you. When he was in high school—"

"Stop, Ryan. Stop with the charming tales of poverty and petty crime. We have a real problem here."

"Fine," she snapped. She loved her tales of poverty and petty crime. It was all she had left of her family. "I didn't know who you were. I did not set out to get pregnant."

"The condom was yours."

Lindsey's, actually; not that it mattered, but it meant she didn't know how old it was, or if it had been compromised in some way. All things she didn't care about that night.

"You think I sabotaged it?"

"I think desperate women have done worse."

"I'm far from desperate, Harrison."

He glanced around her apartment, all her meager possessions on display.

"What a snob you are," she laughed. If he thought she was desperate, he had no clue what desperation really was. Living in a car with a broken microwave under the front seat wasn't even the most desperate thing she'd seen. "Look, let's just be done with the slut-shaming portion of the evening. I'm not interested in anything you have to give me. I will not talk to the press. I won't breathe a word of this to anyone! So you can take your accusations and your curled lip and get lost."

For emphasis she opened the door to the hallway, but Harrison stepped forward and shut the door. He kept his hand braced on the door and leaned over her, close enough that she felt his breath against her exposed chest. Close enough that she could feel the heat from his body.

Memories, unwanted and uncomfortable, settled over her, sunk into her.

She might not like this man, but for one night she had really liked his body.

"I credited you with a great deal of insight that night at the hotel," he said with withering disdain. "I am shocked to learn how wrong I was."

Breathlessly stung, she ducked away from him, but there was no room to run in this apartment.

"Whether the badge was real, whether or not you set out to trap me, none of it matters. If we don't address this situation now, it will only get worse. Tomorrow there will be five men with cameras out there."

"I think you're exaggerating."

"I'm a Montgomery, Ryan. My sister has been the top of every news update for weeks. My father is destroying the state he's the governor of and I'm running for Congress. We are the goddamn news. And if the story breaks now that I had sex with a bartender and got her pregnant? Your life—to say nothing of mine—will be hell. But I have the resources, the legal help and money, to handle it. What do you have?"

"Don't worry about me. I'll be fine."

"That bravery is very endearing. But you have a sister in high school, another one who works as an ER nurse. Do you really want to do this to them?"

"How do you know about them?" she breathed, torn open and vulnerable.

"A preliminary investigation into your life. Right now there are dozens of journalists doing the exact same thing."

"I'm going to kill my brother." God, she could just shake Wes and his overblown sense of justice.

"A sentiment I share, but that won't help us survive this kind of sex scandal."

"Oh my God." She fell back against the counter, the reality of what was happening to them crashing down hard around her. "I'm a part of a sex scandal."

"I see you are starting to get the picture."

"And you're running for Congress."

"I am."

"You're falling behind in the polls."

"Delighted to see you're doing your homework."

His sarcasm was elegant. One of those fencing swords against her raw fists. She didn't stand a chance, and so she gave up the fight.

"All right . . . how do we get out of this?"

"Did you meet Wallace downstairs?" he asked.

"Yes. He doesn't like me."

"No. He doesn't." Harrison laughed. "In fact, he says I should simply ignore the rumors. Ignore you. Ignore your child and just bow out of the race, let Glendale take the seat, and lie low for a few years."

She jumped at this solution because it required nothing of her. "Sounds reasonable."

"But I don't want to bow out of this election. I would like to win it and get to work."

"I'm not stopping you."

"But you are. If I ignore this story, it will eat my career alive. For the rest of my life I'll be the Montgomery who had the sex scandal."

"What do you want me to do about that?"

"Marry me."

Chapter 9

She laughed. She laughed so hard she had to brace her hand against the counter, accidentally knocking her pretty red teacup into the sink, where it shattered. But even that didn't stop her from laughing.

"I'm not kidding."

"And that makes it even more funny. Listen, Harrison, you broke into my apartment. Called me stupid. All but accused me of being a gold-digging whore. I wouldn't marry you if you were the last man on earth."

He nodded as if he accepted that. "You would not be my first choice either. It would be more of a proposition, really. Business."

"You're making it sound worse."

"You've been married once before," he said. "A union you barely survived, if the hospital records are to be believed."

Her ribs caved in on her heart, and for a moment she could not breathe through the shock of having that thrown in her face.

"Those records are confidential," she whispered, wishing she sounded stronger. Tougher.

"To everyone else, yes."

But not to me. That was what he was implying. He was the kind of special and powerful and rich that could reach into her life and shake out every skeleton.

She blanched, getting light-headed.

He reached out to help her and she smacked his hands away. And it felt good, so good that she looked him in the eye and smacked his cheek hard enough that his head snapped sideways.

Her heartbeat pounded in the silence that followed.

"I deserved that," he murmured.

"Damn right you did."

"But it's the only one you'll get."

Underneath his polish lurked something wild. And she remembered in painful clarity how she'd felt both menaced and safe that night in his hotel room. How exciting that had been. But there was nothing safe about him now. Nothing at all. He was all menace.

Harrison took a deep breath and when he smiled at her, she saw a glimmer of Harry. Slightly abashed. Fully human. Reachable. Touchable. More safety than menace.

A lie. She understood that now. It was a persona he could turn on and off at will. A trick, one that no doubt was highly effective with the voters. It had been highly effective with her.

"Let me . . . let me start again," he murmured, leading her toward the couch. She shrugged away from his touch but sat all the same, because she was feeling weak and awful and the soft edge of her red chenille blanket was a small anchor in her reality.

He turned toward the sink, got down another of her red teacups, and poured her some more chocolate milk. After handing it to her, he sat on her little square storage ottoman that was full of her running gear. The fan between them blew in the scent of hot asphalt and grilled meat.

She moaned, low in her throat, turning away from him and the smell and the hot air.

"I haven't even asked how you're feeling," he whispered, leaning forward, his elbows on his knees.

She put her hand over her flat stomach as if to protect the baby from this man's duplicity. This Ken Doll with all that hidden grief, his kindness and coldness. She'd come to terms with this baby, had started to find joy in this little life, started to build fantasies about their future. And he was going to pull all that apart. Change it all.

It was time to get this guy back out of her life.

"The baby is not yours. This whole thing is moot. You can go."

She wanted to press the cool cup to her forehead, but instead she just held it in her hands, meeting his warm gaze with her own hate-filled one.

"It doesn't matter, Ryan. It's only a matter of time before the press finds out you're pregnant, and you are already linked to me." She didn't say anything, staring instead over his shoulder at the copy of *Dulcan's Textbook of Child and Adolescent Psychiatry* she'd been so excited to find on a half-price rack at The Strand. "It doesn't matter whose baby it is."

She sniffed and took a sip of milk. "The baby is mine."

"What I am suggesting is not a marriage in the typical sense. I am suggesting a proposal. A business arrangement."

"If it includes sucking your dick—"

His head jerked back, his cheeks red. *Oh*, Harry was embarrassed. She was small enough to be pleased with that.

"It doesn't. That . . . that night will not happen again. It's not a part of the agreement."

"I'm not interested in your agreement." She stood, but he grabbed her wrist. The warmth of his palm sent something sizzling up her nerves. Something—when he was looking at her like that—that made no sense. She shook off his touch.

"Let me explain, Ryan. And then I'll leave and give you a chance to think about it."

She sat back down, because it was the quickest way to get rid of him.

"We will get married as soon as possible. If I win the election, we'll stay married. If after two years you no longer want to be married—"

"What about you? Are you saying you might want to be married after two years?"

"The best thing for my career is if we get married and stay married."

"Sounds happy."

"I'm not looking for happy. I'm looking for a way to keep doing the work I want to do. But after two years if you want out, we will quietly get divorced after the next election. After which I will buy you a house, anywhere you want. And we will go our separate ways."

"And cut all ties? What about the baby?"

"What about it?"

She gaped. "What about it? You will have spent two years pretending to be a father and then you just . . . vanish?"

"I will also send you monthly alimony and child support checks. The sum of which you can dictate. Within reason. I suppose there might be times I will need to see the child."

Need to see the child. Oh my God, is this really happening?

"You are a cold man, Harrison Montgomery."

"I'm a practical one. Embroiled in a situation that requires me to be as clear as possible. Furthermore, as my wife you will agree to help me campaign; appear in public with me as my doting and totally supportive partner. If at any point word of our agreement is leaked to the press, you and the child will get no money from me."

"What if you don't win?"

"I'm not entertaining that option yet."

"Well, I'm not entertaining any of this yet."

Harrison sat back. "I understand you have your pride. I . . . admire that about you, Ryan. And despite my awful comment earlier, I know you're smart." He glanced around her tiny apartment, including the psychology books on the shelf, before looking back at her. "There must be something you want. Something I can give you to make this rather indecent proposal of interest to you."

She was silent. Overwhelmed. Exhausted and angry. Sad and ashamed.

He took her cell phone from the edge of the bookshelf behind him.

"I'm putting in my cell phone number," he said. "This is my direct line. You have forty-eight hours to give me an answer."

"Or what?"

"Or I am forced to make a statement about you. I would like to make the statement that we've been secretly falling in love and have gotten married in a small private ceremony at the Georgia Governor's Mansion."

"And if I don't agree to your proposal?"

"Then you are a former bartender at The Cobalt Hotel who, with the help of your brother, a dubious DHS agent, is trying to blackmail me."

"That will ruin his career."

"Undoubtedly. It's not like I want any of this, Ryan. He has forced both of our hands."

She took a deep breath and slowly blew it out. "Why can't we just say we're dating? Or engaged? And then just break up when the election is over?"

"Because politicians don't date, Ryan. They are either married or single. And they really don't date pregnant bartenders who live in studio apartments in Queens."

"But you marry them?" she spat. "How noble."

"Marriage will give it all some legitimacy."

There was a knock on the door and then, without

asking permission, that Wallace guy walked in, looking around her home as if it smelled bad.

"This place looks like my shitty dorm room," Wallace said. "Nice loft."

"Fuck you," she snapped, and the venom felt good.

"Oh, she'll make a lovely addition to the family," Wallace laughed. "Your mother, in particular, is going to adore her."

Harrison herded Wallace toward the door. "Give us a second, would you?"

"We need to move," Wallace said. "We're already late for The Carter Center conference."

"I know. I'm hurrying." Harrison shut the door behind Wallace and turned to face Ryan.

He still glittered. She was sweaty and sick and ruined, and he was still more beautiful than any man should be. But his wattage was turned down, the fairy dust wiped away by a certain weariness, a reluctant helplessness.

The glimpse of this vulnerability had a predictable effect on her and because she was an idiot, she wanted to hug him.

Don't believe this, she told herself. *This version of him is an act to get you to do what he wants. Underneath he's the soulless robot who knows too much about your life and thinks you're stupid.*

"Marriage isn't going to fix this, Harrison."

"It won't be easy. But it's a start. My family—"

"Is complicated." She laughed, remembering when he'd said that. For regular people a complicated family might mean their mom was gay, or they had two sets of stepparents who couldn't stand one another. She never would have been able to believe he meant he was a Montgomery, American royalty. "You told me."

"So is yours." He shook his head, a ghost of a smile on his face. "We should put your brother and my mother in a room and see who makes it out."

Ryan refused to smile and Harrison crossed the room.
He hesitated for a moment before picking up her hand.
His fingers were warm and dry against her damp, cold
flesh. "We can make this work, for the both of us."

For a moment they both stared at their conjoined
hands, and she was wondering what he remembered
about her. About that hotel room. What details, if any,
kept him up at night, burning and alone.

Though the idea that Harrison burned, alone or otherwise, seemed unlikely.

Harry burned. Harrison was far too cold for those
memories.

She pulled her hand away.

"I can't do it," she said.

"I hope you can think of this as an opportunity, Ryan.
To change your life. The life of your child. I have resources you can't even imagine, and you can use them
to secure a future for yourself," he said, and with that
he was gone, the door clicking shut behind them.

Ryan put the teacup down on the floor and barely
made it to the bathroom before throwing up.

Harrison went out the back door of the apartment
building, to a tiny alley where his car and driver had
been waiting. Wallace, glancing around for any photographers, opened the back door of the car and Harrison
slid in. Wallace followed.

"Let's get out of here," Wallace said to Dan the driver,
and they turned off 48th onto Queens Boulevard and
made their slow way out to LaGuardia, where the family jet was waiting for them.

"So?" Wallace asked, while Harrison dug his Black-
Berry out of his coat pocket. The thing had been going
nuts while he was in Ryan's apartment. Twenty text
messages. Ten voice mails. Three of those from his

mother. One from the *Times*. Two from the *Journal-Constitution*.

We are in serious trouble.

"Get Bruce on the phone. We need to have a contract drawn up."

"She agreed to your indentured servant idea?" Wallace asked.

"Marriage."

"You say potato," Wallace muttered, but he was getting his phone out, putting in the call to Bruce.

"She hasn't agreed yet. But she will."

"Why don't you just follow in the incredibly long and noble line of politicians who pay their mistakes to go away?"

"Because in the twenty-first century that doesn't work anymore. The world has changed, and . . ." He rubbed at his forehead, at the headache just under the bone that he couldn't reach. "I don't know why I have to keep saying this, but that is not me. That's not the way I want to live my life. Paying off a woman who is pregnant with my baby to be quiet?"

I am not my father. I might have made the same mistake, but I will not do what my father did.

"So you're going to pay her *and* marry her?"

"The campaign—"

"Listen to me, Harrison." Wallace leaned forward, giving an impassioned plea. Harrison usually liked Wallace's impassioned pleas, but this one was going to be in direct contrast to his own goals. "No matter how you spin this, it's going to hurt."

"Everyone loves a love story, don't they?"

"You honestly believe you are going to be able to convince the world that you have fallen in love with a tattooed, foul-mouthed bartender from Philly? I mean, she's beautiful. I'll give you that, but come on. This is the weirdest Hail Mary I've ever seen. This campaign is over."

"What about the next one?" Harrison put voice to his greater fear, imagining the unimaginable. "And the one after that. We don't get a hold of this story, it will ruin my career. I'll always be the guy who knocked up a tattooed, foul-mouthed bartender from Philly, tried to pay her off, and failed."

Wallace sat back, his silence eerily telling. "When you put it that way . . ."

"Right. Call Bruce." It was bleak every way he looked at it, and the only option that left his future open was getting Ryan to agree to this proposal.

"You sure she's going to agree to this?" Wallace asked, lifting the phone to his ear.

"She doesn't have a choice," he said. "Neither of us do."

Chapter 10

The next morning Ryan was awakened by someone knocking on her door, and by the time she got down from the loft and into her robe, that someone was pounding.

"Hey!" she cried, undoing the chain. "Hold your horses."

The moment before she unlocked the two deadbolts she remembered the journalists outside and the easily bribed Mr. Jenkins, and kept the door shut.

"Who is there?" she yelled through the wood, her heart suddenly thumping in her throat.

"It's me, you skinny white bitch, now open up!" Ryan looked through the peephole to confirm. *Right.* Mary from 3B. "Skinny white bitch" was nearly an endearment in Mary's vernacular, so she opened the door.

It was Mary and five more of her neighbors, surrounding Mr. Jenkins.

Everybody looked angry.

The hallway smelled like fried eggs and curry.

"Well, good morning," she said, cocking her hip against the door. "To what do I owe this honor?"

"What the hell is going on outside?" Mary asked. "I can't get to work without getting harassed by about twenty assholes with cameras outside my door."

"Wait . . . what? *Twenty?*"

"At least!" Mary cried.

"They're starting to go through our garbage!" Vasquez from upstairs yelled. "My wife caught one of them coming in through the emergency exit out back."

"I'm . . . I'm sorry." Speaking was hard through the thumping of her heart in her throat. "I'm sure it will die down."

"When?" Mary asked, crossing her arms over her chest, her expression dubious.

"I . . . I don't know."

Her neighbors erupted in outrage.

"Have you called the cops?" she asked Mr. Jenkins, who up until this point and for most of her association with him had remained silent. He was kind of like a silent, balding troll in work pants with a key ring he liked to jangle in his pocket.

"Of course. It hasn't done much good. They moved back to the street for about an hour, but they are right at the doors again. This needs to end," he said, jangling the keys in his pocket.

"You know what needs to end?" she demanded. "You letting strangers into my home."

Jenkins didn't even flinch. "It won't be your home if you don't get rid of the journalists on the sidewalk in front of the building."

"There you go," said Mary, nodding her head in approval. "That's how we do."

Oh fuck you, Mary, she thought but had the good sense not to say. Mary worked as a baker, kneading bread. Mary could tear her apart. Like with her bare hands.

"You can't just threaten me with that, Jenkins. I have renter's rights."

"Not when your actions have a direct and potentially dangerous effect on other residents of the building. Look at your lease."

Holy hell.

"Okay," Ryan said. "I will . . . I will do what I can." She met the eyes of her neighbors over Mr. Jenkins's bald head. They were all glaring at her. Half of them no doubt still pissed about her complaining about the noise after midnight last year. She'd been big on petitions for a stretch there and she did not make friends with the locals. "I promise."

Someone somewhere was making coffee, the smell as powerful as a house fire.

It made her cranky and she shut the door in their faces.

Pushing away the siren song of the three Starbucks within a two-block radius, she grabbed her phone and called her brother.

"Leave a message," his machine said.

"Wes," she said after the beep. "You have to call me. You have to. Because you have fucked up my life in an epic way. You need to make it right." She was pacing between the kitchen and the bathroom. This little part of her apartment had never seen so much activity. "By first of all telling me what you're doing with a DHS badge. You could get in serious trouble for that; and secondly, getting the pack of rabid journalists off my goddamned sidewalk. And third—"

His phone beeped at her, indicating she'd gone on too long.

She hung up and tossed her phone on the couch.

Surely, this morning, of all mornings, she deserved a coffee. A small one. A sip. Just a sip.

She glanced at the clock above the stove. It was eight a.m. She had thirty-six hours before she had to give Harrison her answer.

And if he told the press that she was a bartender who was trying to blackmail him, the press numbers outside her door would only grow. The harassment of her neighbors would only get worse. She imagined Mary might start selling "stories" to the press. Hell, half of them would.

And the quiet, simple life she had been fantasizing about with this baby was totally in jeopardy.

She leaned back against the wall.

Wes had to make this right. He just *had* to.

Her phone, in the cushions of the couch, started to ring and she dove for it.

"Wes—"

"Wrong sibling."

Nora. The sound of her sister's voice brought Ryan to her knees.

They were Polish twins, born eleven months apart. They'd slept in the same bed. Shared secrets and stories and air under the Holly Hobbie quilt their mother had got for them on sale at Woolworth's.

They'd borrowed each other's clothes, beaten up the bullies that called them names, and stolen each other's boyfriends.

Well, that was her mostly, stealing Nora's boyfriends.

And she'd been living in exile for so long.

I'm sorry, she thought. *I'm sorry for all of it.*

"What the hell have you done?" Nora asked. That familiar voice saying familiar words triggered a familiar response.

"I haven't done anything," she snapped back, because she and Nora couldn't have a normal conversation without going for blood. "It's Wes—"

"Wes slept with Harrison Montgomery? I find that hard to believe."

"Really?" she asked, trying to make a joke. Trying to do anything to make all the things wrong just a little bit right. "Because I wouldn't put anything past Wes."

"Oh, that's rich, Ryan. That's so rich coming from you."

Ryan heard the sounds of pots and a pan getting

thumped down on the old yellow stove on Nora's end. She was probably making breakfast. Dad sitting at his spot at the kitchen table, the newspaper pulled apart and set out in his paper-reading tradition. A coffee cup at his elbow, dressed for a job he didn't go to anymore.

Olivia might still be asleep, or just dragging ass on her way downstairs for breakfast.

She and Olivia emailed each other, and Ryan sent her things from the city. Funky clothes and jewelry that would stand out in Bridesburg. But it wasn't the same. It was almost worse, never seeing her in those funky things.

"Are you in trouble?" Nora asked.

"Do you care?" Ryan shot back out of habit. And then immediately wished she could take it back.

"Not particularly. Look, we've got journalists hounding us. Dad stood on the sidewalk last night with his shotgun and some asshole showed up at Olivia's piano practice, asking her questions about you."

"I'm . . . I'm sorry."

"Yeah. And I've heard that before. Olivia has college visits this week. And I know that probably doesn't mean anything to you—"

"Of course it does!" she cried.

"Then make this shit stop. I swear to God, if you blow this for her . . ." Ryan heard the quick inhale of a cigarette being lit. Nora was smoking. Shit was bad if Nora was smoking.

"I'll make it stop," she whispered, running her pinky over the fringe of her red blanket. She didn't know how, but she'd do what she could to make this right.

"Good."

"Can I talk to—"

"No."

Nora hung up. Ryan sat there on her knees beside the couch, listening to the silence for a few moments, before she finally hung up and set the phone back down on the couch.

She did know. She did know how to make this right.

Wes wasn't going to be able to get those journalists and photographers off the sidewalk. Wes wasn't going to be able to fix this. That was Wes's lot in life, making messes he couldn't fix.

And maybe she wasn't smart enough to see another solution, or she was too damn tired to try, but the key to making this stop was in her hands.

And in the end it wasn't even a decision she had to make. She just had to come to grips with what was happening.

Well. Crap.

She got off her knees and sat on the floor, her back to the couch, her legs in front of her. From under the couch, she pulled out the notebook and pen she used to make grocery lists and draft petitions to piss off her neighbors.

There wasn't any other option but to agree to Harrison's proposal. And she could survive anything for two years; she'd been married to Paul for four, after all. She could do this, particularly if it meant giving her baby a better start than the one she could provide on her own. Particularly if it meant protecting Olivia, and Nora and Wes and Dad, from the stupidity of Wes's sense of justice.

What did a congressman's wife do? Smile. Wave. Drink tea . . . she didn't really know what else would be required of her, but she could do it.

She'd done worse.

But she would come up with her own terms for this indecent proposal and she'd look out for her family. The baby and Nora and everyone else back home.

The thought spread, turning to hope. Perhaps this was the way to get back in Nora's good graces. The way to get back home. Being Harrison's wife didn't feel like such a horror show when she thought of it that way.

The phone behind her rang and she reached up to grab it.

Wes.

"You'd better have a good explanation for this," she said, not bothering with hello.

"I was trying to do the right thing," he said, his voice glum and contrite and sad and angry. "I swear I just wanted him to own up to his part in this."

Weary, she laughed. "What are you doing flashing around a DHS badge?"

"Causing trouble," he said. "Look, I've got a call in with Harrison; hopefully I can fix this—"

"You can't, Wes. It's past that. The press is onto the story. They're in front of my house. They're in front of Nora's, harassing Olivia at piano. Dad's going to shoot somebody."

"Jesus . . ." he breathed.

"Yeah. Listen, I got this, but I need you to get me a lawyer. A good one. A . . . scary one."

"Why?"

"Because I'm getting married."

Harrison couldn't believe it had barely been forty hours since Wes Kaminski had burned his life down to the ground, but he couldn't put off his parents any longer. He arranged for a meeting at his campaign office for six o'clock Sunday night, knowing that would keep Dad away. Dad wouldn't show up to his campaign office if he was on fire and Harrison's office had the only water in the city. Dad met Harrison on his own turf. His pathetic way of trying to maintain some power.

"Has she called?" Wallace asked.

Harrison shook his head. He was in the middle of

making phone calls to some of his big backers, trying to reassure everyone that his world wasn't going up in flames, but he got the very real impression that only half believed him.

"You want me to have Jill set up the press conference for tomorrow morning?" Wallace was lying down on the couch in the corner, tossing a tennis ball in the air with one hand and catching it with the other. This was Wallace's deep-thinking ritual.

They'd both slept in the office last night, putting out fires. Jill, his press secretary, tried to quit early this morning. Thank God Wallace talked her down off that ledge.

"Yes." Harrison dropped the pen so he could rub at his eyes with both hands.

"What do you want her to say?" Wallace threw the ball wide, so he had to stretch his arm off the couch to catch it.

"That I'm going to be addressing the rumors regarding my relationship with Ryan Kaminski."

"And that relationship is . . . ?"

"You'll know as soon as I do."

At five, most of his interns and staff had left the building, so it was just the core team still trying to salvage this campaign, still trying to get his education message out over the screaming gossip. At five after five his mother walked into his office in a summer suit with flowers on it, pearls at her neck. A blue purse over her arm.

It was the Patty Montgomery uniform, and he'd seen his mother in some version of it almost every day of his life.

"You're early," he said.

"You have been avoiding my calls and I'm tired of waiting."

She looked . . . rumpled. Which was actually alarming. Even when Ashley had been kidnapped by the pirates, her fate unknown for three weeks, Mother had never stepped out of her home looking less than totally controlled. Her slightly mussed hair and lack of lipstick seemed like a declaration that the Montgomery family was hanging by a thread.

"Your father's office is mobbed. Noelle is fielding calls from *The National Enquirer*. *The Enquirer*, Harrison!"

Just saying the words gave her a minor stroke.

She glanced at the couch where Wallace lay sprawled, not moving at the sight of her, and then sniffed before sitting down on the chair in front of his desk. "You need to tell me what's happening. Your father isn't stepping foot in this building until he's sure a pregnant woman won't come flying out of the woodwork."

"If I had a nickel for every time that's happened," Wallace joked.

"I find none of this funny," Mother snapped, glaring at Wallace before turning that glare onto him. "Who the hell is Ryan Kaminski?"

"Well, Mother, if all goes according to plan . . ."

"Wait. Wait, I want to get a good look at her face when you tell her." Wallace leapt up from the couch to stand beside Harrison's desk.

Harrison sighed, and in a moment's silence gathered all his resources for the fight to come. "If all goes according to plan she'll be your daughter-in-law."

Mother recoiled as if Harrison had thrust roadkill at her.

"Oh, God, it's better than I imagined," Wallace said, clapping.

Mother ignored Wallace. "You're joking."

"I'm not."

"That's a ridiculous plan. Why would you marry some woman we don't even know?"

"I know her," Harrison said, fighting the assimilation of "we." The Montgomery mantle.

"How?"

"She's pregnant."

Mother gasped. "With your child?"

"With his dog, actually—it's very strange," Wallace said.

"Yes," Harrison said. "With my child, but it doesn't really matter, does it?"

"Of course it matters! You are a Montgomery! You need to have a blood test done before you take on this kind of campaign . . . poison."

"It's all poison, Mother. I could come out with irrevocable proof that the baby isn't mine, but I'll still be in the mud."

"Then pay her!" Mom cried. "Do what every other man in office before you has done—pay her off."

"That doesn't always work," Wallace said.

"It doesn't matter," Harrison said, growing sick at the way everyone was able to throw around the idea of paying Ryan off, like she was nothing. Like this child was nothing. "I'm not paying her to go away."

"Don't be ridiculous," Mother said. "It's what men in your position—"

"I'm better than that," Harrison snapped. "I'm better than those men."

"Those men," Mother scoffed. "Like you know—"

"I'm better than Dad!" Harrison shouted, knowing how those words would wound her. How they would rip at her hard façade. She stared at him for one moment with terrible hurt, terrible pain. But he didn't regret saying it. "I know about Heidi. The world may not know what you and Dad did. But I do."

Wallace glanced away, as if he could make himself vanish.

"It wouldn't be the same," Mother said with prickly

care, casting a threadbare chill over a deep embarrassment. "You are not already married."

"I won't do what Dad did."

"I'm the one who paid that girl off," Mom said.

"Then I won't do what you did either." He felt bad for
his mother, he did, but her feelings were just going to
have to be sacrificed because he was exhausted running
from his family's past both in public and behind doors.
"You've been telling me for months I should get married. That it would help me seem more substantial.
More grounded. And now, here I am . . . getting married."

"Not like this! You honestly think a wedding will fix
the gossip?"

"I do. A wedding and a good show." Harrison got out
of his chair and stepped around his desk to lean against
the front of it. "That's where *you* come in."

The rest of the world held her in esteem. They bought
the show she put on with such seamless skill. The perfect hair and clothes, the charity work, the unwavering
support of her husband in the face of whispers and in-
nuendos.

Somehow, no matter how many times she was the silent, supportive wife at the edge of the stage, no one
ever pitied her.

Maybe because everyone knew that Patty Montgomery single-handedly, over and over again, had pulled her
husband from the brink of disaster.

And looking at her—about to enlist her for the exact
same job for his benefit—Harrison felt only sadness.
Pity.

He wondered if his mother remembered who she
really was. Before devoting her life to keeping her husband in a position of power, despite all Ted's efforts to
fall from grace.

He wanted to tell her that it was okay. That he knew

all the truths she worked so hard to keep hidden. For a moment he wanted them to just be honest with each other.

But there was no telling what she would do if he tried to pull down all the walls of the world she had created.

As if she could read his mind, her face changed from frustration to something utterly familiar and hard and cold, and the moment for honesty vanished.

That slightly raised eyebrow, those pursed lips as if she'd smelled something bad, but was too polite to say it—that was the mother of his childhood. The mother with the expression that said *don't come to me with your minor fears and heartbreaks. I would rather not be bothered by your desire for attention or affection.*

As a kid he'd been baffled by that look on her face, because she didn't look that way when they were in public. She gave her kindness to strangers, saved her chill for him and for Ashley.

So effective was that face of hers, that vague air of disappointment and disinterest, that he just stopped wanting anything from her.

It wasn't easy screwing with the balance of his relationship with his mother. He didn't like it. He didn't like needing her. His life was much more comfortable when he kept an icy, businesslike distance between them.

The chill was their comfort zone, and needing something from her made him feel vaguely threatened.

"If she agrees to my proposal, we're getting married. At minimum for two years."

"Two years!" she cried.

"To make it seem at least slightly legitimate. But we will have to convince the voters and the press that Ryan and I are in love. And that's a show that only you can help us pull off."

"You are kind of the Great and Powerful Oz," Wallace said, squeezing the tennis ball instead of tossing it.

"Help us groom her for the role of a congressman's wife." Harrison hoped to appeal to her hubris. "Help us convince everyone that we're happily married."

Do for me what you have done for Dad your entire married life. Make the lie seem real.

"You won't win this election, Harrison," she said, as if she couldn't wait to get that off her chest.

"That's not the point. This election, next election, it doesn't matter. She needs to look the part and we need to act like she's being welcomed into this family. It's the only way any of this works. It's the only way my entire career isn't derailed."

"And if she doesn't agree?" Mother asked. Harrison shrugged.

"We let the press tear her to pieces and hope we can stay above it."

"I'm leaning more toward that option myself," Wallace said, which actually made Mom smile.

"So . . . who is she?" she asked, tucking her purse on her lap and crossing her arms over it. "What exactly are we dealing with?"

"Let me do the honors," Wallace said, pulling from the top of the stack of files on Harrison's desk the report their investigator had made. He cleared his throat and opened the file. "Ryan Michelle Kaminski is a high school dropout."

Mom put her head in her hands.

"Oh wait," Wallace said. "It gets better. Remember that Lip Girl product from about fifteen years ago?"

"No."

"Wallace, let this go, would you?" Harrison asked. Ever since they'd dug up this little gem from Ryan's past, Wallace had been telling anyone who would listen.

"Let it go?" Wallace laughed. "Your future wife was

a teenage fantasy for boys up and down the eastern sea-coast. This is something we need to deal with."

"What is the Lip Girl product?" Mom asked.

"It was this Chapstick stuff that was sweet and sticky and kind of gross, but the whole campaign was around this one beautiful girl putting it on, kissing a man on the lips, and then turning and saying to the camera in a breathless purr, 'Try it. He'll like it.' "

"You're kidding me," Mother said.

"She was seventeen."

"Oh my God," she gasped.

"Look," Harrison said, trying to stop the entire melt-down. "It's bad. We all know it's bad. That's why we need everyone pulling together on this."

Patty's blue eyes slid to his and she made no effort to hide her repulsion. And he knew his mother would help, because she would rather eat her hands than have her family name suffer this kind of ignominy. But she would make Ryan pay.

"I pray she does not agree to this," she said.

"You and me both," chimed in Wallace.

At that moment Harrison's cell phone rang and while everyone else froze in horror around him, he calmly grabbed it off his desk and glanced at the New York area code.

"It's her," he said, which sent Wallace into an explosion of swearing.

He glared Wallace into silence before engaging his phone.

"Hello?"

"Harrison?"

It was a surprise to realize he'd recognize that dry, slightly husky voice anywhere. He turned away from his riveted audience. "Yes?"

"This is Ryan. Look, I'm . . . ah . . . going to take you up on your proposal. But I have my own terms."

He sagged with relief. Now, maybe there was a chance he was going to make it through to the other side of this with his reputation and name at least marginally intact.

"Wonderful. I'll have a driver come and pick you up at your apartment and take you to LaGuardia, where there will be a jet waiting for you. You have a half hour to pack."

"You . . . you can just make all that happen in a half hour?"

"That is only the beginning of what I can do, Ryan. I'll see you in roughly three hours."

"I have a lawyer and he's on his way to Atlanta now," she said, and he imagined her up-thrust chin and was reminded of the woman he met that night in the bar. The woman he'd liked quite a bit.

"Good."

"And you're paying for him."

He almost mentioned conflict of interest but decided against it. He needed her here, married and undergoing some fairly extensive media training as soon as possible.

"Fine."

"All right . . . I guess I'll see you in three hours."

Harrison hung up and turned to his campaign manager and mother, both of whom looked braced for a disaster. "We have a wedding to plan."

Chapter 11

It was amazing how quickly a half hour passed when you spent most of the time freaking out, spinning in circles, and trying not to throw up.

She called her lawyer, then called Jenkins and arranged payment to keep her apartment for one more month; she'd figure out what to do with it when things calmed down. She thought about calling Wes, but decided he'd done enough. And then she tried to pack, but she could only stare at her leather and her halter tops and the cut-offs and thin jersey skirts.

She had six pairs of flip-flops. One of them—her favorite pair—was held together with duct tape. The idea of standing next to Harrison wearing anything she owned was ludicrous.

All of this was ludicrous.

Even her nicer stuff, such as the dress she bought on sale for a friend's wedding last year. Or the cheap business suit she wore to auditions that required that kind of look—it reeked of wrong. Of not at all good enough.

"Screw it," she muttered, and just threw a bunch of underwear and pajamas into her bag with her toiletries and makeup. She'd get new clothes; half this stuff wouldn't fit in a few months anyway. She'd buy a whole set of costumes for this ridiculous role she was going to play and then when it was over, she'd burn it. She'd burn it and take her baby and start a new life.

The sound of her cell phone ringing and rattling against the counter broke the silence in the apartment.

With a shaking hand she answered, "Yes?"

"Ryan Kaminski?"

"This is her."

"I'm the driver who is taking you to LaGuardia. You have a pack of journalists in front of your apartment. I'm idling in the back near the Dumpsters."

"I'll be there in a second," she said and hung up.

She hooked her bag over her shoulder and looked around her apartment one last time.

Once, years ago, she'd thought that it was only a matter of time before her life changed. Before something amazing happened to her. Despite a life that conditioned her otherwise, growing up where she did, how she did, the best she could hope for was an amicable divorce and a kid who stayed out of jail.

Even after what she and Paul did to her family, and then the divorce, she still believed that something fantastic was waiting just around the corner.

That was what modeling had led her to believe. That she was one lucky break, one callback, one random Jumbotron shot at a football game away from her life changing.

Years had passed and she wasn't sure when she stopped believing that. When she just accepted every day at face value. Something to survive and celebrate in equal parts. She'd lost sight of that strange hope and settled down hard into a life that was constantly in danger of collapsing under its own weight.

Money. Work. Now this baby. Her health. Her family. All of those things could crush her life as it stood. And she lived that way—every day. She was just like millions of other people, barely getting by, not making a dent or a scratch on the world they lived in.

Even in New York City, miles away from Bridesburg, she was living nearly the exact same life as if she'd stayed there.

But here she was standing at the edge of life-altering change. Terrifying change. And she was torn between laughing and crying. It was going to be awful; she knew that. Day in and day out with Harrison's judgment and superiority, hand in hand with memories of that stupid night.

And a baby! *His baby!* That he was so willing to walk away from when all of this was over.

What kind of man was capable of that?

The kind of man who would use her and put her away when her use was over. So, she would do the same. She'd get her terms agreed to, change her family's life, spend her two years smiling and waving and doing God knows what else, and then she'd . . . put him aside.

At the last minute, she grabbed one of her red teacups and shoved it in her bag.

A reminder for the awful times ahead of who she was and that she was precious. If to no one else, at least to herself.

Ryan spent the surreal trip from town car to private jet to town car arming and armoring herself with information. She was not going to show up at the Governor's Mansion like some impoverished historical romance heroine who'd been knocked up by the Duke.

Wes had sent Ryan an email full of fascinating tidbits about the Montgomerys, and she studied it like she was cramming for her high school history test.

The Montgomerys were a fifth-generation political family out of Georgia.

They were soldiers and government leaders dating all the way back to the Civil War.

But in recent years, Harrison's father, Ted, had been a very naughty boy. Politically and perhaps personally. Errant whiffs of scandal had dogged him for most of his career, including a nearly fatal car accident with a young woman who was not his wife. After the accident, Patty Montgomery quashed any rumors that Ted and the girl who'd nearly died were anything but co-workers.

But all of that had the faint stench of "she protests too much" around it.

The family ran an extensive foundation that seemed to fund Ashley Montgomery's aid trips.

Harrison . . . well, Harrison was remarkably boring, really. Smug and indifferent in teenage interviews. There was, however, a hilarious picture of him with Chelsea Clinton looking hugely uncomfortable at a prom. His first year at Georgia he'd been a miserable student and a very serious frat boy. After freshman year he transferred to Emory, where he turned things around. Really turned things around. Double major in political science and history, and then he went to Emory Law and then kept going back to get more degrees. Including a Doctor of Law/Master of Theological Studies.

He started a nonprofit organization that served the families of vets, called VetAid.

Dad would like that, she thought before she could stop herself.

When Harry had told her at the bar that he'd never had a boss, he wasn't kidding. This run for Congress looked like his first real job.

"Rich people," she muttered.

"Excuse me?" the driver asked.

"Nothing," she said. She imagined that this fancy car with its fancy driver, whisking her in air-conditioned comfort from the Atlanta airport north of the city to where the houses got bigger and the lawns got more lush, probably had one of those windows she could raise and lower for privacy. But she didn't know where the button was.

"How much farther?" she asked.

"Fifteen minutes."

She closed the email file on her phone, having gleaned as much as she needed for the time being. Basically, she was marrying into a very white, very rich, and pretty boring family.

If it weren't for the sister kidnapped by Somali pirates and Harry (she'd begun thinking about the version of Harrison she'd slept with that night as a totally different person), there'd be nothing interesting about them at all.

Except, of course . . . her. And this baby.

She opened her purse and did her best to freshen up. The green sundress she'd decided on wearing had weathered the travel pretty well except for a dark spot near the strap, where she'd spilled some decaf coffee she'd been unable to refuse on the jet.

Private jet. There had been a time, not so long ago, that she'd thought that was her due. A foregone conclusion in her rosy modeling future. Those ambitions were something that Paul had fanned to life in her. Or at least fanned to a larger flame.

And when they didn't come to fruition, well, that's when she'd learned the reality of marriage. Her marriage, anyway.

Funny to have those dreams come to fruition now.

She pulled her hair out of its bun and brushed it, letting it lie brown and silky across her shoulders. Casting directors, scouts, reps—they all said her hair was her best feature, and so she played it up.

Harry—Harrison—had seemed to like it that night in the hotel room.

If nothing else, perhaps she could throw him off his stride.

Makeup helped with the dark skin under her eyes and the paleness of her cheeks.

Long ago, she'd learned that most people didn't see

past her looks. Her beauty had been her identity for a long, selfish, and miserable time in her life. But now she would use that same beauty as armor to keep Harrison from seeing all the parts of herself she would like to hide.

And by the time the car came to a stop, she looked pretty good, if she did say so herself. And she felt pretty good, too. Not like a sheep to the slaughter, but rather as a fully capable and intelligent woman who was making a decision to improve her future and that of her child.

I can do this, she told herself, and she believed it.

But the moment she stepped out onto a circular drive in front of a redbrick mansion with white columns lit up with dozens of hidden spotlights, her confidence took a hit.

It's called the Governor's Mansion, she thought, tugging on the hem of her cheap rayon sundress. *You knew it wasn't going to be a hut.*

The front door opened and she found herself holding her breath, waiting for Harrison, only to be disappointed when it was Wallace trotting down the steps. He was a handsome man, tall and thin. But it was all ruined by his bad ties. This one was yellow and brown circa 1972.

He stopped a few feet from her, as if she were radioactive and infectious. "You are actually going to do this?"

"Hello to you, too." She peeked behind him, waiting for her would-be fiancé to come out. She didn't want to talk to any of them, but the guy she was engaged to would be better than Wallace.

"He's in meetings," Wallace said, apparently reading her mind.

She thought, *Get better ties,* but his face didn't change. The night around them was thick and lush and hot, and she felt sweat bead up under her hair. *I should have left it up,* she thought. *I shouldn't have bothered trying.*

Because nothing about her impressed this man. Not her armor. Not her beauty. This man wasn't about to get taken in by anything she had to offer.

Her brother had sent some information about Wallace, too. And having read all about his background, she understood him a little better. It didn't make her like him, but she understood what he was doing: protecting his friend.

That kind of behavior was all over his file. A ghetto Robin Hood.

"This isn't going to be a regular marriage," he said.

"I'm aware."

"You know what I've been calling you?"

"I can't wait to hear."

"The indentured servant."

"Aren't you clever?"

"I am, actually." He nodded at the driver, who went to the trunk of the car to pull out her bag, and then Wallace turned to walk back inside.

She wasn't going to start this endeavor being anyone's punching bag. This family might have more money than God, and this handsome man with terrible taste in ties may have more power than she did, but she was no one's fool.

"Do you think your mother would have taken this deal?" she asked, and Wallace paused on the wide white steps. Slowly, he turned. And she saw in his blank-faced astonishment the knowledge of every single sacrifice his mother made years ago on his behalf. He knew exactly what his mother had given up for him.

And because of the file, so did she.

"Would she have taken this deal instead of working three jobs, and living in the shitty housing project on Chicago's south side, all so you could go to the good private school, so you could get the scholarship to Emory?"

"I'm sorry?" he breathed as if he hadn't heard her correctly.

"Your mom," she said, stepping closer. Knowledge was power, and she felt her own power return. "When she found out she was pregnant with you. Do you think if some man had come out of the blue and promised to make sure your life was set up in a way she could never dream of making happen on her own, would she have done that?" She tilted her head, watching him. She didn't want an enemy in this man. She didn't want an enemy at all; the next two years were going to be hard enough. "I think she would have. I think we both know your mother would have done anything for you. Including agreeing to this proposal."

"You think you're like my mom?"

It was obvious he didn't. His curled lip would indicate she wasn't fit to sit next to his mother in church.

"I'd do anything for this baby," she said, brushing her hand over her stomach. "That makes us similar enough."

He was silent for a long time, looking over her head at the lights around the fountain.

"Well, well," he said and then smiled at her again, not particularly kind but not mean anymore, either. "Now who's clever?"

He waited for her while she climbed the stairs.

"All I did was sleep with a guy at a bar," she told him when she got to his step. "A nice guy who seemed like he was having a bad night. If you want to hate someone, hate Harrison. He knew who he was. I didn't."

He nodded slowly, as if mulling over the idea of hating his boss. "Clever and tough. That's good. You're going to need everything you've got with this family."

She glanced around the front of the house, the stunning reality of Harrison's wealth. The stunning reality of what she was doing. Of how unbelievably out of place she was.

"Is my lawyer here?" she asked as they took the rest of the steps together.

"Yeah, he's with Bruce, discussing your amendments to the contract."

"Is there a problem?"

"Well, we're not thrilled with your amendment should he lose this election."

"If it's really awful, I want a way to get out of this marriage."

"He's not a bad guy."

"I might have agreed with you at one time, but now I don't know what he is. And that's why I want to be able to dissolve the agreement if both parties agree when the election is over." She gave him the side-eye. "If your mother was in this situation, that's what you would want her to do."

"All right," he laughed. "We can give my mother a rest."

"What about my other demands?"

"Shouldn't be a problem. Paying the mortgage for your family's house in Philadelphia, setting up a college fund for your sister, for your child, and keeping your brother's name out of the press are all doable."

"And the last thing?"

Poor Wallace looked tortured. "You . . . you really need that in writing?"

"I do."

"Then it's done. No sex."

"No sex. And separate rooms." She could not imagine sharing a bedroom with a man she didn't know, not after years of her own privacy.

If she was going to be spending most of her time pretending to love and be loved by a man who couldn't be bothered to greet her at the door on the evening of their wedding, then she was going to need a place to regroup.

"The Montgomerys have added their own stipulation."

"Really?"

"A blood test when the child is born. The results to be kept private."

She smiled humorlessly. And she wanted to tell him to fuck off, but she had nothing to hide. Harrison had no reason to believe in her; the connection she'd felt that night had been a ruse, the product of grief and her own stupid, wayward heart.

"Fine."

Wallace nodded and opened the front door.

Despite all her efforts to not be one of those historical romance heroines, walking into the marble foyer and seeing the slick hardwood floors beyond, the glittering chandeliers and sconces, she felt like one.

She felt small and alone. And like maybe her dad lost her in a poker game.

At the far end of the front entry—so large that two of her apartments could have fit in it—a door opened.

She wanted it to be Harrison coming through that door as much as she was dreading seeing him again. And now she was grateful that it had been Wallace at the front door; it gave her a chance to regroup. To fortify her walls. To be reminded in no unclear way that this was business. And nothing else at all.

But it wasn't Harrison coming through that door.

"Oh Christ, brace yourself," Wallace whispered, placing his hand at the small of her back as if to help hold her up. His solicitous concern was terrifying.

The woman that came across the foyer to stand in front of Ryan was small, though she gave the impression of being bigger than she was. Her dark suit was tailored to fit her thin body. Her long blond bob was perfect in every way, the highlights subtle, not a hair out of place. Her makeup was the same, elegant and restrained. She wore gold hoops in her ears and a small crucifix on a thin chain around her neck. A diamond the size of a grape on her ring finger.

Ryan knew a stylized look when she saw one, a costume top to bottom created to tell a story, to force a reaction. This woman wanted everyone to believe she was in the background. Nonthreatening. Vaguely forgettable.

But it was a lie.

She was chilling in her practiced innocuousness.

Behind her, another woman came out the door. Blond and rumpled, a pencil in her hair, two phones and clipboard in her hand.

"I'm Patty Montgomery," the woman in front of her said.

Ryan had of course read plenty about her in the files and knew that what she was really wearing wasn't that St. John suit or the god-ugly round-toed pumps, but ego. She was cloaked head to toe in her own hubris.

Unable to resist stirring the pot, Ryan shrugged, as if the name meant nothing to her. Beside her, Wallace swallowed a laugh.

"I am Harrison's mother." She said it slowly, as if Ryan were stupid. Or didn't understand English.

"Nice to meet you. I'm his fiancée." Ryan put out her hand to shake, but Mrs. Montgomery simply sniffed. As far as snubs went, it was expected and unimaginative.

Really? Too good to shake my hand? That's what you're leading with? Ryan thought, surprised by how pissed the lame insult made her. It seemed that all the anger and resentment that she wasn't going to let herself feel about this strange turn her life had taken had found an incredibly handy outlet in this woman.

"Wallace, where is Harrison?" Patty asked, looking past Ryan as if she weren't there. "Reverend Michaels is in the south parlor and he doesn't have a lot of time to wait."

"He's got a conference call with Gibbs in Washington. He should be done shortly."

"Wonderful." Patty gave Ryan another long look. "You have a half hour, I imagine, before the ceremony if you'd like to change."

"Nope."

"No . . . nope?" Patty asked, her perfect eyebrows nearly hitting her hairline.

"This is it. My wedding dress. I got it from a guy in the garment district who only had one eye. It's my lucky dress." She was hugely gratified to watch Patty's face nearly implode with distaste. Honestly, this woman was really too easy.

"Tomorrow morning we have a press conference, and after that you will be doing a school visit. Do you plan on wearing . . . that?"

"I've got some skinny jeans."

"Noelle!" Patty called, and the messy shadow woman behind her stepped forward.

"Yes."

"Clearly, Ms. Kaminski is going to need a new wardrobe. Could you see that done?"

Noelle nodded and wrote a note on the clipboard she carried.

"I'm size four," Ryan said, watching Patty from the corner of her eye. "Size eight shoe. Yellow looks terrible on me, and keep the skirts short. I may be a politician's wife, but I'm not dead, am I?" She laughed, pouring it all on thick. For a woman who just seconds ago had thought she needed no enemies, she was doing

her damnedest to make sure her future mother-in-law
was going to be one.

It was her perverse streak, the rebellion she had
against anything that wasn't genuine. She'd take a hot
mess over a woman pretending she was perfect, project-
ing a lie. She had no patience for that.

And this gut reaction to prove an act was false had
gotten her in more than her fair share of trouble.

"We'll need a stylist," Patty said, eyeing Ryan's hair.
"Tony should be able to come in first thing before the
press conference."

"My hair is fine," she said.

Patty stepped closer, bringing with her the crackling
energy and disapproval of five generations of money
and power. Ryan swallowed. "I don't think you understand that whatever rock you have lived under is gone.
Your sad little existence as a waitress and a would-be
model—it's over. The way you lived your life, the things
you believe, they do not matter anymore. You are a
Montgomery, and you will behave as such, or I'm afraid
you'll find this golden ticket you've managed to weasel
out of my son will vanish. You. That baby. You will
disappear right back into the hole you came from with
absolutely nothing."

"All right, Patty." Wallace stepped forward, but Patty's gaze was so cold that he froze in his spot.

"Is this the same speech you gave that girl who almost
died in the car crash with your husband?" Ryan said,
deliberately baiting the bear, because she'd been taken
out by her knees by this woman. And the only thing to
do when you were going down in a fight was to make
sure you weren't going down alone.

"Ryan," Wallace breathed, as if a warning to take
cover. To tip over that ugly chair and hide behind it. But
she stood her ground, because it was all she had left.

"Do you think not caring makes you brave?" Patty's

low voice cut her to pieces. "It doesn't. It makes you stupid. More than your lack of education, or where you come from, not caring just makes you stupid, Ryan. And you don't know this about Harrison, but he cares. More than anyone else in this family, he *cares*. And you may have impressed him one night in a bar. But you are in his life now and he won't be impressed by you at all. Now, you're getting married in the south parlor. You have twenty minutes."

Patty's heels nearly bored holes in the granite and hardwood floors as she left, Noelle her shadow trailing behind her.

"Holy shit," Ryan said, finally sucking in a breath. Panic roared around her. "What the hell am I doing?"

"Hey, hey," Wallace said, grabbing a stiff armchair next to a table covered in flowers. "Don't pass out. Please don't pass out." He shoved the chair behind her knees and Ryan collapsed gratefully into it.

She put her head in her hands and let her hair fall down around her. A cave that smelled like the shampoo that was still in her tiny shower back in her apartment.

The hole I come from.

I want to go home.

"This is ridiculous," she said, torn between angry tears and hysterical laughter. Because Patty had been right; where she was from, not caring was the only way to survive. Where she came from you learned not to get your hopes up and then you learned not to hope.

After that, all you had left was bravado.

"No. No, it's not." She felt and heard Wallace get down in a crouch in front of her.

She shook back her hair, staring at this strange ally. "Ten minutes ago you would have given me the same damn speech." Oh, now she was turning toward tears. Because this guy had a nice face.

"Yeah, and now I'm telling you to suck it up. Harrison, his career, hell, even his mother needs you to see this through."

"I don't give a shit about his mother," she spat.

"Excellent. Me neither."

She smiled, but sagged farther into the awkward chair. "This is going to be a disaster."

"Maybe," Wallace said. "But you're here. You've come this far and you've done all right."

That made her laugh. "All right?"

"Yeah, you know, better than all right," he said, settling into his pep talk. "The lawyer. Making sure you get something out of this. That your family is taken care of. You're clever. You're tough. How'd you know about the girl in the car crash?"

"My brother sent me some information about the family, and I just put two and two together."

She was tempted to ask him why he was being nice. If it was real. Because she could use something kind, something real right about now.

But tough was lonely. So was proud.

And she had a lot of practice with those things, having lived alone with them for years. Exiled from every Christmas and birthday with her family. Weekends at home, Olivia's performances, Dad . . .

The thought of Dad got her to her feet.

This was how she made things right with Dad. The money her lawyer was making sure she got—that would go a long way toward fixing what she'd done.

She grabbed her leather purse. It used to be one of the nicest things she owned, but now, sitting on the granite floor under the chandelier, it just looked cheap.

I don't care, she thought. *I don't care how I look to these people. I have a job to do, a past to make right, and a future to secure.*

And I'm not stupid.

"Show me where the fucking south parlor is. I need to get married."

Wallace pointed toward the door that Patty and Noelle had vanished through.

"Right." She threw her hair over her shoulder and crossed the foyer.

"Ryan?" Wallace asked.

"Yeah?"

"You were right about my mom." He was running a hand over that ugly tie. "She would have done this, too. For me."

It felt like a blessing. But maybe that's what any kind of approval looked like when you were lying down flat at rock bottom.

Whatever, she thought. *I'll take it.*

She winked at Wallace, which made him laugh, and she opened the door to the unknown beyond.

Chapter 12

Harrison saw Wallace tapping his watch in the study doorway. Harrison nodded and held up one finger. Wallace pulled an exasperated face.

"Hey, Gibbs, I need to go." He cut the analyst off in the middle of a discussion of language use in a new survey they were going to put out regarding fiscal responsibility. "Email me that poll data and I'll look it over and call you back next week." Gibbs agreed and hung up.

"I take it she's here?" Harrison asked, hanging up his cell phone and slipping it into his pocket. He'd been procrastinating, listening to doors slam down the hallway and not in any hurry to join the fray.

Cowardly; he totally understood that.

"She's been here waiting for nearly forty-five minutes," Wallace said, and Harrison gaped at the man.

"Are you chastising me? The man who wanted me to pillory her in the *New York Times*?"

Wallace shrugged, stepping farther into the mahogany-paneled office. It was on the first floor and therefore open to the public for tours, so it fairly reeked of formal inefficiency. But Harrison had never been comfortable in his father's offices. Not since he was twenty-two. In the irrational fear he would be contaminated. Pulled offside by his father's weakness.

The joke's on you, isn't it. The weakness was already in him.

Maybe that was why he was procrastinating, putting

off the ramifications of his weakness. The utter reality of his failure.

"I've changed my mind about her."

This honestly didn't come as a surprise to Harrison. Ryan had the kind of tough-love charm that Wallace would adore. Hell, Harrison had adored it for one night.

Tell me who your best isn't good enough for.

"Don't tell me you're turning into a romantic."

"She went toe to toe with your mom," Wallace said.

Harrison paused while shrugging into his coat. "And she's still here?"

"She's tough, man," Wallace said with a shrug and a smile, like he was talking about some scrappy new pitcher for the Braves.

In Wallace-speak, it was high praise.

"We knew that." He jammed paperwork into his briefcase, the amended marriage contracts he'd signed. No sex, separate rooms, she could leave if both parties agreed should he lose the election, the blood test Mother had insisted be included. This whole marriage was a farce. It wasn't even a very good business arrangement since it was, at its core, a cover-up. "She is tough. Foolish and headstrong. Uneducated, a potential nightmare in the press, she has a loose-cannon brother with a criminal past, to say nothing of that Lip Girl thing. She may or may not be pregnant with my child. She may or may not have orchestrated this whole damn thing."

"You don't really believe that, do you?" Wallace asked. "That she's tricked you?"

"Don't act so horrified, Wallace. Twenty-four hours ago you were saying the same thing."

"Well, as your soon-to-be wife just reminded me, there were two of you in that room and only one of you knew who you were."

Harrison came abreast of his campaign manager at

the door. "If that's true and she didn't know me, she quickly figured it out, didn't she?"

"Or her brother did and she really knew nothing about it."

What if that was the truth? he wondered, but then quickly decided it didn't matter.

"That doesn't change the fact that I barely know her. But what I do know is she is without a doubt the worst possible wife for me."

"Yeah," Wallace said. "If all you are is a politician."

"I'm a Montgomery," Harrison said. "What else would I be?"

The south parlor was the scene of a very strange tableau. Reverend Michaels and Mother sat on the love seat, their heads bent together. One might think they were praying, but Harrison knew better. Plotting world domination perhaps, or at the very least the destruction of one former bartender from Philly.

Dad sat in a chair by the curtains, his tie and jacket gone. A drink in hand. And by the flush on his cheeks, it wasn't his first. Ted was studiously ignoring everyone else in the room, particularly Ryan. As if just clapping eyes on her might hurt his approval rating.

Or maybe he was thinking about Heidi, the young woman he'd used and discarded.

Maybe he was feeling the edges of his own guilt.

Ryan sat in one of the gold brocade Queen Anne chairs, her legs crossed, a flip-flop dangling from her toe. She was reading something on her phone, one finger twirling the end of a lock of hair.

She was chewing gum.

Loudly.

In a house full of lies and pretense, she was startling, viscerally real.

"I think I'm in love with her," Wallace muttered.

"Sorry I'm late," Harrison said, stepping farther into the room.

"Well, well, if it isn't the Golden Boy." Dad wasn't slurring. Not quite. But his words were dipped in ugliness. Ryan lifted her head, a deer scenting danger.

Harrison ignored him. Ignored him so hard he practically shook.

"Not so sanctimonious now, are you, son?" Ted kicked his legs out in front of him, angling his head as if to study Harrison more clearly. "Tell me, how does it feel to be just as human as the rest of us?"

Harrison threw his briefcase onto the chair.

"Nothing to say to your old man? You know if you'd asked me, I could have told you. It's never worth it, son."

"Ted!" Mother's sharp voice rattled the windows, silencing her husband, who took his chastisement like he always did—with a healthy slug of bourbon.

"It's not too late to change your mind," Mother said. She stood and approached him with her hands out. "We can think of another way out of this."

Suddenly, it seemed as if their roles were reversed and he was the one steeling himself, holding himself away from her so as to not get dirty with her barely concealed emotion. Her messy desire for more of him than he was willing to give.

"There is no other way," Harrison said.

"Well, in that case." Dad stood up, bracing himself on the chair until his legs were steady. "Congratulations, son," he said, toasting Harrison with his glass, and then turned to Ryan. He fought the desire to step in front of Ryan and shove his father back into his evil, dark little corner, but that would require acknowledging the man. "Welcome to the family. Welcome all to hell."

"So romantic," Ryan said, and all three Montgomerys turned to stare at her. "Really, how can a girl refuse?" She stood up, tucked her phone back in her purse, and approached all of them. Like Daniel sashaying into the lion's den. "The contracts have been signed. I'm totally bought and paid for, and while I appreciate a good family fight before any wedding ceremony, I've been waiting for close to an hour to get married. I'm exhausted. Sick. And my feet are swelling. So, I'd like to get hitched."

Everyone looked down at her feet. At her flip-flops.

"Harrison," Mother moaned. "You cannot be serious about this."

"I am."

Ryan stood there looking exactly like what she was—beautiful, yes. Stunningly so. Sexy and lush and vibrant. But she was broke, desperate, and uneducated. In terms of improving her life, she'd hit the jackpot with him.

She wasn't here because of any lingering emotional attachment he had to her from that night they'd shared. He didn't share his sister's romantic idealism, the desire to be anyone outside of his name.

Ryan was here because Harrison had been weak.

"Reverend Michaels," he said. "If you would do the honors."

Married. I am married.

She kept staring at the simple gold band on her finger, next to the very not simple diamond ring Harrison had slipped on with the band in a very slick sleight of hand that she doubted anyone had noticed. Engaged and married in one fell swoop.

The diamond was at least a carat and made the diamond chip Paul had given her a lifetime ago seem ridiculous.

"Where'd this come from?" she asked. "The diamond?"

"My aunt's." He didn't look at her, barely acknowl-edged her. "You'll give it back if you break the con-tract."

Right. Contract.

She was married to a man who'd ignored her for the last hour. If he hadn't said her name during the cere-mony, someone watching the event would not have known whom he was marrying. The icy moat he'd dug around himself was impenetrable and despite the sticky heat of Atlanta in the summer, she was cold in his pres-ence and felt naked in her dress.

As soon as Wallace had shut Harrison's car door, Harrison had put up the privacy screen between the front and back seats and poured himself a scotch from the bar hidden in the seat between them. He'd given her a bottle of water, which sat in her lap, condensation making dark spots on her dress.

And then he'd pulled a stack of papers from the brief-case on the floor beside his outstretched legs and didn't look at her again.

He was so big in the backseat, took up so much space. Air.

She tilted her head back so she could breathe.

"Are you going to be sick?" Harrison asked.

His electric-blue eyes watched her in the darkness. It was the first time he'd looked at her since getting in the car. It was shocking, that gaze in the half-dark.

My husband.

That is my husband.

"I'm fine." Her voice croaked from exhaustion and disuse.

The tinted windows made the dark outside seem darker, but it was obvious they were driving closer to the city.

"Where do you live?"

"A condo in midtown," he said looking back down at the files in his lap. He took a sip of scotch.

"Is it nice?"

"Nice enough."

The silence was so thick she could scoop it up in her hands, like wet sand, and make a wall between them as real as the privacy screen between the front and back seats.

"What happens tomorrow?" she asked, because she was perverse and he so clearly wanted her to be silent.

"We'll be giving a press conference at my campaign office. Before that there will be some people at my house to help us get ready."

"Your mother is getting me clothes."

He barely looked at her. "If that bothers you, tell her to stop. Eventually she listens."

"It's fine," she said. "Noelle will probably have a better idea of what I need than I will."

Harrison sighed. Ryan ran her hand over the water bottle in her lap, collecting moisture and then wiping it on her dress.

"I made her angry, and I did it on purpose. I probably shouldn't have done that."

"Everything makes her angry; don't take it personally."

"I'm going to need all the friends I can get."

He huffed under his breath, giving her the impression that friendship and his mother were not going to happen. But she couldn't stop thinking about the way Patty had taken her apart in the foyer. Obviously, Patty didn't like her and that was fine, but that scene wasn't just about not liking Ryan. It was about protecting her son. And Ryan had no clue what went into being a politician's wife, but maybe that was part of it.

Protection.

Part of her job was to keep the illusion alive. To protect Harrison's reputation.

Any other time, she'd call bullshit on that. There were two people in that hotel room, and only one of them knew the whole story. But she'd taken the money. Signed the agreement.

She was a politician's wife.

She thought of all the women standing next to disgraced politician husbands as they made their tearful apologies for screwing other women. Were they there out of love? Or because the heart of their relationship was much like the heart of Harrison's parents' marriage?

Or her own.

She'd survived physical science sophomore year at Flowers by cheating off of Denise Shimansky, so she would survive this by cheating off of Patty Montgomery.

Which meant she was going to have to make nice. Or at least nicer.

"Will someone be writing us a speech . . . or something?" she asked.

"Wallace will have some remarks for us."

"Remarks—is that a fancy politician word for a speech?"

That made him smile, and she felt that same stupid shot of accomplishment that she'd felt that night in the bar. A sense of pride in making this very serious man smile.

Stupid, Ryan. Don't be stupid.

"I suppose it is. Are you okay in front of an audience?" he asked, as if just figuring out that it could be a problem for a future congressman to have a wife who was terrified of public speaking.

"It makes me fart uncontrollably."

His entire face fell in horror and she couldn't help bursting into laughter.

"You're joking," he said, more demand than question.

"Sometimes I get so nervous I cry."

"This isn't funny, Ryan."

"Oh, but it is." She wiped at her streaming eyes. The tension of the day made her laugh even harder until she was doubled up on the seat. "Oh God, your face. So perfect."

"Laugh it up," he said dryly, but he started laughing, too. Well, not laughing, but smiling with his whole mouth, destroying just a bit of that icy chill around him, and it was such a wonderful release that she sort of stopped hating him. For just a minute.

This must be what Stockholm syndrome feels like.

"Seriously, though, are you going to be okay in front of cameras?"

"I've done some modeling work. I think I'll be okay. I'm just going to pretend I'm playing a character. A love-struck woman ready to stand by her man and drink tea and wave at people." She gave him a smile and wave that was part Queen of England, part Dolly Parton. Warmth and distance, all in one gesture.

"That's . . . really good."

"Thank you."

"Why'd you stop modeling?"

"I don't know," she said with a shrug, though she did know. She knew exactly why the work stopped coming, why her agent found it harder and harder to book a job for her. "I've been told I am not always the easiest to work with."

In the reflection of the window she could see him watching her. If she closed her eyes she imagined she would be able to actually feel the heat and weight of his gaze; that was how hard he was staring.

"Doesn't bode well for us, does it?"

"I'm not sure anything bodes well for us."

He went back to his files and she went back to looking out the dark window at the interstate lights, and the silence went back to being uncomfortable.

Part of what she liked about being a bartender was being able to read people. Being able to take all the clues they left in their body language and tone of voice, the way they held their drink or talked to their friends, and add all those things up into an impression. An idea of what they were like, what they wanted, what they were scared of.

Usually within ten minutes of serving someone a drink, she knew why that person was drinking. And sometimes, what the person was thinking.

But Harrison was utterly blank to her. Not only couldn't she figure out what he wanted or what he thought, but he didn't leave her any clues to even try to figure him out. He was a slick, handsome rich surface upon which she could get no footing.

Tonight, however, his family had given her plenty of clues. Plenty of tells. And the story his family told was not a nice one.

He'd grown up in a bowl, he'd said that night in the hotel. Without air.

She wondered, watching him with narrowed eyes, if he was truly this nonchalant. This cool in the face of marrying a stranger. Or if it was a show. After watching his parents in action, she was leaning toward show. Because underneath Harrison's calm surface she would never have guessed he had parents like that.

Ted was a drunk. A bad one. Barely kept in line by his wife.

And all they cared about was what the other was doing that might impact them.

The only thing the Montgomerys seemed to do together was stare daggers into her flesh. How wonderful that loathing her was what they could agree on.

I am the tie that binds.

She traced a drop of water down the plastic side of her bottle and watched him from the corner of her eye.

"That was quite a scene in there," she said. "At the mansion."

He flipped over a page of his file. "Not quite how you imagined your wedding?"

"I never imagined myself getting married again, but that wasn't what I was talking about."

His icy blue eyes met hers, wide with surprise, but then he glanced away, hiding himself again. She'd hit a nerve, she thought.

Smarter women might leave him alone. Go back to staring out the window and gathering reserves for the coming weeks. Smarter women would shut up and not poke at the man in his cage.

She'd never been very smart.

"I was talking about your parents."

He didn't pause, didn't look up. She wouldn't have known he'd heard her if it weren't for the muscle flexing hard in his jaw.

"Complaining about the in-laws already?" He flipped a page so hard it sounded like the paper tore.

"Has it always been like that?"

"What? Dad drunk and Mom furious? Yes. It has always been like that."

"Do you hate them both equally?" she asked. "Or are you saving something special for your father?"

Slowly, so slowly, like the earth turning, he lifted his eyes toward her. "What makes you say that?"

"You barely looked at him."

"I only had eyes for you." His smile was a cold, hard slice in his face. The most ineffective smile ever smiled.

"Why do you hate your dad so much?" she asked. "Is it the drinking?" Honestly, she didn't expect him to answer. There was no precedent set between her and Harrison. Or even Harry, really, who'd managed to tell her very little about himself, all while she was falling headfirst into his bed.

"I don't hate him," he lied, and she laughed.

"Your mother you talked to—not kindly, but you answered her questions. You did her the honor of argument. But your father . . ." She shook her head. "That was a heavy-duty freeze-out. Top notch, really, because you were smiling the whole time."

He shifted in his seat as if he were sitting on nettles. "My father and I disagree on a lot of things politically."

"What was happening during that ceremony wasn't political, Harrison. I may not be smart. But I'm not dumb."

"This whole thing is political. The marriage, you being here. None of this would be happening if I weren't in politics."

She shook her head, enjoying his discomfort, his angry clinging to lies and defenses he'd already created in regard to how he dealt with his family. She wondered when he'd done that, how he'd learned it. Was it something that happened to Montgomerys at birth? Alcoholics were thick on the ground back home and she'd watched plenty of families get destroyed, plenty of husbands and wives and kids turn themselves inside out pretending there was nothing wrong in their homes.

Well, that nonsense would end with her baby. Her baby wouldn't lie to keep the family skeletons in their closets.

"But for your family politics is personal, and I must say, that heavy-duty anger toward your dad, it felt pretty personal."

"Plenty of fathers and sons don't get along. I can't imagine what your father thinks of your brother?" He lifted an eyebrow, sending her what she imagined was usually a cutting glance, but she had nothing to lose. Nothing left to cut. He could not touch her with his poor efforts.

"My father would lie down in traffic for all of us," she said. Or he would have, once upon a time. Now, she couldn't be sure.

"How lovely."

"And your dad, would he do that for you?"

Harrison laughed. "He would only lie down in traffic if it got him good publicity."

"Is that why you hate him?"

"No, Ryan," he snapped. "I hate him because he's weak. He abuses his power. He pretends to be something he's not."

"Oh," she breathed, sort of stunned that he'd actually answered. Sort of stunned that dishonor was at the heart of his dislike for his father. She'd believed that dishonor was part of the political package. The Montgomery reality.

"Why haven't you talked to your sister in six years?" he asked, turning the interrogation over onto her.

She barely controlled the flinch, the instinctive recoil, because that was what he wanted. She'd played this game of polite torture, delicate cruelty, before with her sister and it was poisonous and destructive. But she was very, very good at it.

"That's not true," she said. "She called me just the other morning to tell me not to screw up our little sister's life any more than I have."

"And that's something you've done?"

I screw up everyone's life, she thought. *Just watch.*

"It's why I am marrying you, you know. If it were just me, I wouldn't give a shit about the press. But my sisters. My dad. My brother. This baby. Marrying you and your money will change everyone's lives."

And maybe . . . maybe it will let me back in.

"Why did you marry me?" she asked.

Harrison shook his head and reached back into the small hidden compartment in the seat between them for the scotch. "We've covered this, haven't we? A sex scandal would ruin my career."

"I know what you told me, Harrison. But what your mother said tonight is true—there were other ways to handle this. So why marriage? And I'll remind you I'll know if you're lying."

"Yes, the human lie detector claim. Did you learn that from your years behind the bar or those psychology books in your apartment?" His eyes glittered from under his lashes.

"Oh no," she laughed, fairly convincingly if she did say so herself. "I just look at the pictures in those books."

"Now who is lying?" he asked, his voice a quiet whisper before he took a sip of the scotch.

Oh, he was far better at this game than she was.

Because he'd seen the secrets, the small desires she kept in her apartment, those stupid books. That stupid dream to go back to school. And he would mock it. Diminish it. Just to hurt her, because that was the awful game she'd started.

And she knew nothing of him. Nothing at all.

I can't do this, she thought. *I can't spend every minute of my life playing some kind of chess match with this man, wondering what is real and what isn't.*

She hated the very thought of it, a future spent on high alert, looking for weaknesses to exploit just to wound him. Just to find the human being beneath that façade of his—it made her feel like she was drowning.

Tears burned behind her eyes and she looked away from his sharp gaze.

The wheels hummed along the highway, the world a blur outside the window. "If this is going to work," she said, pressing her hand against the cool glass and then her forehead, "to the world outside, we'll lie our faces off. But you and I . . ."

The words *Let's be kind. We've both been hurt enough* wouldn't come out of her mouth into the horrible coldness between them.

"No lies between us?" he supplied.

She nodded and whispered, feeling more painfully vulnerable than she had all night, "No lies between us."

"I married you because I am not my father. I may make his mistakes, but I am not my father."

"Mistakes?" she asked, his words slipping down along her neck, through the skin down to her bones. Where it hurt.

Me, she thought. *He means me.*

She thought of that girl nearly dead in a car crash and how she'd been pushed aside until she vanished.

"You wanted honesty," he said.

"Yeah, that will teach me, won't it?" She curled away from him, staring out the window at a world rushing by.

Chapter 13

Harrison bought his loft a few years ago in one of his early efforts to prove he wasn't his parents. He used every scrap of his meager savings, collected over the years from his stipend as director of VetAid. He'd also used the trust his grandfather had set up in his name.

Just about everything he had except this loft had been eaten by the campaign. Until the election was over and he was back to earning a living in some capacity, he was as broke as he'd ever been. As he ever wanted to be.

The contract for his driver was paid for.

The jet belonged to his parents, and he was stupidly grateful for it.

The unit he bought was in an old cotton factory, part of the revitalization of unused urban spaces. It was in direct contrast to the home he grew up in on Clifton Road overlooking Druid Hills Golf Club in a leafy neighborhood off of Ponce de Leon Ave.

"You live in a factory?" Ryan stared up at the old brick building.

"Not what you expected?" he asked, leading her into the building.

He took no small amount of pleasure in surprising her. He was still sore from the way she'd slowly pulled him open inside the car, as if all his carefully kept secrets, all those things the Montgomerys hid away so well, were just readily available to her. As if she could just reach into his chest and play tic-tac-toe with what hurt him the most.

He'd hurt her, too, in the car. It had seemed like the only way to get her to back off.

Another reason to stay removed from her. So they could come through this without tearing each other apart.

"You can use the second bedroom," he said as they walked in, and he flipped on the lights. He pointed down the hall toward his guest room, which had a bed shoved into the corner surrounded by boxes and a treadmill he didn't use enough. But it was clean and the sheets were fresh. "It's a little cluttered, but it should work."

"I'm sure it's fine," she said, polite and subdued, which was kind of terrifying in her.

"There's a bathroom right beside it," he said. "Are you hungry?"

His entire floor plan was open concept, and he'd bought the furnished showroom with its modern furniture. The sleek leather sectional and the dining set next to the floor-to-ceiling windows faced a neon downtown.

A metal spiral staircase led up to his bedroom, bathroom, and a small study. The walls were brick and the metal beams across the ceiling were original, and he remembered once upon a time liking that. Liking how different it was from anything he grew up in. How independent it had made him feel.

His sister was halfway around the world saving lives and defying their parents by living in poverty, and he showed his rebellion by buying an industrial loft.

Sometimes he didn't know what the hell he was doing.

In the corner the kitchen was an eat-in counter, and he paid his assistant to grab groceries every week. Most of which piled up in his fridge until he threw them out, but he was glad at the moment to have food he could offer the pale woman still standing at the door.

"Would you like a sandwich?"

Her face tightened. "No thanks."

"You should eat something." He hadn't noticed it until now, but she looked much thinner than she had that night at the hotel. As if something had been slowly whittling her down to bone and muscle.

"Not unless you want me to throw up all over your floor."

He paused while pulling ham out of his fridge. "Is that something you do a lot of?"

Hollow-eyed and exhausted, she looked at him, and he could tell that she was figuring out the distinction between no lies between them and keeping parts of herself safe.

He'd done the same thing in the car, figuring out just how much truth to give this stranger he'd married. It was cold. Calculating. And the only way to get through the next few weeks. To say nothing of the next two years.

Then it occurred to him that marrying her had been his biggest rebellion, and he didn't know how he felt about that. He'd spent so many years putting distance between himself and his family, storing away parts of himself like he was hoarding it. But for what? For whom?

To be his own man. To distinguish himself from the long line of Montgomerys who'd squandered and abused every single advantage they'd had.

He'd spent so much time—every minute of every day since he'd been twenty-two—deciding who he wasn't while still measuring himself with their yardstick. He envied his sister and her clean break from the family, but he could not get where he needed to go without them.

Simultaneously he cared about none of it and too much about all of it.

He felt sometimes that he'd spent so much time polishing all the wrong things about himself, leaving too much of real value to be forgotten, grown over with weeds and rust.

It is the job you've chosen, he told himself. *It's the role you play. You want to be in politics. All those things you don't care about, or don't want to care about—they matter.*

He looked at her, this fierce woman, perhaps liar, he'd married who seemed somehow so rooted in her flip-flops and shabby green dress, who despite all but selling herself to him managed to stand there defiant and totally her own person.

And he was envious of her. Envious of her singularity. Of the way she didn't care about the yardsticks he cared about. He wanted to ask her how she did it.

"I'm going to bed." She grabbed her purse and her beat-up duffel bag and walked down the hall toward his spare bedroom.

Harrison watched her go and then made a sandwich, which he ate standing up. The milk was still good, so he poured himself a glass and stood at his window, watched the headlights on I-75, and toasted his wedding night.

Alone.

Monday, August 26

Before dawn, Harrison woke up to the sound of someone being violently, wretchedly ill.

Ryan.

All of it coming back to him in that confusing place between dream and reality.

He threw pants on and hustled down the metal steps to the bathroom next to the guest room.

Inside it was eerily silent. He knocked quietly on the door.

"Ryan?"

"Go away."

"You sound . . . really sick."

"I *am* really sick. Now go away."

He stepped back from the door, feeling helpless, but then the door opened, revealing Ryan.

Dawn light, rosy and creamy, covered her pale, perfect skin. She wore short cotton shorts that revealed the muscled length of her legs and a thin, tight black tank top like the one from the night in the hotel.

"Hey," he said, blindsided by the reality of her, sick and beautiful in his loft. "Everything . . . okay?"

"Fine." She pushed past him toward the kitchen. The tattoo on her back peeked over the tank top's black edge. The woman's hands, wrapped in seaweed and flowers, her blond hair a cloud around her face. Her eyes closed in some kind of surrender.

She was drowning.

My wife has a tattoo of a drowning woman on her back.

Ryan stopped, turned around, and went back to her room only to come out with a red teacup that he recognized from her apartment cradled in her hands.

As he watched, she got herself a glass of water and took a pill.

My pregnant wife.

"I have teacups," he said. "You didn't need to bring your own."

"I like my own."

"Can I get you something?"

"I'm fine." She sat at one of the high stools that in his memory no one had ever sat on. Ever.

His parents had barely been to his home. Wallace came once to watch a Braves game when his cable got blown out in a storm—which had been an oddly satisfying experience, despite the fact that he didn't care much for baseball. He'd never had a party. The few women he'd dated hadn't been over. If pressed, he would say that he would rather sleep on the couch in his campaign office than upstairs in the bedroom.

What does that say about me?

"What happened to no lies between us?" He stepped around her and into the kitchen to start coffee.

"I have bad morning sickness." She gave him a wan smile before putting her head back in her hands. "I took a pill, but it just takes a while."

He checked his watch. "Are you sure you're up for this?" he asked, taking in her utterly defeated posture. "Because in a half hour most of my staff is going to be here to get us ready for the press conference."

"You bought a wife." She shook back her hair, her smile not quite up to full wattage, but he gave her points for trying. "You'll get a wife."

"We can postpone—"

She stood, uncoiling her body one long, lithe muscle at a time from his stool. "I'm going to take a shower."

His team was good, his mother perhaps the best player of the political game in the world, but he had serious doubts that they were going to pull this off. She looked ill, the distance between them was vast and hurtful, and he felt oddly off center. Aware too clearly of the lies he'd been telling his whole life. Not big ones, not terrible ones like his father, but dozens of little ones, about his family. About happiness. And he wasn't entirely sure of his own ability to carry off another series of lies.

And the pale, sick, and angry woman who was sup-

posed to help him tell those lies seemed completely incapable of looking him in the eyes, much less pretending
to be in love.

This, he thought, *is going to be a disaster.*

Wallace arrived full of ebullient congratulations in a
hideous purple tie. Jill brought donuts and a marginally
better outlook than yesterday. Dave, his assistant, silent
and steadfast, made coffee.

"Where's Ryan?" Wallace asked.

"Getting ready." It was on the tip of his tongue to tell
Wallace that this was never going to work. The press
conference, the sham marriage—they should just quit
while they were ahead.

But then Mother arrived with Noelle in tow, carrying
armfuls of shopping bags. And he would not admit his
misgivings in front of his mother.

"Where is she?" Patty asked, sniffing the air for Ryan.
"I have her wardrobe."

And as if the sound of her voice had been the starting
bell in a boxing match, Ryan came out of the guest
room, wearing a denim skirt and a faded blue Pabst
Blue Ribbon beer tee shirt.

"She wore that just to piss off your mother, didn't
she?" Wallace whispered, biting into a second glazed
donut. The remnants of his first were all over his tie.

Harrison didn't answer, but he imagined that Ryan
smiled when she'd put on that shirt, thinking about Patty's reaction.

"Good morning," Ryan said, looking oddly meek
with her wet hair unbound, her face pink and freshly
scrubbed.

It was weird. He'd seen her sad, horny, angry, scared,
and worried. Never meek.

He put a hand against the small of her back, feeling through her shirt the tension of her muscles, the heat of her skin. "Let me introduce you to my team. You remember Wallace?"

"Of course." She deliberately sidestepped his touch and he dropped his hand. The smile she gave Wallace was enviously genuine. "Nice tie."

"Thanks," Wallace said. "Nice shirt."

She tugged on it, suddenly self-conscious, as he introduced her to everyone else.

"I want to thank you in advance," she said, shaking hands with Jill and Dave. "For how much patience you're going to need with me. I'm not familiar with any of this and I'm probably going to need more help than anyone knows, but I promise, I'm taking it seriously."

"That's . . . very good to hear," Jill said, clearly still skeptical, but that was Jill's natural state.

"Cool," Dave added, unable to stop staring at Ryan, who even without makeup, the bright sunlight washing over her through the windows making her seem pale and fragile and thin, was shockingly beautiful.

When Ryan saw the shopping bags on the couch where Noelle had put them, her eyes lit up.

"For me?" she asked, and Noelle nodded.

Without another word, Ryan grabbed the bags against her chest and vanished back into the bedroom, without once looking at him.

"Well, that's a good start," Wallace said, looking over at Jill and Dave, who both nodded. Harrison had to admit she had a way about her that could be really disarming when she tried.

"A good start?" Patty scoffed as she settled into an armchair beside the television. "You honestly believe she can make a room full of journalists believe you're in love. She's acting like a kicked dog who won't even look at you. She won't let you touch her."

"We'll be fine." He pushed aside his mother's worries because they so mirrored his own. "Wallace? Let's see your remarks."

Dave handed out coffee to everyone and Wallace passed out copies of his remarks.

"No one will believe you met at an art gallery," Mother said, crossing out a line.

"We need to decide how much truth we can tell and how far we can stretch a lie," Wallace said.

"I can't imagine she's been in an art gallery in her life," Patty said. "She looks like a woman begging for change outside—"

"How about we just say New York," Harrison said.

"You can't talk about any of her background," Mother continued. "Or her family. No education, no—"

Ryan emerged from the bedroom, her heels a steady, strong click on the hardwood of the hallway. She came to stand in the wide doorway, an eye-searing vision in a scarlet suit that hugged her body, ending in a flared skirt at her knees. A pair of dark heels made the most of her already extraordinary legs. Everywhere Harrison looked—her hair in a tight bun, her lips stained with color, her eyelashes dark and sooty, the fit of her suit, the red covered buttons marching down her chest and narrow waist—everywhere he looked she was perfect.

"Isn't it rude to talk about someone when they're not in the room?" she asked.

He was on his feet and Wallace, next to him, was, too.

It wasn't that her beauty had altered. The rawness of her looks, the sexuality that could so easily blind a person from seeing anything else about her, was muted. Secondary. This woman in front of him with the perfect makeup and hair and sharp suit—she looked smart and focused. She glowed with a sly light. A warmth and an intelligence.

"Holy shit," Wallace said.

"You look beautiful," Harrison said, and her eyes sliced through him.

"What did you say once?" she asked, stepping farther into the room, made of confidence and swagger. She was a flame—all of them, with the exception of Mother, helpless moths. "This is the least of what I can do?"

He tipped his head, caught in the edges of her bewitching smile.

"A suit is easy," Mother said, picking up a cup of coffee from the edge of the television table. "Let's talk about what we're going to do with your background."

Ryan sat down on the arm of the sofa, close to Harrison but still somehow very far away, in a perfect imitation of Mother's posture. Her distance.

"What would you like to know?" she asked, and even her voice was different. Slower, the consonants rounder. Not quite Atlanta proper, but not quite Queens anymore, either.

Mother leaned forward and as he watched, Ryan cataloged all of his mother's nuances, what she did with her hands, how she cocked her head. The position of her feet. Ryan made dozens of minute changes, but the effect was huge.

She transformed herself.

Harrison allowed himself to feel just the smallest amount of hope that maybe they could pull this off.

But Mother's smile was cruel. "Let's talk about your first marriage."

Either they'd pull this off or Ryan and Mother would get into a fight on the coffee table. At this point it could go either way.

Ryan had met more than her fair share of mean girls. Bitches, who thought that because they had money, or bigger tits, or lived on the other side of town, or had fucked her boyfriend at one time or another, had one up on her.

Patty Montgomery was just another mean girl.

And Ryan was here to prove that she could do this. She could dress up and play the part of Mrs. Harrison Montgomery, despite being wildly unprepared for the role.

But it was a pretty good bet that Mrs. Harrison Montgomery shouldn't hit her mother-in-law with her teacup, so she swallowed the urge and renewed her promise to play nice.

Though flashing the scars left by her marriage in a room full of strangers made her feel painfully exposed. Harrison's staffers, she could feel them all watching her. So, she adopted some of her mother-in-law's icy distance. Those hooded eyes, the clenched jaw.

And the chill felt good. Like insulation a foot thick between herself and the past and everyone in this room.

Except Harrison.

She wasn't sure there was enough insulation in the world to make her forget he was there.

"His name was Paul," she said. "We got married when I was twenty and it lasted for four years."

"How did you meet?"

"Paul was dating my sister."

"Your sister? And you—"

"Stole him? I guess you could say that, though he wasn't much of a prize. My sister was in nursing school and when I got the contract for Lip Girl, he became very interested in me. I thought we were in love, but he was far more interested in the money I was making."

"How charming." Patty's sarcasm was a sharp blade and Ryan was not totally impervious. She shifted in her seat, trying not to lose her temper. This was part of it, wasn't it? Part of what she'd signed on for. The tea drinking and waving and getting browbeaten by her mother-in-law.

"I hardly see how this is relevant?" Wallace asked, but Patty held up a hand, silencing him. Ryan realized that Patty wasn't going to stop this little interview until she was chewing on Ryan's bones.

Just another mean girl, she told herself when she felt herself wobble. *And not even the worst you've ever seen.*

"How did this fairy tale end?" Patty asked.

"Mother—" Harrison tried to step in and Ryan appreciated it. She did. But this was her fight.

"No, it's okay." Ryan looked over at him, standing with his arms crossed over his chest, the city through the window behind him. If she had her choice, he'd never know this. She'd never talk about it. "Things with Paul were fine for two years, rough for another. Terrible . . . really, really terrible for one more."

She thought of her hospital record, the clinical description of broken bones and black eyes. Scrapes and cuts. A woman thrown down stairs and punched in the face.

Harrison had seen those hospital records. Understood that she'd been beaten up and still went back to the guy, and she was as aware as anybody else that blaming the victim was ludicrous, but it didn't quite stop her from hating herself.

Her skin prickled with heat, all along the side of her face and down her neck.

She cleared her throat. "I had told Paul, stupidly, that my father had saved scrupulously over the years five thousand dollars for each of his kids. Which was hard, miraculous really, considering his salary. He gave it to us when we turned eighteen to use however we wanted. Nora, Wes, and I all got our money, but he still had Olivia's. Kept it in a safe in the attic." She ran a thumb over the hem of her skirt. Over and over again. As if the past were a smudge there and she could just rub it off. "Paul had expensive habits, and the money I made with Lip Girl was gone. All of it, everything we had was gone, and one night, Paul . . . Paul got a gun from some friend of his and he drove us home to my father's house, where he forced . . . he forced my father to give us all of his money, including my youngest sister's five thousand dollars."

"And you were an accomplice to this?"

"You could say that."

"And what would you say?"

"I thought . . ." Again the thumb over the edge of her skirt. A nervous tic. A tell. *Stop it, Ryan. Stop.* But she couldn't. She could sit here and talk about this, but she couldn't totally pretend it was easy. Harrison was watching her, and she wanted to look at him, gauge how he felt about the woman he'd married. But she knew that if she looked, she'd never be able to tell. And that was in so many ways more devastating than his mother's outright disdain. "I thought if I wasn't there someone would get killed. Either Paul or my father. Nora, if she decided to be brave."

"You were protecting your family?" Patty asked, clearly not believing her.

"That's something you understand, isn't it?" she snapped, because yes, that was what she'd thought, and how dare this woman who had done her own damage to her family judge her? "Our methods might be different, but our goals are the same."

"You and I are not at all alike," Harrison's mother spat.

"Let's talk about education," Wallace jumped in as if to rescue her.

"What education?" Patty put out her claws. "She's a high school dropout!"

It stung. It shouldn't, it was somehow the least of her sins, but it still stung. "Well, I had at the time gotten a fairly substantial modeling contract."

"And that worked out so well for you, didn't it? The horrid Lip Girl thing."

"Enough," Harrison snapped, sounding almost exactly the way Patty had sounded last night talking to her drunk husband.

Are we all just doomed to step in our parents' footprints?

"It's fine," Ryan said. Her pride couldn't change the facts. "She's right. My modeling career failed. My marriage failed. Not much has worked out the way it was supposed to."

"Except for seducing my son, you mean?" Patty asked. "That has worked out perfectly for you."

"She didn't seduce me, Mother."

Oh, but I did seduce you. I just thought you were seducing me right back.

"You honestly believe she didn't know who you were?"

"It doesn't matter!" he snapped and Ryan jumped, strung so tight she felt she might crack like ice.

"Harrison," Ryan murmured. "Don't get mad. It's okay."

"No. It's not!" Harrison surged forward into her line of sight so she turned away slightly, so she couldn't see him again. For some reason, all of this was possible only if she wasn't looking at him. "Mother, you can leave."

Ryan gaped at him.

Patty gaped at him.

"I'm not joking. We've got to work together, and all you're interested in is tearing her apart. It's not going to work if you're here."

The room pounded with silence.

"What happened to your fine speech?" his mother

asked, coming slowly to her feet. "About needing my help to make everyone believe you're in love."

"If this is your 'help,' we can manage without it."

Patty gathered her purse, the air thick and awful.

As much as Ryan would love having Patty gone, it had been made pretty clear to her that she needed Patty. That of everyone in this room, Patty was the most likely to make them convincing.

Ryan reached for Harrison, touching, just barely, the edge of his coat jacket. As if that was all she could bear.

"It's okay," she breathed. "You don't have to—"

"I do," Harrison said, glancing at her and away. *God*. He was really angry.

"But what if we do need her help? It's kind of an all-hands-on-deck sort of situation."

"You'll be fine. Better than if she's here constantly rattling your cage." He lifted his hand to touch her shoulder, but she flinched away from him before he could. It had been instinctive. Uncontrollable. A safety measure.

Well, that's a problem.

In the doorway, Patty saw how she'd flinched, and paused. "You have to touch him," she said. Her eyes were bright, and if Patty were a different kind of woman, Ryan might think she had tears in her eyes. "If you want people to believe you love him, then you have to touch him. You have to smile and hold his hand no matter how you feel about him. Or what he's done." She swallowed, her hand at her stomach. A strange moment of weakness. "Or how he's hurt you."

The words cracked through the air and Ryan came to her feet as if she might say something, but then Patty was gone, Noelle behind her, and the door closed. The moment over.

Harrison stared at the door. Ryan stared at Harrison.

"Well," Wallace said, into the uncomfortable silence that followed. "Let's get back to work."

Slowly, everyone sat back down. Dave filled up everyone's coffee cups.

"Would you like some?" Dave asked her, and because she was giddy with stress and would gladly kill someone for a cup of coffee, Ryan laughed. She laughed so hard she slipped sideways off the arm of the chair right up against Harrison.

The laughter clogged her throat and stopped.

The feel of him warm and alive filled her with a painful want. A shocking need. Not for sex, but for comfort. For him to put that arm around her and tell her they would be okay.

She would be okay.

But that wasn't in the agreement.

And so she couldn't have it.

She got to her feet and crossed the room, sitting in Patty's chair by the television. With great care and effort, she pulled her arms and legs back into the position she'd copied from Patty.

She lifted her chin, folded her hands over her knee, and smiled at the room as if just a little bit interested in whatever they had to say.

"It's eerie," Wallace whispered, watching her.

Harrison turned away, as if what she'd transformed herself into held no more interest for him than what she'd been before.

Chapter 14

Ryan was back in that damn car, sitting beside her husband, who wore a handsome summer-weight suit that fit him like a dream. The safety pin holding up her skirt bit into her back and she shifted to try to get away from it. Outside the world was hot and bright, the concrete city just coming to life. Commuters in bus shelters, pedestrians waiting on corners for the lights to change.

It could have been New York in some ways. The trees were different. The street signs. But it could have been a corner in Brooklyn, or Queens. Manhattan.

Cities were cities, she thought.

She looked down at this suit she wore, the shoes, the sleek black bag.

Women are women, she reminded herself. *This is just a costume. You are still you.*

Though suddenly on the edge of this press conference she wondered, bleakly, which woman she was beneath this dress. Which version of herself. The world-weary and judgmental bartender? The brash and angry model? The selfish girl? The terrible sister? The worse daughter?

The terrified mother, going to extreme measures for her child?

She pressed a hand to her nervous stomach.

"Are you all right?"

"You keep asking that," she said, trying to find the right kind of distance between them. She was thrown off by him tossing his mother out of the house. No one had jumped to her defense in many long years. And she'd thought herself well past the point of wanting some man to step in.

And she hated that he'd done it.

And she kind of loved it, too.

He touched her hand, his fingertips warm over her knuckles. She bit back the gasp that rose in her throat. Of surprise. Of pleasure. Of a sort of dismay at her own weakness.

Nora would be laughing right now. Sitting back with a cigarette and that knowing look on her face. Boy-desperate, her sister had always called her. As if crazy was never enough. Not for Ryan.

The minute Ryan got boobs, she'd fallen in love with the effect they had on men. She'd loved the way men looked at her, the way they fell so frantically in lust with her. Like getting up her shirt and into her pants was the most important thing they'd ever do in their sad lives. She'd let her boobs and the men they'd brought around her door become paramount in her life. Sacrificing her family. Her career. Her well-being.

Boy-*stupid* was really more like it.

And then she'd found Paul, or Nora had, actually; Ryan just plucked him out of her sister's hands and then let him run right over her. Let him run all over her whole family. All because she'd been so crazy for him. So hot-headed and lusty.

Because the way they fought and the way they fucked— in her young mind, that had to be love. As if only the most dangerous emotions, those feelings bordering on out-of-control, could mean something.

And here she sat in a beautiful suit, living a lie, beside a man who hated her and she wanted him to touch her. Wanted a distraction from the nerves and doubt in her stomach. Wanted to feel, just for a moment, like she was important and capable.

All you've ever been good at is sex, her sister had said the night she found out about her and Paul. *It's all you'll ever be good at.*

She tucked her hands into her lap, making fists so hard the knuckles showed white under her skin.

"Are you nervous?" he asked.

"Piece of cake." She waved her hand, making a joke. Clinging to her bravado. She'd said no lies between them, but this—her fear, his misgivings, her mistakes—they were hers and hers alone.

The car pulled to a stop outside of a storefront property done up with red, white, and blue bunting. Posters that said "Montgomery, a New Hope" in the windows.

Wallace stood out front, checking his watch.

"Where does he get his ties?" she asked.

Harrison looked up and smiled. Actually smiled.

"No idea," he said. "You ready?"

No. No, I'm not.

"As I'll ever be."

Wallace opened the door, and she took a deep breath of the hot air laced with the smell of asphalt and sugar and grease from the donut shop on the corner. As if to prove to herself that it was happening, that she was doing it, she watched herself slide her hand over Harrison's. Putting together the heat and touch of him with the sight of her small, pale hand on his. She remembered them with a sort of breathy lightness in that mirror that night, the sight of his body behind hers, her breasts pulled out of her shirt. His hands at her waist.

She shook inside her skin.

Oh, his hands.

He glanced back, surprised at her touch. His eyes first on their hands and then her face, and she could tell he was pleased in some way and that there was a crack in his icy demeanor and she saw, deep down, that he was nervous, too. She saw deep down a glimpse of what she'd seen in him that night in the bar. The messy reality, the frail humanity.

Oh, she thought, her heart hammering into her throat. *Oh, you are there.*

She squeezed his hand like she had that moment at the bar when she'd reached through the barrier between them. Starting that night, this whole arrangement, in motion. Had she never done that, she wondered if they would have ended up in bed.

Not that it matters, she thought, and was surprised to realize that she wouldn't take it back. If not touching him that night meant that they would not be here, she wouldn't change what happened.

Because of the baby. Because for better or worse, her life had finally changed. She'd finally found the guts to stop floating.

"We can do this," she whispered.

"You think?"

"Fake it till you make it, right?"

"Our family motto."

"Harrison," Wallace said, leaning into the car. "We need to get going." And just like that the crack in him disappeared. He was once again smooth and perfect and without failing.

He nodded and stepped out of the car, pulling her with him. You'd think it would be harder, or perhaps require something superhuman on her part to take this last step, but in the end it was simple.

She just followed him.

Wallace introduced them and Harrison, more rattled by this morning's events than he really wanted to admit, led Ryan by the hand through the front doors and to the small podium with the microphone the team had set up early this morning. There were ten journalists in the room, and as soon as he and Ryan came to a stop behind the podium still hand in hand, flashes started going off.

"Thank you, everyone, for coming today," he said, once the original flurry of photos were taken. "I'm sorry for the short notice, but things have been moving pretty quickly and now that everything is official, I'd like to introduce you to Ryan Montgomery. My wife."

A general gasp, and then an explosion of questions and flashes.

He expected Ryan to cower away from the sudden high-voltage attention, but all she did was laugh as if she were delighted by the surprise they'd given the journalists.

Harrison gave all the journalists the order in which he'd answer their questions and Ryan stepped in closer, until they were touching from shoulder to hip.

In his life he'd done plenty of press conferences. He'd given speeches, won debates, argued in front of the State Congress. Hell, he'd even negotiated with Somali pirates. But he'd always done it alone. All alone, never with anyone by his side.

It was disconcerting having her there.

It was disastrous having her there.

"Phil," he said, pointing to the reporter from the AP. "Go ahead."

"What do you say to critics who believe this is all a press stunt?" he asked.

"I don't think of marriage as a press stunt," he said, and pointed to a woman in the back row. "Agnes, go ahead."

In the back row Wallace lifted his hands to his head, the first indication that Harrison had answered the question wrong. Three questions later Wallace was all but imploding in the back, and for the first time in his career Harrison felt a press conference get away from him.

All because Ryan was standing too close. Her hand in his was sweaty and kind of cold. She was pressed right up against his side and he could feel her breast against his arm. Her hip against his. Her other hand crossed in front of her body, holding onto his elbow.

Like they were in love and she was thrilled to be at his side.

She leaned in closer to him, her mouth behind his ear. "You all right?" she breathed.

Great. Even she knew he was bombing.

She lifted a hand to tuck a piece of hair off his forehead, a tender moment that the photographers captured in full.

Her smile was full of secrets, of inside jokes. It was the most intimate thing he'd ever experienced in a room full of strangers. Horrifyingly, he felt his body react as if they were alone. As if that smile were real.

It's an act, he told himself. *Just an act.* But it didn't seem to do any good.

His brain buzzed, empty and useless.

"Where did you meet?" Bill Maynard, the journalist from the *Journal-Constitution,* was a big man with a gray beard and a hard-on for bringing down the Montgomery family.

"An art gallery," he said, and then realized that wasn't quite the lie they'd agreed on. And his brain was blank; he couldn't remember what lies he was supposed to tell and what truths. What questions they'd decided to deflect and which to answer.

"Harrison is not quite telling the truth," Ryan said, stepping up to the microphone, giving him a wink over her shoulder. "We met outside an art gallery. I was on my way to work and we ran into each other."

"You were working at a bar?" another journalist asked, and he could feel the temperature in the room change. Grow feverish. This was going to be one of the details they avoided. They'd agreed on that back in his loft.

"I was," she agreed with a smile. "I worked as a bartender and modeled when I could get the work."

"You were the Lip Girl, weren't you?" Maynard shouted, and in the back Wallace thumped his head against the wall, his eyes closed.

"A child of the eighties, I take it," she said brightly, flirting slightly with the uncharmable journalist. To Harrison's surprise, the guy actually smiled. "I was the Lip Girl. And no, I won't do the slogan." A few of the journalists groaned. "And yes. I was seventeen."

Oh God, she wasn't supposed to say that. They had agreed not to bring up the Lip Girl thing. "I was at a Philadelphia Eagles game with my family, and a casting director saw me on the Jumbotron and offered me an audition. I grew up in North Philly and the opportunity to go to New York, to see some of the world, to make money—it was a thrilling experience for a girl like me."

"A girl like you?" one of the journalists asked. "What do you mean?"

"I'm a high school dropout."

All the journalists dropped their heads, scribbling away.

She glanced back at Harrison like this was a sore spot between them and he squeezed her hand, trying to convey to her how badly they needed her to get back on script. "I have my GED and I've taken a few college courses, but after the Lip Girl campaign I got married, too young as it happened, and when I got divorced I was too busy trying to make a living to go back to school. But I plan on changing that as soon as possible."

They had not discussed that in his loft, and he wondered if it was true or not.

"Why get married?" another journalist asked. "Why now?"

"Because we're not children," she said. "We're adults and we know what we want. I know our marriage is not what anyone would expect. We're vastly different. But . . ." She looked down at their hands, switching the grip so their fingers were intertwined, and the sensitive skin between his fingers grew hot. "I think that's what is so amazing about Harrison." She gave him a shy smile and then swerved back toward the script. "He doesn't see the differences between people. He sees what we share; he sees the things in all of us that make us human. That bind us together. That's what matters to him. Those are the things that I love about him. There are plenty of people out there who think he's far too good for me. And there might be a few people back in my neighborhood who think he doesn't deserve me. But that doesn't matter. Not to him. And not to me. I look forward to helping his work with the campaign. With VetAid, with school reform. I look forward to being his wife."

Oh God, it was such a speech. He glanced over at Wallace, who was staring, mouth open, eyes wide with delight. He might have written some of those words, but never had anyone dreamed she'd deliver them like that.

"Are you pregnant?" Maynard asked.

She looked at Harrison with such fondness, he couldn't help for one starstruck moment to believe her words.

"I sure hope so."

And then she leaned in and pressed her lips—dry and trembling—to his.

The room exploded in more flashbulbs and she broke away, smiling and blushing, and he put his arm around her shoulders, curling her into his chest.

"That's all the time we have," Harrison said. "We've got an appointment later today at the Carthright School to see how their charter program can be adopted state-wide and possibly nationwide. Thank you for your time."

There were more questions and more flashes fired off, but Harrison slowly led her through the door into his office, where they would stay until the journalists filed out.

The moment the door closed behind them, he grabbed her hands.

"You . . . you were amazing."

"I need to sit down."

"What?"

"Sit. I need to sit."

He realized she was shaking, her skin clammy and pale. "God. Okay." He helped her down on the couch and she immediately put her head between her knees.

Quickly, he grabbed the garbage can by his desk and brought it over to her. Unsure of what to do but feeling outrageously grateful and in awe, he sat beside her and slowly rubbed her back until she sat up again.

"You went off script," he said.

"I couldn't remember what we'd agreed on," she said. "My mind went blank."

Mine too, because you were holding my hand. Because you are so beautiful in that suit. Because no one—not ever—has stood by my side.

"So I just 8 Miled it."

"8 Miled?"

"That movie with Eminem? He's doing this rap battle and before anyone can use his past against him, he just admits to all of it."

"You got that from a movie?"

"You've never seen it?" She sat up, her color returned.

"You should—it's a good one. I'm guessing you don't see a lot of movies?"

"I saw *Lincoln*."

She laughed. "Of course you did."

How in the hell did they start talking about this?

"Whatever your inspiration was, you did an amazing job." He still stroked her back, because it felt good and she was letting him. But then suddenly, they both seemed to realize he was touching her. And there was no one in the room to witness it, to make it count toward anything.

Let me touch you, he thought, stunned by how badly he wanted to. *Let me just touch you.*

She smiled slightly and shrugged away. "It was good, wasn't it?"

"I'm not sure I have words to convey how great it was." He walked to his desk, searching for distance.

"Well, you were going down the tubes."

"I was."

"I thought you were supposed to be the pro."

"I am. I just . . . I've never had someone by my side before." As soon as the words came out they seemed too important. Too large a confession, as if he'd just shown her something he meant to keep secret. He checked his cell phone just to have something to do, to seem busy.

She was looking at him as if she could sense beneath his Montgomery persona that absolute ache of loneliness. The rot of distrust.

The door was flung open and Wallace came in, beaming and starry-eyed. "I'm going to kiss you," he said to Ryan. "I'm going to kiss you right on your smart mouth."

Her laughter was bright and perfect, and Harrison felt himself on edge at the sound of it. At the merry reality of their relationship.

He hated you, he wanted to say. *Just a few days ago.*

"Is that okay, Harrison?" Wallace asked, shutting the door behind him. "That won't be weird, will it?"

"Not any weirder than the rest of our lives," he said, pretending to still be absorbed with his messages, when in truth he wasn't really seeing any of it.

"Let's settle on a high-five." She lifted her hand for Wallace to smack.

"We can do better than that," Wallace said, and he pulled her from her seat and hugged her. "You were something else out there. I can practically hear our poll numbers skyrocketing."

Ryan relaxed into the hug with a laugh and a sigh, as if somehow Wallace had known just what she needed.

Shame pierced him and spread through his body, pumped right along with his blood. And with it came jealousy.

"Come on," he said, putting his phone away. "We need to get to the Carthright School. The show is not over."

Chapter 15

Stupid Ryan. Stupid, stupid Ryan.

She'd thought this would be so easy—to keep the private and public personas separate. Touch in public. Truth in private. Lie in public. Silence in private. One touch from him and she was a mess. One wholehearted smile in her direction and she felt giddy. She felt stupidly welcome.

That press conference had been more difficult than she'd imagined, owning up to those things in her past that brought her such embarrassment, that despite the years between now and then she couldn't quite shrug away and say, "Well, I was just a kid."

And then afterward, in his office.

I've never had anyone by my side before.

He'd said that and she knew it was the truth of him. But then he had to run away behind his wall of cold indifference.

They stopped in front of a small two-story building that was obviously old but had been refurbished lately. The front steps were painted white. The red brick had been blasted clean. The sign out front covered in bright-colored children's handprints said "The Carthright School."

"What are we doing here?" she asked. Beside her, Harrison was back to being cold. Indifferent. Glued to his phone.

"We're going to visit the kindergarten class. It's a new full-day program that the charter school is trying out,

and we're hoping it might be a viable program for public schools."

She nodded. "Will there be press?"

"A few." He really wasn't giving her anything to work
with.

"What should I do?" she asked, pointedly. Finally, he
looked up from his phone.

"I'm sorry," he said. "We'll see the classroom. I'll talk
to the principal and the teacher, and the kids will probably give us some kind of program."

"No remarks?"

"No remarks."

How hard could it be? she wondered. *Tour a school.
Watch some kids do . . . whatever kids did.*

"That should be easy."

The kindergarten room was chaos. Even worse than
happy hour that day when the Yankees won the Series
and the refrigeration unit went on the fritz.

Those CNN shots of Oklahoma after that tornado—
the kindergarten room kind of looked like that. Debris.
Lots of debris.

And it was loud. All the kids in the room were yelling
at the top of their voices. The kind of loud that pierced
her eardrums and pounded behind her brain.

One boy ran past in a dragon costume, another behind him with a fake wooden sword over his head like
he was going to bring it down and cleave the kid in half.

Mrs. Tellier, the principal, a small black woman with
thin braids and serious eyes who had been giving them
a tour and explaining the program of child-directed,
play-based learning, plucked the sword from the boy's
hand.

"As you can see, the kids go from station to station at
their own discretion."

Discretion, she thought, watching kids dumping water from a bucket into a table filled with sand, creating an ungodly mess. *What discretion?*

Mrs. Sawicki, her kindergarten teacher at All Saints Catholic School, who used to make her sit in the corner when she refused to color inside the lines, would have had someone's hide for that.

After the quiet of the hallways and the other classrooms, where kids were studiously bent over desks, raising their hands to ask questions, the bright, sunny kindergarten room seemed like total anarchy.

A tower of blocks collapsed to the floor with a loud rattle and bang.

"Oh my God," she breathed before she could stop herself. And that earned her a surprised look from Mrs. Tellier.

"Is it always like this?" Ryan asked, her nerves fraying.

"Some days more than others," Mrs. Tellier said with a nod and stepped farther into the room where a woman—the teacher, Ryan guessed, or perhaps warden? Or prisoner?—was sitting at a table with three children working on . . . Ryan couldn't even tell what they were working on. Writing their names? In Greek?

Beside her a boy dumped out a bin of Legos, the sound making her jump. There were now roughly seven thousand pieces of Lego on the floor.

Who is going to clean that up?

In the corner there were two girls standing next to a garbage can filled with shredded tissue paper. They were putting it on each other's head, handfuls of the stuff falling down on the floor.

A boy walked out of the bathroom, pulling up his pants. His hands dripping wet.

Please let that be water.

Was this the kind of stuff kids did? She realized she

actually didn't know any children. Not one. When Olivia was born she'd been too wrapped up in her own life to give a shit. Nora had been the babysitter. The one who cared.

"You all right?" Harrison asked.

"Fine," she lied. She thought she might pass out.

Mrs. Tellier caught the teacher's eye, and the young teacher managed to get all the kids over onto the carpet by singing a little song about putting their hands on top of their heads and being quiet.

Astonishing.

There was a reporter with them—Maynard, the guy from the *Journal-Constitution*—and a photographer who was on Harrison's payroll, who took pictures of Harrison and Mrs. Tellier, talking about how full-day kindergarten helped mothers get back into the work-force. Ryan crept closer to the carpet, fascinated by the scene as all the kids listened to Mrs. Knight telling a story.

How did she get all of them to listen? To sit still? It was like watching someone tame lions.

Half of them had their fingers in their noses, but at least they were quiet.

"Hello, Mrs. Montgomery," Mrs. Knight said when Ryan got close enough. Mrs. Knight had the whole teacher thing down pat. Kind-seeming and borderline frumpy, she wore sensible shoes and a cardigan sweater with lambs' heads as pockets. She was the sort of person Ryan imagined that kids liked. That they felt comfortable around. The kind of woman that kids threw their arms around because they could.

No kids had ever thrown their arms around Ryan.

In fact, every kid on that carpet was staring at Ryan like she was an alien right off the ship.

"Hi," Ryan said, giving the blinking, gaping children a sort of half-wave.

"Who are you?" one kid asked.

"I'm Ryan," she said.

"That's a boy's name."

"So I've been told."

"Is that your husband?" A girl pointed toward Harrison behind her.

"He is." She barely managed not to say, *Can you freaking believe it?*

The look on the little girl's face was far from impressed. In fact, she looked like Harrison gave off a stink.

"We're reading *The Kissing Hand*," Mrs. Knight said, "about a raccoon who is going to school for the first time and is a little scared and misses spending the day with his mom."

Looking into the crowd of kids, she could practically tell who the book was supposed to help. The girl with her thumb in her mouth, the boy with the red-rimmed eyes, and another boy sitting far away from the group in the corner pulling strings from the edge of the carpet.

"Would you like to read it?" Mrs. Knight asked. Her expression had grown more baffled than friendly, and Ryan realized she was just standing there, not saying anything.

Because she didn't know what to say. She didn't know how to do any of this. How to be a politician's wife on a tour of a school and more terrifyingly, how to be around kids.

And she was going to have one.

Soon.

Behind her, Harrison was still deep in conversation with Mrs. Tellier, and Ryan thought, *Why the hell not?*

"I'd love to," she said, and Mrs. Knight handed her the book, standing up from her seat so Ryan could sit down.

"I don't want her to read the story," a boy complained.

"Me neither," another kid agreed.

"Too bad," Ryan said on instinct, which made them open their eyes real wide, but they shut up.

Ryan tried to situate herself in the chair, which was too sloped, and her skirt was too short, and the whole thing was unbelievably awkward.

"I can see your underwear," a girl in front said, and Ryan snapped her legs closed and tried to tuck her knees sort of under her while sitting on the very front of the seat. "They're blue."

One little boy put his hand—sticky and hot, and she wondered where the hell he'd had it that it was so sticky and hot—on her leg. "I can't see the picture," he said.

"I haven't started yet," she said with a wide fake smile.

What a super idea, Ryan. Just super.

"*The Kissing Hand,*" she read, and opened the first page.

"You have to say who wrote it," a little girl took her thumb out of her mouth long enough to say.

"Why?"

"Because it's important," a little redheaded boy nearly yelled at her. "Mrs. Knight always reads who wrote it."

"Okay, okay," she breathed, and started again.

By page three most of the kids had crept closer, and the kids in the back had gotten up on their knees so they could see.

"I can't see," one kid whined.

"Everyone needs to sit on their butts."

As a unit they gasped. "You said 'butt,'" the peeping Tomette in the front row whispered, scandalized down to her Barbie shoes.

"I meant . . ." What was an acceptable butt substitute? "Tush."

She started reading again, but by page five she'd

lost them and she glanced up to see what they were looking at.

Harrison, standing at her shoulder, smiling.

Not real, she told herself, because she wanted so badly to bask in the false warmth of that smile. She wanted to smile back and maybe even reach up to touch his hand, lace their fingers together.

"Sorry to interrupt," he murmured.

"It's okay," she said.

"I saw her underwear!" shouted the girl in the front row.

The corners of Harrison's mouth flattened with suppressed laughter and she felt herself blushing.

"Keep reading," a chorus of kids chimed in.

"Jonah's touching me!" one kid shouted.

"Jonah," she said. "Stop touching people. Where I'm from you get arrested for that."

The little boy Jonah pulled his hand back into his lap.

"Go ahead," Harrison said. "I'll just listen."

And then, to her amazement and dismay, he sat down right next to the boy who was plucking at the corner of the carpet. Harrison stretched out his legs and leaned back against the wall, all of his attention on Ryan, but the boy next to him was staring at Harrison.

Ryan kept reading, but she was distracted by Harrison. Two kids fell away from the group to pick up other books from the shelf, but Mrs. Knight herded them back toward her.

One boy in back lay down and fell asleep.

I am going to be a great mother, she thought sarcastically.

In the back row, Harrison was leaning over so the boy could whisper in his ear. Whatever it was, it seemed serious, and Ryan put more effort into reading so no one else would look back there.

When she finally closed the book, Ryan was relieved.

She'd never expected reading to twenty kindergarten kids would be so stressful. She was sweating a little.

And how discouraging that she was so bad at it.

"Let's say thank you to Mrs. Montgomery," Mrs. Knight said, stepping in.

"Show us your underwear again!" one of the kids yelled, and Ryan gratefully jumped up from the wooden chair and gave Mrs. Knight her spot back. Ryan retreated to the back of the room to stand next to Mrs. Tellier.

Harrison put his hand on the little boy's head he'd been talking to and gave it a little shake. Which made the boy laugh. Beside her, Mrs. Tellier made a low noise of surprise.

"Michael has had a rough time of it lately," she whispered. "His father is still in Iraq, and home life has been difficult."

Harrison approached and Ryan forced herself not to take a step back, not to keep the distance between them that would give her the illusion of emotional safety. Instead she reached for his elbow, tucking her hand inside, smiling as he pulled her closer.

"Give this to Michael's mother, would you?" Harrison asked, giving Mrs. Tellier a business card. "VetAid helps the families of military personnel in these situations. I think we can help with the custody arrangement."

"I'm sure that would be a relief," she said. They left the classroom to a chorus of kids saying goodbye.

"I'll send you our enrollment numbers," Mrs. Tellier said. "And we can discuss the ramifications of a charter school in Fulton."

There were a few more pictures, and then Ryan and Harrison were back in the car.

As soon as they were pulling away from the curb,

Ryan undid the top few buttons of her suit and kicked off her shoes.

"Oh my God," she said. "That was so . . . loud."

"I didn't think it was that bad," Harrison said.

"Not that bad? It was like a war zone. Did you see that mess? That teacher is going to be there for hours trying to clean up that sand table. Who gives kids sand? And water! Indoors? That's nuts!"

"I'll drop you at home," Harrison said, chuckling, "and then head back to the office."

Exhausted, Ryan nodded and leaned her head back against the headrest.

"You did a great job," he said.

"I showed them my underwear."

"Well, they seemed to like it."

"They were just so . . . intense."

"I understand that's generally the way kids are."

She swung her head sideways to look at him. "Do you like kids?"

He shrugged, which was a terrible answer, and she knew it was a terrible answer because if asked three months ago if she liked kids, she would have done the same thing.

"We're going to have one," she whispered.

He arranged his tie and pulled his phone from his pocket. "Truthfully, I haven't given the child much thought."

"Because of the election?"

"Because you made it very clear that night in your apartment that the child was yours."

Right. So she had. But she doubted that had any bearing on what he thought about their child.

"That's a bullshit answer," she said. "You're telling yourself that to make it easier for you not to care. You should just say you don't care."

"It's not that I don't care . . . it's that I honestly haven't thought about the baby as anything besides a problem to solve."

A problem to solve? Who says that about a person?

"I don't want the baby to be born into a place so cold."

"Atlanta—"

"Your loft," she said. "Your family. This charade between us. I don't want the baby to feel that cold."

"I doubt an infant understands anything about his or her parents' relationship."

"When did you understand your parents?" she asked. He was still looking at his phone and she could hear the whooshing sound of emails being sent to the trash can. The silence went on so long that she didn't think he was going to answer her and she closed her eyes, letting the car rock her toward sleep.

"I was young," he finally said. "A kid, I guess, when I knew my family wasn't like other families. That my sister and I were props more than people."

"My child won't be treated that way," she told him, willing him to look at her. Willing him to understand how important this was to her. For two years or two minutes, her child would not know a second of what he'd known his whole life. "Harrison," she said when he wouldn't look at her.

"You are a Montgomery now," he said. "And considering how well you've done today, I don't know that you'll have a choice."

He went back to his phone and she went back to staring out the window, her hand over her belly as if she could already protect the baby from the chill of her husband.

Chapter 16

Yesterday had been an unparalleled success and somehow at the same time a crushing disaster. Harrison went over the complexities of it while making espresso the next morning.

Press conference: success.

School (outside of Ryan flashing her underwear to some kindergartners): success.

And the victories were because of her—she'd nailed it. Just nailed it.

Every single other moment between them: disaster.

That conversation about the baby on the way home from the school, those had been the last words she said to him all day. When he got home from work, armed with takeout, she'd been asleep, or at least very unwilling to talk to him when he lightly knocked on her door. He'd eaten chicken lo mein by himself, ears tuned to the slightest sound coming from her room.

At some point, watching the blinking lights of airplanes across the night sky, he'd realized he was going to be a father.

He'd nearly dropped his lo mein.

Of course, intellectually he *knew* that Ryan was pregnant. That was why they were married. Why they were perpetrating this grand lie. But it had never fully occurred to him that he would be a father. It didn't matter if the baby was his, or if they got a divorce in two years. That baby would be born into his home. His life.

I'm going to be a dad.

And honest to God, the thought had never occurred to him before.

And frankly, that thing she'd said in her apartment about the baby being hers—that had been fine with him. An easy excuse not to care.

And then she'd called him on it and he had the vague sense that he should do better.

Be better.

This morning he filled up Ryan's red teacup with water and set it down in front of the stool he now considered hers. Because she'd sat in it once. He set the prescription bottle with her morning sickness pills next to it.

She should be eating more, he thought. Considering he'd seen her eat half a donut in all the time they'd spent together, more shouldn't be too hard.

There was an apple in the fridge and he set it down next to the teacup. Stepped back. Shifted the teacup. Considered cutting the apple into slices.

From the hallway he heard the nearly silent sound of her door opening and the pad of her feet coming down the hardwood floor.

He found that he was bracing himself for the sight of her. Holding his breath, even. Not only for her beauty, fragile and bold at once, which seemed impossibly to knock him off stride every single time he saw her, but because he felt so damn bad about yesterday.

And he wanted, in some small way, to make everything that was wrong between them just a small bit better.

She came out of the shadows in glimpses—white thigh, chin, a swinging arm, and then she was there, in her shorts and tank top, her dark hair tucked behind her ears.

Her eyes diamond bright and hard.

Still angry.

"Good morning," he said.

Her eyes raked over him, leaving him cold in his thin tee shirt.

"I made you breakfast." He pointed needlessly at the water and apple.

The frozen tundra between them thawed for just a moment when she smiled. "My favorite."

"I haven't seen you eat much."

"The doctor tells me my appetite will return at some point."

"But shouldn't you be eating for the baby?"

"Let me worry about the baby."

Yeah, the shirt wasn't nearly enough. He needed a winter jacket just to be in the room with her.

"Look, about yesterday," he said. "I didn't mean to sound cold about the baby. I just haven't had much of a chance to get my head around it."

She sat down on the stool and took a pill, washing it down with the water. She picked up the apple and considered all sides of it before taking a careful bite.

"Ryan—"

"I think maybe the less we talk about the baby, the better off we will be," she said, staring at the apple and then taking another bite.

"I'm just telling you the truth," he said, spreading his arms out wide against the counter, feeling her slip farther and farther away until he would be stuck on his iceberg and she'd be stuck on hers. And that was a long, cold way to spend two years. "That's what you wanted. The truth between us, and the truth is, I haven't thought about the baby as something real. Not yet."

"Do you believe it's yours?" She seemed shocked to

have asked the question and she quickly shook her head. "No, don't answer that."

"I think I should answer. I think we should talk about this."

"Fine. Do you believe the baby is yours?"

"I believe you when you say it is," he said. Such a law school answer, such a political splitting of hairs. He was almost embarrassed to have said it, but it was the truth.

"What the fuck kind of answer is that?" she asked, slicing through his bullshit.

He shrugged. "It's the one I have."

"Well, it sucks. *You* suck." He blinked at her and she threw the apple at him. He ducked, and the apple hit a cupboard and fell to the hardwood floor with a thunk.

He stared at the apple and then at her and back to the apple again. She'd thrown that at him. An apple. At his head! "Are you insane?"

"No, Harrison. I'm a Kaminski. And you can try to change me, and you can give me all the fine suits and speeches written by someone else you want, but underneath it, I'm Ryan Kaminski, from Bridesburg, and this is how we argue."

"You can't—"

"Oh, I can, asshole—"

A pounding at the door stopped her from finishing that sentence, which was probably a good thing.

"I was trying to apologize," he said as he walked by her toward the door.

"Well, your apologies suck."

Yeah, you've made your thoughts pretty clear on that, he thought, and jerked open his front door.

Wallace came in with armfuls of newspapers and a genuinely jolly mood that was so large, it shoved all their animosity toward the far corners of the condo.

"Hello!" Wallace said. "I come bearing gifts! For the

woman of the house—" He set a to-go cup of coffee down on the counter in front of her.

"I'm not drinking—"

"It's decaf, honey," Wallace said and she slumped in her chair, her hair slipping over her face. As Harrison watched, her shoulders shook.

"Are you crying?" he asked, astonished. Was that what it took to win this woman over? Lukewarm decaf from the coffee shop down the street?

"No," she snapped, and then gave Wallace a warm smile. "Thank you."

"Most welcome." Wallace turned with a flourish. "And for you, Harrison, Golden Child, I bring good press." He plopped down the armful of newspapers, which Harrison immediately began to rifle through. They weren't on the cover of any paper, but the *Journal-Constitution, USA Today,* the *Wall Street Journal,* and the *New York Times* all had stories of them in inside sections. All accompanied by a picture, most commonly the one of her kissing him.

They look happy, he thought. *Whoever that couple is, it seems real.*

"We are incredible actors," she said, tapping the picture.

"You are," he said. "I just follow your lead."

"Well," Wallace said, "before you start thinking it's a clean sweep, Maynard from the *Journal-Constitution* isn't buying it." Wallace flipped the paper open to an op-ed piece and started to read. " 'The Montgomery Family has lied so often and with such flagrant disregard for voters' intelligence or morality that this new love match of Harrison's reeks of just more of the same.' "

"Ouch," Ryan said into the silence after Wallace threw the paper down.

"Maynard has never liked me," Harrison said.

"Well, he'll be out for blood in the next few weeks.

So, just be careful. But fear not," Wallace said. "I did some polling—"

"Wallace," Harrison cried. "We don't have the money for polls."

"We'll find it. In fact, I imagine we might find it easier than we think, because . . ." Wallace pulled a creased paper out from his back pocket. "We're doing great. Like . . . better than great. Like I haven't seen numbers like this. Ever."

Harrison's eyes scanned the numbers. They had sky-rocketed. He was blown sideways by something like joy. But not quite. Happiness, but not really.

Relief.

Harrison was relieved.

That was where his pendulum swung: between relief and stress, and no farther.

"It worked," he said, beaming up at her, and she blinked as if his face were the sun and it was too bright and then . . . she smiled. Right back at him.

Animosity. Apple-throwing. The icebergs. His family. It was all gone. And it was like the bar the night they met. Just two people and the chemistry of kindness.

And his pendulum strained toward happiness.

"I'm glad," she whispered.

"Good," Wallace said. "Because we have a little over two months. The fundraiser with your sister at the end of the week. And two more rallies after that, a debate, a thousand press events and community center speeches, and then, if we can keep this momentum . . . we should be in the clear."

Harrison nodded, not really listening to Wallace, and he reached over for her and before she could duck away, or stop him, he pulled her into a hard hug.

Her face against his chest, the weight of his arms around her shoulders, his hands wide against the smooth bare skin of her back revealed by her tank top.

To his surprise, his pleasure, she sighed into the sensation, caught unaware without her guards, and she sank right into that hug. His starved body soaked up the contact.

"Thank you," he breathed against her hair. "Thank you."

For a man who seemed to only ride around in the backseats of cars, sit behind a desk, and occasionally blow press conferences, he was fantastically well built. She knew this because she was currently face first against his chest.

He was lean but taut; not ripped, but hard-seeming. The muscles in his back and arms rippled as he stroked her hair.

The gesture sent a surprising hot wind through her that felt suspiciously like desire.

Weird. Because she'd thought sexual desire had been overrun by stress and nausea. A general dislike and confusion toward Harrison.

But the Internet had warned her that, too, would come back. For some women, with a vengeance.

Don't let me be some women, she thought. How much more tenuous would this situation be if she wanted Harrison? As in really wanted him.

"Well, you haven't won the election yet," she said, finally coming to her senses and pulling away. She stepped back and even that wasn't enough, so she went around the counter to pick up the apple she'd thrown, the chunks that had splintered off. Then she realized she had no idea where the garbage can was in this kitchen.

It was time she learned, if this was her home.

It was time to figure it all out if this was her home.

"I'm going to need to find a doctor," she said. "An ob/gyn."

"You can call my doctor," Harrison said. "He'll have someone he can recommend."

She wanted to resist that, wanted to make it harder somehow, but that would have been pointless. "Thank you," she said.

"I'll text you his number," he said, and then took a deep breath. "I have to go pick up my sister in Bishop, Arkansas, this week."

"Is that . . . do I need to go with?" Bishop, Arkansas, sounded terrible. And hot. And . . . terrible.

"Need? No. But if you'd like—"

"Actually," Wallace said, "we could use her at the League of Women Voters luncheon . . . with your mother."

"You're going to leave me with your mother?" she asked. "Without a chaperone?"

"I don't know how much trouble you can get into with the League of Women Voters."

She put the smashed apple on the counter and lifted an eyebrow. Shockingly, he laughed.

And her reaction at this point was so predictable it was ridiculous. Ten minutes ago she'd been throwing an apple at his head, and now he was laughing and it made her want to smile. It made her want to investigate that bare chest a little further.

"Well, before you worry about that," Wallace said, "you're heading to Sweet Bliss Bakery today to talk about small business in Decatur."

"Me too?" she asked.

"Yes, you too," Wallace laughed. "You and Harrison are attached at the hip until he leaves for Arkansas. Welcome to marriage and the campaign."

Wallace drove over to Sweet Bliss with them, briefing Harrison on the remarks he would make at the bakery.

She couldn't say she understood the finer points of tax breaks, incentives, and relief, but she figured it was part of her job to at least try and pay attention.

"Unemployment numbers came out yesterday," Wallace said.

"And?" Harrison asked, glancing up from his notes.

"It's bad."

Harrison sighed the kind of sigh she understood so well. Sometimes there was just so much wrong, it was hard to figure out what to try and change first.

The bakery was a funky storefront on a cool, leafy business street lined with cafés and park benches. Inside, it was crowded with people, a few reporters and the owner, Sandy, a smiling Mexican woman who jumped out from behind the counter to welcome them.

"There's Maynard," Wallace whispered, his eyes trained on a guy she recognized from the press conference on the far side of the bakery, and Harrison nodded to confirm he heard him, while continuing to shake hands with every person in the room.

Ryan stepped back, fading into the woodwork and the loaves of bread, trying to breathe through her mouth. Because the smell of baking bread and cookies didn't smell good now; it smelled sour.

Proof that God could be so mean.

The stop was a short one. Harrison had a coffee and a Danish, and sat at a table and answered questions about tax breaks for small business and incentives for entrepreneurs.

"I have a question," Maynard said when things were winding down. She saw Wallace, in the back of the room, glance up, his entire body taut at the sound of Maynard's voice.

"Shoot," Harrison said, and took his first sip of coffee, which now had to be cold.

"It's for your wife."

Every eye turned to her where she sat on a stool beside the counter, a cup of tea at her elbow.

Instinctively she wanted to flinch or narrow her eyes and demand to know what they thought they were looking at, but she smiled instead, hoping she looked delighted and surprised. Like she knew what the hell she was doing.

"All right," she said.

From the corner of her eye she caught Wallace and Harrison share a quick look of fear, which did nothing for her confidence.

"Unemployment numbers came out yesterday."

"Not good, are they?" she said.

Maynard blinked, and inside she did a victory dance. "No. They're not. Particularly for women. Women are the fastest-growing demographic in unemployment."

"What exactly is your question?"

"Do you have any insights into that?"

Wallace on the far side of the room stood up as if he were going to put a stop to the whole event, but she knew if they did that without her answering the question, all the good press from today would start to fade away and Maynard's voice would get louder.

She remembered her brother after finding out she was pregnant. *You're broke. Alone and about to have a baby.*

Had she stayed in New York, she would have applied for unemployment.

So yeah, asshole, she thought. *I have some insights.*

"I don't think we can talk about women and unemployment unless we talk about reliable and affordable day care, or health care, or safe neighborhood schools. Raising children falls more often than not on the mother's shoulders, and sometimes it's impossible to hold down a job and be pregnant. Or hold down a job and keep our kids safe and cared for."

"Amen!" Sandy, the owner of the bakery, shouted from her spot behind the counter. "I couldn't start this bakery until my kids were in school full time and able to get themselves home from where they were being bused."

"There you go," Ryan said, pointing at Sandy. "That's my insight."

A few other people started clapping, and while sweat trickled down her spine and her head went fuzzy, she caught Harrison's eye.

The summer before her mom died she was on a T-ball team, a Bridesburg neighborhood thing sponsored by the Gas 'N Go. But Ryan had taken that shit seriously. She'd stood at first base with her mitt up, her eye on the ball, waiting for her chance to make a play. Any play.

Dad had stood in the tall weeds past the first base line, smiling at her like she'd invented the game.

Proud.

That's how he'd looked at her.

That's how Harrison was looking at her now.

Like she'd invented the damn game.

Ryan smiled at Sandy, and then, because she was nearly light-headed from stress and relief and the sour smell of sourdough bread, she reached over and squeezed her hand.

Sandy hauled her into her arms and the way Ryan was sitting, her face went right into her boobs. Which made both of them laugh.

Flashbulbs went off.

Harrison stood up and came over to her, helping her off the stool, wrapping his arm over her shoulders. "Thanks, everyone!" he said, waving and saying good-bye, and within minutes they were settled in the back-seat of the town car again.

With Wallace, the grinning, bouncing maniac.

"You are a goddamned natural!" he cried, all but punching her in the shoulder.

"A natural bullshitter," she laughed.

"Maynard thought he had you," Harrison said. That smile flirted around his lips, his eyes were glittering, and she'd never seen him so . . . shiny. This was the Harrison on the video footage. Harrison Montgomery the candidate. And all that shine, all that glitter, it was falling down on her, too.

It was heady stuff.

"But he didn't!" Wallace cried, and he and Harrison went on to break down the event and her performance.

She felt herself blushing. And it was hard to breathe, actually.

Growing up, she'd thought she was a part of a clan. A team. The Kaminskis. Someone in that house always had her back, always made sure she was okay. She knew that if it was required, people would go to war for her. And she would do the same for her sisters and brother. Her dad.

They were never alone when they had each other.

But she'd been kicked off that team and she'd been alone. Really, really alone for a long time.

But not anymore.

In the strangest places she'd found herself another tribe. An unlikely team.

She turned her face toward the window so they wouldn't see her crying.

Chapter 17

The morning that Harrison was leaving for Bishop, Arkansas, it was raining. A dark day pressed against the floor-to-ceiling windows, and a fog obscured the view of the city and the trees she'd gotten used to in the last few days.

And oddly, it matched her mood.

It was weird that she would be alone here. In his house. Without him.

"Other than the Voters luncheon, you won't have anything on your schedule," Harrison said, putting his suitcase by the door. "Have you called the doctor?"

"I have an appointment tomorrow."

He nodded, as if that were all that needed to be said about that.

For all their team spirit, the baby was still a no-man's-land between them. Never discussed. Sometimes she got the sense that he wanted to change that, ask her about it, be involved, but perversely she wouldn't allow it.

She had to stop herself from getting sucked so totally into this huge life of his. He could use her for the campaign and she could like it, even love it. The meetings and the events. The glitter by association. The teamwork. It was exhausting, but she felt like she was a part of something.

And that was seductive.

But something had to remain hers; not everything could be used as fuel for his campaign. And the baby was what she was clinging to. The baby and her red teacup and being stubborn and perverse for the sake of being stubborn and perverse.

"What are you going to do?" he asked.

"Sleep, mostly. I have to call my landlord and end my lease."

"What about your stuff?"

"My brother is going to box it up for me."

"He can send it here?"

"He was going to deliver it personally and then stick around for a week," she said, straight-faced. "He can sleep on the couch, can't he?"

"Is that a joke? That's a joke."

"Is it?"

In the end she couldn't keep a straight face and they both smiled, cracking the strange tension of his leaving and the doctor's appointment.

From the back bedroom she'd been calling home, she heard the ringing of her cell phone.

"I need to go get that," she said, putting down her teacup and ducking out of the kitchen and away from Harrison.

The room was dark, the curtains still drawn. The bed she slept in was shoved in the corner, covered in amazing gazillion-thread-count sheets and blankets. In the corner was a treadmill, which might explain her husband's physique if it weren't covered top to bottom in boxes.

She sat down on the edge of the bed and grabbed her phone from the windowsill where it was charging.

The number had a Philly area code.

Nora. It was Nora. She must have gotten word from

the bank that the mortgage had been paid and maybe that a bank account had been set up in Olivia's name.

She suddenly had two hearts, one in her stomach the other in her throat.

For a moment she allowed herself to imagine the words coming out of Nora's mouth: *Come home. We miss you.*

"Hello?" she said, her eyes closed, daring to hope.

"What the hell have you done now, Ryan!" Nora snapped.

"What . . . what do you mean?"

"I got a call from the bank today. I have to go down there and sign papers because the mortgage has been paid off and an account has been set up in Olivia's name and I'm in charge of it?"

"Why are you making this seem like a bad thing?"

"How'd you get the money?"

Don't, she told herself. *Don't make it worse. Don't be awful just because she is.* But in the end, she'd bitten her tongue enough in the past few days and she couldn't anymore.

"Well, you'd never believe this, but I made enough sucking dick—"

"Ryan!" Nora exhaled, long and slow. "Can we talk seriously?"

"You're the one who called with accusations, Nora."

"Okay. How did you get this money?"

"I married Harrison Montgomery. It's all part of our prenup."

The shocked silence on the other end of the line should have been satisfying, but her world was too messed up. "You *married* him?"

"I did. If you ever read a newspaper, I imagine you'll see my picture." She almost told Nora about the baby, but the poor baby had been through enough the past few days.

"Are you . . . okay?"

Ryan closed her eyes against the sting of tears, but somehow that wasn't enough. She had to climb up onto the bed and lie there in a fetal position, her head buried in the mound of blankets on the unmade bed.

"I don't know," she answered truthfully, unsure of where that would get her with her angry sister.

"Are you in danger?"

My body, no. My heart, maybe?

"No. I'm . . . he's nice."

"And you're such a good judge of men?"

"I would have thought you'd be grateful!"

"Don't tell me you did this for us?"

"Who else would I do it for?"

"Yourself! Oh . . . God, Ryan. I don't . . . what the hell am I supposed to say to that?"

"I don't know," she whispered, beyond exhausted. Beyond defeated. "Can we start with thank you?"

"Fine. Thank you."

The connection buzzed with silence. "Dad . . . Dad misses you. Olivia's harassing me all the time to get you to come home . . ."

"What are you saying, Nora?"

"I'm saying come home."

She lifted the phone away from her face and covered her mouth with her hand so her sister wouldn't hear her sobbing.

"Ryan? You there?"

"Yeah," she said, her voice thick, and she knew Nora could tell she was crying. "Thank you, but I can't right now. In a—"

"What?" Nora's tone was sharp. Hurt.

"I can't come home right now. I'm in the middle of this campaign . . ."

"Six years you've been begging to come home and now you're too busy? Isn't that just fucking like you?"

"Nora, I can't just walk away."

"Do what you want, Ryan. You always do."

Nora hung up and Ryan did, too, and pushed the phone away, as far as she could.

"Ryan?" It was Harrison and she lay there, stretched out across the bed, watching him in the doorway. "Was that your sister?" He knew she'd been waiting for Nora to call.

Flush and wicked with some reckless wind, she did not sit up.

Fuck you, Nora. Fuck. You. I do what I want? Hardly!

But maybe it was time to start.

Harrison was nice.

And her sister made her feel like shit.

And in the end, really, wasn't this what she was good at?

"Yes," she answered. "It was Nora."

Harrison stepped into the room. She stretched out her leg, loving the way he could not stop his eyes from following the movement.

"I want to give you these," he said, lifting a set of keys and a scrap of paper. "The keys to the condo and the code for the garage. I'll have the car, to get Ashley. But in the future you can use it whenever you need it." She took the keys and the scrap of paper and set them down on the windowsill with her phone.

"Would you like to sit down?" she asked.

To her great surprise, his weight made the mattress dip and she scooted up to higher ground so she wouldn't roll into him.

"Are you okay?"

She pushed her face into the sheets for a second, wishing she could just melt into them.

"Not yet," she said, her voice muffled in the sheets. "But I will be."

"What did your sister want?"

She tilted her head to see him. "The bank called about the mortgage and the account set up for Olivia."

"She wasn't happy?"

"Nora might be physically incapable of happy."

"I'm sorry. I know you had hoped . . ."

"She told me I could go home."

"Really?" Oh, he sounded so happy for her. How novel to have someone happy on her behalf for once.

She waved her hand, as if dispersing that happiness like a swarm of little bugs. As if it didn't matter, as if it didn't sit on her heart hard enough to leave marks.

"What about you?" she asked. "Are you happy to go see your sister?"

He nodded, his face different . . . calm, relaxed. Sweet.

"Tell me about her."

His smile was fond and it made her chest squeeze with envy.

"Ashley's . . . better than the rest of us. She sees the best in people. Works hard on behalf of people who most of the world forgets. She can be brave and headstrong and trouble . . . lots of trouble."

"I think I would like her."

"You probably would. Are you missing yours?"

"Every—" Her voice cracked. "Every day."

Harrison shifted on the edge of the bed so he faced her more fully, and she wanted to touch him and be touched by him. She wanted to feel good and wanted. To make someone else feel that way.

She wanted what they'd had in the hotel room.

"Will you tell her about me?" she asked, wanting to matter. To someone. "Your sister?"

"I'm guessing she knows already. The news."

"Right," she said, embarrassed. "Of course."

For some reason, in this hushed room with both of

them wearing so little, she found it hard to hold on to her defenses. They rolled off her fingers like marbles. Hard and real, but irrelevant.

"That night," she whispered, "at the hotel, it wasn't a lie. Not for me. I didn't know who you were. I wanted . . . I wanted you for you."

"I know."

"Now you know? What's made you change your mind?"

"You." His hand was an inch from hers. Less than an inch. If she moved her finger she'd touch it, and what kind of domino effect would that have? If she touched his hand, would he touch hers? Would he touch her face, her neck, her breasts? The sudden ache between her legs? "You can put on a show, but I don't think you'd lie."

"Was it a lie for you?" she asked him.

He lifted his hand and it stalled halfway between them.

Do it, she thought, *please. Touch me.*

And then he did. With a tender hand he stroked back the hair on her forehead, tucking it behind her ear. She swallowed a gasp, like some still and silent thing just waiting in the deep for a spark to bring her back to life.

And his touch was that spark.

"No. It wasn't a lie. I wanted you and that night, I think I would have done anything to have you. But I'm not that man," he told her. "I'm not . . . Harry."

"Are you sure?"

His smile gave her that familiar gut punch of happy. "You've met my family."

"You're not your family." That came out a bit more fierce than she'd expected. She could blame Nora for that. And for this painful compulsion in her body, that in the dark landscape of the last few months was too bright.

"I'm not?" His thumb traced the side of her face, touched, just briefly, the corner of her lip. "I'm sure most of the time that is all I am."

Her breath shuddered in her lungs and she felt brave, of all things.

"Don't you wish—"

"I was someone else? No. Not really," he said, cutting her off. His blue eyes the color at the center of a flame.

She thought he might kiss her and she thought she might let him.

But then he stood. His touch gone. The moment over.

"But I was a different man that night, and it was nice," he said at the door, his hand against the door frame.

She knew better, she did, but somehow Ryan wasn't totally convinced.

Saturday, September 7

It seemed like her appetite returned just as a small silver bowl of peach cobbler was set down in front of her at the League of Women Voters Annual Community Luncheon. She'd picked her way through the crab cakes and a wedge salad, but not even sitting next to Patty could kill her sudden hunger for the cinnamon ice cream on top of peaches that literally melted in her mouth.

"Perhaps smaller bites?" Patty murmured out of the side of her mouth.

"You gonna eat yours?" she asked back, pointing at Patty's cobbler with her spoon.

The luncheon had been actually quite nice. It was held in a ballroom at the Hilton filled with pink and white lilies and chandeliers and more blond hair than could be naturally possible. Patty, in front of a room

full of other people, had been subdued. Chatty, even.
And as much as it pained Ryan to admit it, Patty in her
natural habitat (which seemed to be a ballroom filled
with rich women) was pretty impressive. She knew everyone and was gracious to everyone, particularly the
women who looked like they would have happily ignored her.

There was a steady stream of women waiting to talk
to her, ask her questions. Ask for help and advice. Noelle, beside her, took steady notes, and accepted business cards from women who wanted appointments.

Patty remembered everyone's name! It was miraculous.

Patty was kind of the Queen Bee.

And Ryan was a little in awe.

Ryan had her own lineup of women who wanted to
talk to her. Most of them just wanted to coo over her
ring and ask backhanded questions about Harrison and
how they met. She sensed a few astonished and sour
grapes and imagined that many of the beautiful and ac-
complished women in this room had believed themselves perfect for Harrison.

And they would be.

Too bad, ladies! she thought, entertained by the idea
that Ryan Kaminski from northeast Philly, with her
own potent mix of hot sympathy sex and a defective
condom, beat out all these rich women with their pedi-
grees and diplomas for the most eligible bachelor in Atlanta.

The ballroom was emptying out, and staff in white
shirts and black vests came out with the big trays to
take away the dishes left on the tables. Luckily, they
were starting on the other side of the room, leaving her
plenty of time alone with the desserts at the table.

"Can I sit down?"

It was Noelle behind her. Noelle with her terrifying efficiency and her blond hair pulled back in the tightest bun ever conceived outside of the Russian Ballet.

"Are you talking to me?" she asked through a mouthful of ice cream.

Noelle glanced around the mostly empty ballroom. "Yes, Ryan. To you. Can I sit down?"

"Sure," she said with a shrug. "Hand me that one, would you?" She pointed toward one of the uneaten cobblers on the other side of the table.

"Are you kidding? That's someone else's food."

"She didn't even look at it."

Noelle grabbed the silver dish and set it down in front of Ryan with a thump.

"You can have some if you want," Ryan said, hoping she wouldn't want any. "It's really good."

Noelle put down a stack of files and didn't so much sit as kind of collapse into her chair.

"Do you have a plan for when this is over?" Noelle asked.

"I'm going to take a cab back to the condo—"

"No, I mean, when this . . ." Noelle twirled her hand around the ballroom. "When this charade you're a part of is over."

"Why?" Noelle, surrounded by the wilting flower arrangements and empty tables, seemed like a sorority sister at the end of a bad night. Ryan put down the silver bowl. "You okay?"

"Like you care?"

She shook her head, marginally entertained at the sudden venom from the quiet girl. At least it was something she understood. All these backhanded women with their double-edged compliments left her off balance.

"Would it be easier for you if I didn't care?" she asked.

"Why in the world would you care about me?"

"Why wouldn't I? You haven't done anything to me."

"My boss wants to annihilate you."

"Well, I didn't say I cared about your boss. As far as I can tell, you are not the same person."

"Oh, God, there are days I'm not sure if we are." Noelle put her head in her hands as if her skull were just so damn heavy. "I started working for Patty ten years ago, right out of college, and I thought I was so lucky to get the job, to get the chance to work with the Montgomery family. I thought I would be *doing* something. Something real."

"You don't think you are?"

Noelle laughed. Like really laughed. It was very strange. "I'm helping a vindictive and paranoid woman strangle her family. And lie over and over again to the voters of this state."

"Noelle, maybe this isn't the best place for this conversation," she breathed, looking around to see if any of those backhanded women were lurking behind flower arrangements. Was this a mental breakdown? She'd witnessed more than her share of women losing it in public places, but never someone as locked down and together as Noelle. She was blinking a lot, but that could be the bun. Ryan patted Noelle's fist beside her files. But at first contact, Noelle jerked her hand away.

"No. Don't. Oh, God, the last thing I need is you pitying me. I've made my own decisions. But you need to have a plan."

"I'll be okay, Noelle, don't worry about me. But what are—"

"Patty has asked me to find your ex-husband."

The ice cream she'd eaten congealed in her throat and she choked. "Paul?"

"I can put her off, but she'll find him." Noelle took a

deep breath and picked up her stack of files. "You seem like a nice woman. I admire the way you're not backing down and frankly, I think the best thing for Harrison would be getting away from this family, but it won't happen. Get a plan. Get one now. And get out."

Chapter 18

It was late when Harrison got home from Arkansas three days after he'd left. It was late and he was a mess. He was a black hole; he was antimatter.

And so, when he got into the condo he went right to the liquor cabinet. Because what black holes needed was to get blind drunk.

"Harrison?"

He barely managed not to do a spit take.

"Ryan," he said, turning to find her on the couch, an unfamiliar red blanket over her legs. "I thought you'd be in bed."

"What time is it?" She sat up and he saw that she had her laptop wedged next to her body. She was sleepy and rumpled and . . . here. She was here in his lonely apartment. His lonely life. And for one acidic and strange moment he was so damn glad. Glad that he wasn't alone. And that it was her on that couch, rubbing her eyes, feisty and wrong in every obvious way, but somehow right in ways that he couldn't quite capture.

"Two . . . maybe three."

"In the morning?"

He smiled into his drink. "Yes."

"How was Arkansas?" she asked. Harrison finished off what was left in the glass before pouring himself some more. "Not good, I take it?"

"Fine," he said, before shooting that drink back, too. He said fine because that was what he was used to saying. Because that was the answer his mother told him to make when asked anything.

Fine. Everything is just fine.

And because he didn't know how to put into words all of the ways that things were exactly *not* fine. And because . . . he didn't know where he stood with Ryan. For a second the other day in her bedroom when he'd handed her the key, he'd nearly kissed her. And she would have let him; she all but spelled out her welcome in those languid lines of her body.

But he couldn't. And now he was glad he hadn't.

He'd realized the last few days in Bishop that the reason his night with Ryan had been so amazing was that they had come together as equals. On every level. And that happened only because he'd lied.

"What happened to no lies between us?" she whispered.

He poured himself one more drink and then went to sit on the opposite side of the couch. She set down the computer and curled her legs under her, making sure the red blanket covered her toes. Perversely he wanted to fling back that blanket, reveal her toes. Her long legs. Her beautiful self.

"My sister is in love."

"That's bad?"

"She's in love with a bodyguard, that man Brody who got her out of Somalia. But he has worked for some very bad people in the past. In particular, a dirty former senator who was selling arms to even dirtier people overseas."

"Oh my God," she breathed.

"Well, it gets worse. Because that senator was murdered in Cairo this morning, the security company Brody was working for is now under investigation. He will undoubtedly get subpoenaed, and in order to try to keep the blowback from hurting my sister, I made it clear that Brody wasn't good enough and he had to break it off with her."

Somehow the words did nothing to convey what happened in that back alley behind a bar in Bishop, Arkansas. The way he saw another man's heart break wide open and all his self-loathing and despair come pouring out.

Brody had been in ruins and Harrison made it worse—he used it to his own end. He took all that self-loathing and turned it into a tool to drive the man away from his sister.

He moaned, in his throat, staring blindly out the window at the night.

"What I did," he whispered, "was exactly what my mother would have done. Exactly. Protect the family, no matter who it hurts."

"Ouch."

"Yeah," he laughed humorlessly, remembering Brody's resigned, dead eyes. Ashley's livid, tear-filled ones. "Ouch. But he was already there; he knew they had to break up. If it was any other situation maybe it could have worked, but he was protecting really bad guys. He's on his way back to Washington, D.C., to face the whole shit storm."

"I meant ouch for you," she said.

Oh don't, he wanted to say. *You'll kill me with your sympathy and I don't deserve it.* "I doubt Ashley sees it that way. I'm pretty sure she hates me right now."

"Well, she's a grown woman. And her own person, so she can make her own decisions. It's not fun having your brother interfere in your love life." She ducked her head, catching his eye and smiling. "As I well know."

Right. Wes. He remembered with sudden clarity that night in New York, how her faith in Harrison's ability to save his sister stemmed from her faith in her own brother.

"What if . . . what if we brothers in our efforts to protect our sisters end up doing all the wrong things?"

Have we done the wrong thing? That was part of what he was asking. *Is our strange relationship proof that Wes fucked up your life in much the same way I am fucking up my sister's? Making sure that happiness is more elusive than it needs to be?*

She didn't answer the question, and the suspicion that he'd done the wrong thing with Brody and Ashley felt more and more confirmed. Nearly cemented, even.

Your brother didn't treat you like you were your own person and I've turned around and done the same.

If we were any other family, he thought but realized he was just giving himself and his behavior an excuse.

"Where is Ashley? Wasn't she supposed to come here with you?"

"She's still in Arkansas, waiting for Brody to come back to her."

"Is she coming to the fundraiser?"

"I have no idea."

He heard the rustle and shift of the blanket, felt the cushions dip as she moved. *She's leaving,* he thought, and he couldn't blame her. He felt sick himself. Sick about the way he'd had to talk to Brody, sick that Ashley had finally found happiness with the wrong man at the wrong time.

But she didn't leave. She sat right next to him, her knees still curled up so they pressed against his side, her kneecaps practically in his armpits. She touched him, briefly, softly brushing the hair over his ears.

His breath escaped his chest in a rush.

"That must have sucked," she said.

Words beyond him, he nodded.

"Do you think this is going to hurt your campaign?"

"Yes. But mostly I think it's going to hurt her. It's going to open her up to all kinds of pain."

"Well, that's unavoidable, isn't it? She's in love, and that's kind of what love does."

"My family doesn't do love, Ryan."

"Nonsense. You just said your sister loves this Brody guy. And you clearly love your sister."

He jerked away from her touch, frustrated and uncomfortable.

"How was the luncheon?" he asked, changing subjects. "Did they serve the peach cobbler?"

"How'd you know?" She laughed.

"They always serve it. It's famous."

"It was the most delicious thing I've ever had. I ate nearly every serving at the table."

"I'm glad you're eating. How . . . how was the doctor?"

He could not hide his interest and she sat back slightly, as if that interest were slightly repellant. Or perhaps just totally unexpected. *Oh, man,* that's where he was with her.

She was surprised that he would be interested in the results of her doctor's appointment.

And he was too much of a coward to try and change that impression, in fear that she didn't want him to be interested.

"He said now that my appetite is back, I need to concentrate on gaining the weight I lost."

"Did he say everything else was good?"

"I'm officially ten weeks, they count from my last period, not when we had sex and I heard the heartbeat."

"Really?"

She smiled at him because his voice had kind of cracked. "I go for an ultrasound in a few weeks."

Ask me, he thought. *Please ask me.*

"Would you like to come with me?"

"Yes. I would."

She smiled, and then he did, and it didn't feel awkward at all to touch her. He squeezed her hand, the smooth skin of her palm against his. She wore a loose shirt, the sleeve coming off her shoulder, and he imagined sliding his hand up her arm. To that velvet place at her elbow. Higher, to the curve of her shoulder; his fingers would find the edges and ridges of the muscles there. And then across her chest, the fluted collarbone under his fingers, the flat of his palm just touching that tender skin at the tops of her breasts.

Between his memory and his desire he could feel the pound of her heart under his hand, hear the hitch of her breath in his ear. He found himself bending, turning toward her, his arm reaching across the back of the couch as if he could just pull her against him. Into him.

It was what he wanted; at this moment he wanted it more than he wanted anything else.

But he was a Montgomery, doomed to live a rather incomplete life.

And he'd signed a contract promising he would not expect this of her. That sex would not enter into this arrangement.

And how could he deny his sister this and take it for himself?

"How did things go with Mother?" he asked, pulling his thoughts away from sex with the surest device at his disposal: a conversation involving his parents.

"Maybe you should have another drink," she said in a dry voice.

His head shot up. "How bad was it?"

"It's not selling-weapons-to-bad-guys bad, but it's not good, either."

"Just tell me."

"Your mother is looking for Paul."

"Your ex? Why?"

She shrugged. "Leverage against me? Who knows what she's thinking."

He groaned and leaned forward, resting his head in his hands. She touched his back, one long stroke along his spine, and then she stopped and he wanted to beg her to do it again. He wanted to pick her up and pull her into his lap, forget the alcohol, forget his family, forget the thousands of ways everything could fall apart tomorrow and just . . . breathe her in.

"Noelle told me. She said I should have a plan for when this is over."

"Didn't it just start? We've been married less than two weeks."

Her smile was sad. Grim, nearly.

It took a surprising amount of courage, it really did, for him to reach over and touch her hand. To gather her fingers in his. He expected with every breath for her to pull away. To sit back on the far side of the couch or to stand, leaving him alone in this dark room with his dark thoughts.

And he didn't want that.

If this was taking advantage, he wanted that. Whatever it took to try and feel better. That's how despicable he was. He didn't care.

"I think . . . I think I'm going to go back to school," she said to the blanket in her lap. "Take some college courses."

"Really?"

"I'd like . . . well, I don't know what I'd like. But I'm interested in psychology, and there are some night classes at Georgia Tech that I can take."

"I think that's a great idea. And you have most of the textbooks."

She laughed, and he was so stupidly pleased to have made her laugh. "I'll save so much money."

Money. He sobered, his stomach bottoming out for the hundredth time tonight. "I can't send you to school right now."

"I don't expect you to," she said. "I'll get financial aid—"

"You won't qualify. Not anymore. Not as my wife."

"Oh." She sank a little farther into the couch. "I didn't think about that."

He couldn't have predicted what came out of his mouth. For all his scrupulous plans for so many years, things had been going batshit wrong in his life lately, so it shouldn't have been all that surprising when he opened his mouth and just told her the absolute truth.

"I'm . . . I'm broke, Ryan. I mean, like . . . I've got nothing. Between the campaign, getting my sister out of Somalia, and the stuff we set up for your family—I have nothing left. I'm running on credit. And that is truly about to run out."

She turned wide eyes toward him. "Are you kidding?"

"It won't be like this forever; it's temporary. When the election's over and I'm back at work—"

"What about the private jet?"

"My parents'."

"Your car?"

"The contract was paid; when it runs out, it's over."

Her dark level eyes just stared at him and he didn't know what she was thinking. But he'd never been broke before and he was amazed at how guilty it made him feel. Like he'd done something wrong.

"I'm sorry—"

"Don't." She shook her head. "You're just never quite what you seem, are you? I have some money saved. I'll see where that gets me."

They sat there in heavy silence for a long time. "Tell me," he whispered. "Tell me what you're thinking."

"I think for a guy surrounded by so many people, you seem awfully alone a lot of the time."

He imagined climbing the stairs to his bedroom with

her. He imagined undressing in the half-dark and sliding under the sheets where he would find her, warm and
welcoming, and he would pull her close, close enough
that he could feel through their skin, their bones and
muscles, the beating of her heart.

Sex wasn't part of the fantasy; they were entirely too
estranged for that. And he couldn't shake this sense that
he was taking advantage of her. But he imagined comfort. A hand in the darkness. Warmth where he was
cold.

She stood, gathering her blanket and her laptop, and
he knew the reality would be him taking those stairs
alone. Climbing into his cold bed alone. Staring at the
ceiling alone and thinking of her.

He grabbed her hand, pressing it quickly to his lips
just to taste her, because though he could not imagine
how they would get to his bedroom, it didn't mean he
didn't long for it with every cell in his body.

"Stay with me," he whispered. To his utter astonishment, he begged. "For just a little while. Just a little
while longer."

He held his breath waiting for her to make up her
mind. Wondering why every quiet moment between
them felt so dangerous, as if they were alone in a vast
minefield.

He thought again of his sister and Brody, the way
they seemed to genuinely care for each other, find comfort in each other. The way Brody broke it off with Ashley despite the devastation it caused him, because he
knew it was the right thing for Ashley.

Harrison believed they were in love—his sister and
Brody. And he believed that their love was good and
selfless and in any other world, if Ashley were born in
any other family, that love should have a chance to
thrive.

But Ashley was a Montgomery, and that meant any

emotion that could not be spun into gold for them had to be crushed out of existence.

This thing between him and Ryan—it was selfish. An agreement to keep them all safe. That practically guaranteed they'd never care for each other.

That is who I am.

That is what I know of love.

"Never mind," he breathed.

Shit. Shit. Shit. Shit.

She'd gotten used to the political candidate. The man she'd signed the contract with, who saved all his smiles for voters, who projected warmth and compassion to everyone but her. This guy . . . on the couch, with the drink and the messy hair. All that confusion and grief in his eyes. This guy needed her—not to dress up and pretend to be someone else, but needed her warmth and her ear and her compassion—*damn it!* It was Harry, and she liked him.

Really liked him.

Which was why she should leave. Because they'd signed contracts that made liking each other nearly impossible and punishable. Because she would throw herself into his fire without thought, without care, until there was nothing left of her.

Because when she liked this guy—historically—it made her do reckless and foolish things. With a sudden spasm, like the shutter on a camera opening and shutting super fast, she remembered those foolish things. Her body remembered. Her skin, her breasts, between her legs—they twitched with memory.

"Never mind," he said, and coiled to stand.

"No," she said and sat down next to him, the blanket gathered in her lap. "I'll stay."

A plane flew across the night sky, red lights blinking in the distance. But he was silent, as if asking her to stay had exhausted what he had left of conversation.

"What was Arkansas like?"

"You've never been?"

"No," she said, unmistakably sarcastic. "I've never had that pleasure."

He turned to look at her, half-smiling. "Now who is the snob?"

Desire like speed entered her bloodstream and she felt every inch of her skin, so close to every inch of his.

"Point taken," she said after a while.

"It was nice. Really nice. She's met some good people, and Bishop is a nice community. She started this shuttle service for senior citizens."

"She's been there, like, less than a month!"

"I know," he smiled, "she's remarkably determined. And she doesn't see obstacles. This thing with Brody, she only sees that she loves him."

"She believes love conquers all?"

He lifted his nearly empty glass in a toast.

"Do we admire that?" she asked, trying to jolly him out of his bad mood the way she had that night at the bar. "Or make fun of it?"

"I don't know." Oh, he seemed so lost when he said that. Not at all the confident politician, the gleaming freshly minted Golden Boy of Georgia Politics.

He seemed like a man who hadn't been loved in a very long time. If ever.

And as shitty as her family life was now, it had been amazing at one time. She had been loved and loved well by all the people she needed.

Harrison never had.

"Oh goddamnit," she muttered before leaning forward, pitching forward, really, right into his chest. Her

arms slid around his neck, her belly pressed against part
of his shoulder.

His entire body jerked at the contact as if he'd been
startled awake from some dark sleep.

"What are you doing?" he asked. His hand without
the drink in it landed against her back, his touch sear-
ing through her shirt and the light sweater.

Oh God, the thoughts she had. The memories of that
night, the feel of him in her hands, her arms. The way
he tasted. Smelled. She wanted to add a second chapter,
a whole new set of memories.

"I'm hugging you. This is a hug."

"Oh."

He put down the glass and turned slightly in the
couch, embracing her fully, pulling her up against him.
Cheeks, chests, arms all touching. The blanket in her
lap kept her from crawling into his and she supposed
she should be grateful to that red blanket, but in actual-
ity she thought she might burn it tomorrow.

Her body's hunger, its desperation after weeks of being
numb, was shocking. It hurt almost like blood flow returning to a leg that had gone to sleep. She wanted him
more than she'd wanted anyone. Ever.

The Internet was right. And she was one of those
women for whom desire roared back, fueled by hormones and a certain lush new way of living in her body.
Her breasts felt weighted, her skin like velvet. Between
her legs, blood pounded like some kind of tribal drum.

Oh for fuck's sake, she thought. *Let's not go overboard.*

"What if . . . what if I needed to kiss you," he breathed.

Chapter 19

YES! Her body cheered. *We can do that! Kisses for everyone.*

"Harrison." There was a world of doubt in her breath that she couldn't hide. Confusion. Worry. A finely tuned sense of danger.

It wasn't just the contract they signed that made her worry. What would they do tomorrow? How would sleeping together change the very delicate balance they'd managed to create? How would she pay in days to come for taking what she wanted right now?

They both leaned back but didn't let go. She fisted her hands in his shirt, her nails biting into the skin of his shoulders. His heart was pounding so hard she felt it under her hands, could see it in his throat. She stared at that throbbing skin, wondering when the world was going to burst into flames.

And then he kissed her.

And the world wasn't engulfed in flame. It was she that was consumed.

She clutched at his shoulders and his hands swept around her hips to pull her into his lap, but they were stopped by the stupid soon-to-be-ash blanket, which she pulled and yanked out of the way until it was gone and she could find his body with hers.

There, she found his chest with her breasts. His arms with her hands. The hard erection in his pants with her belly.

Yes. Oh, God. Yes, finally, she thought, pushing herself against him because she'd been waiting for this. Even while pretending she didn't want it. Didn't need it.

She'd been wanting this.

Wanting him.

He ate at her mouth, using his thumbs against the hollows of her cheeks to open it wider so he could devour her. And that's what she craved; not just sex. Not just contact. She wanted to devour and be devoured.

"Ryan," he breathed, pulling the sweater up and over her head and then yanking down the thin straps of her camisole until her breasts were revealed. He bent her back over his arms and licked at her breasts, pulling her nipples into his mouth, sucking until she cried out. Until everything began to coil inside of her, burning hotter and tighter.

Fuck. She was going to come. She was going to come like this.

The pain of this pleasure was nearly too much and she had to share it, enlist his help in carrying this load, and so she sucked at his throat, so hard he lifted his hips, high and hard against her, his cock nudging into her.

She ran her fingers through his hair, using her nails against his scalp, and he hissed, his skin twitching. He reached both his hands around her hips, grabbing rough palmfuls of her ass, and she cried out, smacking her hands down on the back of the couch to hold herself up, to keep herself from slipping into a pile of messy woman on a man's lap.

He pulled her and pushed her against him. Rough and hard and fast and urgent. Like he couldn't get close enough.

"Are you . . . ?" he panted, licking her throat, sucking her earlobe into his mouth, all while his wicked hands held her against him. The perfect grip. A dreamy jail. "Is this hurting—" His voice cut off on a loud groan.

"Good. So good. Keep—" No. She didn't want to keep going like this. She needed more. She needed him inside of her.

Just the thought of it—that slow penetration, the way her body would yield, but it would still sting a little, how heavy and thick he would feel, how right and foreign at the same time—brought her panting toward orgasm. Quickly she reached between them and unbuckled his belt. He caught on and reached under her skirt for the edge of her panties. She shifted to help him pull them off, but he grabbed the thin silk at her hip and twisted it around his hand, the elastic and silk burning into her skin until the fabric ripped and fell away.

He tossed her torn underwear on the floor and she pulled down the zipper of his pants and pushed aside the cotton of his boxers until he was a reality in her hand, hot and damp just there at the tip. Her mind was blown blank by lust, her body pained by want. By need. By a desire so sudden and so hungry she was almost scared the feeling wouldn't go away. They could fuck each other until they couldn't move, but this fire in her blood would not be extinguished.

On her knees over him, holding him still, she slowly lowered herself down, felt the push of the broad head, right there, right where her body wept for him.

She hung her head, shaking.

Oh. God.

"Ryan," he panted, as if he were running right alongside her in a marathon. His hands slid over her ass, up her back and back down, unable to make up their mind where to stay. "Condom."

"I'm already pregnant," she breathed, her forehead against his collarbone, his cock easing slowly, slowly inside of her. "And there hasn't been anyone but you for four years."

"What?"

"Four years. I'm clean. You?"

"Ryan?" She felt him jerk as if to see her better, but they could save all their confessions and secrets for later. Now. Now they were busy with this.

"Tell me," she demanded.

"I'm . . . I'm clean." Of course he was; he was Harrison Montgomery.

She took him all the way. Her body split, her legs shaking.

His skin twitched under her hands. Against her. Inside of her.

She felt the breathless want turn into something real; it grew weight and heft and she lifted her hips, circled them, fell back against him, again and again, lifting the cumbersome weight of her desire up and off the ground until it had a life of its own and she could not move fast enough, hard enough. His hands on her hips did not hold her close enough and she closed her eyes and bit her lip and reached and reached and reached.

Harrison groaned and swore, sweat running down his neck, the hair at her temple, wet from his sweat or hers she didn't know or care. All she cared about was the orgasm, just out of reach. Suddenly he lifted her and turned, laying her down on the coach, and he followed, covering her head to foot. His pants falling down to his knees. He gripped the armrest of his couch, spread her legs with his, braced himself against the floor, and pounded into her. Loud and sweaty and raw and real.

So real. So authentic.

It was them. Just them. No act. No charade. No pretense.

Finally, she thought, *here we are.*

She reached between them, placed her finger against the hard, buzzing edge of her clit, and in one wild and ecstatic burst of light and sound and pleasure she screamed, her body blown to bits.

As if from a long ways away she heard his answering shout, felt him shaking against her, and she stroked his back, hugged him hard to her.

And waited for the regrets to show up, one by one, like moths finding the only porch light for miles.

What have we done? she wondered, combing her hands through his hair.

She didn't know what the next moment looked like, much less tomorrow. Or the next week.

How did this change everything?

The aftermath of all that lust was fear. Fear that she'd messed it all up again. She'd gotten to someplace good. Really good. She had friends. Work she was proud of. A team that counted on her.

A baby for whom she had to build a future. A safe, loving, caring future.

And this sex could really mess it up.

"Are you okay?" he asked, bracing his hands against the cushions by her rib cage.

She nodded, attempting a smile, though her body wasn't totally back online. There were still parts of her she couldn't feel. Her legs, for one. Her left arm.

When she shifted away from him he slipped out, and she felt the messy wetness of them between her legs.

"I'm . . . uh . . ." he said, sitting down hard on the other side of the couch, his damp pink penis slouched resting against his leg. "Wow."

She forced herself to move, to sit up, and then stand on wobbly legs.

He lifted a hand to catch her if she fell.

"I need to go to the bathroom," she said, and then walked across the room to the hallway toward her room. In the hall, out of his sight, she put one hand on the wall to prevent collapse. With every step, instead of stronger, she felt weaker.

Mistake. Mistake. Mistake.

In the dark bathroom she closed the door and crumpled down on the toilet.

She had half a mind to hide here until he got tired of waiting and she heard the creak of the stairs as he went to his room.

A minute passed. Another.

And there was only silence from the other room. He was more stubborn than she was.

She considered just slipping into her bedroom from here. They could simply not address that desperate, hungry sex at all and then tomorrow, they could just pretend nothing had happened and keep plugging away in this strange, estranged pretend relationship they were in.

But when she stood and caught sight of herself in the mirror over the sink, she knew she couldn't hide.

You are a grown-ass woman. And grown-ass women don't act like teenagers terrified of how a man makes them feel.

She cleaned herself up, brushed her hair. Her teeth. She felt, more than that first night or even that awful ceremony at the Governor's Mansion, like something had changed. That sex, hell, that *hug,* had shoved things aside, revealing what she'd rather keep hidden.

She wanted Harrison.

She liked him.

Staring at her reflection in the mirror, the lips swollen from kisses, the beard burn on her cheeks, the wild hair and wilder eyes, there was no pretending.

I had sex with my husband.

She put her hair back in a ponytail, went into her

bedroom for clean underwear and a new tank top, and then headed back out to the kitchen to face the music.

The music, in this case, being a devastatingly handsome man, standing at the kitchen island, his arms braced wide against the counter. His head bowed.

My husband.

And his own regrets were so obvious they were written on his body, in the way he stood. The lines around his mouth and between his eyes when he looked up at her. He didn't know what to do any better than she did.

And she was wholly comforted by that.

"I think we're in breach of contract," she said, attempting a joke.

He smiled, a brief flash, gone before it really had a chance to settle in. "I won't tell if you won't."

"Then we're in the clear."

"Ryan," he sighed.

She lifted her hand, her stomach, her heart, her lungs shrinking. "Please don't say you're sorry," she whispered.

"I'm not sorry. I'm not. But . . ." He blew out a long breath and ran his hands through his hair. "I feel like I've taken advantage of you."

Something inside of her cringed. Her pride? "Taken advantage of her" alluded that their power dynamic was so skewed in his favor that she didn't have a choice. Or that he didn't think she was capable of choice.

"No. That was me taking advantage of you." That hunger she'd had for him was embarrassing now. Hormones—she'd blame the hormones.

He watched her for a long while and she crossed her arms over her chest, feeling slightly too naked in her shirt. Too naked under his gaze.

"Nothing has to be different," she said.

"It feels like everything is," he said. "We had . . . Christ, Ryan, that sex . . . are we supposed to pretend like that didn't happen? Because I don't know if I can do that!" He walked around the island toward her and she took a quick step back. Which of course stopped him in his tracks.

What would happen, she wondered if she said, *I kind of fell in love with you that night in the hotel. I know that sounds ridiculous, but I'm kind of wired like that. And now . . . now it's that night in the hotel and this night on your couch and I can see love again on the horizon and that's not what I need right now. You look at me like something you've taken advantage of, and I'm trying to build a new life for this child. A life with love and acceptance. Full-throttle warmth.*

And I don't think that's anything you know how to give.

"It was an emotional night," she said. "And I think maybe . . . we both just needed some comfort."

"Are you honestly telling me that's all that was?"

Part of her wanted to ask him what he thought it was, demand answers from him, but those answers might be worse than not knowing.

She had a path; for the first time in her life, she was working toward something, and she couldn't let that be derailed. Not for sex. Not for more of this man's honest smiles. Not for the scraps of attention and affection he offered when he was circling his own personal rock bottom.

He'd offered her a way into a better life and she, while he'd been gone, had created her own exit strategy. She couldn't sacrifice that now. She was going to be a mother. Her baby didn't deserve a compromise.

"Comfort and hormones," she said with a shaky laugh, as if inside she weren't in shambles.

He looked like he was trying to figure out if he was offended.

"I'm glad it happened," she said in a rush, throwing

220 Molly O'Keefe

the words into his increasingly cold silence. "I'm glad I was here. Tonight. You needed a friend."

"Right." He did nothing to hide his bitterness. His recriminations were not pointed at her, but rather himself. The weakness he'd shown her, the vulnerability, it didn't sit easily with him.

Her favorite thing about him, and he would eradicate it if he could.

"Don't. Don't do that."

"I don't have friends, Ryan."

I know. I know you don't and that's why I have to be careful.

"You do now." She took a stab at bright and cheerful, but it fell closer to solemn vow.

His laughter was dark, tinged with disbelief, but his manners, his well-established sense of self-preservation, that shield he'd created between who he was and what he was, kicked in and he graciously ducked his head. A strange bow that broke her heart. "Thank you, then. For being here. I'm . . . I'm glad you were too."

Dad used to love nature shows and she remembered being sick once, a real bad stomach flu that required the couch so she wouldn't wake up her sister and the big yellow Tupperware bowl by her side, endless glass bottles of 7UP and Dad keeping watch in his easy chair.

In the middle of the night the fever broke and she woke up to a dark room with the television muted.

On the screen were mountains rising up out of the sea. Green, forested cliffs and endless blue water dotted with ice.

"They're called fjords," Dad whispered from his spot in the easy chair. "Glaciers made them."

Glaciers made her and Harrison. They were gone now, but the deep and far and wide distances had been scraped away and sex wasn't going to bring them any closer.

It is better this way, she thought, stepping backward into the shadows of the hallway.

Tuesday, September 10

Harrison heard what she said. He did. They were supposed to pretend that nothing had changed. That the sex, and the comfort and care she'd shown him, had not happened. He understood that was what she wanted.

And he even understood why she would think that was for the best. She had a future she needed to protect, a home with warmth and love, and he was the guy who'd destroyed his sister's chance at happiness.

So he got her reluctance.

But he could not seem to get on board with it.

The morning of the fundraiser he set a plate with a scrambled egg on it next to her teacup and the prescription bottle. It was a peace offering, kind of.

And a statement that he could not totally pretend everything was the same as it had been yesterday.

He didn't know what he wanted from her, but he did know that this weird half-in/half-out relationship was not it.

But she came out of her room, grabbed the teacup and the bottle, shot him a wan, close-mouthed smile, and then disappeared back into her room, ignoring all of his symbolic scrambled-egg messages.

Right, he thought. *That was lame.* He got that. If he was going to entice her friendship and trust out of hiding, he needed better bait.

She avoided him the rest of the day, coming out in time to leave for the fundraiser in a strapless black dress that ran over her body like ink.

"You look beautiful," he said, wishing he had more words to tell her how he felt. How she moved him.

She smiled, but didn't look him in the eye.

"You clean up nice yourself." She reached over and adjusted his tie. It was one of those sweet moments between wives and husbands, even fake ones, that he'd somehow gotten used to. That he found himself longing for.

He reached for her hand but she was moving out of reach. Looking more nervous than usual.

At the hotel, Wallace called him aside.

"We've got a problem," he said.

"What kind?"

"Brody is here. He'd like to see your sister."

"Have you told her?"

Wallace laughed and held up his hands. "That's your job, man."

In a moment of clarity, he realized he couldn't let his mother's behavior be his default position anymore. Protecting the family name at the cost of the family was ridiculous. And if Brody was back here for a second chance, could it be a second chance for him, too.

Harrison walked down to the loading docks near the kitchen. He pushed open the door, letting in an eddy of hot air and stink from the dumpsters. At the sound of the door opening Brody spun to face him, his face alight with hope that crashed and burned at the sight of him.

"Not who you were expecting?" Harrison asked.

"I'm here to see Ashley." His words were like a planted flag. And the way he stood, arms over his wide chest, legs braced for whatever might come his way, it was obvious he wasn't going anywhere until he saw her.

"I gathered." Brody looked like he hadn't slept in days. Or perhaps been near a mirror.

"Look, man," Brody said. "Nothing is different. I could still get pulled in on this weapons thing. I'm still me, and she's still her, but . . . I love her."

Harrison nodded, leaning against the cement door frame.

The truth was he wasn't so far ahead in the polls that this wouldn't matter. It would. Glendale would use this and there would be another series of smear ads on television, with plenty of attention paid to the fact that Brody had dark skin, something that still mattered in some parts of the country.

But his sister's happiness felt bigger than his election. Than appeasing people he didn't know.

"What makes you think she feels the same?" he asked. "She waited for you, Brody. Showed up here wrecked because she didn't seem to mean much to you."

He'd used Ashley to protect himself before and that mistake was hard to live with. He wouldn't make it twice. He was here to serve Ashley. To see her happy, and if that meant Brody, then he'd deliver Brody.

"She means everything to me," Brody said, his voice low and rough, conveying enough emotion that it made Harrison uncomfortable. Brody wasn't a man who lied. Or exaggerated his feelings. The ache rolling off of him was real.

"And I'd like to prove that to her if I could just . . ." He pointed at the kitchen over Harrison's shoulder. "Get inside."

"I can't guarantee she'll agree," he said. "But I'll see what I can do. Wait here. I'll send someone with her answer."

So after he made sure his sister wanted Brody there, he surprised everyone at the fundraising dinner and let him back in. Like a Trojan horse of potentially bad press, he let Brody in to the event to see Ashley. To give Brody a shot to make it right.

A shot for both of them to make something right.

"You sure that's a good idea?" Ryan asked him when they were backstage watching Ashley, his bright, wide-eyed, optimistic sister, make her way through the crowd with Brody, her dark and dangerous foil, at her elbow.

"Does it matter?" he asked. "Look at her—she's happier than I've ever seen her."

He turned to find Ryan watching him. There were times when she dropped that wall she had erected, when she was so utterly and totally revealed to him that he couldn't believe there was any point to pretending they didn't want each other. Didn't like each other.

"I'm really proud of you," she said. Previous to this moment he'd never thought that was something he needed—to make her proud. He'd never really thought of making anyone proud, and the second she said those words, he realized he never thought of it because he'd never had it in his life.

It was like a unicorn.

And God . . . he'd had no idea what he was missing.

"Ryan," he breathed, curling his fingers through hers until their palms touched.

At his touch, while he was feeling so exposed, she just locked herself down. Closed up. Vanished behind a fake smile, taking with her the pride and all that connection, leaving him on the outside.

They both waved and smiled under hot lights that suddenly felt ice cold.

Chapter 20

After the fundraiser was over, the lights turned off, the stage partially dismantled, Ryan all but ran from Harrison. From that arm around her waist, the heat of his body at her side, the way he sometimes watched her as if she were a riddle he was trying to figure out. Which was hilarious. She wasn't the one with different personas.

She was just Ryan Kaminski trying to make this shit work.

Her purse and comfortable shoes were in the suite they'd been using as a staging area and she headed up there, her feet and head aching. All she wanted was to go home, pull the covers over her head, and sleep for a week.

That wasn't entirely true; she wanted to go home, pull the covers over her head, and talk to her sister. The Nora from years ago, who had good advice and loved her.

I miss my sister.

She stopped for a second, her hand braced on the burgundy wallpaper in the hallway. There was a raised pattern on it, interlocking squares, and she traced it with her fingers until she could move again. Until she could breathe past the rock on her chest.

Nora, she thought, *I wish . . .*

She forced herself to keep moving forward, her heart a shriveled raisin in her chest, ruined by wishes.

She walked in just as Ashley and Brody were walking

out, and everyone stopped on either side of the thresh-
old.

Brody, even more handsome, more austere up close,
slipped his arm around Ashley's waist, a silent show of
support. Ashley leaned back just slightly against him
and the two of them wore their happiness, their affection for each other, like his-and-hers matching sweaters.

It would be nauseating if she weren't so damn jealous.

"Hi," Ryan said, holding out her hand to shake Ashley's, like a job applicant. Part of her yearned for the
job, of sister or friend, or something to this woman that
Harrison so clearly loved. And the other part was exhausted by all the yearning. Furious over its sudden appearance.

Stop wanting shit, Ryan.

"I'm—"

"The wife no one told me about." Ashley slung her
purse over her head so it hung across her chest and then
pulled her long brown curly hair out from under the
strap. Brody smoothed it down her back.

"I . . . no one told you? Harrison . . ."

"They don't tell me anything." Ashley shook Ryan's
hand, giving her a long, appraising up-and-down. "This
is Brody. My . . ." She glanced at him. "What do I call
you?"

"Let's stick with Brody," he said with a twinkle in his
dark eyes.

"So, not lover?" Ashley teased. Ryan glanced down at
her feet, aching inside of her shoes.

"So what's the story with you and Harrison?" Ashley
asked. "Mom told me about the contract."

"That would be the gist of the story."

"Do you love him?"

She gaped, no answer available.

"Do you like him at least?" Ashley amended.

She understood what Ashley was doing and why she

was doing it. It was the exact same thing she would have done for Nora, or Wes back in the day.

Ashley had her brother's back. And as awkward and strained as it was between them, she was glad someone was looking out for Harrison.

"I like him. Admire him. But it's complicated."

"I understand complicated," Ashley laughed. "And I gotta say, you two put on a good show up there. I believed it."

"That's my job." To her horror, her voice cracked.

"Are you okay?" Ashley stepped forward and put a hand on Ryan's arm, and she found herself wanting to grab that hand and spill the whole story. So at ends, so lost in this thing between her and Harrison and so lonely at the same time, she was unsure of what she would say if she did open her mouth.

So she smiled instead, something she'd gotten very good at.

"Don't you two have somewhere else you need to be?" she asked.

Brody and Ashley shared a quick glance full of silent conversation.

"Go. Please," Ryan said before one of them lied and said it was all right. "My problems are hardly worth anyone changing their plans for."

"You sure?"

"Absolutely."

Ashley dug into her bag for a second. "Crap, I was going to get your cell phone number, but I must have left my phone in the bathroom. I'll be right back."

She took off, leaving Ryan standing there with Brody, whose silence was so pronounced it was a physical thing. She shot him a wan smile.

"You ready for this?" he asked.

"For what?"

"The Montgomery circus."

"I'm one of the stars, I think," she said. "The bearded lady or something."

"It's different on the inside," he said. "When they love you—"

"Harrison's not like Ashley," she said quickly before he could say another word.

"No one is like Ashley. But Harrison isn't as cold as he seems to be."

I know, she thought. *I know, and it would just be so much easier if he were.*

"And maybe you're not as hard?" He cocked his head, watching her.

She laughed. "We don't . . . It's not . . ." *It's not what you guys have,* that's what she'd been about to say but that sounded ridiculous, so she just shook her head. "I'll be fine."

"I was telling myself that, too," Brody said with a half-smile that was devastating. Good God, the man was handsome. "And you know, fine is plenty until you get a taste of happy. Once you're happy, it's all over for you."

"Okay, okay, I found it." Ashley came back into the room with her phone. "Give me your number before I run out of battery."

They exchanged numbers and then Ashley pulled Ryan into a hard, fierce hug and Ryan stood there, wrapped in a sister's arms again, not her own, but that didn't seem to matter. It felt good.

And she crept dangerously closer toward happy.

Ryan woke up Thursday night, something she'd been doing more and more of. Heartburn, having to pee, a sudden desperate craving for Oreos dipped in peanut butter—all those things were ruining her sleep on any given night.

She shuffled from her bedroom down the dark hall to the living room, where the television was still on, the volume very low.

He sat in a corner of the couch, his tie pulled loose, the buttons of his shirt open. His eyes riveted to the screen. The light from the television and the latest of Glendale's last series of smear ads were flickering over Harrison's face.

The campaign had hit a rough patch. Maynard was not letting up. The op-ed pieces were getting more pointed. He'd been all over talk radio talking about how the Montgomery family had failed the people of Georgia, and that Harrison was no different than his father, and he wanted to see the reign of Montgomerys in Georgia politics stopped.

And Glendale was coming after him with everything they had. Radio ads, billboards along I-75; you couldn't watch the local news or listen to the radio without three or four ads for Glendale, and at least half of them smeared Harrison.

They did more press. And still more. But the scales were tipping out of their favor.

"Turn it off, Harrison," she said softly and he jumped, startled. The stony lines of his face curved into a weary smile.

"Did I wake you up?" he hit a remote with his thumb, and the screen went black, the condo plunged into thick darkness.

"No," she said, turning on the lamp as she walked past it to the kitchen. "I'm just hungry."

"I had Dave pick up some more graham crackers."

Oh, she didn't know what to do with those little things he noticed. Those small domestic kindnesses. "Thank you," she said, and grabbed the box from the cupboard and poured herself some milk.

Going back to her room had been her plan, but she couldn't leave Harrison out here, torturing himself with his opponent's smear ads.

"Why are you watching that garbage?" she asked, dunking her graham cracker in milk.

He shrugged and rubbed a hand over his face. "I don't have an answer that sounds sane."

"Isn't the debate tomorrow?"

"Yep."

"You're neck-and-neck in the polls, Harrison. And without that guy's budget, you just have to trust that the message and the work that everyone's doing will get to the right audience."

"Is that what I have to do?" he asked, shooting a weary smile over his shoulder.

She handed him a graham cracker, which he took. And then she held out her mug of milk for him to dip the cracker into.

"Is this a pregnant thing?" he looked dubiously at the milk.

"It's a childhood thing. Try it."

He did, and then lifted the dripping graham cracker to his mouth.

"Not bad," he said after he ate it, and she handed him another.

"Can I ask you something?"

"Shoot."

"Why are you doing this? Running for office? Why now? I mean . . . is it all about trying to fix what your dad broke?"

"Is that such a bad reason?"

"Well, it's kind of overkill, isn't it? Dedicating your life to sweeping up after your dad?"

Harrison broke the graham cracker in his hands into smaller squares and then smaller ones. "I knew I would be going into politics. I wanted to go into politics, but I knew everything I did would be measured or colored by what my dad had done. And so from the very beginning I was thinking about that. About who I was in comparison to my dad."

"Who are you when you're on your own?" She swirled her cracker through the milk in a slow figure-eight pattern.

In the long years of exile from her family she'd figured out who she was outside of the confines of that neighborhood. Outside of that last name. And they had been hard years, but she realized, suddenly, that they'd been good years, too. She'd figured a lot of shit out.

He was silent for a long time and that wasn't a good sign; he was quiet only when he was thinking.

Maybe the guy needed a little more exile to answer that question.

"I want to serve the public," he said. "I want to help people who need it. I want to make people's lives easier in fundamental ways. And I think government, in its purest form, can do that. I can do that."

His earnestness, his absolute conviction in his ideals, made her chest tight, as if her heart were suddenly too big for her ribs.

"Your mom told me the first time we met that you cared." She watched cracker crumbs bob and drown in her milk because she couldn't quite look him in the eye. "That you cared more than anyone else in the family."

"Ashley—"

"Ashley's not even on the same curve," Ryan said. "But all these smear ads, all these Maynard op-ed pieces, you can't change them. Those things they say about your dad, they're true, and trying to keep them covered up or ignore them, it only feeds that fire."

"You saying I should 8-Mile it?" She glanced up in time to see a dimple, and then it was gone.

"I'm saying you need to get a little more Zen about it."

"Zen?" He scoffed. "I don't think that's something I can do."

"You should try," she said, and handed him her last graham cracker before heading back to her bedroom.

"Ryan?"

Don't turn. Just keep walking. Pretend you didn't hear him.

But that would be ridiculous and cowardly, so she turned.

He was going to ask her to stay. She knew it. It was written on his face, in that lonely slump to his shoulders. He was going to ask her and she wanted to. So badly she wanted to sit down next to him on that couch and comfort him with her body. And be comforted by his.

"Thank you," he said.

"You're welcome," she said, and then rushed into her room before she gave in to the mercurial demands of her foolish heart.

On a cool morning in October, Harrison and Ryan worked at the Atlanta Community Food Bank, boxing and sorting food for the Thanksgiving event that would be taking place in an hour.

The director of the food bank, a kind but stern woman named Abby, worked with them. Abby was talking about the food bank's initiatives and kept using the words "food insecure."

A term that made Ryan snort-laugh through her nose.

"What . . . ?" Abby looked over at Harrison on the other side of the warehouse, as if he might explain why his wife was laughing at the thought of families going hungry. But he wouldn't have the answers. For all his compassion, he didn't have any idea what it meant to be hungry.

Sorry, food insecure.

"What is so funny?" Abby asked.

"I'm sorry." Ryan shook her head. "It's just the term. 'Insecure.' When you're a kid and you're hungry and you know there's nothing at home for dinner and won't be until the end of the month, 'insecure' isn't exactly the right word."

"What word would you use?" Abby asked.

"Scared. Food scared."

Out of the corner of her eye she saw Harrison put down a box and turn to stare at her.

"Your family didn't have enough food?" Abby asked.

"Some months my dad's disability check didn't cover everything, and meat was always the first to go. Then vegetables and fruit. Milk. Even the powdered stuff for emergencies. Then the macaroni and ketchup. If we were lucky, we'd only have to get by without dinner for a few nights."

"What did your father do?"

"Drove buses for the city until he slipped on some ice and hurt his back, and then we lived on his disability. Which could get us through as long as no one needed new shoes, or the car kept running. And I guess I've never really thought about this, kids usually don't, but I can't imagine how my dad must have felt those nights."

She pushed hair off her shoulders as she knelt to pick up another bag of rice. "It must have killed him knowing he couldn't always give us a good meal . . . I can't even imagine what he'd call it. But I doubt it's 'insecure.' Food anger? Food rage?"

"Mrs. Montgomery—"

"Please, call me Ryan." She still wasn't used to "Mrs. Montgomery" and frankly didn't think she ever would be, considering her mother-in-law.

"I think you'd be a great spokesperson for us."

"For hunger, you mean?" She laughed, but no one

else did. Harrison was staring at her over the boxes he'd stacked. Abby was doing the same.

She could feel the blood pounding in her cheeks, sweat dripping down her sides from her suddenly sticky armpits. Oh, this attention sucked.

"Yes, in a word," Abby said.

"That's . . . I'm . . ." She glanced at Harrison, hoping he would bail her out with some kind of story about how busy they would be in Washington, how badly he needed her on the campaign, but he just kept those level blue eyes on her. "I'm not really . . ."

"You'd be great at it," he said. "Perfect, I think."

Her ears buzzed and she laughed, a wheezy, empty thing.

"Look," Abby said. "I know you're busy, but perhaps after the election you can come in and talk to us."

"That's . . . We'll be . . ." she stammered into silence.

"Just think about it. We'd love to have you," the director said, and then quickly checked her watch. "Let's open the doors!"

After the food was handed out and the photos were taken, Harrison was back in the limo with his wife.

When she thought he wasn't looking, she'd unbuttoned the top button of her skirt and pulled the thin fabric of her yellow-and-green print shirt over her stomach. Her clothes were getting uncomfortable lately; she wouldn't say it, but she did that sort of thing a lot.

And tried to hide it from him.

He wondered what she would do if she knew how badly he wanted to strip those clothes off her, reveal her in the sunlight so he could soak in the sight of her, learn the reality of her so his dreams, his imaginings, his pre-dawn fantasies of her would be made more real. More concrete.

So this whole damn relationship of theirs would be made more concrete.

This charade that they were living was wearing him down. The closer they got to the election, the more real the next step in his life, the more he wished they could have those moments back on the couch. The more he wanted to just stop . . . pretending.

At first the charade had been in public, the smiles and hand-holding. The kissing and whispers. The united shoulder-to-shoulder front they presented to everyone. But now . . . since that night in September, and maybe since before then, maybe gradually, minute by minute since they'd been together, the tide had turned and the time when they were alone felt like the large lie.

The chill with which they handled each other. The careful indifference, as if showing the other how they might care, or how they were invested in each other, might somehow tip this boat over.

And what then? he wondered. What would be the great disaster if he let his wife—his goddamned *wife*—know what he thought. How he felt. They'd said no lies between them, but all they did was pretend not to be so painfully aware of the other. Staring out windows, taking phone calls.

It was his childhood all over again. But worse, somehow. A thousand times worse. Because he knew what he was missing out on. What *they* were missing out on.

It seemed impossible that the woman who had stayed with him, held his hand, let him into her body, comforted him, counseled him, shared her graham crackers, now stood beside him a stranger, pretending at love.

"You should think about it," he said to his wife. "Working with the food bank."

She looked out the window, even harder if such a thing were possible.

"You'd be good."

The sound she made was partially disbelief, but he couldn't be sure because he couldn't see her damn face.

Fuck this, he thought on a sudden wave of anger, and he rolled up the partition between the front and back seats. They did not need any witnesses for this half-formed idea of his.

Chapter 21

"Look at me," he barked, and she whirled to face him, stunned and disgruntled by his tone.

"What is with you?"

"What is with me is how we get in the backseat of this car and pretend like we don't know each other."

She blinked, as if confused. As if he didn't make sense. As if he were speaking nonsense.

"Tell me." With one hand he reached around her, between her body and the seat, until she was shifted toward him, his hand at her back. She was so slight, so small, it took almost no physical effort on his part to pull her halfway across the bench seat.

"What are you doing?" she asked, slapping her hands down against the leather seats to stop herself.

"What is the lie?" he asked. "When we're alone, or when we're out in public?"

"What are you talking about?"

"Don't do that. Don't pretend you don't understand." He bit off the words right in her face, and he watched the anger ignite in her. Felt it in her body, and he liked it. Liked the reaction. Wanted more. Wanted anything that was real. "I can't keep it straight anymore. What is real and what is pretend. Do we like each other? Do we love each other? Are we indifferent? Is it hate we feel when no one is watching?"

He'd pulled her close enough that he could smell her breath. Gum and orange juice. The lotion she wore, something sexy and flowery. And beneath that her skin. He could smell her. Like an animal he could smell her.

His cock got hard. His cock got very hard.

"Are you my wife?" Boldly, recklessly, he took his life in his hands and put his free hand on her knee because he knew this woman was capable of taking off his head if she chose. And suddenly, he dropped the idea that he was taking advantage of her. This wasn't about the power that came from money or connections or big houses. Or the contract they'd signed.

This was about the power of choice.

And she could choose, right now, to stop him.

Or she could let him in.

He could stop waiting for them to be equals because in this, they were. They always had been.

Her skin was warm under his touch and he slid his palm up higher on her leg, until he felt the silk lining of her skirt on the top of his hand, the trembling muscles of her leg under his palm.

A flush climbed out from the demure edge of her suit jacket and he watched it cross the boundaries of her collarbones, up the pale, beautiful length of her neck into her face. Her panting breaths gave away her secrets; so did her dilated eyes. Her hands at her sides, opening and closing as if they couldn't make up their mind.

"If you want me to stop, I will," he breathed.

"What are you going to do?"

"Put my fingers inside of you. Make you come."

The sound she made was part laugh, part sex sound. The sound she made when he pushed inside of her.

The blood in his veins nearly boiled.

"Do you want that?" he asked.

She nodded and he laughed, pressing the smallest, most tender kiss to the corner of her lips.

"Say it," he breathed into her mouth.

"I want that."

Another kiss, and when she turned her mouth to kiss him back, to send them furious and rabid into each other's clothes, he pulled away. "Say the whole thing."

She grabbed his head in her hands, holding him so she could stare right into the center of his brain, his soul. Whatever he expected from Ryan, he always somehow got more. Something more hot. More fierce. As if his imaginings were somehow clichéd, watered-down boy fantasies, and she came at him a whole woman.

"I want you to put your fingers inside me and make me come, and then I want you to lick your hand clean."

Good Christ. Done. He was done. She'd just finished him.

There was no careful seduction, no balancing of the scales, no waiting to see if what he wanted was okay with her. Instead she spread her legs, tipped her hips, and he breached the damp silk of her underwear, finding beneath it a hot welcome.

She hissed as his finger slid inside of her and jerked when his thumb, searching through her curls and those tender folds of skin, found the bead of her clitoris.

Her fingers clenched the fabric of his suit jacket and he wanted to rip it off his body so he could feel the bite of her nails against his skin again. But his hands were full and she did not seem at all invested in taking off clothes. His or hers.

The hand at her back slipped farther down between her body and the seat, grabbing her ass so he could hold her still, for his driving fingers.

She cried out and he pressed his mouth to hers. Not a kiss. But a way to silence her.

"Shhh," he breathed against her.

Her sighing response tipped up at the end into a cry and he kissed her for real, his tongue in her mouth. She bit at him, sucked at him, and then pulled him all the way against her until he fell to his knees in the foot well beside her.

It was mad and wild and totally silent. Fucking her with his fingers, devouring her with his mouth. She coiled and jerked, hips beating against his chest. Her hands in his hair now, pulling until his eyes watered and it didn't matter. None of it mattered because she was coming.

He felt it with his fingers—the squeeze and clench and flutter of muscles, the liquid coating his fingers, the way her breath hiccupped into a sob.

"Ryan," he whispered. Not a question, not a demand, just her name, formed in his brain, birthed through his mouth. Ryan.

"Finish it," she whispered, and he leaned back to catch her eyes, twinkling and sexy and destructive in all ways.

God. She was so beautiful. So sexy.

Not looking away from those eyes, still on his knees before her, he took his hand from between her legs and put his fingers in his mouth.

Her body twitched. His cock pounded.

She lurched up from where she'd fallen back half against the window and he scrambled up to the seat beside her, both their hands fumbling at his zipper like he was a bomb about to go off. Finally, she had him out of his pants, her fist curled around him, and then she bent, slipping her lips around him. The hot, wet suction of her mouth nearly did him in immediately but he closed his eyes and tipped his head against the back of the seat, determined after all these weeks thinking about her touch that he would not explode at the first touch of her tongue.

She moaned low in her throat, the vibrations rattling through his skin, through his muscles and bone, to echo in his own throat.

She twisted her grip and then dropped her hand and took him deep in her mouth, until he felt the head of his cock brush the back of her throat and then, somehow, impossibly, like a dream from when he was a teenager, even deeper.

"Oh, God, Ryan," he breathed.

He stood no chance against that, and he slipped his hand around the back of her neck until it felt like he controlled her in his grip, like he moved her.

And she surrendered to it.

Oh, God.

He eased her back and then because he was so turned on and she was so willing, he pressed her back down again. Just a little. Just enough. And then again. And again.

Her hands came up and clawed at his jacket, gripping it in her fists.

His orgasm destroyed him. Shook him from the ground up, and he was helpless in its grip. In her grip. Her soft mouth still around him as she swallowed. He put his hands in his own hair so he wouldn't accidentally pull hers. Wouldn't accidentally hurt her.

Even wrecked by that orgasm, he was still pushed to the edges of his control by what he felt for her.

Again, he thought when he could think again. *I want that again. Over and over until all the bullshit between us is gone. Until all that's left is how we make each other feel.*

There was a subtle knock on the glass between the front and back seats, and he swore.

She groaned, covering her face with her hands.

"We're here, sir," came the muffled voice of Dan, his driver. "Back at the loft."

"Do you think we could tell him to go around the block a few times?" he whispered.

"There are beds inside that loft," she said, and he rolled his head to face her.

"All my staff and my family are also in there."

"What?" She jerked backward.

"Sorry, it was Wallace's idea. A kind of State of the Union Party and Debrief. I forgot to mention it."

"Yeah, you did," she muttered. But they'd been so busy, racing from event to event. And frankly, despite his fantasizing about this, he'd never thought they would get to this point. Half naked and replete in the back of the limo.

But they could not hold onto the heat between them, and the chill settled around them as he and Ryan adjusted their clothes.

"Who are we when we go inside there?" she asked, staring up at the building.

"I don't know."

"You think this is arbitrary, don't you?" she asked. "The way I'm trying to keep our public and private lives separate. You think I'm being difficult?"

He shook his head. "I don't know why you're doing it, but I know it's not just to be difficult."

"Because I need to have something to call my own," she told him, her face stark in the sunlight. Her lipstick gone, her eyeliner smudged. "Something that doesn't get used by you."

"Used? Is that what you think I'm doing?" *God. Say no. Please tell me no.*

"I think you would drag me under," she said. Her eyes—those eyes cut right through every lie he wanted to believe about them. "And never even know you were doing it."

Ryan used to have this dress that she loved. It was her mother's old prom dress, and she'd let Nora and Ryan play endless hours of dress-up in it. It was a gauzy thing covered in sequins, more classy and elegant than the jeans and flannel shirts and tennis shoes they saw Mom in every day.

In the end, before she and Nora outgrew dress-up and each other, from a distance the dress looked awesome, but close up it was obvious every single one of those sequins was in danger of falling off. Threads were pulled everywhere.

Walking into the condo full of staff and Harrison's parents, she felt like that dress.

What had been the point of that? she wondered. Of Harrison initiating it and Ryan letting it happen.

Right, she thought, stopping herself from shrugging off the responsibility, *like you just let that blow job happen. You just let him fuck your mouth like some kind of porn star. Like you didn't love it.*

But she did. She'd loved all of it.

And she could have stopped him, he gave her ample opportunity to, but in the end, like the horny poor-decision maker she was, she'd jumped right in.

And if no one were in this condo right now, she would let it happen again. Maybe on the kitchen island. And again, upstairs in his bedroom, and then maybe again in the old claw-foot tub in the bathroom.

What am I doing? she wondered, trying to get as much distance between herself and the temptation of her husband as possible.

Wallace gave everyone the great news that Harrison had pulled ahead in the polls. He also let them know that the fundraiser had been a success and they could keep the scheduled television spots in the next two weeks.

"But now is not the time to relax," Wallace said, rallying the troops, who looked about as exhausted as she felt. Only Harrison seemed to glow. And glow harder after every event.

He really was made for this, she thought.

Or maybe it was just the blue balls making him glow like that.

"Let's stay on point, let's keep our message out there. Let's not get sloppy," Wallace said. Everyone cheered and good-naturedly called him coach, and then they all dug into the muffins and fruit that Harrison had had delivered.

The only problem was Ted Montgomery. Like a vulture sensing eminent death, he'd been circling Harrison's victory.

"Why are they here?" Ryan asked Wallace, after his speech.

"I invited them." Wallace poured himself a coffee and grinned at her over the edge of the cup.

"What? Why?"

Wallace shrugged.

"You're flaunting our success, aren't you?"

"Rubbing it in their faces," Wallace agreed without a shred of shame, before leaving her to talk to staff.

Harrison seemed to be making sure there was at least the distance of the room between him and his father, and most of the staff were doing the same, watching the Montgomerys like they were a cancer that might spread.

Noelle and Patty were talking in the kitchen area. Noelle's eyes darted toward Ryan over the top of Patty's helmet hair and then guiltily away.

Paul.

In the whirlwind of the campaign, in the war of attrition between her and Harrison, she'd completely forgotten about Paul.

And the Paul bomb could detonate and destroy this team. All this work.

Ryan kept her eyes on Patty and Noelle and when

Patty left the kitchen, and when it wouldn't look too obvious, Ryan swept in and cornered Noelle near the muffin tray. Taking a second to take stock of what was left: about twenty bran muffins and only one banana. And the banana ones were the best.

How many muffins were too many? she wondered. Three? Because she'd had three and a half already.

Nausea no longer ruled her life. She woke up at eleven weeks pregnant and the nausea was replaced by a bottomless pit of hunger and food cravings that made no sense. She wanted to take that banana muffin and salt it before shoving it in her mouth. She wanted to roll that muffin in hot sauce.

"Hi, Ryan," Noelle said, cool and unreadable.

"Noelle," she said.

"You want to eat some food off my plate?" she asked.

"Very funny."

"How about that one?" She pointed to a paper plate on the edge of the sink with a whole strawberry on it. Who took a strawberry and didn't eat it?

"I'm fine. I wanted to ask you if you knew anything more about what we'd talked about at the luncheon."

Noelle stiffened. Her eyes darted around the room and when she saw Patty over near the windows talking to Jill, she relaxed.

"No," she answered. "Nothing."

"You would tell me, right?" Ryan asked.

Noelle nodded, rolling her eyes behind her glasses.

"Okay," Ryan said, wondering why every exchange with this woman seemed so difficult. She reached for that last banana muffin, but Noelle grabbed her arm.

"I . . . I need a favor," Noelle said.

"From me?"

"Of course you."

"Secrets and now favors? Next are you going to invite me to a slumber party?"

Noelle just blinked at her. Unamused.

"What do you need?"

"Wallace. Is he dating anyone?"

"Is that . . . are you joking?"

Noelle blushed bright red and turned away. "Forget it."

"No, no, stop." She put a hand on Noelle's arm to keep her from walking away. "I'm sorry—you just surprised me is all."

"It's stupid," Noelle breathed, shaking her head.

"Do you like him, or are you asking for, like . . . political reasons?"

"Look at him," Noelle muttered, staring at Wallace balefully through her eyelashes.

Ryan turned to watch the guy, wearing a bow tie, as he talked to Jill and Harrison.

"He is handsome."

"Handsome," Noelle said, like the idea was an insult. "The guy is brilliant."

"Oh, well, that too." *Aren't I a shallow creature?*

"And what he's doing . . . I just . . . I admire him is all." *Oh, I know that feeling. That poison-tipped edge of admiration.*

"You should tell him that."

Noelle scoffed. "In case you haven't noticed, I'm the enemy."

"I wouldn't go that far."

"Look over there." She jerked her head back to where Harrison's parents were standing alone next to the windows.

"Like I said. You are not your boss. Or your boss's husband."

"I just feel like . . ." Noelle watched Wallace from the corner of her eyes, like a pining puppy dog in glasses. "Forget it."

"Like 'what have I got to offer that guy'?"

"That's exactly how I feel."

"Don't sell yourself short, Noelle. You've got plenty to offer."

Noelle laughed and set her paper plate down. "You don't know me, you know. You're hardly an authority."

"True. But I want you to have something to offer. Just like I wanted to have something to offer to this campaign. And maybe . . . maybe that's the first step."

Noelle narrowed her eyes, the professional cynic. "Yeah, maybe. Thanks. You know, everyone is totally impressed by how well you're doing. You are kind of killing it."

"Damn right," Ryan muttered with a smile, though she was secretly pleased that people thought she was killing it. She rather thought she was too.

"I'm not sure if you've considered it, but . . ." Noelle rearranged the things left on her plate—the strawberry stem, the melon rind, the half-eaten donut. "You're going to need some help in Washington, like an assistant."

"I hadn't even thought of that. It's already kind of getting difficult keeping things straight, and Wallace is organizing both Harrison and me and I know he's stressed." *Man, me with an assistant. Dad would totally get a kick out of that.* "Do you know someone?"

Noelle's mouth fell open. "Yeah. Me."

"You're asking me for a job?"

"Maybe. Yes."

"I thought you wanted to be a part of something."

"With you and Harrison, I would be."

"Oh." The sound just slipped out of her because she did not know what to do with this feeling in her chest, this unbearable lightness. The sudden and strange pride in herself.

"Let's talk after the election," Ryan said. "In the meantime, go talk to Wallace. Tell him you like his ties. Men go nuts for women who compliment them, even when they're lying." Ryan gave Noelle a nudge, largely so she could be alone with the muffin tray. Noelle balked like a teenager crossing a dance floor to talk to a boy she liked, but in the end she did it. She walked across the room and joined whatever conversation Wallace was having. And Wallace, once he saw her there at his elbow, opened up his circle and included her and within moments they were arguing.

Which she imagined was like foreplay for these awkward brainiacs.

"You ready to be a congressman's wife?" a voice asked at her elbow, and she turned to find Ted Montgomery, holding a glass of orange juice he'd been doctoring with a flask of vodka in his jacket pocket, smiling at her.

It was difficult not to physically recoil.

It was strange to have such a strong visceral reaction to him because he looked like a time-machined version of the man who'd finger-fucked her to orgasm in the backseat of a car.

"Is it much different than what I'm doing now?" she asked.

"Well, I suppose that depends on what kind of woman you are?" There was something in his voice, just an inflection on the word *woman* that made the question . . . not okay. Very not okay.

"How do you mean?" She crossed her arms over her chest, wishing she had something more physical between them. A brick wall. A thousand miles. Harrison.

"Well, are you going to play the game that's required of you? Can you shovel shit while dishing it out?"

"That's not part of the job as I see it. Harrison—"

He laughed at her like she was a little girl showing him a piece of art and she felt her North Philly instincts rising up. She imagined grabbing that plastic tray of muffins and bashing it over his head.

"My son is a lot of things, Ryan. But he is not cut out for politics. He's too idealistic, too easily conned. You think you're the first woman who has tricked him?"

"What the hell are you talking about?"

"Ask him about Heidi." Ted stepped closer, his eyes taking a walk all over her as he leaned over to take the last banana muffin from the tray. "You picked the wrong Montgomery, sweetheart, if you wanted to fuck yourself into an easier life."

She gasped, a thousand swear-rich insults running through her head, but she could only gasp like an offended debutante.

"What's going on here?" It was Harrison, and Ryan turned away toward the fridge, blinking away embarrassed rage tears.

"You're talking to me now?" Ted asked. "All it takes is getting within three feet of your wife?"

"What do you want?"

"You know your mother and I are a little concerned at how quickly this woman has embedded herself in your campaign."

"She's my *wife*."

"Look, you want to prove you're better than me? Fine, you've done it. You married her, but don't give her the power to mess up your future."

"You're drunk." Harrison crowded his father away from the kitchen island and caught his mother's eye. Patty put down her teacup to come over. "Sending Dad to do your dirty work, Mother—that's a little beneath you, isn't it?"

"I did no such thing," Patty said.

"Really, I'm supposed to think Dad cares about my political future?"

"Think what you want, Harrison," Ted said. "You always have. But of course I care."

"Right, now that your career is nearly over, I should have guessed you'd care about mine. I think it's time for you both to leave."

Ted put down the muffin, and he and Patty gathered their things and left as if he understood he'd used up whatever benevolence Harrison had for them.

Patty, in the doorway, looked over her shoulder at Harrison and Ryan. And Ryan thought about all those people getting on the *Titanic,* looking back at the friends and family they were leaving behind.

The only difference was that Patty knew she was climbing onto a doomed ship.

When she met Patty in that foyer weeks ago, she never would have imagined that she would feel pity for the woman. But as their eyes met across the room, her heart practically broke for her.

"Are you okay?" Harrison asked once they were gone.

"Fine."

"What did he say?"

She thought about bringing up Heidi, or telling him how his father had sleaze-bagged all over her, but decided not to. It was what Ted wanted, to drive a wedge between them.

"Nothing important," she said with a weak smile.

"That's a lie." Harrison's voice was cold, his eyes narrowed. "Did he hit on you?"

"So what if he did, Harrison?" She sighed.

"So what if my father hit on my wife?"

"Your fake wife, remember? And I think your dad kind of hits on everyone."

"That doesn't make it okay."

"No. And it doesn't make it my fault, so stop glaring at me."

Harrison picked up the muffin that Ted had put down. "You want this? I know the banana ones are your favorites."

"No," she lied past the lump in her throat. *They're just muffins,* she told herself when she wanted to read all sorts of things into the fact that he noticed she liked them. *And you did eat three of them. The whole room probably noticed.*

Harrison threw the muffin away and went to talk to Jill.

Don't think about it, she thought, closing her eyes. *Don't think about it at all.*

But in the end, she couldn't quite stop herself.

What did Harrison have to do with the woman who nearly died in that car crash with Ted?

Chapter 22

Monday morning they were down at the office bright and early, getting ready to film additional television spots. But ever since Ted had talked to her at the party, their shtick was off.

Unable to handle her husband's chilly silence, on Sunday she tried to give him a hard time about keeping the condo so cold penguins could survive in her bedroom, but he'd only turned up the heat without argument.

This morning she'd asked him to make her a decaf latte from the espresso machine he treated like an expensive car, which she usually openly mocked. And he did it without once trying to explain the machine's magical inner workings.

He'd placed the perfectly made latte in front of her with a smile that was miles away from his eyes.

I'm the one who is mad, she'd thought. *I'm the one who is supposed to be cool.*

He was robbing her of her righteous coolness.

"Harrison," she said in the car heading downtown through the milky dawn. "What's wrong?"

"Nothing."

"Is it about your dad? Because there's nothing to be upset about."

"My father hits on my pregnant wife and there's nothing to be upset about?"

"Fine, yes. Be pissed. He's a shitty guy. But why are you upset with *me*?"

"I'm not."

"Right," she scoffed. "Is it because you think he's right? You regret bringing me into the campaign like you have?"

"No!" he said so quickly and fervently she could not doubt him. Which frankly was a relief. She didn't want to believe that Ted could plant seeds of doubt in her husband's mind, but his behavior since the party had been so strange.

"Then what's wrong?"

"I'm trying not to pull you under, Ryan," he said, throwing her words back at her. "I would think you'd be grateful."

The conversation was far from over, but they arrived downtown and Harrison was out the door, turning to help her because his manners were flawless.

"Harrison," she sighed.

"Like me or hate me, Ryan. Make up your mind."

Stunned by his rebuff, she followed him into the office.

As off as it was between them, inside the office it was business as usual. The team honestly seemed to need her. They asked her opinion on which tie he should wear for the spot—she pushed for pink, they wanted blue; compromise was met at purple.

They talked about having her in the spots.

"She's too pretty. She'll upstage him," Wallace joked.

"Very funny," Harrison said.

"I'm not joking."

"Do you have the notes on the speech?" Harrison asked her, tying his tie without a mirror. Because he was that guy. After the spot, Harrison was giving a speech at a community center in Kirkwood. For that she would

be there, standing in the background, hands clasped behind her, smiling until his speech was over.

"Yes," she said, slipping into her black heels, her feet
already protesting. "We're changing the part about college tuitions."

"No. The part about tax breaks for children's pro-
gramming."

"Right." She shook her head. "Sorry."

Maynard from the *Journal-Constitution* kept asking
her questions after events and after a while, the other
journalists got in on it too. She couldn't say she knew
the answer all the time, but Wallace prepped her pretty
well with sound bites that seemed to mollify the press.

And truthfully, she enjoyed answering the questions.
She enjoyed having the answers. She'd enjoyed these
powwows before, this sense of . . . team. And she never
once would have considered it was a bad thing until Ted
said that yesterday. She never suspected she would have
the power to poison anything of Harrison's.

And whether it was fake or not, she liked the way
Harrison had looked at her the last few weeks. Like
they were partners. Like he was proud.

No one had looked at her like that. Not in a very long
time.

And she was just vain enough, or maybe just needy
enough, to love it.

And miss it now that he wasn't looking at her at all.
And it was childish; she knew that. She'd been the one
so dead set on keeping the walls up between them. But
she'd liked that he'd been trying to get over them.

Exhaustion rolled over her like a sudden fog.

"You know," Wallace said as he walked past her,
"this is a pretty straightforward meet and greet. We
don't actually need you to come, if you need a day to
rest."

Harrison's head came up. "Are you okay?" he asked. "Are you tired?"

"I'm fine," she said, though a day off was a lovely idea. It had been late night after early morning for about five days now and she could use a baby-growing nap. Or three. And to be left alone with whatever remained of the catered breakfast from yesterday.

But she wasn't about to stay home, not when this *purpose* was waiting out there for her.

Everyone in the room shared quick glances. "Really," she said. "I'm fine. My doctor said I was doing great and as long as I was sleeping at night, I could help campaign."

"We kept you out until one a.m. last night," Harrison said.

"And woke you up at seven," Jill added. "And that's pretty much the latest morning you've had."

"I think we can give the good-luck charm a break," Wallace said.

"Good-luck charm?" she asked, spinning on her heel to look at Harrison, who was sort of blushing against the door.

"It's not . . . That's—"

"That's what we've been calling you," Wallace said, interrupting Harrison. "This whole campaign hit overdrive since you came on."

"Well, it sounds like you need me. So, let's get going." She grabbed her makeup case from the edge of Harrison's desk. She'd gotten good at putting on her makeup in the back of the car. One of the million little things she'd gotten good at in the last few weeks.

"You can stay home," Harrison said, turning to the door without looking back at her. "We'll be okay."

"Harrison—"

"Stay home, Ryan."

"But . . . are you sure?" Disappointed didn't begin to

describe this feeling. She was ready to take her role as good-luck charm seriously.

"I'm sure. You should rest."

And then they were all gone, whisked away into cars to go film the TV spots, leaving her alone in this office that wasn't hers, in this life that wasn't particularly hers either.

Thursday, October 17

Without the campaign work to distract her, Ryan couldn't stand the suspense about Paul anymore and frankly, she was pretty sick of lying down and letting the Montgomery family do what they wanted with her. So Thursday afternoon she drove herself to the Governor's Mansion—which felt like a big deal after weeks of being driven everywhere like a delivery that needed to be dropped off.

And she went looking for the lioness in her den.

"Patty around?" she asked, walking into Noelle's office, which was right outside the closed doors of Patty's.

Noelle, quick as she was, only gaped for a second. Ryan was on a roll, so she just pushed open the double wooden doors to reveal Patty working at her desk.

She glanced up at the intrusion and lifted a perfectly sculpted eyebrow. And then removed red reading glasses and set them on her desk.

"Do we have an appointment?" Patty asked.

"No. This is more of a casual thing," she said.

"I'm afraid I don't—"

"You don't have anything scheduled for the next hour," Noelle said, earning her a scowl from Patty. And if Ryan could hand out merit badges, Noelle would be first in line.

"Lovely," Patty sat back. "Would you like coffee or—"

"No. What I would like is to know why you're trying to hunt down my ex-husband."

Patty shot a withering glance over Ryan's shoulder.

"Don't you dare blame Noelle," Ryan said. "She was showing more respect for your son and his campaign than you have."

"Noelle." Patty stood up behind her desk. Once upon a time Ryan might have quaked in her boots, but she'd seen behind this woman's façade and wasn't impressed. "Shut the door on your way out."

The door clicked quietly behind her.

"If you find Paul, it will bring down Harrison's campaign," she said. *Through me.* That she didn't say.

"You credit him with that much power?"

"He would say anything to hurt me. Make up any kind of lie, just to see me go down, and I would pull Harrison down with me. We both know that."

And she wanted to defend herself. To tell Patty, who undoubtedly wouldn't care that she was a different person than the woman who'd married that kind of guy. Who'd been so attracted to his ruthlessness.

Who'd let him touch her and hurt her and then touch her again.

Ryan's name in Paul's mouth would turn all the changes she'd made in her life into nothing.

"If voters saw him, all that would matter was I am the kind of woman who'd married that scumbag, which would make my marriage to Harrison totally suspicious."

"Yes," Patty agreed, coming around the front of the desk. Sunlight streamed through the windows to fall on Patty's face. For any other woman the sunlight would have picked through and highlighted flaws. Wrinkles and weird coloring spots. But not Patty. She looked flawless. "That is what I imagined."

"You hate me so much you'd bring down your son's campaign?"

Patty's eyes blazed. "I love my son so much that I would see that man dead before I allowed him to hurt Harrison's campaign."

"You'd have him killed?" Ryan cried, and Patty rolled her eyes.

"Good God, such theatrics. No, I was looking for him so I could pay him to keep his mouth shut."

Ryan sagged so hard and so fast her ankle turned in her boot.

"Come, sit down before you fall over."

All out of righteous fury, Ryan stepped to the chairs in front of Patty's desk and sat. To her surprise, Patty sat in the chair beside her.

"You were right all those months ago—we are more similar in many ways than we're different. I would do anything for my family."

"Except hire a hit man," she said, trying to make a joke.

Patty lifted an eyebrow as if it wasn't beyond the realm of possibility.

"Oh, you have to be kidding," Ryan said, unsure of anything.

Patty smiled and crossed her legs at her trim ankles. "In all honesty, I'm glad you're here," she said, leaving Ryan wondering what exactly her mother-in-law was capable of. "Harrison won't talk of losing this election, so you and I should probably come up with a contingency plan."

"He's not going to lose."

Patty shot her a wry look. "Harrison is not here; neither is Wallace. No one will get offended by some honest conversation."

Oh, that was hilarious coming from her. "I don't want a contingency plan if he loses."

Patty took a breath and eyed her carefully. "He will lose. Someday. He might win this one and lose the next. It's your job to keep him focused. Moving forward. He can't slip backward into the comfort of VetAid—"

Ryan stood up. "Stop. Right there. I'm not his campaign manager—"

"That's right." Patty stood up. "Campaign managers come and go. You are his wife. His partner."

She shook her head. "Our marriage is not like yours."

"Are you trying to allude that there is a greater depth of feeling between you and Harrison? I will have to remind you I was at your wedding ceremony. I read that contract."

"No, I'm alluding to the fact that I have a life of my own. Plans. Things that I want."

"Well, they're hardly more important than the campaign, are they?"

At one time she might have agreed. Drunk on the team spirit and the sense that she was fighting for something good and right, she might have agreed. But then Harrison told her to stay home, dismissed her. And it had hurt. And then he'd done it again the next day. And then because her feelings were hurt, she did it the following. And suddenly they were spinning in separate orbits.

If I am more important than this campaign, she realized, *I'd better act like it. I'd better make plans.*

"There's no shame in sacrifice," Patty said.

But at what point does the sacrifice become meaningless? When it's no longer appreciated? Or valued? Or when you no longer even realize what you're sacrificing?

"Have you ever loved your husband?" she asked.

"That's irrelevant, isn't it?"

"We're talking about marriage."

"We're talking about politics."

Wasn't that just a classic Montgomery answer.

"You never loved him?"

"I loved him very much."

Patty's cool smile didn't stick, it flickered and wavered on her face and then finally fell away, revealing a pain more profound for its unexpectedness.

"Is that so hard to believe?" Patty asked, running the flat of her hand over the edge of her desk as if it were a loyal pet she was stroking.

Oh, God. Patty loved Ted and he cheated. Over and over again he cheated. And she just kept sacrificing, trying to make up the difference.

"I'm sorry," she breathed, because she didn't know what else to say.

"Don't be. Teddy's behavior was never a surprise. I just thought . . . I thought I could change him. I thought I could make him see the man I saw when I looked at him, all that potential. He's . . . he really is a good man. Decent. Caring. He's just very . . . weak."

And so she had to be even stronger.

"Why didn't you ever run for office?" Ryan asked. It seemed a sudden shame that this woman and all her talents was relegated to cleanup duty. To smiling and waving at the side of the stage. Sacrificing more than she probably even knew. "You seem far more suited for it than Ted."

Patty tilted her head at Ryan and laughed.

"I'm not kidding."

"I know you're not and it's flattering, but, no, it's not anything I've considered. And at my age—"

"Hillary Clinton is older than you, isn't she?"

"Well, that's . . . just . . . I don't . . . ." Patty was actually blushing, and it was so deeply strange, Ryan felt the urge to get the hell out of Dodge.

Ryan stood up. "You should think about it, because you'd be pretty awesome at it. I'm sorry I barged in here."

She walked out of the office and past Noelle, who glanced up at her with wide eyes.

"Don't give up on her yet," Ryan told Noelle. "You might still get a chance to do something important with her."

Friday, October 18

It was eighteen days until election night, and Harrison had nothing to do. There was no town hall meeting, no fundraising to do. No staff meeting. Nothing.

The calm before the storm, Wallace called it. What could be done was done. And what was coming was prepared for, so Wallace gave everyone the night off.

Which was suspicious, actually. The way Wallace had been making side eyes at Noelle during the breakfast party a few weeks ago made him think his staff was out somewhere getting wasted and having sex, while he was in the small den off his bedroom writing thank-you letters and clearing out his personal email in-box.

And ignoring his wife.

You would drag me under and never even know you were doing it. That's what Ryan had said.

And it was the truth. And it paralyzed him with self-loathing.

His father's nonsense about putting Ryan into a position to ruin his campaign was ludicrous. She was making his campaign. Things had only been going better since she'd gotten involved, and so he just kept asking more of her. More and more and more of her.

And what did he give her in return? Media scrutiny and sleazy run-ins with his father.

Day by day, he'd been forcing her into the mud where he lived.

Down below him, he heard the creak of the couch as

she got up for something to drink or to go to the bath-room. There was a constant hum of music from her laptop . . . she was a big fan of Maroon 5.

Occasionally he caught himself listening for her when there hadn't been any noise for a while, wondering if she was asleep. Wondering if she was thinking about him.

That scene in the car, it haunted him. It woke him up from a sound sleep. Distracted him in the middle of meetings. The other day, standing in front of a podium at a library, he'd lost his way in his speech thinking about that sound she'd made, that whispering sigh that turned into a cry at the end when he'd slipped his fingers beneath her underwear.

Perhaps other men, with different pasts, with differ-ent parents, with different plans for his life, would be able to understand how to blur the lines they'd laid down at the beginning of this relationship.

But he didn't. Every feeling he had felt leveraged be-cause of that contract, felt dirty because he wasn't sup-posed to feel it.

Because he was his father's son there was something in his bloodline, something in his genetic code, that found a way to ask what he shouldn't ask.

And it wasn't just the sex.

It was how well she was playing her role. How per-fectly she adapted. How she rose to every challenge. How she winked and flirted with all of those journalists when they'd thought she'd cower and run at their ques-tions.

When Wallace had called her his good-luck charm, it had all been hammered home and in one fell swoop, he ended it. Because he was using her in every way.

And if he wanted to argue with himself, defend his actions by claiming to care for her, that was even worse. Because it was a lie he was telling himself.

He didn't care for people. Not like Ryan would want to be cared for.

Loved. She would want to be loved.

And he didn't know how to do that.

So the least he could do was try and protect her from his family.

Downstairs the floor creaked, and he shook his head clear from his thoughts and forced himself to settle back into his work.

Buried between press releases, updated schedules from weeks ago, and Wallace's efforts to get a group of staffers to play basketball on the weekends, he found a series of emails from Ruth Corlo, mother of Michael, the boy in the kindergarten class he and Ryan had visited shortly after their marriage.

Michael had been sitting alone while Ryan read the story to the class and there had been something about the boy's posture that he recognized, the sideways glances at the group and the stubborn set of his shoulders. He wanted to join the group of kids sitting at Ryan's knee, but something had been holding him back. Weighing him down.

It didn't take much to get it out of Michael; he was just a kid, after all.

Michael had told him that his dad was coming home from Iraq and his mom was scared, because the last time he'd come home all they did was yell at each other.

He'd given Mrs. Tellier his card to give to Michael's mother. She'd emailed right away and he'd tried to answer her questions personally, but lately he'd just been too busy, so he got the acting director of VetAid to step in.

Ruth Corlo had just sent him a thank-you note for his help.

Things aren't great, she wrote, *and might not be for a*

long time. But they are better, thanks to you and your organization.

When he started VetAid, he'd gotten drunk on the very specific pleasure that came from seeing a need and being able to fill it.

But those moments in the campaign, after events when he and Ryan stood onstage or walked through a community center, talking to people and shaking hands and answering questions. The policy meetings with Wallace, the staff meetings, the ideas and brainstorming. The plans. They felt right on a whole different level.

And Congress, Washington, D.C., whatever trajectory followed, he couldn't wait. His sister once told him that the work she did, the stuff in the camps, the disaster relief—she felt compelled to do it. Like she was more herself in those situations than at any other time.

That was exactly how he'd felt these last five weeks. More himself, his purpose fulfilled.

There was a scratch at the door to his den just before Ryan poked her head in.

"You busy?" she asked.

Yes, he thought, the sight of her filling him with a sort of panic. Busy ignoring her. Busy trying to pull this desire for her out by its corrupt roots.

"No, I'm not busy," he said, pushing away from his laptop. He shoved the pile of dirty dishes on the corner of his desk behind the printer and grabbed the socks off the floor and threw them in the shadows in the corners.

"I've been doing some research," she said, stepping onto a rug just inside the room. "And I am not going to go to Washington with you."

Chapter 23

"Once you are elected, you have to go back and forth from Washington, D.C., to Atlanta a few times a year to keep everyone happy," she continued. "But I can stay and take some psychology classes at Georgia Tech, maybe help out at the food bank . . ."

"And not have to suffer living with me?" He tried to make it a joke, but it didn't come out that way and they both knew it.

The room was hushed, the moment heavy, and he didn't know what to say about it. Or do about it.

Every time he looked at her, all he was aware of was how much he wanted her and how wrong that felt.

"That good-luck charm thing," she said. "You know it's not true. You're ahead because you're the right guy for the job. And the world knows those ads are bull-shit."

He waved it off. Painfully. Her being good luck had been true, and now it seemed he was working hard to make it untrue.

And she'd backed right off since that Monday. Choosing not to come with him on any more events unless he asked.

And then he'd stopped asking.

Why, he was not sure.

Because I want her to be beside me because she wants to be.

That sounded ridiculous; he understood that. They'd signed a contract. He was in fact paying her.

But he wanted her to want to share this with him.

See, he thought, *she was right. You would drown her and not even notice.*

"I was sort of thinking you wouldn't have to suffer living with *me*," she said, her eyes carefully someplace else. "You'd be able to work and I wouldn't get in the way of anything."

"You're not in the way of anything."

"Well, I'm not really *in* anything, am I?" She tried to make that sound like a joke, but it didn't work. The night broke open around him, revealing all kinds of ache.

"I know you've stepped back from the campaign, and that's fine, but you can come back anytime." He stood up from his desk, stepping out of the golden pool of lamplight into the shadows by the door where she stood.

I'm sorry, he thought, remembering the morning he told her to stay home. The way she'd been unable to hide the disappointment. The hurt. She'd backed off because of him.

God, somehow this complicated relationship had gotten even more complicated.

"But isn't this ideal?" she asked. "I mean, it's not like we have a real marriage. Why continue pretending?"

There were a thousand answers he could give right now. Polished, political, perfect answers, the types of which he'd been giving to almost every question asked of him in the last month.

But instead he was silent. Totally silent.

Because he couldn't stop thinking, *what if we stop pretending?*

What if we just stop?

"Jesus Christ, Harrison, I've watched you talk nearly nonstop for weeks now and the second we're alone, you're silent. I can't . . ." She shook her head, shoved her fists into her pockets, and stared, unblinking, at the corner of his desk. "Ever since Paul destroyed my life, my sister . . . my whole family has made me feel like I'm good for nothing." She sniffed and nearly smacked away the tears that had the audacity to fall from her eyes. He reached for her, but she stepped back.

"Don't," she whispered. "Don't touch me. It's the hormones. Let me just finish this." She took a deep breath. "I think I've been believing them, my family, for years. Proving them right, while I pretended not to give a shit. The crappy jobs in bars, the bullshit modeling, the fucking . . . psychology textbooks, I collected and read like they mattered at all in my life. It was all nonsense. My life was nonsense."

He wished he could touch her. Wished he were that man who knew how to just casually reach past the wall she'd put up, because she needed to be touched. Hugged. Comforted, the way she'd done for him over and over again. But he didn't know how, not without her permission.

And not in the silence of his house. Not without a witness making it somehow . . . less real. An act. A show.

Not a gesture of his affection and care.

Fuck. I am just like my parents.

"And then you come along with this . . . proposal. And this campaign, and you give me this stupid little part in it—"

"Nothing about you is stupid. Nothing."

"Everything," she spat. "Everything about me has been stupid. Because I started to believe that maybe I could be a part of this thing you're building. And maybe I could build something of my own, too. With school and the food bank. And you. And then, God, Harrison, the sex . . ." Her eyes, wet and wild, met his. "It's been four years since I've let anyone touch me. Four years. And I didn't have sex with you lightly. Not in New York and not here. Then . . . I don't know what happened, Harrison. You said you didn't agree with your dad, that you don't think I could poison the campaign."

"I *don't* agree with him!"

"Then why did you push me away? For God's sake, I'm being as honest as I can be; at least try to do the same."

Honest. Fine. "I don't want to take advantage of you."

"Take advantage of me?" she cried. "This is a job, Harrison. You are paying me to smile and wave and talk to the press."

"But we had a contract about the sex."

"I could have said no. I would have if I wanted to. I'm not your servant or a kid you picked up off the streets. I'm not scared of you or impressed by your money. I want *you*, Harrison, just you. You have an overinflated sense of your power if you think you're taking advantage of me. You can't take from me what I don't want to give."

I want you, Harrison, just you.

He had no idea what to say to those words. How to process them.

Once when he was young, and his parents were filming a radio spot with his whole family, Harrison had gotten a cold and lost his voice and his mother had done a casting call to replace him.

It was ridiculous to remember that now, but there it was.

"Who was Heidi to you?" she asked.

The world went still. Soundless.

"Harrison?"

"Is that what my father was talking to you about?"

"He said I wasn't the first woman to try to con you. She was the girl in the car crash?"

He turned away from her, back to the desk, that safe island of thank-you notes and emails, but she grabbed his elbow. She grabbed him, pulling him back to her. "How do you know about that?" He finally found his voice.

"My brother sent me some information about your family when we got married, just so I would know what I was walking into, and then, later, I was able to put it together."

"Did it say she was pregnant?"

"No," she gasped. She still held onto him, her fingers stroking the weave of his shirtsleeve, like she was petting him. He wondered if she even knew she was doing that. "Tell me."

"Heidi was a twenty-five-year-old intern from Iowa during Dad's vice-presidential campaign. She was bright and beautiful. Ambitious. Very ambitious."

"You think she slept with your dad to get ahead?"

"She slept with *me* to get ahead."

Her mouth fell open and he reached out; with his thumb against her skin, he tilted her mouth closed. Her hand at his elbow, his fingers at her cheek—the little points of contact that were somehow paramount, somehow keeping him on his feet.

"I've never told anyone that."

"Harrison," she sighed, the word, her eyes, her whole body saturated with sympathy.

"It's okay," he said. Though it wasn't really. Like a wound that never saw sunlight or fresh air, it just kind of festered, hidden away. He remembered the pain of realizing he was being used as if it were ten minutes ago. "I'm not the first twenty-two-year-old kid who thought he was falling in love."

"Doesn't make it any less awful."

"True. It was awful."

"What happened?"

"I met Heidi her first week on staff. We went on a date a week later and not long after that, we had sex for the first time. I didn't want anyone to know about it; I thought I'd get in trouble. So we were hot and heavy for about two months, and I brought her to the house a few times under the guise of work. In hindsight, I should have seen it. The way she was always angling for my dad, but . . . I don't know, I was young and stupid and I wanted to believe she wanted me for me. After a while she stopped returning my calls and she got harder to pin down about seeing each other. And then the rumors started about her and Dad. I didn't believe it, but then Dad and Heidi got in the car accident and they both lived, but she had a miscarriage."

"Did you think the baby was yours?"

"I absolutely did. I was . . . I was totally devastated. But then I overheard my parents fighting at the hospital, and Heidi was only one month along, so the baby couldn't have been mine—we hadn't had sex in months. And then Dad . . . Dad confessed to the whole affair. My mother said she'd take care of it and as soon as Heidi could travel, she was gone."

"All that were left were rumors?"

"There were always rumors about my dad. About women and drinking and corruption, but I never believed them. When I was younger, my dad walked on water, but once I saw what happened with Heidi, I could never look at him the same way."

"Heidi was far from innocent."

"That doesn't make the way my family dealt with it any better, does it? She'd miscarried, nearly died, and my mom gave her money, doped her up, had her sign a confidentiality agreement and then sent her away. I mean, I thought the whole point was to hold ourselves to a better standard. She was an employee and half his age. The power dynamics of it all are totally skewed."

"I'm not Heidi."

"I know you're not."

"No. I don't think you do. I'm not Heidi angling after the family dynasty. And I'm not Heidi getting used and discarded, either."

He turned away, because he really didn't believe that. There were a thousand forks in the road between them—different ways things could pan out. And almost all of them involved her getting set aside with a bunch of cash once she'd served her purpose.

Unless I can convince her to stay, he thought, but he knew that everything he'd done toward her, every hot-and-cold moment, only alienated her further. Pushed her to this point—of proposing separate lives. Separate homes.

"This explains a lot about how you reacted to my being pregnant."

"I'm sorry for that," he said, turning back to her. "For the way I acted in your apartment."

"That's why you wanted to marry me," she said. "The thing you said about making your father's mistakes."

Her fingers were still touching him, and he knew, he really did, that he should step away, break the connection, but he didn't want that. He didn't want that at all.

He wanted more connection.

Like a dog begging for more affection, he pressed harder into her hand.

It was odd how little he knew about her, how narrow their association was. For instance, he didn't know what her face looked like in sunlight until that first press conference (beautiful, was the answer); he didn't know what she liked on her tacos, what she took in her coffee. He didn't know if she had nightmares or remembered her dreams at all.

She'd slept on her stomach that night at the hotel, her hair a curtain he'd lifted with his fingers so he could watch her for a few moments longer before leaving.

But he knew that she was fierce. Loyal. Proud. Funny. Smart. In some ways smarter than him and Wallace, with all their degrees and experience.

If he reached forward—just a little, not even a full extension of his arm—he'd touch that big button. The body beneath it.

"Do it," she breathed. Startled, he looked up, caught her eyes. Caught her reading him like a book, all those things he thought he kept so secret.

"Touch me."

Without thought he put his hand to her stomach, that button, the small curve of her tummy beneath it. And then both of his hands were on her, his arms around her. His body finding those places on hers where they fit, somehow. Where all their edges didn't clash or cut. Where their unlikely softness found an answering softness.

She kissed him. Or maybe he kissed her; he didn't know. They kissed. Carefully. Like they'd never kissed before. It was their first kiss here, in the middle of their messy reality. She tasted like mint tea and Chapstick and something strong and bittersweet.

He wrapped his arms around her back and picked her up, just lifted her off her feet, because despite the size of her spirit, and her attack, and her bravery, she was actually quite small. He kept forgetting that. Kept forgetting that she was tiny. And pregnant.

With his baby. And suddenly, thinking about the baby while holding her in his arms—that changed things. That changed everything. He'd been alienated for a very long time, and now he wanted to be welcomed in.

"I don't know how to ask for things," he said. "Real things. I mean, my parents didn't exactly support that kind of behavior."

"You're a grown man, Harrison."

"That only makes it harder."

She hummed, kissed his throat.

"You just open your mouth and ask, I suppose," she said.

"I don't want you to stay here," he said, pulling away to see her face, flushed and beautiful. Soft and rounder than she'd been just a few weeks ago. But her eyes were sharp. "I want you to come with me. I want to watch your body change and go to doctor's appointments. I want to be there when the baby is born."

"Then I'll come with you," she whispered, and kissed him while he carried her into his bedroom.

Their clothes fell off without any effort on their part and when he laid her down on the bed, it didn't feel like his bed, like the place he'd spent so many lonely nights. It felt new.

She was soft and supple under his hands and he found himself obsessed with learning the edges of her, her exact perimeters. The curves at her breasts, her hips, the tops of her thighs. Her belly. The span of her rib cage, the circumference of her wrists, the distance between her chin and collarbone.

The exact beats per minute of her heart against his.

And then, that belly, its upward arch, the downward slope, the tautness of the skin just under her belly button.

"It's changed," she breathed as he pressed kisses there. "It's round."

It's beautiful. So beautiful.

He rolled her to her side, cradling her against his chest, his arms wrapped around her.

Pressing his forehead against her shoulder, he prayed for strength or softness or a sign that this was the right thing and that he could keep doing the right thing. That he was strong enough to be the man he wanted to be with her.

"Please," she whispered pushing against him.

That was all the sign he needed. With a groan, he entered her from behind.

And it was lazy. And sweet. And new.

But also familiar in the most perfect way.

Like they'd been doing this all along.

She cried out, burying her face in the pillow. Her breasts in his hands trembled as she shook and after a moment, after she laughed and blew her hair out of her face, she reached for him, rolling to her stomach and pulling him up onto her back.

He thrust into her, into that hot, clinging welcome, and he felt her thrusting back, meeting him halfway. More than halfway.

It was the most honest and giving thing he'd been a part of.

And it felt so damn good to be a part of it.

It felt so damn good to lie there with her in his arms, sticking to each other as sweat dried on their bodies.

"Why are you called Ryan?" he asked. It was late, but neither of them seemed inclined toward sleep, as if reluctant to let this go.

"They thought I was going to be a boy and so they only picked out a boy name."

"It didn't matter that you were a girl?"

"Dad said it would make me tough."

He laughed against her shoulder. They were spooned, her back to his chest, and he was tracing the outside edges of her tattoo with his fingers. Every once in a while she would flinch away.

"Ticklish?" he asked.

"Yes."

"Tell me about your tattoo," he said, tracing the woman's blissed-out face. "It's really beautiful."

"It's Ophelia." She rolled farther onto her stomach so he could see the whole thing. The flowers and the gauzy dress floating around her. The flowers around her feet, twining up her leg.

"Hamlet's Ophelia?"

"She's drowning in the river."

"Dying for love?"

"I got it after my divorce."

A reminder. She didn't have to say it. He leaned forward and kissed the vines dragging Ophelia to her watery death.

"I'm not him," he felt compelled to say.

"I know.

"I went to see your mother yesterday," she said after a while.

"Why?"

"The Paul thing. She was looking for him so she could pay him to be silent."

"That sounds like my mother."

"She loves your father. Or did, at one point."

He pushed his face into her hair, unwilling to think of how much pain that kind of love must cause.

"Is there a way to do this," she whispered, "so we don't turn out like them?"

"Of course." He wrapped his arms around her, willing it to be true.

And then she turned in his arms, kissing his lips, wrapping her arms around him, drowning him in a different kind of love.

Chapter 24

The phone ringing beside the bed woke her up. Seven a.m.

Harrison had left an hour ago, pressing a kiss to her forehead and telling her he'd see her later. She'd tried to get him to get back into bed with her, but he'd laughed and urged her to sleep. Which she'd done immediately.

She fumbled for the phone, knocking over the clock and a glass of water.

"Hello?" she croaked when she finally got the phone in her hand.

"Ryan?" It was Wallace and something in his voice made her sit up. "We need you. Get down here as soon as you can."

Twenty minutes later she was on her way to the office, feeling slightly like Lip Girl to the rescue.

We need you, were seriously heady words.

Her body was still warm in the memory of last night, in all the things that she and Harrison had said to each other and all the things they hadn't yet. This unlikely relationship had become even more surprising and she didn't even bother to stop herself as she tipped back again into love.

She got out of the car and walked into the office where she was met with a solid wall of anxiety. Everyone was staring at their computer or phone, watching something on the screen.

Her stomach dropped into her shoes.

Paul. It had to be Paul.

This wasn't Lip Girl to the rescue. Lip Girl doesn't save the day, she ruins the politician. That's how this story goes.

"Is it Paul?" She asked, convinced that on every single screen it would be her ex-husband, smarmy and awful, spouting horrible lies, or even worse truths, about her.

"Worse," Wallace said, looking twenty years older. His skin ashy, his eyes dull. It was Wallace, defeated. Harrison came up behind him, his golden patina rubbed down to steel.

"What could possibly be worse?" she asked.

"Heidi," Harrison said. "She's given an interview about all of it. The money. The baby. The affair. All of it."

Her head buzzed. *Impossible,* she thought. *That's impossible.*

But of course it wasn't.

It was just like opening the door expecting to see a terrible storm raging, and instead finding a nuclear holocaust.

"How bad is it?" she asked.

"As bad as it can be," Harrison said. "It's over."

"What's over?" she asked.

"The campaign," Harrison said. "Maybe my career."

"Don't say that!" she cried.

"You haven't seen it, Ryan," he sighed. "It's bad."

"Then show me the video. Let me see how bad it is."

The men, like machines that had just stopped, didn't move and so she walked past them to Harrison's office. "Come on," she said, forcing them to follow her. She stood at the door and let them walk in past her and then she closed the door behind her. The roar of the outer office turned to a hum through the wood.

Her stomach ached and her hands were sweating but she kept her cool. Someone had to. Someone had to have perspective. Wallace walked around Harrison's desk and opened his laptop. "So, the interview was aired on

WSB and WAGA, and Glendale is already putting up some television spots, talking about the ad. He did a radio interview with Scott Slade this morning, and I'm sure there will be more to come." Wallace clicked around on the laptop but she was watching Harrison who stood by the window in a sheet of early sunlight, hair sparkling, eyes stern, his arms crossed over his chest. They'd made love last night. Slow and steady, his arms around her. They told each other secrets. The lovely, innocent ones that stitched them closer with affection and delight.

It was not perfect between them by any stretch. But it was honest and real.

And worth fighting for.

He was worth fighting for.

She just needed to convince him of that.

"Here you go," Wallace said and flipped the laptop to face her. Harrison turned to stare out the window and she wondered how many times he'd watched this footage. How sick he must feel.

Bracing herself she turned toward the screen.

A woman about her age, wearing a dark winter coat, stepped up to a microphone held by a person off camera. Wind kicked up and blew blond hair across her face, which she pushed away with a mittened hand. Behind her was a ranch-style house surrounded by a dry, yellow winter lawn filled with kids' toys and Mother Mary in a bathtub altar. Mary was kind of tipped over, leaning against the tub, having a rest.

"Go ahead," a voice said offscreen. "Just repeat what you told me."

"It's Maynard!" Ryan said, and she turned to see if Harrison recognized the voice, but he had no reaction.

"When I was twenty-five, I worked as an intern for the Montgomery family during Governor Montgomery's vice-presidential campaign. In that time . . ." Heidi glanced up at the camera and Ryan saw this woman's pain from years ago, fossilized by years and plans gone wrong. Maynard had unearthed all that emotion, and Heidi was furious and ready for revenge. "I had an affair with Ted Montgomery."

Harrison sighed and put his hand against the window as if his legs were losing strength.

"Our sexual relationship resulted in a pregnancy. Ted Montgomery drove me home one night. He was drunk and we were in an accident. I broke four ribs, my arm, I was unconscious for three days, and when I woke up I found out I had lost the baby. At that time, Patty Montgomery offered to pay all my medical bills and more on top of that to go home and never mention my relationship with the Montgomerys."

"And you agreed?" Maynard asked. Was it Ryan's imagination or did he sound triumphant?

"I didn't have any insurance. My parents would have had to sell the farm. I . . . I didn't have a choice."

"Is there something you would like to tell the Montgomerys or the voters of Georgia?"

She looked dead center in the camera. "The voters of Georgia need to know the kind of people they're electing. Harrison Montgomery knew what his parents did and he let it happen."

"Oh my God," she groaned, and stumbled back into one of the chairs in front of Harrison's desk. The leather was hot from the sun pouring in the windows and she barely felt it burn the skin on the back of her legs. "Can't we sue her or something?"

"It's the truth," Harrison said.

"What about Maynard?"

"He was just doing his job," Harrison said. "And pretty well, too. No one else has found Heidi."

"So what do we do?" she asked, stunned to see these two powerful, intelligent men so defeated. "Do we get out there and tell people how she lied to you? How you didn't know about the baby or the affair until it was all too late?"

"What's the point?" Harrison asked.

"The point is your campaign! Your honor. Your . . . our future." *Oh God,* she suddenly realized in a whole new way what Patty meant by keeping Harrison focused.

And then she realized that Patty would never get a chance to be the woman she could have been. She'd never have a chance to hold an office because of all the mistakes she'd made for her husband.

There was a terrible lesson in there.

"The point is you, Harrison."

Harrison shrugged, as if none of it mattered. As if there weren't something bigger at stake. "We concede."

Wallace nodded.

Ryan wanted to tear out her hair.

"These are your parent's mistakes, Harrison!" she cried. "Not yours."

"You heard what she said," he countered. "I knew about it. I have known about all of it, and I've done nothing but keep the family secrets. I'm just as guilty as they are."

There was a knock at the door and Harrison yelled, "Go away!" just as Ryan opened it.

It was Noelle, her hair back in that bun, her eyes serious behind her glasses.

Wallace sighed. "If you're here to tell us how pissed off Patty—"

"No," Noelle said. "I'm not here for Patty, though she's a mess. I swear her head about spun around. Ted's already drinking. It's kind of a shit show at the mansion. I'm here because I have an idea," Noelle said.

"Come on in." Ryan opened the door wide. "We need ideas."

"We need to do a press conference and give a statement. Like ten minutes ago."

"That's hardly an idea," Wallace criticized, and Noelle's cheeks turned red. "The same bullshit press conference voters have seen from every politician in a scandal, with the contrite hand wringing and the dutiful spouse—"

"That's where we flip it." Noelle turned and pointed to Ryan. "Ryan. We get Ryan to address this. She gives the statement, Harrison answers questions."

"That's ridiculous," Harrison muttered, but Wallace didn't jump in with his agreement and Harrison turned to look at his manager with horrified eyes.

"No, it's not," Wallace said, the light coming back on behind his eyes.

"She's kind of a press darling," Noelle said.

"This is a great idea. A great idea," Wallace said, and started spinning into action calling reporters.

"You're not listening to me," Harrison said. "I'm not going to let Ryan stand up there and tell any more lies!"

"I won't lie," she said. "We'll come clean. We'll come totally clean. Oh my God, Harrison, think of how good this will feel."

"And it might not work," Wallace said. "But it will set you up for the future."

"The future," he scoffed, and turned around again.

Ryan approached Harrison at the window.

He was staring down at a woman pushing a stroller across the street, a baby's black curls, like dandelion fluff, visible past the side of the sun visor.

"This isn't your fault," she said.

"I knew this was going to happen," he said. "At some point, this was inevitable. Secrets don't stay secret forever."

"I told you, you should have 8-Miled it," she said, trying to make a joke.

"I'm so sorry you're in this."

"I'm not," she said, and he rolled his eyes toward her. "I'm not sorry at all."

He looked at her, really looked at her. And she realized how she'd gotten used to his gravitas; what had made him stand out in that bar among the lesser men had grown commonplace. Which made it impossible to doubt him when he said, "You will be. It's going to get worse."

Within the hour they managed to get the press conference put together and Harrison's campaign office was once again full of reporters. Ryan stood at the podium, Harrison at her side, and had a serious case of déjà vu.

And just like before, the second she was done with her prepared statement, reporters' hands shot up.

"Harrison, did you know what your parents did?" asked Agnes, a woman she'd grown to like a little over the last few weeks.

Harrison stepped forward. "I was twenty-two at the time," he said. "I understood that my father and Heidi had an affair and that my mother was paying Heidi money to leave and not say anything."

"Did you know about the pregnancy?" Agnes asked.

Ryan squeezed Harrison's hand, urging him to just tell the whole truth. Harrison had decided that because Heidi hadn't brought up the affair the two of them had, he wouldn't either. Which Ryan had thought was pretty generous, but Harrison had been adamant that the scandal was scandalous enough.

Which was more than true.

"I wish I could say I didn't, but I did," he answered. "The way my sister and I grew up wasn't by any stretch normal. And there wasn't room in our lives for us to have opinions. We served the campaigns and other than that, we were quiet. It's ugly as I look back on it, and obviously my sister learned far faster than I did to be her own woman. I'm still trying to understand what my parents did and why. And I know that's not a great answer, but it's the one I have."

"What about your marriage, Harrison?" Maynard, standing in the corner looking smug and exhausted, drew the attention of everyone in the room. "Is Ryan pregnant?"

"That's a private matter between my wife and me," Harrison said.

"Don't you think your family has lied to the people of this state enough?" Maynard shot back.

"I'm pregnant," Ryan said, stepping forward, trying to stop the small fire of Maynard's animosity before it spread through the room and they had a dozen journalists demanding more and more answers. "We were going to wait to announce it after the election, but now is as good a time as any. Harrison and I are having a baby. I'm due in April."

"My math isn't great, but that would mean you were pregnant before you got married," Maynard said.

"This press conference is over," Harrison said, lifting his hand against the explosion of flashbulbs and reporters' questions. And with his arm over her shoulder, he escorted her away from the podium and back into his office while Wallace and the rest of the staff wrapped up the press conference.

The silence between them in the office throbbed. It pounded. They stared at each other, white-faced and shocked.

"Why did you tell them that?" he asked.

"Because we're being honest."

"Do you have any idea what they are going to do to you now?"

She did, a little. The ocean had been chummed and the sharks were circling and because Harrison was already in the water, she'd thrown herself in with him.

"We're in this together," she said, with more hope than anything else, because she could feel him putting distance between them where last night there had been none.

"You should leave. Right now," he said.

In answer, she sat down on the couch, staking her fragile claim in his life.

It was proven to her over and over again in the following weeks that there was nothing the world liked better than pulling a person down off a pedestal. Harrison and his family were destroyed in the press.

And then they went after her.

And not being a man she couldn't be sure, but it seemed like there was something viciously gleeful about the way the world went after women. She went from respected wife to dirty whore in three news cycles.

And then the Lip Girl footage surfaced.

After weeks of it being a nonissue, it was everywhere.

And the media ate it up, as if that seventeen-year-old version of her kissing a man and then turning around and saying "try it, he'll like it" in impossibly tight jeans was all the proof everyone needed that she was no good and never had been.

There were people outside their condo holding signs that said "slut." She was accosted outside her doctor's office by a man urging her to repent her sins all while he did his best to grab her ass. Harrison shoved the man away, much to the delight of the photographers who had started following her.

Someone threw an egg at her at a daycare ribbon-cutting ceremony.

Even going to the grocery store was an event. It got to the point she had to seriously consider if the errand was worth leaving the condo for.

But Harrison campaigned. Nineteen hour days, head up, eyes forward, ignoring the viciousness people tried to throw at him. Unless it was about her, at which point he defended her to the ground.

But he was losing. They all knew it.

The night after the footage was released everywhere, she woke up alone in Harrison's bed, which wasn't unusual these days. She stared at the ceiling listening for the clack of his laptop keys, but she didn't hear it. Didn't hear him downstairs pacing from the windows to the door.

The other few nights she'd gone to find him, he'd shrugged off her concern. Her touch. Putting distance between them with platitudes and chilly kisses. She gave him some room, because she understood that this sucked for him on a seriously personal level, and there wasn't much she could do but be there and wait for him to work through it.

She shuffled downstairs, prepared to find him in front of the TV watching the smear campaigns, but the television was dark, as was the rest of the condo.

"Harrison?"

"Ryan?" His voice came from the back bedroom. "You all right?"

He came out of the bedroom just as she walked up to the door. "What are you doing?" she asked.

"I'm going to bed," he said.

"Down here?"

"I don't want to disturb you."

"Disturb . . . Harrison?" she couldn't believe he was saying this with a straight face. "What is happening here?"

"You need sleep, and I'm working late . . ."

"Stop, please. Stop talking like this is reasonable. Is this about the Lip Girl thing?"

"Of course it is!" he snapped.

She gasped. "Do I have to defend my seventeen-year-old self to you?" she asked, stunned and pissed.

"Do I have to explain to you how much it kills me that you're being dragged through the mud, just for being in my life?"

He was ravaged in the shadows, torn apart, and she felt like a triage nurse unsure of what to address first. His guilt, his self-exile?

"Do I have to explain to you that lying in bed next to you and our baby makes me wish I could go back in time and never go to New York and demand you marry me?"

"Don't say that," she said. "I don't wish it. I don't wish that at all!"

She reached for him but he stepped away. He lifted his hand, which wouldn't have stopped her, but the anguished guilt all over him—that stopped her in her tracks.

"It's better this way," he said.

And then he turned around and closed the door behind him, leaving her alone in the hallway. The furnace kicked on and warm air blew down on her from the vent in the ceiling.

He'd turned on the heat. For her.

Wait it out, she told herself as she climbed the stairs back to his bedroom. *Until after the election. When this is all over, he'll come back around.*

But it was more hope than belief.

Chapter 25

The morning of the election, Harrison slipped the scrambled egg he'd made for Ryan onto a plate while she was in the shower and he set out her red teacup full of water. The prenatal vitamin and the Compazine.

At some point he'd started doing this for her every morning. And kept doing it even though he couldn't look her in the eye, didn't sleep beside her at night.

He put his head in his hands.

I've failed her so much.

There was a knock at the door and expecting Wallace, the only person who showed up at his condo in the early morning hours as if it were normal, he yelled, "Come on in."

The door opened and to his shock, it was his parents standing there. Or versions of them, anyway.

The polished strangers he'd grown up with were nearly broken. Stripped of the reputation they'd fought tooth and nail for, they looked painfully human. Frail. Old, even. Dad especially.

"What the hell are you doing here?" Harrison asked.

Dad glanced at Mom, who was the talker, the answerer of questions, the person first in the doorway, but she rested her hand against the door frame as if her engine had just stopped.

Dad swallowed, his chest lifting and falling with heavy breaths as he looked at his wife, and Harrison could not imagine what emotions swam between them.

But it was obvious that they were big and they were killing them.

"I resigned this morning. It will be on the news, shortly, I'm sure," Ted said, and then cleared his throat. "We're going to visit your mother's sister in Arizona."

Harrison blinked. Mother's sister, or "that intolerable hippie" as she'd been called in their house, was about as last resort as it got.

"We just . . . wanted to let you know," Ted said. The two of them still lingered in the doorway.

Mother lifted dry, ravaged eyes to his and he flinched from all that was revealed.

"Don't," he said, before she opened her mouth. He could not take her apology now, years too late when she had nothing left to lose.

"Son," Mother whispered, "we're so sorry you got dragged into this—"

"Don't pretend to be pained on my behalf," he snapped, the freeze giving way under fire. Under a terrible burning anger. Being angry with his parents was safe. It was familiar. It was totally okay, and he latched onto that with a vicious kind of glee. "I've been a prop my entire life. You've manufactured your sympathy in whatever passes for your heart because that is the emotion some polling group told you to feel when your son loses everything he has spent his life working for."

Mother's ravaged guilt turned to surprise, and if he hadn't spent thirty-two years in her company, he might have believed her. "Is that what you think? That I am pretending to feel bad for you?"

"Yes, Mother," he said. "That is what I think. That is what I have been taught to expect from you. Don't break character now."

"Stop! Both of you, just stop!" Ted cut in, using a hard voice Harrison had not heard from his father in a very long time. Both Patty and Harrison turned to him as if astonished that he could speak. "This is my fault. All of this is my fault. And I've turned all of you into liars in order to keep my secrets. And I'm sorry. I'm more sorry than I can say. But I didn't want this life. I never wanted it. Not for a single minute."

"What are you talking about?" Harrison asked.

"Politics, the family fucking business. I knew what it did to people. How it tore families to pieces. But your mother . . ." Ted shook his head.

"Don't you dare throw that in my face. Not now," she breathed.

"I'm not throwing anything in your face," Ted said, holding out a hand to his wife that she all but slapped away with her eyes. "I'm just trying to explain to Harrison how we got here. How our family got so broken."

"And that's *my* fault?" she asked, and Harrison could only watch as his parents detonated right in front of him. "Because I wanted you to realize a tenth of your potential. Do not pretend for one minute if you'd become a teacher or a football coach or some other piece of nonsense you would have been a better man."

Mother's words sliced through Ted, leaving him smaller than Harrison had ever seen him. Tiny. Beaten.

"I'll be in the car," Mother said, her head held high as she turned and walked out of the condo.

"She's probably right," Ted whispered, staring at where she had stood. "But it's a nice dream, being a better man. A better husband. Father." Ted turned swimming eyes toward Harrison. "Listen, son, I know you have no reason to take my advice, but God, let Ryan go. Let Ryan out of this life. Give her the chance to be human far away from politics. Far away from us. If you care for her at all, it's the best thing you can do for her."

"Are you honestly trying to tell me you care about her?"

Ted pursed his lips. "I . . . I just don't want to see any

more people hurt. And if she stays she'll be hurt. You know that, son. We'll be in touch," he said, and then he, too, turned and left, shutting the door behind him.

Harrison sagged against the kitchen island, the granite countertop cold beneath his fingers.

Dad's words, they only made solid the feeling he had every day watching Ryan slog through the filth that he'd brought into her life.

She'd be better off away from him. From this life of his. From what this life would do to her, what it would ask of her. From this agreement he never should have drawn up.

In the bathroom, the shower was shut off and he imagined his wife drying off her body. Wrapping her hair in a towel. She used lotion in a blue bottle that smelled somehow like nothing else. He knew because when he was in the bathroom, he put it on his hands and felt closer to her for it.

My wife, my wife, my wife, he thought. Harrison was very good at not being selfish; for years and years he'd sublimated his minor and petty wants for what was good for the family. His father's campaigns. And then his own political aspirations.

She was the only thing he'd really been selfish about and it had blown up in his face.

In her face.

She deserves better, he thought.

He was going to have to concede tonight. And then he was going to have to let her go.

"I just can't believe people are buying this," Ashley kept saying later that night as they watched the election returns in a suite at the Hilton downtown. His sister, his staff, Ryan—they were all gathered around the television as if their watching the ship go down would change its outcome.

"I'm going to concede," Harrison said. "Put us all out of our misery."

"But what if . . ." Ashley asked, ever the optimist. His sister who didn't see obstacles. "What if things change?"

"They won't," Wallace said. He grabbed the bottle of champagne that he'd ordered from catering about five months ago, when things had looked brighter for them, and took a swig right from the bottle before handing it over to Noelle, who did the same.

"Come on," Ashley said, her wild brown curls blown so smooth. Even his sister had been forced to change in order to fit into this world he'd created. His wild, passionate, compassionate sister who grew gardens in the desert; she'd been groomed to fit into this tiny glass box that was his world, and it was the most unnatural thing he'd ever seen. "Let's give him the time he needs."

His sister pressed a kiss to his cheek and he closed his eyes at the contact. Uncomplicated and warm. Honest. Why did that have to be so rare in his life and given to him by the only two women who never really fit in it?

"I'm going to call Glendale and concede. And then we'll go down and address the staff," he told Wallace, who nodded, silent and grim-faced. All his manic energy had drained right out of him; even his red tie seemed subdued. Defeated. Harrison thought maybe they should hug it out or something, but then Wallace and his champagne bottle were gone and the moment was over.

The big suite was empty except for his wife in that wing chair across the room.

He grabbed his jacket and pushed his arms through the sleeves, finally making eye contact with Ryan, who was watching him with hot, dry eyes. In so many ways she was the smartest person he knew, savvy and wise about people, about what motivated them. She was a natural psychologist, but he wondered if she knew what he was about to do.

"You want me to come down there while you make the speech?" she asked.

"Of course."

She was gorgeous wearing a blue suit, edged with subtle elegant sequins, her hair pulled back into a sleek knot. She was wearing pearls. *Pearls*. That woman from the bar—she wouldn't have been caught dead in pearls. But it was a lie. Everything was a lie except for the cornered-rabbit, brittle look in her eye that he'd put there.

"And then you can go," he said.

Who did he think he was kidding? she wondered. *Himself, maybe.*

But not her. Definitely not her.

Brody had been right; she'd had a taste of happy and now nothing else would do.

"Go?" she asked, arching an eyebrow at him. "Where?"

"Home, I imagine." Harrison fixed his tie the same way she'd seen him do it a thousand times before.

She knew what he meant; she found herself braced for it because the last few weeks he'd been maneuvering them to this place.

But she needed it confirmed. Spelled out in black and white.

Because if he meant to dismiss her, she would not make it easy.

"The condo?"

"You still have your apartment in New York."

"No."

"We'll put you up in a hotel for the time being."

"Hotel," she breathed.

She felt sick about the way this election was turning

out. For Harrison and for herself. It was an awful experience hearing people talk terrible shit about you day in and day out. Things she didn't deserve but somehow had to take because she was a public figure. And not responding, ignoring every asshole that called her a slut and gold digger, was making her crazy. Turning her inside out with anger and a strange paranoia.

She didn't deserve this.

But it was happening, and they had to figure out a way to survive it.

But it seemed Harrison, who had clutched at her, naked and raw and human, and was now unable to look at her, was going to throw in the towel.

Ryan stood, glad for her heels because it got her close to getting up in Harrison's face. "I never pegged you for a coward," she said.

"Are you telling me you actually want to stay here and continue to get dragged through the mud?"

"Yes." Unequivocally yes. "I won't say it doesn't suck; it does. But if this is where you are, it's where I will be."

He shook his head, tugging the cuffs of his shirt past the edge of his jacket.

"The clause in the contract. I'm agreeing to let you go."

"Well, I'm not offering to leave."

His eyes flew to hers and she saw there the fierceness with which he wanted her. The desire he had for her, which was nice, but a cold comfort as he was pushing her away with both hands.

"You wanted to stay here, remember?" he asked. "You said I could go to Washington and you'd stay here. It was what you wanted."

Oh, how obvious he was being, so cutting and solicitous at the same time, as if being polite would make it better.

"Yeah, that was what I wanted before you fucked me like your life depended on it."

"Look, it didn't work. In the end the act didn't work."

"Then let's stop acting!"

He stared hard at her, right through her. Right through that threadbare old prom dress of Mom's, the blue sequins she wore now, the boots from that night at the hotel. His eyes blazed through every version and every persona and she had no idea what he saw.

But for the first time in maybe ever, she knew exactly who she was, and she was ready to fight to be seen.

"That's what I'm doing," he said, and her jaw snapped shut so hard she bit her tongue. "I'm stopping the act. Look at what is happening to you, Ryan. Can you look at me, at this situation, this marriage, and say it's any better than what you had with Paul?"

She gasped, stunned that he'd bring up Paul.

"First of all, you are nothing like Paul. And this marriage is nothing like what I had with him—"

"I'm not beating you up," he said. "I'm not threatening your family, but isn't being with me diminishing you? They're calling you a slut, Ryan. Because of me! And you're pretending like it doesn't matter."

"Don't, Harrison—don't take responsibility for something that isn't your fault!"

"Then whose responsibility is it?" he demanded.

"Sometimes things just are," she said, but he wasn't buying it. "Fine," she continued, flush with bravery. "I'll stop pretending. I'm falling in love with you. And I think you're falling in love with me too."

Her words echoed and re-echoed as if she were at the bottom of a well, dark and deep.

His face didn't change, as if her confession didn't even register. The words bounced off the stone rock face of him.

"Harrison?" she asked.

"This was a mistake we shouldn't have tried to make right."

She sucked in a furiously wounded breath. He was so persuasive, so believable as this cold, heartless man that she was scared he would believe it. He would convince himself.

And he would be lost to her. Totally lost.

Take it back, she thought. *Take it back. You have to. We don't stand a chance unless you take it back.*

But he didn't.

This is when sacrifice ceases to matter. Right here. Right now.

When he no longer cared that she would give him everything.

"Fuck you," she breathed. "You want a divorce, come and find me."

Chapter 26

Harrison conceded. He made his gracious speech. He thanked his staff, his voters. He promised that he wasn't done, was far from done, that he would keep working for the people of the great state of Georgia. And he looked into all those faces and he was amazed that they believed him.

It wasn't that he thought he was lying. Or telling the truth. He was just hollow. Words falling from his mouth without any meaning.

Staff left, and Jill was crying. Again. He patted her back, said some reassuring words, and she left, telling him she believed in him. Would work with him again once he was ready to come back.

Ashley left, back to Bishop. "Stop being such an idiot," she said, through her driver's-side window. "Stop pretending you like being a son of a bitch and get over yourself."

"Take care of that man of yours," he said, ignoring her insults.

"We take care of each other," she said. "That's the way love works."

He watched her go until her taillights became just two of hundreds on the highway out of town.

"Ryan took your car," Wallace said, coming up on his left. He smelled like champagne and defeat.

"What?"

"She took your car back to the condo, got her stuff, and left."

"With my car and driver?"

Wallace nodded.

Harrison sagged. Would have fallen backward onto the pavement outside the Hilton if Wallace hadn't been there with a friendly hand on his shoulder.

"You must have pissed her off good," Wallace said.

"I told her I wanted a divorce."

"Why the hell would you do that?"

"Because the whole thing was a bad idea. My life is all wrong for a woman like her."

"Your life. God, man, you talk about being a Montgomery like that's all you got."

"It is."

"Bullshit. Your feelings for her, it wasn't an act. It was never an act. Every time the two of you walked into the room the place lit up, because it was obvious that you felt so much for each other. I know you, Harrison, and you can't act that well. That's why the whole world fell in love with her at the beginning, because they saw the truth of her. Sure, we gave her some things to say, put her in some fine clothes, but that was all just frosting. She's real and honest and all the skeletons are out of the closet now. She's perfect for you, jackass; you're just being stupid."

I'm falling in love with you and I think you're falling in love with me.

"This whole proposal wasn't fair for her. She had no idea who I was."

"Yeah, and I think that's why you married her. Come on, I'll give you a ride," he volunteered.

"Aren't you drunk?"

"I stopped drinking hours ago."

"Then . . . yeah, I'll take a ride."

They crossed the parking lot to a beat-up blue hatchback.

"Don't I pay you better than this?" Harrison asked,

staring at the rust that threatened to take over the tire well.

"Don't speak ill of Denise—she's fickle."

"Maybe I lost this campaign because my manager is crazy."

Wallace gathered up an armful of paper coffee cups and burrito wrappers from the front passenger seat and tossed them in the back.

Harrison sat on something squishy, but he didn't care enough to investigate.

They drove in exhausted silence across town.

"Why do you wear such ugly ties?" Harrison asked, past the point of being polite.

"Slander. They're not ugly."

"They're terrible."

Wallace smiled. "My mom bought them for me, every year for my birthday since I was a baby. Most of the time she could only afford things from the thrift shops."

"I know I pay you enough to buy new ties."

"I don't want new ties," he said. "I want to remember where I came from. How my mom always prepared me for something better."

Harrison looked out the window, the green of Atlanta rushing by.

He'd just pushed his only shot of something better right out of his life and then sealed the door, ensuring he'd suffocate. Alone.

Ryan had brought hope with her. Change. Laughter. Happiness.

Love.

Everything he'd never thought he'd have. Everything he'd never been prepared to receive. They were gifts left unused because he didn't know what the hell to do with them.

Wallace came to a stop in front of his building. The windows of his condo were dark and he realized she wasn't going to be up there. Her red cup, her suits, the blanket and laptop on the couch. Her sweet skin in his bed. Her hair tangled in his fingers.

That was all gone.

"You want to come up for a drink?" he asked, because he did not want to be alone in that condo with the ghost of her and the failure of his campaign.

Wallace squinted up through the windshield. "I want to come up and get blind drunk."

Blind drunk sounded good. Sounded right.

I think I've made a mistake, he thought. *I think I've made a terrible mistake.*

"Let's get to it, then," he said, and led Wallace up to his condo.

Where every minute he felt worse and worse.

Dawn did the house no favors.

"This is it?" Dan, the driver, asked. Clearly he wasn't all that impressed with 238 Belgrade Street. She couldn't blame him. Dawn's light had nothing to do with the chipped paint on the windowsills. The torn screen in the door. The broken cement steps. The whole house, the whole row of old houses, their plain brick fronts, just seemed to sag, exhausted and worn down.

The Burg had changed, fancy coffee shops and stores that sold throw pillows had crept in along the fringes, but the heart of it was the same. Working class. Working poor. Lots of Polish and American flags hanging limp from white metal railings.

"The old homestead," she said. They'd split up the drive, she and Dan, but the twelve hours had been long and she was punchy with exhaustion and nerves. "You want to hear a joke?"

"No."

She ignored him. "My girlfriend asked me to kiss her where it's smelly, so I took her to Bridesburg."

"That's disgusting."

It was. But she used to think it was funny.

"Is . . . anyone home?" he asked.

If I'm lucky, no.

She got out of the car and checked under the window air conditioner for the key they always kept taped there. It was a new air conditioner, but the key was still there.

Some things never change, she thought, both comforted and terrified by the thought.

"Go ahead and go. You must be beat," she told Dan after she grabbed her bags from the trunk of the car.

"You sure?" he asked, looking up at the house like it meant to eat her. Maybe she shouldn't have filled so many hours of that car ride telling him how much her sister hated her.

"Sure. Go. Get yourself a hotel room and some room service." She opened her purse and started to give him some money.

"Stop, Ryan," he said, putting his hand over her purse. "I'm not taking your money. Look, I want to say, all that shit that went down with Harrison? It's bullshit. Don't let that noise get to you."

The distance from Atlanta and the election helped her understand that, but it wouldn't change the fact that Harrison had just exiled her.

Man, wasn't that a familiar story. Constantly getting kicked out of her own goddamned life.

Enough of that nonsense.

"Thank you, Dan," she said, and kissed his cheek.

"I hope I'll see you again," he said. "You and Harrison, you guys made sense."

She laughed out loud at that. "Nothing about us made sense," she said. "Not one thing. But thank you." She kissed his cheek and then stood on the curb, her beat-up duffel bag at her feet, and watched him drive away.

The house loomed behind her, full of all of her mistakes and memories.

And she was done being kept out of it. Done being ignored and pushed aside.

Key in hand, she opened the broken screen door, letting it rest against her back as she put the key into the lock, but before she could turn it the door opened.

Nora stood there in a bathrobe, a coffee cup steaming in her hand.

How was it possible in the six years that had passed since she'd seen her sister, Nora hadn't changed at all? It was as if this house had some kind of magic hold over time.

She still looked just like Dad. White-blond hair, pin straight and cut off at her chin. She was square and sturdy, but small all the same. For years people made the mistake of underestimating Nora because she was cute. Her face was heart-shaped porcelain dominated by blue eyes and a wide pink mouth.

Her nickname in the neighborhood had been Kewpie for a while, until she got caught kissing Jason Marx behind the Gas 'N Go, and then she was called Gas 'N Go.

This neighborhood did not look away from your mistakes. Mistakes got poked at until the blood was all gone and you got numb to the pain. It was what everyone thought made them tough growing up here, but really all it did was make it harder to leave. Make it harder to fit in anywhere else.

And her sister—smart, beautiful, tough, and resilient— was the proof of that. She could have gone anywhere, been anything, but this neighborhood made you believe this was the only place you belonged.

"Nora."

It was all she could say, because every single speech she'd concocted over the years felt stupid now. Being contrite didn't work anymore, because she'd done her penance. Being belligerent didn't work either, because she was too damn old to hold onto these grudges.

"Nice suit." Nora jerked her chin out as her eyes took in the glittering sequins. The pearls. The fantastic shoes, none of which she'd taken the time to change out of after leaving the hotel.

"It's too tight." She pulled at the waistband and too late, she realized that she was drawing attention to the small bulge at her stomach. The last thing she wanted her sister to know was that she was showing up on her doorstep in a two-hundred-dollar suit, all her things in a duffel bag, and pregnant.

"Where's your husband?"

"Atlanta."

"He lost?"

Ryan nodded.

"Because of that bullshit with his parents?"

"Can I come in, or do you want to keep interrogating me out here?"

As an answer, Nora took a sip of her coffee and Ryan could smell it. Irish Cream. Nora's favorite. She was going to make Ryan beg. Of course.

"You said I could come home."

"And then I said you could go fuck yourself."

"I can't apologize to you any more than I have," she said, taking sips of her own pride. "I have nowhere else to go and even if I did, I wouldn't go there. I want to come home, Nora. I want to see Daddy and Olivia. I want . . ." A giant gulp of pride and courage. "I want my family back. It's been six years. Isn't that long enough?"

Nora didn't say anything, her blue-gray eyes unreadable, her posture unforgiving.

Ryan had nothing left to cling to. No pride. No animosity. No hurt feelings. Nothing.

Just as she opened her mouth to say please, Nora stepped aside.

"Come on in," she said.

And for the first time since that night when Paul had robbed her dad of all his hard-saved money, she stepped back into her home.

"Thank you," she whispered, walking past her sister, unable to look at her because then the floodgates would open and she'd be a crying pregnant mess in sequins on the old beige carpet.

The house was the same and yet not. The same blankets were thrown over what looked like a new gray couch. The mantel over the fireplace still held the shrine to Mom, the candles and the wedding picture. The snapshots of Mom in the hospital, red-faced and beaming, holding each of them as babies. Nora's high school graduation portrait was shoved in the back and in the front there was a new one of Olivia, sitting in a spotlight, bent over the keys of a grand piano—playing her heart out.

The television was new, but it sat on the same fake wood TV stand, the corner broken in from some wrestling match between Wes and one of the Sullivans down the street.

Dad's recliner was still there. The stuffing coming out of a split at the arm.

The smell was the same. Coffee and Lysol.

Upstairs a shower came on and all the pipes throbbed and clanked at the pressure. Part of the soundtrack to her childhood.

She put her fingers to her lips and closed her eyes. Feeling in utterly equal measures the pain of having been gone, the relief at finally being back, and the strange and surprising gratitude that she'd managed to grow up and past the person she'd been when she lived here.

She'd thought for so long that this was her home. That part of her rootlessness was that she couldn't come back here. But she realized the truth in this moment. It wasn't really her home. Not anymore.

If Nora had let her come back after Paul, she might never have changed. Not really. Certainly she never would have met Harrison or gotten pregnant. But she would have stayed some version of the girl she'd been in these four walls.

Angry, mean, prideful.

Thank God, she thought, *thank God I got away.*

"How long do you need to stay?" Nora asked.

"I . . . I don't know. A week, maybe."

"Your room is still empty. You'll have to move some boxes, but it's yours."

In every variation of her homecoming that she'd imagined over the years, this nonplussed, undemanding version of her sister never made an appearance.

"Why are you doing this?" Ryan asked. "Why now?"

Nora had always been good at bad news. Ryan remembered when Nora looked her right in the eye and said Mom wasn't coming home from the hospital. That she would die in that room in Eastern, attached to the tubes and the machines. Nora had held Ryan while she cried in those stiff-backed hospital chairs. They weren't even a year apart, but Nora handled grief as if it were Play-Doh. While everyone around her was wrecked with sadness, she was able to just roll hers up into smaller and smaller pieces until she could put it away.

"Because you're here," she said, point-blank. "And you weren't before. It was easier to tell you to stay away when I wasn't looking at your face. You look like shit, by the way."

Ryan laughed, not that it was all that funny.

"And I missed you too."

"Nora?" Dad yelled from the kitchen, and her heart dropped into her stomach. "Who you talking to?"

Nora lifted an eyebrow and stepped so close, Ryan felt the edge of her coffee cup in her sternum. "You do one thing, one thing to hurt that man, and you'll never step foot inside this house again. I don't care if you're pregnant or not."

Ryan sucked in a quick breath. "You saw the news?"

"No. I looked at you. I'm a nurse, Ryan. And you have always been a shitty liar." She took a deep breath and walked to the kitchen doorway. "I've got a surprise for you, Daddy." Her tone implied that the surprise was an Ebola infection.

The kitchen was bright, the sunlight from all the back windows a kind of beacon, and she followed that light to stand beside Nora in the doorway.

Daddy, in an old pair of work pants and a gray Eagles tee shirt probably as old as Ryan, sat at the head of the beat-up Formica table, the newspaper separated and opened around him in his complicated paper-reading ritual. He wore a pair of half-glasses, which, when she shuffled guilty and anxious into the room, he slid up onto the wild shock of white hair on his head.

Age had not been kind, and he looked a little like one of those wizened troll dolls with the crazy hair.

"Is that . . ." he whispered.

"Hey, Daddy." At the sight of her father, the same but older, thinner, and more delicate somehow in that bright sunlight, the tears stormed the gates and she was overrun. So many years gone. Wasted. For what? "It's me."

Daddy glanced from Ryan to Nora.

"Don't look at *me*," Nora said, cutting across the kitchen to the coffeepot. "She just showed up at our door like a stray cat."

His throat bobbed and his hands opened and closed into fists, and she would do anything—anything at all—to change the fact that the sight of her gave him any pain.

"I told her she could stay here," Nora said.

"Really?" Daddy asked. "Will wonders never cease."

"She paid off the mortgage," Nora said with a shrug. "Started that fund for Olivia. The money she took has been paid back."

"I figure I forgot about that money a long time ago," Daddy said.

Please, Daddy. Please just get up from that chair and hug me.

And then he did; he got to his feet, the aluminum chair sliding across the old linoleum with a screech. Ryan set her bag down. Dad took a step and so did she, and then she was flying across that kitchen into his open arms. His familiar Old Spice–scented hug.

"I'm so sorry," she breathed, over and over again.

"I know," he said, stroking her hair like she was ten again. "And . . . I am too. We all are. It's going to be okay. It's all going to be okay."

It wasn't. Maybe not ever. Not after Harrison and the election. Her heart broken in that suite in Atlanta. But it felt so good to hear her dad say it after all this time.

"What's going on?" another voice asked from the back steps that led into the kitchen from the second floor.

Ryan whirled to see her little sister, Olivia, standing in the doorway.

Not so little anymore, she thought with a pang.

Olivia was a beautiful young woman. Tall and thin, with wet brown hair sliding down her back. Her wide brown eyes glanced from her to Daddy to Nora, taking it all in.

"Hey, Liv," Ryan said.

"You're back."

Ryan nodded, and Olivia slowly stepped off the last stair and crossed the kitchen. "Nora let you in?"

"I didn't really give her a choice."

That made Olivia smile, and Ryan stood in a kind of breathless wait. A painful limbo.

"Thanks for the dress you sent on my birthday."

Ryan smiled. She'd been sending Olivia tee shirts and dresses from vintage shops in the Village since she'd left Philly. And they emailed each other fairly often.

"Did it fit?"

"It's far too tight and way too short," Nora said.

Olivia, to Ryan's nearly anguished delight, rolled her eyes and Ryan didn't wait for Olivia to come to her, she just pulled her sister into her arms and hugged her. Olivia, after a minute, hugged her back. Hard.

"Nora told me about the college fund," Olivia whispered. "Thank you."

"I'm sorry I've been gone so long," she whispered, feeling the weight of all the things she'd missed in this girl's life. Boyfriends. Friendships. Broken hearts. All the concerts and practice.

"Come on, Olivia," Nora said. "Eat some breakfast; I'll get dressed and get you to school."

Nora walked past Ryan, dodging the hand Ryan reached out for her. Glaring at her over her shoulder, making it very clear that Ryan could come back in the house but Nora would not be so easily won over.

Two down, she thought, her arm slung over Olivia's shoulder, while Daddy stepped behind the stove talking about making his girls some toads in the hole.

After breakfast, Nora took Olivia to school and Ryan nearly fell asleep at the table.

"Go on up to bed," Daddy said, kissing her forehead.

"Where are you going?" she asked, wanting to linger in the warmth of his smile for as long as she could.

"Had a little fire down at the hall; we're going to start

fixing it up," he said, referring to VFW Post 2. Dad's home away from home.

"I'll come with."

"You look like you're about to fall over. Go on up to bed."

There was no point in arguing, so she climbed the old steps, skipping the second one and its squeak, out of habit, too exhausted to count the memories buzzing around her. Her room was dark but still impossibly smelled like Jean Naté and mothballs. The boxes got shoved onto the floor on the other side of the mattress by the window, and she fell face first and dreamless into the worst of the sag in the middle of her old bed.

Hours later, she woke to her sister shaking the mattress with her foot.

"Hey, get yourself up, sleepyhead."

"Is this a joke?"

"No. It's six o'clock."

"In the morning?" Had she been asleep for almost twenty-four hours?

"No. At night, and I've got to get to work. There's meatloaf downstairs, but you need to make sure Olivia does her homework and doesn't just practice all night."

"Practice . . . right." She rolled over and pushed her hair out of her face.

Nora, in blue scrubs, her hair held away from her face with a thick silver barrette, stood in the tiny space between the bed and the old beat-up dresser with all the Roxy Music and The Cure and Morrissey stickers on it from her emo music phase.

For a moment, the sight of her sister right there shrunk her lungs down to nothing.

"You got these?" Nora asked, tossing a bottle at her. Ryan didn't react fast enough and it hit her shoulder.

"Prenatal vitamins? Yes."

"Have you had an ultrasound? Because you can come into the ER later and I'll—"

"I've had an ultrasound. I wasn't due back at my doctor in Atlanta for a month. Everything is fine."

"You planning on staying for a month?"

The accusation was painfully clear.

"My life literally imploded, Nora—"

"Your life is always literally imploding."

"Look, I'm sorry everything about me is too damn messy for you. But I'm not a kid and you can't wound me anymore. You've hurt me all you can hurt me. So stop wasting your energy."

For a second they just stared at each other. Years and miles and more hurt feelings than should be held in a lifetime between them. But they were sisters. And that still mattered to her.

"I don't want to fight with you," Ryan said. "We've wasted so much time doing that."

Nora laughed and wiped her lip with her thumb, looking like a boxer getting ready to go back in the ring. "We're Kaminskis—that's all we know how to do."

Oh if that wasn't a crutch, she didn't know what was.

"Well, I'm a Kaminski," she said, throwing off her blankets and getting to her feet. God, this room was tiny. Why did it seem so big in her memory? She opened her bag and pulled out some yoga pants to pull on. "And I'm giving it up."

Nora laughed deep in her throat as if the idea were a joke, and Ryan sighed. "I am not the girl I was," she said. "I'm not picking up men and letting them tell me who I am."

"Really?" Nora asked. "You're telling me you showing up here, pregnant and broken-hearted, has nothing to do with a man?"

"It's me and the baby right now. That's it."

"That's it?"

The doubt in her sister's voice made her want to punch her in the nose, but she was rising above those instincts.

Downstairs there was a pounding on the door, and Nora swore and turned on her heel. "If that is the Davies boy from down the street coming back here to sniff around Olivia, I am going to kick his ass," she said, stomping down the steps.

Ryan threw on a tank top and ran after her sister. Because watching her sister kick a boy's ass was still a pretty good time around the Burg.

Ryan got to the bottom of the stairs just as Nora pulled open the door.

"Listen, you little shit—"

But it wasn't the boy from down the street.

It was Wallace.

Chapter 27

"You brought him here?" Ryan asked, following Wallace out the door to his rusted hatchback. She was wearing Olivia's bunny slippers but no coat, and the November wind off the Delaware cut right through her. "In that?"

"Can we leave my car out of this? And yes, I brought him here, because for two days he's been doing nothing but drinking and talking about you. And I can't take any more of it. So you get him."

"What if I don't want him?"

"This is your husband?" Nora asked over her shoulder. Wallace nodded.

"Weren't you just saying none of this was about a man?" Nora asked, and she could hear the smirk in her sister's voice.

"Wallace, this is my sister Nora. Nora, this is Wallace." They exchanged cool nods. *Oh man,* it suddenly occurred to her why she'd liked Wallace so much. He and her sister were so much alike.

"Ryan," Wallace said. "He wants to make things right."

"Then he shouldn't have made them so damn wrong."

"Bring him in," Nora said.

"Nora!" she protested.

"Let's get him inside," Wallace said, ignoring her. Nora and Wallace worked without her to get Harrison out of the car and into the house. They dropped him on his back on the couch and Wallace pulled the afghan over him.

"There you go," he said. "One husband delivered. I left Noelle at the hotel, so I'm going to get back to her."

"You can't just leave him here," she said.

"I can," Wallace said. "I am. He's in bad shape, Ryan, and I think he needs you."

"Well, I'm sick of being what he needs when he's in bad shape!"

Olivia was on the stairs and Daddy came in from the kitchen. Nora was barely keeping a straight face.

Wonderful, it was now a family affair.

"Whatever," Wallace said, throwing his hands in the air like it was that easy. "Work it out. I gotta go—I'm just about asleep on my feet."

Nora shut the door behind Wallace.

Harrison was wearing his suit pants and a white shirt that looked like he'd spilled either bourbon or coffee on it. She leaned down to sniff him. Bourbon. Definitely bourbon.

When she'd said come and find me, she'd never expected him to come in person. She expected one of those jump-out-of-the-bushes guys who deliver envelopes and say "you've been served."

But he was here. On the couch. Grandma's crocheted American flag blanket tossed over his shoulders.

"What are you doing here?" she breathed.

He snored in answer.

"That's your husband?" Olivia asked, seemingly fascinated and grossed out as only a teenage girl could be.

"Sort of," she whispered.

"Sort of like Paul was a sort of husband?" Daddy asked, his tone incredibly clear. *Has he hit you? Does he hurt you and make you think it's your fault? Does he demean you and take from you?*

She shook her head. "Whole different realm of sort of."

Daddy took off his glasses. "Well, you better come on into the kitchen and explain it to us."

Harrison tried to scrape away the metal band around his skull without opening his eyes, but somehow it wasn't coming off. It just kept getting tighter. And disturbingly, he couldn't really feel his hands. And it was so hot in the condo. Like super hot. Had Ryan turned off the AC again? She liked to make these stupid penguin jokes and they'd been waging a stealth war over the thermometer.

"Is he waking up?"

"I think so."

He pried open his eyes only to find five people staring down at him. He blinked, thinking he might be dreaming, but no, it was real. In a surreal twist on *Snow White and the Seven Dwarfs,* he was lying down on a couch, surrounded by one girl and four old men with various amounts of hair on their heads and faces and in their noses, wearing what looked like head-to-toe camouflage outfits.

The Dwarfs were going on a military mission.

"Where am I?" he tried to say, but it only came out as a creak from a throat that felt like asphalt and gravel.

"You want coffee?" the girl said.

He tried to say no thanks but it came out like "blergh firfe."

"He foreign?" one of the old guys asked.

The one with wild white hair and reading glasses perched on the end of his nose shook his head. "No clue."

"What *do* you know?" another man asked.

"I know he's on my couch and we need to get going."

"We taking him with?"

Harrison tried to say "no," but it came out as sort of a "gaaaaahhhh" sound. He had no idea where they were going, but he wanted no part of it.

"I'm not hunting with foreigners." One of the old guys walked away.

"You gonna be all right with him?" the leader of the Dwarfs asked the girl.

He realized she was sitting on the arm of the couch he was lying on and he was hot because he was practically swaddled in an American flag.

What the hell?

He found his hands and rubbed at his eyes. Not a flag, a blanket that looked like a flag.

"Sure," the girl said. Something about her seemed really familiar. The smile. Or her eyes.

How do I know her?

"If I have trouble, Ryan's upstairs," she said, and he sat up. *Ryan?*

"Where am I?" he asked.

"Philadelphia." The girl stuck out her hand. "Nice to meet you. I'm Olivia. You're my brother-in-law."

Brother-in-law. Olivia. Philadelphia.

Holy Christ, that wasn't a dream. Wallace and Noelle had driven him here to try and win back his wife.

"This . . . isn't the best first impression." He tried to sit up and get unswaddled at the same time, which made him lurch right into a beat-up coffee table, sending an empty coffee mug onto the rug. He tried to pick that up and nearly bashed his head on the corner of the table.

God. Please. Kill me now.

"And I'm Robert Kaminski. Your father-in-law," the white-haired man said, glaring at him over the reading glasses.

He finally fought free of the blanket and sat upright. His father-in-law stepped back to give him room with the two remaining Dwarfs, who weren't actually Dwarfs at all but clearly former soldiers, if the camo was authentic.

"I'm Harrison," he said. "Harrison Montgomery."

His sister-in-law winced and waved her hand under her nose. "You stink, dude."

Awesome.

"Mr. Kaminski," Harrison said. "It's good to meet you."

Robert ignored the hand Harrison held out to him. He was short and square, his white hair giving him a certain Einstein mad genius look, and it was very obvious he was not impressed with Harrison.

"I . . . ah . . . how long have I been here?" Harrison asked. It was dark outside the windows.

"It's five a.m.," Olivia said, jumping off the couch. "You've been passed out for about twelve hours."

Harrison scrubbed a hand over his face. The last thing he remembered was a truck stop in Virginia; he'd wanted to go home, having sobered up enough to realize that showing up on Ryan's doorstep unannounced might not be the best idea. But Noelle got him another fifth of bourbon and they continued north.

One of the older men in camouflage stuck his head around the doorway on the far side of the room. "We better get going, Robert," he said.

"Go wake up your sister," Robert told Olivia. "I don't trust this man."

"I'm not—" He didn't quite know how to finish that thought. *I'm not going to hurt anyone?*

He'd already done that to Ryan. He'd hurt her so badly, she'd had no choice but to come back here to people who'd shoved her out of their lives as effectively as he had.

Guilt and shame rippled through him again. For the

last two days since she'd left for Philly, anytime that happened, he'd tried to numb the pain with alcohol.

Just like his father must have.

"We're going hunting," Robert said. "I'll be back by dinner. Olivia, wake up your sister and get yourself to school." He lifted a gnarled finger to Harrison's face. "Don't steal nothing."

And then he was gone, taking the rest of the men with him, leaving Harrison feeling about three inches tall.

"Don't worry about him," Olivia said. "He's just like that."

"I'm not . . . I'm not here to hurt anyone."

Olivia nodded, looking so much like Ryan it hurt to imagine the days when Ryan was that young and that trusting. "You're here to get Ryan back?"

That had been the plan, if he remembered correctly, that he and Wallace had cooked up, around dawn the day after the election. He'd realized that losing the election didn't hurt half as bad as losing Ryan. As losing what they had been building, as losing the hope of a future different than his past.

Something better.

He'd told Wallace that and Wallace, the secret romantic, had called Noelle and convinced her to drive them to Pennsylvania so Harrison could woo back his wife.

It seemed impossibly stupid now, sober and sick and foul smelling.

Woo her back, what a joke.

"What have I done?" he groaned, burying his aching head in his hands.

"Look, you're here," Olivia said. "You showed up. My piano teacher says that's half the battle. Just showing up. So, next what you're going to do is shower, because you stink. And then Ryan's bedroom is the second door on the right. Go say hi."

"She's not going to want to see me."

"Nora says the day Ryan isn't interested in seeing a guy is the day we win the lottery."

"Nora doesn't know your sister," he said, anger cleaning out the sludge in his veins. Along with this father of hers trying to give him grief for hurting Ryan, when he'd spent the last six years hurting her.

If this was where Ryan came when things got bad, she needed a softer place to land.

Olivia's mouth twisted in some unreadable expression of doubt or agreement, he had no idea which.

But then she handed him the mug of coffee in her hands and pointed to the stairs. "We won't know unless you try."

In his hung-over state, Olivia was totally the boss of him and he did as she told him, climbing the stairs up to a narrow second floor and the bathroom at the top of the steps. It was old-fashioned, covered in pink hexagonal tiles that matched the sink and the tub with the black-and-white-and-purple shower curtain.

He imagined Ryan growing up in this bathroom, doing her hair, putting on lip gloss. Figuring out her beauty. He wanted to hear about it, about all of it. Those stories she told him, they were funny and sweet, but there was a darker side, and he wanted that too.

All of her, that was what he wanted.

After his shower he couldn't face putting on his clothes again, so wrapping a thin Snoopy towel around his waist he gathered up his dirty stuff and walked over to the second door on the right. The pale wooden door covered in an elaborate piano practice and performance schedule was closed, and he sincerely hoped he had the right room and wasn't about to see Wes again.

Heart in hand, he eased the door open and to his relief, his wife's scent curled out around him. Like a cartoon, it circled his head and coalesced into a finger beckoning him forward. He stepped into the shadows of the room and saw in the light from the open door his wife's body on the bed, covered in blankets, her dark hair on the white pillow.

His hands got damp at the sight of her, and his stomach, already fragile and unhappy, squeezed itself into a tiny space behind his liver.

He was nervous. Nervous like he had never been before.

And he didn't know what to do. Getting into bed with her seemed like a presumption of the worst kind. But going back downstairs in a towel was ludicrous.

"You coming in?" she asked, lifting her head from the pillow, her eyes glittery in the half-dark.

"I didn't . . . do you want me to?"

"You're letting in cold air, so come in or leave."

Not quite a welcome, but after the scene in the hotel suite, he knew she wasn't going to make this easy. And he didn't deserve to have it made easy.

He closed the door behind him and tossed his dirty stuff in the corner. The room was tiny, the double bed taking up most of it, so he climbed into it from the foot, until he was lying down next to Ryan. The pillows were thin little pancakes and he doubled them up under his head.

"Hi," he said, unable to help smiling. Because she was here. And she was pretty with her frown and the messy hair and the crease from the sheet over her face. And he'd missed her.

"What are you doing here?" she asked, making it very clear she was not happy to see him.

He shifted on the bed, lying on his side, propping his head up on his hand, and her eyes followed the movement. Stroked over his arms, his bare chest, down his stomach.

The desire was unmistakable.

Well, well, he thought, *maybe she's not as mad as I thought.*

"I wanted to apologize, for all the stuff I said in the hotel room."

"All the *stuff*?" she said, her tone cold. Mocking. He should have come up with prettier words, but he was in ruins. Hung over, exhausted. A dog relegated to a dog-house.

"I never wanted to hurt you."

"It seemed to me like for most of our relationship that's all you've wanted to do."

"I'm sorry . . . I'm sorry it seems that way. In the beginning," he said.

"And then again, at the end."

"No." He shook his head, sure in that at least. "I was mad, but not at you. *For* you, yes."

She snorted like she didn't believe him, and he was all out of pretense.

"I want to start over again. I want a chance to make it work, to try and see if what we have is real."

"You don't know? You can't figure out what feelings are real and which ones are fake? You're a bigger mess than I thought."

"That's not what I meant—"

"Then what *do* you mean?"

He took his life in his hands to touch the side of her face, the fall of hair over her shoulder. A small study in softness, delicate variances between velvet and silk.

"No contracts. No agreements. Just you and me. I don't want you to feel like you have to do something because of a piece of paper and I don't want to feel like I'm taking advantage—"

Her open-mouthed kiss silenced him.

Stunned him.

Made him glad he'd used the toothbrush he recognized as hers in the bathroom.

*We are kissing now. We were fighting and now we're
kissing.*

"What—"

"Shut up."

She was giving him no time to process it. She licked at
him. Sucked at him. His lips, his tongue. Her hands slid
down his body, over his belly to his cock beneath the
towel.

Now or never, her touch said.

And he absolutely wanted now.

Again, his brain was kind of primordial goo, but he
figured if they were having sex that had to be a good
sign. Relieved and ecstatic, his arms swept around her,
hauling her body up against his. He pulled down the
blankets she was under and tugged her tank top up over
her head, revealing her beautiful breasts, the swell of
her stomach, and he fell on her like a man whose execu-
tion had been stayed. He kissed her skin, sucked on her
nipples, and cupped her flesh in his hands with more
gratitude than he thought he was capable of feeling.

It is going to be okay. We are going to be okay.

That was how he translated her exigency.

She kicked her legs free from the blankets and rolled
over onto her back and he followed her, not done with
his gratitude or her breasts.

Her fingers ran through his damp hair, sending cold
drops of water onto his shoulders. He was surprised
they didn't sizzle against his skin.

And then she pushed on his head. The instructions
were clear and he was more than happy to comply, and
he kissed his way down over her stomach, rubbed his
cheeks against the curve of her belly, and felt a flutter of
something there against his cheek. And then another, a
solid thump against the taut flesh of her abdomen. His
heart tripped over itself and blood flooded his body,
prickly and hot.

"Is that—"

"Shhh," she said, and kept pushing him down.

Later, he thought, they would talk about it later. Because this urgency of hers, this command, it was so fucking exciting. She owned him right now; down to his bones he was hers.

He slid down, pushing her legs out wide with his body. She curled one long, smooth leg over his back and he felt utterly surrounded by her. Cocooned in her softness and her scent and her sleepy warmth. It was sexy and real and home in a way.

In a basic, elemental way.

I belong here. Right here. All my life this is what I've been missing. This is what I've wanted.

"Lick me," she breathed, and he opened her with his fingers, spread the pink lips, breathing over the revealed flesh until she twitched and groaned and arched toward him. "Now."

He chuckled as he set his mouth on her. Careful and reverent, trying to let her in on his feelings by the way his tongue circled the hood of her clit.

"Harder," she whispered, arching into his mouth, lifting her hips into his face. "Suck me."

Oh God. He sucked her into his mouth, worked his tongue over her clit. She didn't want soft. She wanted hard. Fierce.

And he felt the answer rise up his blood.

"Use your fingers."

He slid his hand between them, easing a finger into the damp, clinging heat of her body where he could feel the twitch of her muscles.

"More."

He groaned against her skin, sliding another finger into her. She arched against the bed, her muscles strung taut. His mouth, his fingers, they were tools put to her use and he fucked her, sucked her, until she was gripping his hair in her fingers, licks of pain radiating down his skull, across his neck, his back, down to his hips and around to his cock until he felt like he was made of her electricity.

"God . . . yes!" she cried and groaned and shook, and he held himself still against her. Still so he could feel all of it, every twitch and pulse.

She let go of his hair and he crawled up over her body, nosed away the arms she'd thrown over her face. Her cheeks were pink, sweat rolled down the side of her face, and when her eyes blinked open he smiled down at her, feeling this moment blend into every future moment between them.

"Hi," he breathed and leaned down to kiss her, but she ducked sideways and then pushed against his shoulder, until he rolled away from her.

His brain was slow and muddy and his body electrified and single-minded, so it took him a second of watching her pull on clothes from her bag at the side of the bed before he caught on that she was leaving.

"Ryan?"

"You were always so worried about taking advantage of me."

He leaned up to kiss her neck, to cup his hand over her shoulder, but she shrugged away and stood.

"You know what makes what we have not taking advantage?"

She waited for him to answer, but he didn't say anything until she turned around. Something was happening, some tidal shift, and he had no control over it. And he could see the anger in her eyes, hot and mean, and he braced himself for what was going to come.

Ryan was going to tear him apart.

This is how she felt, he thought with stabbing premonition, *in that hotel suite.*

"Love," she spat. "Love makes it all right. It makes

everything we've done a gift freely given and joyfully received. And I could have freely given you everything I had, but you couldn't have received it as a gift. Because you don't know how to do that. You took advantage of me, Harrison, because you don't love me."

He got up on his knees in the bed and reached for her. Luckily, the room was so small she had nowhere to go and he had her hands in his before she could maneuver around the bed.

"Ryan—"

"Now I've taken advantage of you. We're even." She didn't have to pull her hands too hard; he let her go. The stack of his clothes he'd set by the dresser got picked up and flung in his face. "Get dressed and go."

Chapter 28

Ryan sat at the kitchen table, in her old spot. Her ass had left an impression on the red cushion of the seat. But her ass didn't fit in it like it used to. Nothing fit her like it used to.

This is not my home anymore.

That man upstairs, he is not my home anymore either.

It's just me.

The baby rolled, as if putting up its hand to be counted.

You and me, kid, she thought. *That's all we need.*

She took another sip of orange juice and waited to hear the squeal of the back steps as Harrison came down.

How strange to feel so cold. So . . . strangely solid, where for so long she'd just felt liquid and weak, as if her center of gravity was constantly shifting, constantly causing her to fall in and out of her own balance.

She pushed away the juice because Nora always bought the kind with a ton of pulp and she hated drinking through her teeth, and she started to work on her to-do list.

Divorce.

Figure out where to live.

Get back to school.

But where? she wondered. She had no interest in going back to New York or in staying too long in Philly.

Which left the rest of the world.

Or Atlanta.

Georgia Tech and the Food Bank.

Atlanta is a big city, she thought. And she didn't have to be exiled from what she wanted in fear of bumping into him on the street.

She was tougher than that.

Good lord, what she did upstairs just proved that, didn't it?

She shook her head, astonished at her own audacity.

The front door opened and then slammed shut and the jangle of keys hit the table in front of the window, and it was the sound of Nora coming home. It had been the same sound since Nora got a set of house keys after Mom died and Daddy started driving the night route.

"Anyone home?" Nora asked.

"In . . ." She cleared her throat. "In here."

Nora arrived in the doorway.

Her top was different, a scrub shirt covered in yellow suns and puppies with sunglasses—which while ridiculous on its own, seemed like a terrible sign of a world out of order when worn by Nora. There was something splattered across the front of her blue scrub pants. Mud. Or worse. The morning's makeup was gone. Her hair, wet or greasy, hung around her face. No sign of the barrette.

"Are you okay?" she asked, knowing there was a good chance her words would get thrown back at her. But there was no way she couldn't ask.

For a long moment Nora's face was blank, as if she didn't understand or hadn't heard the question, and then she shook, her whole body, just one sharp, short shake. The kind of thing that used to make their mom say "a ghost just walked over my grave."

And then she smiled. Wan and weak, but a smile all the same.

"Fine. Long day. You alone?" Nora asked.

"Olivia is at school and Daddy's gone hunting."

"Hunting," Nora laughed. "That'll be interesting."

Nora hung up her coat on the rack by the back door and poured herself a cup of coffee from the pot.

"It's cold," Ryan said, trying to make nice. "You might want to nuke it."

Nora drank it cold like it was a testament to her orneriness and sat down in her old seat across from her.

"Are you sure you're okay? You seem . . ."

Nora glanced sideways at the bathroom door in the corner, her bottom lip caught under her teeth, and Ryan realized Nora was barely holding it together. She pushed aside her coffee cup and reached for her sister's hands.

At the touch of her fingers Nora gasped. She gasped like she'd been holding her breath all day.

"My whole life is about managing," she whispered. "Manage doctors, manage patients, manage other people's grief and anger. And then I come home—" She stopped, shook her head, and yanked back her hands.

"Come home and what?"

"I've hated you for a long time, Ryan," she breathed. "And it wasn't about Paul, or even the money or hurting Daddy. It was because you left. I spent so long imagining you in New York City, living this glamorous life far away from this place."

"It wasn't glamorous," she said. "It was a studio apartment that smelled like cabbage rolls and a string of jobs I got because of my boobs. And being lonely. Lots and lots of being lonely. Don't . . . don't envy that. You were here. And a part of a family."

Nora's lips twisted, the old indication that she was trying not to cry. "I never got a job because of my boobs."

"It's because you were hired for your brain. And your boobs are tiny."

That brought Nora's head up, her mouth open, the laughter running out before she could stop it.

"I love Daddy and Olivia and I wouldn't change that . . . but sometimes it feels like I don't have anything of my own. I just stepped into Mom's shoes."

"Nora, I'm sorry. I'm sorry I was such a shitty sister. I should have been here to help."

"I didn't win any prizes either. And look at you, Ry." She laughed. "Pregnant and alone and back in the Burg?"

"But you won't stay." Nora shook her head. "It's obvious. You're moving on."

That wasn't Nora kicking her out again; it was her sister realizing she'd changed. That Ryan was different, and it was about the biggest compliment she'd ever gotten from her sister.

"Where's your husband?" Nora asked, blinking her eyes until the sheen of tears went away.

"Upstairs," she said, wondering what was happening in her sister's head. What kind of trauma she'd seen to make her so vulnerable. "Getting dressed, and then I imagine he's leaving."

"You're really gonna split?"

"It wasn't a real marriage."

"You're pregnant, Ryan. That makes it pretty real."

The memory of his face when he'd felt the baby moving against her belly. Those small popcorn pops she still hadn't gotten used to. He'd been transformed by delight. By excitement.

Leaving would deny him any more of those moments. And deny her the joy of sharing those moments.

"He circles back around me when things fall apart," she said. "I don't know what kind of marriage we can make out of that."

Nora laughed. "Helping each other through the bad times? I'll take that kind of marriage. Does he treat you bad when things are good?"

She thought of that partnership, the way he held her

hand in front of reporters. Asked her opinion in all those meetings.

"No," she whispered. "I just don't know if any of the good times were real for him. In fact, I don't know what was real between us."

"Well, he's here now. Nothing more real than this place." Nora made a low noise in her throat and finished her coffee. "Want me to get rid of him for you?"

Ryan laughed. "No, I think at thirty-two years old, I can fight my own battles."

"You love him?"

She nodded, because it was true. The truest thing she had in her life besides the baby. "Not that it matters; I don't think he's got it in him to love me."

"Then the asshole doesn't deserve you."

"Simple as that?" Ryan whispered through a throat made thin by emotion.

"Simple. As. That."

Ryan's smile gave way to laughter, and the laughter opened her heart up to something so powerful and painful she could barely stand it.

She'd been alone and without love for such a long time her body had gone numb, but it came flooding back.

"I think . . . we, you, me, and Wes, we got real good at hiding all the things that make us lovable," Nora said. "All the softness and all the . . . sweetness, because it hurt when Mom died. Because being soft and sweet wouldn't put food on the table. We hid those things so well we forgot where we put them. But you got plenty in you that's lovable, Ryan. I'm sorry I, or Paul or anyone, made you feel different."

Ryan grabbed her sister's hand again, clung to it across the old table.

The silence between them was broken by the squeal of the back steps as Harrison made his appearance, wearing his suit pants and bourbon-stained white shirt. He was scruffy and bloodshot and coming down the steps of her childhood home, where she'd dreamed vivid dreams about love and Prince Charming, and her solid and cold heart was not impervious.

It wanted him. Her stupid heart. Her stupid body—both wanted him. Thank God her brain knew better and was driving this ship.

I am my own damn Prince Charming.

She'd used him in her bedroom. Used him the way she'd felt used. And she'd tossed him away like he'd tossed her away.

It felt good.

And shitty.

And she didn't know what to do about any of that.

"Hey," he said, pausing on the steps when he saw Nora and Ryan.

"Well, hello," Nora said, putting aside all her strange and sudden vulnerability in exchange for her familiar sarcasm. "You're not bad-looking when you're conscious."

"And clean," Harrison said, with a shy smile that nearly destroyed her.

"You want some coffee?" Nora asked.

"Badly."

Ryan sat there like a silent bump on a log, ignoring Nora's wide-eyed look while Nora went and poured Harrison a cup of coffee and nuked it.

"We're out of milk. But sugar is over there," Nora said, pointing to the square Tupperware container on the counter next to the fridge. "I'm afraid the latte machine is busted."

Harrison ignored the sugar and all of Nora's jabs and leaned back against the counter, drinking day-old reheated coffee like it was no big deal. Like he did it every day, when she knew for a fact that he was unnaturally devoted to his espresso machine.

"I'm afraid I didn't get a chance to meet you properly yesterday," he said.

"Because you were passed out cold on my couch," Nora said with a slicing smile.

"Exactly. I'm Harrison, Ryan's husband."

Nora and Harrison shook hands. "Sorry to hear about the election."

"Thank you; there will be others."

That surprised her.

"Hopefully you won't lose those."

Harrison smiled. "Hopefully."

"When are you leaving?" Ryan asked Harrison, cutting through the bullshit small talk.

"I'm not leaving," he said.

"What?"

"I'm not leaving." He shrugged.

"Maybe you didn't understand me upstairs?"

"What happened upstairs?" Nora asked.

"Oh, I understood you," Harrison said, his eyes on Ryan as if Nora weren't even in the room. It was like that first night at the bar all over again. Nothing existed but him. "But I don't think you understand *me*." He crossed the room and leaned over the table. "You can use me like that all you want, Ryan. But I'm not leaving."

The back door was thrown open so hard it bounced off one of the kitchen chairs, and Ryan jumped, nearly bonking heads with Harrison.

Daddy poked his head in the door, his hair wild, his grin even wilder. "Girls! We need all hands on deck!"

"Did you actually shoot something?" Ryan asked, getting to her feet and rushing with her sister to the back door.

"Bucky hit a big white-tail with his truck!" Dad lit up

like he used to, that smile in the corners of his mouth. "Come on, clean up the back table. It'll be just like the old days."

Just like them, but somehow, painfully not.

Why didn't you ever call me? she wondered. *Why didn't you ever reach out? I was your daughter as much as Nora and you just let me be gone for six years.*

Dad vanished from the doorway and she turned to find Harrison watching her, reading her expression like he knew what she was thinking. The sweetness of being back home, tipping just a little toward bitterness.

And he probably did know what she was thinking. That was maybe the consolation prize of their marriage. Instead of happiness, they had this awkward knowledge of each other. This terrible understanding that couldn't ever be turned into something warm. Something useful.

It just was.

The backyard was bare in the November afternoon. Their patio furniture was shoved in the corner, the trash cans had tipped over in the night, and raccoons had thrown the garbage around like it was a party. The chain-link fence in the back was rusted and falling down in places, covered in junk that had gotten stuck against it in the wind.

There was nothing lush or pampered or cared for about this lawn.

And her dad and some of his old army buddies were going to bring in some roadkill and butcher it on the patio table.

"Harrison!" she yelled. "We need you."

"You trying to drive him away?" Nora muttered under her breath as she walked by, going out to the yard to help.

Showing him the real me, she thought.

"What's happening?" Harrison asked, standing in

the doorway with her. His shoulder brushing against
hers.

"Dad's going to butcher a deer they killed on the
highway. He needs your help."

To Harrison's credit he only nodded, finished his terrible coffee, and handed her the cup. His hand caught hers
for a moment, his fingers tracing the rings on her finger.
The engagement and wedding rings he put there . . . what?
Two months ago.

God, how quickly things could change.

"You're still wearing them," he said.

"I forgot to take them off." She started to pull them
off her finger, but it was difficult with this water weight
that was beginning to make her fingers and feet swell.

"Leave them," he said, taking her hand and kissing
her fingers.

"Harrison—"

"I'm winning you back, Ryan," he said with that shy
smile. It was fascinating, that smile, an indicator of
some side of him she'd never seen. "But first I gotta go
butcher a deer."

He said it like he knew what he was doing and then
was gone, out to the old garage in his dress shirt, walking past the garbage and the weeds as if they just weren't
there.

When Harrison said for better or for worse in the Georgia Governor's Mansion, he'd never once expected this.

Holding down the hind leg of the dead deer while his
father-in-law used a hacksaw to cut the deer right down
the middle of its belly. All in an attempt to win back the
affection of his wife.

Harrison turned his head and gagged into his shoulder.

"You all right there?" Robert asked, still hacking his way through skin and muscle.

"Just fine," Harrison managed to get out.

It was freezing out in the yard and he had no coat, and none of the Dwarfs or his father-in-law seemed interested in loaning him one. And he got it—it was both a test and a punishment. He'd belonged to a fraternity for a while; he knew how this worked.

Harrison wasn't entirely sure how Robert was going to come at him or how much leeway he was going to give the father who had shunned Ryan for the last six years when it came to the hard time the man wanted to give the new son-in-law.

"How much meat you think we're going to get off this thing?" Robert asked the guy named Bucky, who as the driver of the weapon that had felled this creature sat in a lawn chair drinking beer while the rest of them worked.

"Seventy pounds, if you're careful," Bucky said, draining his third bottle.

"Call some of the folks down at the hall," Robert said over his shoulder to another one of the men. "See if we can't put some of this meat in the freezers of families who need some help this winter."

"That's good of you," Harrison said past the hideous burn of bile in his throat.

"We take care of our own around here," Robert said. *But you didn't,* he thought, thinking of Ryan's face as she watched her father in the kitchen. *You left her in the cold.*

"Ryan told me about that VetAid thing you got going," Robert said.

"Families of vets need help, too."

"That's good of you."

Harrison smiled. This was as close as they were going to get to hugging it out.

"So Robert?" one of the other hunters on the far side of the table said. "You never told us Ryan got married."

"Again!" another guy yelled.

"You weren't invited to the wedding?" asked Bucky.

"No, I wasn't," Robert said, sawing with a little extra force. Harrison moved his fingers farther out of the way.

"That's what happens when you don't talk to your daughter for six years. You miss out on some stuff," Harrison said.

"Oh ho!" Bucky cried. "He's got you there."

The back door opened and Ryan stood in the yellow square of light, a sweater wrapped around her body. "Anybody need anything out here?" she asked.

"Your husband needs a barf bag," Robert said, watching him from the corner of his eye.

Ryan winced.

"I'm fine," he lied.

"I could use another beer," Bucky yelled, and Ryan went back inside.

For a second, the only sound in the backyard was the hideous scrape of saw through bone.

"You want to fill me in on what's going on between you and my daughter?"

"If you wanted to know anything about her life in the last six years, I imagine you could have picked up the phone."

Robert stopped butchering and stood, facing Harrison carrying a saw with blood dropping off its serrated edges, but Harrison wasn't scared. He was cold, hung over, starving, nauseated, and ready to fight on behalf of a woman who hadn't seen anyone fight for her in a long time.

"You got something to say, I figure you should just say it," Robert demanded.

The back door opened and Ryan came out carrying

beers, but she stopped on the top step as if sensing the dangerous mood in the backyard.

"For a guy who welcomed her home with open arms, you could have welcomed her home a lot sooner," Harrison said.

"She came running here because she had nowhere else to go, which makes me think you must have made sure she didn't feel too welcome with you," Robert said.

"You're right," he agreed. "I did. I lost everything a few days ago. Everything I thought I wanted. The election, my career, my future. But I wanted to protect Ryan from how terrible my world can be. How ugly. How cold. How unforgiving. So I sent her away. And that's the thing about losing everything," he said, catching her eye, telling her and her father at the same time. "It makes you realize what you really want."

"And you want my daughter?"

He nodded, and the distance between him and Ryan vanished. The men, the deer—it all fell away, and the world was revealed in stark lines. Belief or doubt. That was all that mattered.

"You think I don't see you?" he asked her, ignoring his father-in-law and his friends. "You think I don't understand how every time you've hit rock bottom people shove you away, leave you alone?"

He could hear her breathing. Over the wind. Over the pounding of his heart, he could hear her breath.

"I'm not leaving," he said. "You can do whatever you want to me. I'm here."

"What if I leave?"

"Then I'll follow you."

"You think it's that easy?"

"Easy?" He laughed. He laughed so hard it hurt, and then he held out his arms, looking down at the dead deer on the table, her father carrying a gory hacksaw. "What part of this looks easy to you?"

Ryan handed Bucky the beer and headed back inside, ·
the swish of her skirt like a red cape to his inner bull.

"I missed her every day for six years, almost picked
up the phone a million times," Robert said, looking
suddenly older in the twilight. Suddenly weighed down
by a life that had not been easy.

"Why didn't you?" Harrison asked.

"Too proud?" Robert shrugged. "Trying to keep the
peace with Nora? I don't even know anymore. But I'd
take it back. Every minute, I'd take it back."

"You need to tell her that."

Robert nodded and straightened his glasses, but instead of going in there and telling his daughter he loved
her, he bent back over the deer.

"This is your chance," Harrison told Robert, who
only grinned and shook his head.

"I think it's yours, son."

Harrison stepped back. This wasn't how he was going
to prove his love.

He turned on the hose and held his hands under the
ice-cold water and cleaned off the blood and the regret.
He splashed the water over his head and face, and the
shock of it cleared his head.

He loved her and she needed to know that.

Chapter 29

What he wasn't expecting was a kitchen stuffed full of people making drinks and putting out food. Apparently, butchering a deer in your backyard was reason for a party around here. And when he walked in, conversations halted and they all turned to look at him.

"You Ryan's husband?" a woman wearing a Flyers hockey sweater and carrying a casserole dish filled with what looked like Tater Tots and bacon asked.

"I am. You know where she is?"

"I'm here," came her voice from behind him, and he turned to see her at the table. "You're a mess."

He spread his arms out as best he could so she could really get a good look.

"If my mother could see me now?" he joked. Across the room, Nora threw him a kitchen towel and he used it to wipe the water off his face and hands. The shirt was a lost cause, but he refused to take it as a sign of his own chances in this kitchen.

"Maybe we should go out front," Ryan said, standing up.

"Truth in private, lies in public?" he said, and she stilled. "That hasn't worked so well for us, has it?"

She looked at him point-blank with sad, worried eyes. "What are you doing, Harrison?" she breathed.

"Figuring it out, I guess."

"By butchering a deer?"

"If that's what it takes."

"Your world—"

"Fuck that, Ryan. Your world. My world. I don't give a shit anymore. It's us. You and me. The baby. It's our world and it looks like whatever we want it to look like."

The crowd in the kitchen had gotten larger, people gathering from the dining room, and their audience watched like a good audience should, avidly, eyes wide. Food and drink forgotten.

He was embarrassed, slightly mortified, but at this point he would strip naked for her.

She still seemed dubious and he thought of how badly he'd botched it between them. After the election and then upstairs in her room. She deserved better, so with both hands he tore open the box where he kept everything he felt. All those things he'd tried to make go away because no one in his life ever valued them.

"I've been far from happy for so long. But you made me feel good and whole for the first time in my life. You made me feel like I was worth more than I'd ever thought I was. I want that back."

"You made me feel that way too," she said, crossing her arms over her chest. "I saw the person I could be with you, and that was exciting. And I wanted that. The food bank and going back to school and being a part of your team. But I can be that person without you, too."

"Damn straight," some audience member called out.

"That's true," he said, cleaved in half with pride and dread. "Is that what you want?"

She shrugged. "Maybe we should just be grateful that we've shown each other what's possible and leave it at that."

"I can't leave it at that because I love you," he said. "I love you. I love you more than . . ."

"Butchering deer?" someone asked.

He ignored the peanut gallery. "I can't even finish that thought. Because there's nothing in my life that comes close to you. Everything is a distant second to you."

She was silent and dry-eyed and as the silence stretched on, their audience began to share sideways glances. He was losing her. The walls she'd retreated behind were too high.

"Why?" It was a voice from deep in the corner, by the sink. The crowd shifted and Nora appeared, holding a Yuengling bottle braced against her hip. A small blond pit bull in an apron.

"Why . . . what?" he asked.

"Why do you love her?" Nora said, tilting her head toward Ryan. "What's so special about my sister?"

"Everything," he said, caught off guard.

Nora made a buzzing sound. "Lame answer, asshole." The crowd laughed.

"Stop," Ryan said, coming forward, her hands out as if she were going to send both of them back to their corners. Nora shot him an "are you really this dumb" look over Ryan's shoulder and his muddy brain finally caught on.

Nora was giving him a boost over Ryan's high walls.

He reached for Ryan, cupping her face in his clean but cold hands. Her eyes were wide and filling with tears that she systematically blinked away.

"You don't have to do this," she whispered, but he could see that deep down, she wanted it.

"I love you because I've never had anyone by my side before. Because you inspire me to look at things differently. Because for the first time in my life I want someone to be proud of me. I love you because you make me better. You make my life better."

"Yeah, that's nice and all, but that's all the shit she does for you." It was Nora again, right over Ryan's shoulder, like the declaration of love police. "What about *her*?"

"Your sister is tougher than Maynard," he whispered to Ryan, who didn't smile. *Right.* She just kept blinking away those tears, too tough to let them fall.

"You're fierce," he said. "Loyal. Smart. So . . . so smart, Ryan. Smarter, I think, than you even know. You're a fighter who leads with her heart no matter how many times it's been beaten up. And you're kind, too. And that seems minor, but in my world . . ." He cleared his throat, but the ball of emotion didn't go anywhere. It got worse, in fact, and he felt tears building in his own eyes. "I haven't known a lot of kindness. You changed my life at that bar, showed me what was possible between two people when someone is brave. When someone is kind. I want to return that favor every day. For you. For our baby. Our family. I want to wake up every morning and make you happy. As happy as you've made me."

"You gonna say something about how hot she is?" Nora asked.

Ryan flinched in his hands and he shook his head, looking into those brown eyes with the dark edges. "I've doubted my worth," he whispered to her. "I've felt alone, just like you have, and if you let me in, Ryan. If you let me love you, I promise you'll never feel that way again."

He dropped his hands from her face and stepped back. He couldn't force her to trust him. He couldn't force her to do anything. A guy in the doorway to the living room clapped, and Harrison did a little bow before he shot Ryan a half-smile, trying to hide his doubt and his fear and his worry.

"I'm . . . I'm going to take another shower," he said, and then headed up the stairs, leaving the kitchen behind.

She would come to him on her own, or she wouldn't.

* * *

Once Harrison was gone, the kitchen exploded around Ryan but she barely heard it.

"How come you never say that kind of shit to me?" Janet Baker asked her husband, who'd been the guy clapping in the doorway.

"Bring me another beer and I will," he shot back.

Something got thrown. Someone swore. A bunch of people laughed.

"That was freaking awesome," Grace Kerns said in a hushed and reverent voice, and other women agreed.

Ryan agreed. Harrison's speech was awesome. It was like something out of a movie. But still, somehow, she couldn't move.

"What are you going to do?" Nora asked, coming to stand beside her, staring at the stairs with her like it was a crime scene.

"That person he described, is that really me?" she whispered.

"It's how he sees you."

Ryan laughed. "I'm not brave. I'm . . . scared to death."

Letting Harrison in, all the way in and trusting him not to hurt her. And letting him trust her not to hurt him—that would be the bravest thing she'd ever done.

"Why'd you make him say all that?" she asked her sister.

"Because that's the shit you deserve, Ryan," Nora said. When Ryan looked down at her, she saw the sister of her childhood, returned to her somehow. And her gratitude was overwhelming.

"Thank you," she breathed.

"You're welcome, but I really don't understand what you're still doing down here." Nora swatted her butt

with the towel over her shoulder and then retreated into
the high-fives of the rest of the women in the kitchen.

Ryan remembered that first press conference, and
how putting her hand in his and following him out of
the car had been so surprisingly easy. She just did it. She
just changed her life.

And taking the back steps to the second floor one by
one was the same way.

Easy.

While at the same time impossibly difficult.

She was brave and cowardly all at once. Relieved and
terrified. Excited and worried. Laughing and crying.

As if she'd been living with every emotion on mute for
years and now she felt it all at full volume. Love amplified everything. It amplified her. She was suddenly capable of thousands of things she'd never dreamed of
before. Things she wouldn't have had the ability to even
see.

She skipped the second step, her hand at her stomach
over the growing baby. She nearly ran down the hallway
to the bathroom. She eased open the door and then shut
it quickly behind her so the cool air didn't get in. She
could see the shadow of him through the shower curtain, the solid shape and size that somehow managed to
fill all the empty spots in her life.

Silently, she shed her clothes, her heart leaping around
her rib cage like it wanted out, and then she eased back
the edge of the shower curtain.

"What—" he cried, turning to face her, a long, soapy
trail of shampoo falling over his eye. He smiled when he
saw her, swiped the shampoo away, and quickly rinsed
the rest of it out of his hair. "It's you."

"It's me." Goose bumps covered her body and she
wrapped her arms around herself.

She was naked and cold and he sidestepped slightly so
the hot water reached her.

Such a stupid thing to make her cry, but it did. A sob broke out of her.

"Hey," he breathed, reaching for her, wiping the tears away with his thumbs as fast as they fell. "Hey, what's wrong?"

"I'm happy."

A slow smile spread across his face. "This is you happy?"

She nodded and wrapped her arms around his neck, pressed kisses to his face. His cheek, the corner of his eye. And she felt his big, wide hands sweep around her, sliding up and down her back as if he couldn't touch enough of her.

"I love you," she said.

He rested his head against her shoulder and she cupped his neck with her hands and they stood holding each other up, the warm water running over their faces, into their mouths and eyes, but neither moved.

It was a strange moment of relief. Of homecoming.

"Thank you," he said.

She stepped closer and pressed her hips against his, suddenly hungry for him. For the tenderness she'd known in his arms. She wanted to erase what had happened between them in her bedroom, that cold and angry act that bore no resemblance to the beautiful sex they were capable of.

And then the hot water, suddenly, viciously, turned cold.

They both screamed and scrambled out of the shower, dripping onto the pink tiled floor.

She swept back her wet hair. "Welcome to my world," she laughed.

Harrison sobered. He grabbed a towel and bundled her up and then wrapped the old Snoopy one around his waist before picking her up in his arms.

She wrapped her arms around his neck, her fingers squeezing water from the tips of his hair.

The walk to her bedroom was brief but drafty, and then he closed the door behind them and dried her off before settling her under the covers. Shivering, she watched him dry off and then join her.

"It's our world," he told her. "It's what we make it. Parts of you. Parts of me. The baby. It's what we want."

He was propped up on his elbow over her and she slipped closer into the crack between his chest and the mattress, filling every space available to her. His erection was warm and hard against her belly and she reached between them to touch him.

"You know what I want?" she asked, her fingers circling the head, tracing the veins along the side.

He smiled, rakish and handsome, and leaned down to kiss her breast, making his way to her nipple. His hand slipped up her thigh and she spread her legs so she was open to his touch.

Love and lust collided between them and she was ready, unbelievably ready for him, and he shifted over her and slid into her perfectly. There was no doubt. No acceptance she wasn't sure she wanted to give.

"You," she breathed into his mouth as they began to move. "All I want is you."

Chapter 30

"I have never seen one woman eat so much fried chicken," Harrison teased, opening the door to the condo. She stepped past him, feeling tight and full and miserably pregnant.

"The last piece was a mistake," she said, putting a hand to her stomach. The baby kicked her in agreement. Or disagreement; it was hard to say. The baby kicked a lot. And rolled and stretched, putting little hands against her belly and little feet against her spine and pushing with all its baby might.

"You all right?" he asked, smoothing his hand over her distended stomach. The baby kicked him too. Harrison grinned at the feeling and she grinned at seeing him so happy.

So peaceful.

Those smiles of his had multiplied like rabbits. Every day there were more. Easygoing smiles. Self-effacing smiles. Wry. Shy. Delighted. Flirtatious. Sexy. In those monthly trips to see his parents in their new house, his smiles had been pained, resigned. But more recently, slowly, they were becoming warm.

Being out of office was good for Ted and Patty. Their marriage wasn't anything that Ryan wanted to emulate, but it was better functioning than it had been, largely because Harrison insisted on keeping everything out in the open, giving secrets no chance to fester.

"You tired?" he asked.

"Always." She smiled. But tonight more than usual, because they'd rolled out the Pregnancy Nutrition Awareness program at the food bank today and there had been nonstop press interviews.

"Come on," he said. "I'll walk you to your door."

"Harrison," she sighed.

After leaving Philly and coming back to Atlanta to try out this new life of theirs, instead of getting a divorce and dating, or having her move out, an expense neither of them could really afford right now, he'd suggested that they keep separate rooms.

And she'd agreed.

"I've never had a roommate," he'd said.

"Then you're in for a treat."

And it had been. It had been five months of getting to know each other. Of special dates and ordering in. Both of them had tried to cook for the other with nearly disastrous results, but they'd pressed on, and now Ryan could make tortilla pie and peach cobbler and she made a bunch of it.

The baby loved peach cobbler.

Harrison bought a barbecue for the small patio and was getting pretty good at not burning chicken.

Nora came to visit and they'd had a party.

And then another one a few weeks later. Both of them sort of surprised by the number of friends they had.

They made out on the couch, went to movies. Had brunch with Wallace and Noelle a few times a month. They argued about what to watch on TV.

And every night he walked her to her door before going upstairs to his room.

"Don't you think it's time we were done with this?" she asked. "Dating in our own house."

"You don't like it?"

"I love it, but I also love that big bed upstairs and

waking up to your pretty face every day." She squished
his cheeks together and kissed his pursed lips.

"Are you saying you're sure?" he asked, kissing her
cheeks, her eyebrows, her nose.

"I am so sure I love you it's nearly nauseating. What
about you? Are you sure?"

"Couldn't be surer," he said, walking her back toward
the couch. "Can we still make out on the couch?"

She laughed. "I don't fit on the couch with you anymore."

As if to prove her wrong he arranged them there, her
surrounded by pillows, him with her feet in his lap.

In the corner were the stacks of baby items from the
baby shower/wedding party Nora and Olivia had thrown
for them in Philly last month.

The neighborhood had amply supplied them with casserole dishes and Eagles football onesies.

Nora and Olivia had promised to come to Atlanta
when the baby was born.

"To help," Nora had said. "Someone's got to make
sure you're doing it right."

But Ryan wasn't stupid; Nora was going to be an
amazing aunt. The very thought of it always made Ryan
cry.

"Wallace came to see me today," Harrison said, dig-
ging his thumb into the sole of her foot, making her
groan and nearly pee her pants.

"How are he and Noelle doing?"

"Good. He ah . . . mentioned the mayoral election
next year."

Ryan jabbed him in the stomach with her big toe and
grinned up at him. "Did he? And what did you say?"

"That I would work for him if he wanted to run."

"What?" she cried. "That's not what he meant,
was it?"

"Initially, no, but I think he left thinking about it.

He'd have to let someone get him some new ties, but he'd be a great mayor."

"But what about you? Aren't you interested?"

"Nope. Not right now. Already I'm spending a week a month in Washington with VetAid, and you're going to school and so busy with the food bank. And with the baby—"

"We could make it work."

"I don't want to make our family work," he said. "I don't want to put any pressure on this kid or us to be anything that we're not."

"No danger of that," she laughed. "But if you want—"

"I'm so happy. Happier than I've ever been. And that purpose I was looking for," he said, pulling her closer to him. It was awkward. She was awkward, but laughing they made their way into each other's arms. "That purpose is you," he whispered into her hair. "You and the baby."

She was like a watering can these days and her taciturn husband, who was constantly acting like a cheesy Hallmark movie, was not making it easier on her.

"The purpose is *us*," she said. "The three of us. We are the purpose and the point of everything. But, I have another proposal for you."

"Can't wait."

"The second you think you want to run for mayor, or congressman or President of the United States, let's talk about it. We can decide together."

"The same for you. You want to be mayor or senator or President of . . . you think I'm kidding, but I'm not." She was blushing and crying and swollen and needed to pee, but she sat still while he kissed her. "You can do anything you want."

She groaned against his lips, pressing a hand low on her belly where the uncomfortable throb she'd been feeling off and on for the last few hours turned sharp. Painful.

"You're having contractions, aren't you?" he asked and she nodded, gripped in the teeth of a bad one. She'd been having Braxton Hicks for the last few days, false contractions that sure as hell didn't feel false.

"Off and on all day, but it's worse since dinner. I think . . . I think this might be actual labor."

All the calm of her polished husband vanished and he looked stark raving terrified. "This is real?" he asked, leaping to his feet, pulling her up carefully with him.

She could feel him getting ready to take the situation in hand; he was already reaching for his phone to call the doctor and looking over to the door where her hospital bag sat waiting.

But she stopped him, took his beautiful face in her hand, and cherished this moment before everything changed. Before their world of two became three. It was beautiful what they had, and what they would have. And sometimes she could not believe her luck, but then she reminded herself that she and Harrison had each other because they were brave.

Well, that and a faulty condom.

She pressed a kiss to his lips, tasting her own tears there.

This is real.

"A unique, not-to-be-missed voice in romantic fiction."
—Susan Andersen

MOLLY O'KEEFE

THE **CROOKED CREEK RANCH** TRILOGY
CAN'T BUY ME LOVE
CAN'T HURRY LOVE
CRAZY THING CALLED LOVE

THE **BOYS OF BISHOP** SERIES
WILD CHILD
NEVER BEEN KISSED
BETWEEN THE SHEETS

www.molly-okeefe.com

 MollyOKeefeBooks   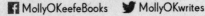 MollyOKwrites

BANTAM